30 DAYS TO SAVE THE WORLD

a short story anthology

presented by

WCX WRITERSCONNX

LOST bajan BOOKS

30 DAYS TO SAVE THE WORLD

Cover art by A.W. Frasier
Concept by Rodney V. Smith
Compiled by Rodney V. Smith, Vanessa Carley, Ina Ramos, Eliza Solares
Edited by Debra Goelz, Melody Grace Hicks, Cardin Watts, Fiora Voss

For information contact:
info@lostbajanbooks.com

ISBN: 9781738018406
ISBN-13: 9781738018406
First Edition: November 2023
10 9 8 7 6 5 4 3 2 1

Dedication

To all of the dreamers and those who dare ask that one question that defines us writers: "what if?"

30 DAYS TO SAVE THE WORLD

a short story anthology

Table of Contents

FOREWORD
by Van Carley

Writing can disembowel and leave us staring at the pages where we just spilled our guts. Other times, we're spilling tears from laughing at what clever wordsmiths we are. The trouble is, we often do this alone, so when we discover a community with other writers, it can be difficult to return to the echoes of our solitude.

When I joined Wattpad over a decade ago, it was to have a place for my writing to exist and share it with others. Soon after joining, I discovered the community side of the platform and realized there was a void in my writing life that I didn't know existed. Each week I entered what was known as the SciFriday contest, hosted by volunteers who ran the Science Fiction profile. There was always a different prompt and word count requirement. Before this, I had never written much science fiction, so it became an enjoyable way to expand my storytelling wings. Imagine writing something intergalactically compelling in three hundred words. It's a challenge! Week after week, I entered and noticed the same usernames among the participants. We'd read each other's entries, cheer each other on, and celebrate when someone won. (Spoiler, I may have snagged a win).

Those early Wattpad years were such a great time as I navigated my place in its community, and explored my writer voice. It also taught me the value of a writer community.

But why am I telling you this?

I've spent most of my Wattpad years meeting amazing writers who I now consider friends. We even built the WritersConnx community together and we continuously look for ways to celebrate our members. So when Rodney (@iamrodneyvsmith) tossed out the idea to create a blockbuster summer Sci-Fi for our next anthology project, I pulled up an imaginary chair and said "tell me more".

From there, the idea grew into a countdown to save the world, with each day to be written by a different author, and I found myself remembering those glorious SciFriday contests. Who would have thought that I'd go from being a writer fumbling to write Sci-Fi to then helping organize a mega blockbuster alien invasion anthology?

Part of what makes this endeavor exciting and unique is that no one is rushing into the battlefield to fight extraterrestrials. In fact, no one is saving the world. Instead, we're exploring the human side of a massive disaster and how people might react if they believed they only had thirty days to live. Would we spend it with our loved ones? Attempt to check the boxes on our bucket list? Or would we allow dark thoughts to take over, and decide the fate of others with the edge of a sharp blade? I knew the project would be a hit, so it was no surprise how thrilled everyone was when we announced it in our WritersConnx Discord server.

Since then, I've been nothing but impressed with how our contributors have stepped up their game and have taken critiques and suggestions from our editors like champs. Writing can be very personal, and it takes guts to take what you've manifested in your thoughts and formulate them into actual words for people to judge. You're allowing readers into your mind. It's a vulnerable place to be, and not easy.

What I love most about this anthology is the distinct writer voices in each story, and one of our editors, Fiora Voss, said something that I really liked. She said it feels like she's getting a glimpse into the minds of people she had only seen in chats, and how the stories reflect their authors. However, not necessarily in plot or concept, but style, focus, whether they're funny or serious, and despite each entry being unique, the stories are united.

I couldn't agree more.

We have a fantastic batch of writers who have thrown their talents into this project. Some were even called upon last minute and delivered truly amazing stories on short notice. When a writer can cause Rodney to run back to our team chat and fangirl over what he just read, which happened many, many times, then we know our writers have genuinely given us their all. I'd like to believe it's because of how invested people are and their trust in our vision. The atmosphere has been buzzing with us breathing as one unit, pushing for this anthology to be a success.

I couldn't be prouder, and as you turn the pages to read story after story, you'll find out why.

Van Carley,
Mistress of Anthologies, and WritersConnx Admin
@van_carley

PROLOGUE

about the author

***Rodney V. Smith** is an Author, Filmmaker, Visual Artist and Award Winner. 30+ years screenwriting and producing indie films, and reading all of the books.*

2018 Watty Award Winner, his mission is to complete all 12 books in the comedic vampire series HOW NOT TO VAMPIRE. He is one of the founding members of WritersConnX.

THE ARRIVAL

by Rodney V. Smith

HARRISONBURG, VIRGINIA, USA

JULY 27, 3:14 AM

"What the fuck is that?" Harlan Withers shrieked, finger pointed directly up at the sky above.

He was lying on his back, smoking a joint on the roof of the Waffle House where he worked, so there was no one else around to shriek at, but when things just appear out of nowhere, sometimes a man's got to shriek.

His finger should have been pointed at something *in* the night sky, but while that was *technically* what it was doing, what was going on was a hell of a lot more complicated than Harlan's brain was currently equipped to handle.

The wide open sky was gone. The splash of stars that Harlan enjoyed watching the hell out of every night was now obscured by something impossibly huge. Distant circles of blinking red and blue lights were scattered across a black, unmoving expanse that seemed to go on forever in all directions, all the way to the horizon. The night sky had been obstructed in the blink of an eye as if it had never existed.

Harlan dragged his gaze from the *thing* high above, over to the half-smoked blunt in his hand. It was his nightly mid-shift treat, and while it gave him a decent buzz to get through the next couple of hours until the morning crew arrived, it had never given him hallucinations before. His gaze returned to the sky, where his finger was still pointing, and then the enormity of exactly what he was seeing hit him all at once: it was *a fucking U.F.O.*

A gust of wind struck him, plastering his hands down at his sides, the gravel on the roof biting into his exposed skin. *No dammit, he didn't want to die like this, lying on his back on the roof of the Waffle House. It wasn't fair! He hadn't even finished his joint, and that shit was expensive—*

Two seconds later, the wind died out. Harlan swore he heard the rattle of cars and trees getting the shit shaken out of them, but at that point, all he could think of was getting the hell off the roof. He needed to tell someone right now!

"MARIA! CALL NINE-ONE-ONE!" Harlan screamed as adrenaline, fear, and absolute-fucking-panic kicked in with a vengeance. Maria probably couldn't hear him from inside the kitchen, but Harlan had left the back door propped open with a cinder block, so there was hope. His phone was nothing but a brick since a customer had thrown it at the wall last week, and he still had to get a new one.

He crawled to the top of the roof access ladder. This wasn't the wisest move on Harlan's part since he was nice and properly stoned, adrenaline or not, and he stumbled to catch his balance. He swayed for a long moment on one leg, then grabbed the metal handles.

He caught a glimpse of the closeby I-81, headlights becoming taillights and vice-versa as the occasional car sped on into the night, somehow oblivious to the monstrosity above them.

"DAMMIT, MARIA! GET OUT HERE!" Harlan climbed down the ladder, throwing furtive glances skyward as if the craft was going to vanish as quickly as it had appeared, but it hung in the sky as if it had always been there. As if it *belonged*.

The heavy kitchen door slammed open then rebounded with an audible thump off the filthy black dumpster that Felix kept putting too damn close, every damn time. If you pushed too hard, like Maria just had done, the door would whack you in the face pretty good if you weren't paying attention. Maria wasn't paying attention, and she yelped as the door caught her.

"Goddamn Felix!" Maria swore as Harlan jumped to the ground. She glared accusingly at Harlan. She knew better, but people loved to blame him for everything. "What you screaming about now, Harlan?"

He spotted Maria's phone lying by the dumpster where she had dropped it and snatched it up, completely ignoring his injured friend. "We gotta call somebody in charge right now, Maria!" he insisted. "We got aliens!"

"I thought you was out here smoking weed, not meth."

"Look!" Harlan jabbed an angry finger at the sky. Maria rolled her eyes, making it clear that she didn't have time for this shit, but she glanced up. Apparently, she didn't quite register what she was seeing and actually turned back to Harlan, mouth already opening to deliver her usual caustic insult about Harlan's intelligence. But then she shook her head and checked the sky again, this time very, very slowly.

"What the *fuck* is that?" Maria whispered. "Harlan, what did you *do to the sky*?"

Glaring at Maria, Harlan dialled 911. "Me? I ain't done nothing! It just popped out of nowhere, I swear!"

"Is that a flying saucer, Harlan? It's too big!" She gasped as she made the sign of the cross. They both took in the underside of the distant ship above, tracking all the way from one horizon to the next. The ship vanished into darkness on all sides. "Where does it end, Harlan? Where does it *end*?"

"Nine-One-One, what's your emergency?"

Harlan gulped and tried to sound as sober as possible. "Yeah, I'd like to report a flying saucer?" He tore his gaze away from the craft and walked across the back alley.

"Sir, this is the emergency line—" The operator had an impatient tone. She probably got calls nightly from every crazy human in a twelve-mile radius, but she wasn't having it tonight, not on her watch.

"Ma'am, I swear this isn't a prank, but I don't know who else to call. Can you get somebody there to go outside and look at the sky? Please?"

"I don't know why I'm doing this," the operator said, then sounding like she had covered her headset, "Jerry, you wanna take a look outside at the sky?" Back to the phone. "Please hold."

Feeling suddenly lost, Harlan looked back at Maria, who had sunk to her knees on the rough asphalt of the back alley and was praying. She never took her eyes off the craft.

The alley behind the Waffle House was barely that, just a 20-foot section of paved ground that gave the trucks barely enough time to make deliveries. The asphalt gave way to scrubland and overlooked the I-81. Three almost full dumpsters with standard-issue graffiti were lined up against the back wall next to the kitchen door. The familiar yellow WAFFLE HOUSE sign towered over the squat brick building, making up for the lack of the trademark yellow awning around the roof. Instead, they had large light-up yellow letters that spelled out WAFFLE HOUSE, the signal to travellers on and off the interstate to come get their food with the occasional side-helping of don't give a fuck.

The sheer impossibility of the moment crashed home to Harlan then, and he wanted to sink to the ground in that back alley and just give up. What was the point of anything? Everything he had known about life and the way things worked was pointless in the face of that *thing*. Like Maria said, it was just *too damn big*. Something that big had no damn right hanging around in the sky as if it was a perfectly reasonable thing to do.

"Where does it end, Harlan?" Maria still whispered like it was a prayer. *"Where does it end?"*

"Hey!" someone yelled from the side of the alley close to the parking lot. Harlan and Maria turned to see an older man with bottle-glass thick glasses, glowering at them impatiently. "Restaurant's open, right?"

Harlan gestured weakly toward the alien craft in the sky. "Yeah, but… are you seeing this?"

The man turned to look and then shrugged as if giant alien spaceships were an everyday occurrence. "Yeah, I seen it. Kinda hard to miss, but tell ya what: get me some coffee and some scrambled eggs, and you can come on back here and gawk at it all you want."

Harlan stared blankly at the man, then turned to Maria, his mouth on automatic. "You heard the man, Maria! Customer wants his food."

That seemed to snap her out of it. She wiped her tears on her apron as she stood, blinking as if seeing the man for the first time. It was a surreal *tableau,* with them all standing in the back alley of the restaurant, kind of like one of the Renaissance paintings he'd seen on the internet.

Harlan tried on a smile that felt plastic. "Find yourself a seat, and we'll get right to you, Sir."

The man shrugged and vanished behind the side of the building. Maria smoothed her apron with shaking hands, but she actually seemed calm. Harlan watched her cautiously as if she was about to explode, and when that didn't happen, he looked at the phone in his hand.

The screen was black.

"I think they hung up on me," he said and handed the phone back. Maria pocketed it into her apron. "You gonna be okay?"

"There's a fucking *alien ship* in the sky, Harlan. What do you think?"

"I don't think any of us are going to be okay. I mean, look at that thing." He swallowed, still fighting that feeling of being completely lost. "What do we do now?"

She gave him a long, almost hopeless look. "What we always do, Harlan. Whether it's a hurricane, a fire, riots, floodwater up to the roof, or even a damn tornado, we stay open *no matter what.* Waffle House don't close for nothing, short of the end of the world. So what we do right now, is we go back to work until *that* happens."

Harlan took another look at the sky and couldn't help but shudder. In the distance, tires screeched, followed by a sudden crunch. At almost the same instant, sirens blared into the night air. It seemed like people were slowly discovering that life had changed forever.

"I think the end of the world just began," he said.

20,000 FEET OVER CHARLOTTE, NORTH CAROLINA, USA 3:15 AM

His new co-pilot was still dozing as Captain George Delmar eased American Airlines Flight 866 into what was supposed to be a routine descent to the Atlanta Hartsfield-Jackson International Airport. That, of course was the moment that his entire world went to shit.

The familiar sight of the US Eastern seaboard 20,000 feet below vanished, replaced by an impossible black mass, now only 4000 feet below, and closing.

George had time to note the various unfamiliar patterns of light that had replaced the lights of various small towns, these new alien lights seeming to go on almost forever across the uncomfortably close surface.

The proximity alarms shrieked that Flight 886 was about to crash into the ground and that something needed to be done immediately. George's life flashed across his mind, and there were so many regrets, so many things he still wanted to do–things like not turning off the autopilot a minute ago, just because he wanted to keep his skills sharp and not just let the computer handle it.

George eased down on the stick, his training and self-preservation instincts kicking in, determined to at least level out the plane to avoid a crash. He must have yelled or something because his co-pilot (what was his name again?) jerked awake and then leaped into action without a question, realizing that some kind of disaster was imminent. The two men pulled the plane out of its low-angled descent, coaxing it into a climb, away from a fiery death.

"Holy shit!" George breathed, half laughing. "I think we made it–"

George would later think that it was as if physics had just realized something was clearly out of place, and was determined to set it right again. Impossibly huge objects do not pop into existence without displacing something else, and in this case, that something else was *air.*

The wind hit then, buffeting the plane higher with the force of a hurricane.

"Oh shi–"

WASHINGTON D.C., USA - 3:37 AM

The President of the United States needed just a moment to collect his thoughts. He felt detached, almost like he was watching himself be the leader of the free world. But who could blame him? All he needed was a moment, just a moment…

He pressed his forehead against the cool, thick bulletproof glass and watched the scenery pass by, trying not to look up at the *thing* that had replaced the sky. The thing that terrified him to the core of his very being.

His Chief of Staff was desperately trying to get him to pay attention to the various video calls from the Chiefs of Staff, but it was impossible to concentrate. Everything turned into background noise, so *insignificant* in the face of the monstrosity overhead that went from horizon to horizon.

Someone said something about adapting the protocols, but he wasn't listening. There *wasn't* a protocol for something like this.

He watched the multiple cars that had pulled onto the shoulder of the freeway. A man gawked at the sky from the hood of his car. A woman on a cellphone, screaming. Too many on phones. They wanted answers, answers he couldn't provide, at least not yet.

Cadillac One, the armoured car known as the Beast, was capable of reaching speeds of 120 mph but had never needed to sustain those speeds through its various incarnations over the past twenty years. The President had never seen it go anything over 40, but then again, he'd never had to travel this far in it before, especially with his wife and daughter in tow, away from Washington DC, away from under the shadow of the flying saucer.

For the sake of safety, they couldn't risk flying anywhere, and he understood why, but he still wasn't looking forward to driving over 900 miles West. The plan was to be on Air Force One by midday and then to fly West to a nuclear bunker deep in the Rockies. The President would be able to coordinate the response from there and hopefully stop his generals from freaking out and bombing anything.

The country would be in full panic mode as soon as they woke up and saw an alien craft in the sky, and his generals were already talking about tactical strikes as if this was some *wargame* and that millions of lives weren't at stake.

The Beast braked and then slowed just enough to creep past the wreckage of a six-car pile-up. A dazed-looking man, his shirt covered in blood, turned toward The Beast, maybe hoping for help. He seemed to lock eyes with the President, for just a moment, as impossible as it was through the tinted glass, but then he turned to look at the sky. Then, the moment had passed, the Beast accelerating back to full speed, the crash and the bleeding man nothing but a memory

The President of the United States took a deep breath He couldn't help those injured people, not like that anyway. He had to take care of everyone. He was ready.

"Have we established contact yet?" The President finally asked.

CABLE NEWS NETWORK
3:44 AM

Breaking news! Reports are coming in that an enormous alien craft of possible extra-terrestrial origin has appeared over the Eastern seaboard of the United States.

All flights have been grounded, effective immediately, as there are continuing reports of multiple downed and missing aircraft with many feared dead. Possibly hundreds.

A representative from Homeland Security has issued a statement that all branches of the armed forces have been placed on high alert and the Pentagon has gone to DEFCON-1.

A nationwide state of emergency has been declared. We repeat: a nationwide state of emergency is in effect immediately.

Officials estimate that the craft is approximately two thousand miles in diameter and spans all the way from Southern Ontario in Canada, to the area near Disney in Florida.

We'll be continuing to report on this unprecedented state of emergency, so stay with us, your number-one source for news.

DAWLISH, UNITED KINGDOM - 7:44 AM

Millie Carpenter looked away from the news report on her mobile, heart pounding, wondering if anyone else on the train had seen the clip with the headline that simply screamed ALIEN INVASION.

The cute boy across from her glanced up as well. He had a bad haircut and sat in the same seat every morning with his headphones on as if he was auditioning for early adulthood. His face was pale, eyes wide.

Their gazes met briefly, and all at once, she knew that he had seen the same clip she had. Just to be sure that she wouldn't make a complete arse of herself, she held up her mobile screen for confirmation.

The boy nodded, slipped off his headphones, and leaned forward to *actually* talk to her. Wow. Just wow.

"It's got to be some kind of joke, right?"

"It seems pretty legit. It's all over the internet."

"Bloody Americans, right? Always the centre of the universe. At least it's over there and not hitting us."

Millie opened her mouth to say something witty and charming, anything to keep this boy talking to her, maybe even ask her name just like in the movies. She never got the chance.

The wind hit then, rocking the train as it crept along the tracks on its regular commute along the coast. This wasn't new for anyone who rode the Dawlish commute, and Millie, like everyone else almost expected it.The wind kicked the waves up and over the train in the worst weather. The trains had even been outfitted to deal with the water, and nobody hardly got wet anymore. *This* wind came out of nowhere, an unnatural force that moved everything in its path, including water.

Millie watched with horror as the biggest wave she had ever seen engulfed the train.

It was the longest three seconds of Millie's young life, but then, just as quickly as it had begun, it was over. She suddenly realized that she had found the young man's hands in the chaos, and they clutched each other's fingers tightly.

They looked at each other and didn't let go.

***

The craft sat locked in geosynchronous orbit with the Earth. Anyone asking would have assumed that its direct center was over Washington D.C., maybe even directly over the White House itself. Just like in the movies.

Satellite imagery would later confirm that, for whatever reason, the *actual* center of the craft was over the Waffle House off Interstate 81 in Harrisonburg, Virginia. This detail was lost on everyone, including the inhabitants of the diner, except for a tall man in a suit who sat in the corner booth with a single cup of coffee in front of him, waiting for someone or for something to happen.

It was five days before the craft communicated, beaming a 10-mile-wide, glowing blue number into the sky directly below. For good measure, just to make the point, at 12 AM Eastern Time, every screen in the world flashed with a giant number, in what could be considered a friendly and *nonthreatening* font:

30

about the author

***MB Dalto** is a bisexual New Adult romantic fantasy author, best known for her Watty Winner TWO THOUSAND YEARS, her Watty Shortlister CUT TO THE BONE, and Watty Longlister LADY MUTINY. She is a Wattpad Creator and contributor to both Paid Stories and YONDER.*

When she is not hiding behind her laptop, she is reading fantasy novels, playing video games, and drinking coffee.

THE PROPHET

by M.B.Dalto

SOMEWHERE ALONG ROUTE 95, NEW YORK, USA
AUGUST 1, 3:34 AM

Though Aaron's fingertips were frozen from being out so late, and his neck ached from constantly looking up above him, he was unable to tear his gaze from the glowing blue '30' hovering in the sky above him.

There was something else, something beyond the number, but he couldn't quite focus–

He was filled with the knowledge that *he alone knew what the number meant.*

For the first time in his life, he was the most important person on Earth, and that emblazoned numeral would forever remind him of that. Everyone would hear his message, and he'd finally be respected. Maybe even worshiped. They'd see him as a prophet. Perhaps even a *god.* And his days of delivering pizzas for Reading House Of Pizza would be over. But first—

Headlights pierced the ethereal fog surrounding him. As he stumbled toward the lights, his bare feet crunched the dead leaves on the forest floor. He swore he had shoes at one point— who rode a bike barefoot? And speaking of, where was his bike?

The driver lowered the passenger window of a gleaming black Rolls Royce. A car fit for kings. Or for prophets.

"Uber X for… Aaron?" the driver asked as he leaned over the passenger seat, peering at Aaron like the car shouldn't be for him. "Aaron *Campion*?"

Talk about timing.

He knew how he must look in his striped polo shirt of red and green to match RHOP's signature colors, paired with stained khakis, and— well, he *did* have sneakers. Somewhere… Navigating his way through the woods barefoot in the middle of the night should have disturbed Aaron more than he did, but he was on a mission. A mission of the utmost importance. *Something* had come to him in that fog, and he knew that he needed to share it with whoever would listen. The knowledge he possessed was the most important information that could befall human ears, and Aaron alone was tasked with the responsibility to share it.

And share it he would.

Climbing into the car, he felt the familiar comfort of his phone in his pocket. He wouldn't need to wait until he returned home to tell his friends—né, they would be his *followers* now!—about his divine mission. From this day forward, he would be known as *Aaron the Prophet*, delivering a hell of a lot more than just your large cheese with extra pepperoni in thirty minutes or less.

But as he stared at his screen, his heart sank into his stomach to the point of nausea, which didn't help the caffeine headache gathering behind his eyes. The phone was dead. Useless. All he could see on his screen was that same illuminated '30' as it was in the sky, as if it had been burned into his brain like the ghost of an image on an outdated plasma television. Now he would need to wait longer for his friends to find out. For the world to *know*.

Defeated, for now, Aaron settled against the back seat of the Uber fit for a Prophet. The driver adjusted his rearview mirror as if to see him better. Yes, look upon your Prophet.

"You really going to Reading? That's over a hundred miles away, but lucky you, it's already paid for."

Of course, it was paid for. He was the Prophet. Once he shared his prophetic teachings with the world, money wouldn't be an issue. In fact, they would be paying him for his wisdom. And this Uber driver was going to be the first of his lucky future followers.

Leaning forward in his seat, Aaron smiled.

The driver looked over his shoulder. "Well," he said.

But as Aaron opened his mouth and began his very first sermon, the driver removed one hand from the wheel to cover his ear, then the other, interrupting Aaron's message as the car swerved. But even worse? Aaron crossed his arms over his chest, deciding he would not share his wisdom with this miscreant.

"*What the hell is wrong with you?*" The driver screamed though the only thing Aaron saw wrong was the guy's poor driving and insolence. "Do you need to go to the hospital or something?"

Aaron again opened his mouth and told him that other than his lack of shoes, he was perfectly fine, but this time the driver removed both hands from the steering wheel to cover his now-bleeding ears.

The Rolls swerved into the opposite lane, nearly crashing headfirst into an oncoming car. Horns blared as the Uber swerved back into the correct lane avoiding a collision, but the car slammed to a stop, and the driver turned around to glare at Aaron.

He drew back in shock at the man's behavior. As the first person to be gifted with the words of the prophet, the man's reaction was baffling.

"I swear to God, if you open your mouth again, I'm going to drop you off in the middle of nowhere and get you permanently banned from the app for this *bullshit!*"

Matching his glare, Aaron decided this man was not worthy of his efforts. He pretended to busy himself by looking at his unusable phone screen, but really he was silently considering the numerous versions of eternal punishments he could exact upon the infid

The car pulled back into traffic and Aaron tried to make himself as invisible as possible. Prophet or not, he wasn't going to take the chance that the driver would toss him out and he'd be forced to walk all way back to Reading

***

Aaron calmly requested the Uber drop him off at Benchwarmer's Coffee & Doughnuts, his preferred café, but instead, the driver screamed and swerved up onto the curb in front of the Reading Police Department, generating more screams of surprise from the innocent bystanders along the sidewalk.

"OUT! GET OUT!" the driver screamed.

He opted not to tell the driver to have a nice day as his food service experience had trained him, instead slamming the car door behind him as he stepped out onto the street that he hoped would one day be named after him. *Aaron Avenue*. He could picture it now.

The sidewalks at the center of town were congested with the bustle of foot traffic, and what appeared to be abandoned cars lining not only the sides of the street but backed up the entire length of the main throughway. News crews congregated outside of the police station, watching the front entrance as if waiting for someone or something to happen. Others were looking up at the sky at something that shouldn't *matter to a prophet, something that the Prophet didn't need to see, no…* He had a message to deliver.

The urge to share his news drove him onward. Coffee could *wait*. There was chaos everywhere, and if anyone was going to understand the importance of the information Aaron had to impart on the human race, he'd need a police escort to keep the riff-raff in line. Like a Pizza Delivery Saint, he straightened his tomato-stained polo shirt and headed toward the entrance.

He pulled open the heavy glass door into the station, which was packed full of angry people. And he, their Prophet, was there to assist

"Aaron?" he heard from behind him. Turning on his heel, he saw his friend and co-worker, Charles, being escorted by two armed police officers down the hallway of the station.

"Oh shit, Aaron! Where have you been, man? We haven't heard from you for days, and now the world has gone crazy—"

"Enough of that," one of the officers growled, yanking Charles's arm so abruptly it practically knocked his friend off his feet.

Aaron had many questions. Mainly why had Charles been arrested? He was going to demand answers, and as their Prophet, the officers of the law must *obey*.

Redirecting his trajectory, he approached the officers, and Charles by association, with the best swagger he could muster on bare feet. Straightening his spine and puffing out his chest, he tapped the officer on the shoulder, something not-Prophet Aaron would never have considered. But today was a different day.

The same gruff officer stopped at Aaron's touch and glared at him over his shoulder, his free hand reaching for the taser attached to his belt. "Can I help you?" he snarled.

Of course, they could help him. By releasing his friend, obviously.

"Let him—"

But he couldn't even finish his sentence before the officers each took a step back, yelling as if they'd been stung by a swarm of bees, and Charles slunk down between them gasping, his eyes filled with horror as he struggled with his hands cuffed behind his back. The officers clapped their hands over their ears as they writhed on the floor like overturned beetles, eyes wide and mouths agape as they stared at him.

As evident by the cacophony of screams, the other nearby officers and visitors were all doing the same—shunning him as if he was the devil himself. Didn't they know he was anything but? He was the *Prophet.* He was there with a message for them. His message would help them all through what was to come, in peace and without confrontation. *Why couldn't they understand this?* Without it, *they were doomed.*

Aaron turned back to Charles, ready to try one more time to let his friend know his very Prophetic news, but the officer had already stepped between them, scowling at Aaron

"I am going to have to ask you to leave, *sir.*" The sarcasm was dripping from the formality.

"But—"

The officer yelled, "OUT!" Cutting Aaron off before he could say another word. "With your mouth shut, or I will break your mouth for you– swear to God!"

With his heart racing and his palms sweaty, Aaron exited the police station. This was now the second time he had attempted to gift his knowledge to humanity and twice that he was so rudely cut off— and he of all people, threatened!

As soon as he honed his prophetic powers, he would smite the heathens where they stood.

But the panic of not sharing the information he was given clenched inside his chest. He had to tell someone… *anyone*… it felt like it was literally eating him from the inside out, this inability to share his parables.

"Excuse me, sir?"

A "sir" without sarcasm. She already had Aaron's attention. A young reporter, perhaps in her early thirties, with perfect hair and makeup, smiled as she sprinted toward him as if trying to beat the rush of news crews anxious to speak with the most important person ever to breathe the same air as them.

"You just came from the police station, can you tell us what's going on in there? We heard a noise, like a thousand birds shrieking from the inside of a tornado. Was it connected to the invasion?"

This was it. The perfect opportunity for Aaron to get his message out to the world—the local news broadcast. With so many news outlets present with their reporters and their cameras, he was certain he'd find someone there who would want to hear his story and learn his message.

Keeping his mouth closed this time, Aaron nodded vigorously.

"Great," she said, looking back to her cameraman. He pointed to a spot on the sidewalk, and Grace positioned herself as directed, clearing her throat and straightening her spine.

Aaron kept his attention on her, sidling up beside her where she directed. She smelled like pineapple— the perfect pizza topping. The cameraman placed his headphones over his ears and positioned his camera on his shoulder, and gave the reporter a thumbs up. Aaron's heart skipped a beat. They could very well give him his own daytime talk show after this.

"This is Grace Weathers, reporting from the streets of downtown Reading. I'm joined by—"

The reporter paused and looked to Aaron as if to ask him his name, but he wasn't going to delay any longer and lose his chance to finally share his message. He snatched the microphone and confidently stepped in front of her so that the camera was focused wholly and entirely on him.

And this time, he didn't stop speaking when Grace Weathers cowered away from him with her hands over her ears. Even the shouts from the passersby did not stray him from his righteous cause. Although the cameraman winced, with his headphones on, he seemed less bothered than the others and motioned for Aaron to continue with a twirl of his finger— the camera was rolling, and this was going to be shared with every Channel 6 viewer that day.

Aaron felt like he spoke for hours, sharing his knowledge and imparting the divine truth, and his story would be told for generations to come. It was *that* important, and now the world would know it too. The movie about him would win Oscars, and his memoir would be an instant New York Times Bestseller.

And when he was finished—when he finally disclosed all he needed to say —he let out a sigh of relief, a sense of resolve settling upon him. Though the cameraman gave him the thumbs-up, Grace Weathers ripped the microphone out of his hand, and Aaron swore she snarled at him.

Where was the praise? The falling over in exaltation?

"I don't know who you work for or what you're trying to do," she said, but if you do anything like that ever again, I will have the authorities after your ass. In fact—" She arched her neck as two policemen exited the station. "Officers! We have another fanatic over here!"

But Aaron was already waltzing down the sidewalk towards home with the weight of the world's salvation lifted off of his shoulders.

***

By the time he returned to his rundown basement apartment and kicked over the piles of RHOP pizza boxes that should have gone out in last week's recycling, it was just about time for the *Channel 6 Action News At Noon*. Aaron wasn't normally a viewer of the local news—or any news for that matter. Current events depressed him, and he chose to live with a far more optimistic outlook than the talking heads cared to deliver.

Though the electricity seemed to flicker, as uncertain as his cell phone's reception had been, a few meaningless wiggles of the television's wires proved effective enough to generate a clear picture with somewhat coherent sound. And just in time, he surmised as he tossed the remote control aside into yet another pile of pizza boxes and settled in to watch his spectacular debut, just as the theme played and the introductions began.

Aaron's leg bounced impatiently as he endured the interminable weather update (overcast with unnaturally high winds and the chance of dense fog, with a 100% chance of flying saucer, ha-ha) and the traffic alerts (heavy congestion from too many people trying to evacuate, but viewers are urged to await instructions and not add to the traffic).

Was all of this happening because of *him*? Was his ascension to becoming a Prophet the beginning of the Endtimes?

Only when the Breaking News chyron flashed across the bottom of the screen, did he lean forward to give the program his undivided attention. The news anchors looked even more exhausted than the traffic and weather people, with disheveled hair, unkempt clothing, and bags under their eyes. Like they had been broadcasting nonstop for days. *Fascinating*.

"Today marks day five since the unidentified craft has made its appearance in the skies above the eastern seaboard. Citizens have crowded into the streets to get a view of the immense craft that now blocks the sky for millions. Homes and cars have been abandoned in the mass panic sweeping over not only the state but the country. We go now to Grace Weathers, live from the Reading Police Department, for more."

Grace appeared on the screen, her perfect makeup melted, her hair like a rat's nest, balls of cotton poking out of her ears, and dried blood on her jaw, as she began her segment.

"As more reports are coming in, this unidentified object could possibly be affecting not only our electronics but also the sanity of our citizenry. Earlier today, I had a first-hand experience with such an affected individual. We must warn you that what you are about to witness is somewhat disturbing and uncomfortable, so if you have sensitive hearing, we advise you to turn the volume down."

Aaron turned up the volume all the way just as the recording from earlier began. There was Grace Weathers asking Aaron to introduce himself, and there he was taking the microphone from her as he prepared to tell the world the most important message they had ever heard.

Aaron almost fell from his chair in anticipation. This was it. In a moment everyone would be enlightened and enamored not only with his message but also, with *him*.

He didn't blink as he watched himself on the screen. Standing there in the last Reading House Of Pizza uniform he'd ever have to wear. After today, it would be only the finest silks for this Prophet. Not that it mattered. He'd be revered either way.

He watched himself open his mouth to speak.

An ear-splitting, gut-wrenching eardrum-piercing howl of a wounded animal slowly dying made Aaron fall out of his chair. He slapped his hands over his now-bleeding ears.

"Stop! Stop!" he begged, but the noise was relentless and maddening. "Make it stop!" Giving up, he army-crawled across the floor, daring to uncover his ear just long enough to pull the television's power cord from the wall.

The silence was deafening even after the screen went black.

Was that what others had heard when he attempted to deliver the most important news ever? Was his information so valuable that even sound waves could not support the pure knowledge of his teachings?

Speaking would do no good, then.

Writing, however… Yes! That's it!

He could write it all out, like a gospel or a manifesto.

He scrambled from where he lay and gathered up every pizza box he could find. He didn't have time for fancy journals or expensive paper—a Prophet needs to be resourceful. A conveniently discarded pen was underneath the couch, and soon the living room was littered with the tools of his opus.

And he spent hours writing everything down. This would be the world's instruction manual to carry on. To live their best lives from that day forward. And if not for Aaron—for the information he obtained and the message he would share—the world could very well end.

But it wouldn't. Because thanks to the Gospel according to Aaron, everything about the future was going to be *perfect.*

***

The smell of old pepperoni tickled his senses, and as he lifted his head, the oily cardboard from the pizza box beneath his head stuck to his face. Aaron focused his eyes on the darkness of his house. He lost track of time and didn't remember falling asleep, but it didn't matter now that he had fulfilled his purpose and recorded all his teachings for the world to read.

Before gifting his corrugated masterpiece to the world, he'd admire it one last time. Then he'd stack the boxes up for their final delivery, but—

"What the hell?"

His heart raced. He opened and closed the covers. One after the other.

"No, no, no!"

All of his writing… his message. His wisdom and his warnings—

Every sentence. Every profound teaching. It was unreadable. His perfect words were replaced with jibberish.

Box after box, only incomprehensible scribbles and scrawling.

His message… the most important message in the world.

It was gone.

Calm down, Aaron. Just do it again. You were tired last night.

He opened an unused box, all set to start over. When the fate of the world is on your shoulders, you don't complain about having to do extra work.

His pen was poised over the cardboard.

He blinked.

The cardboard stared back at him.

What was the message he'd been sent to spread around the world to save humanity?

His head pounded as he tried to recall, but the harder he tried, the deeper the throbbing in his temporal lobe pulsed, worse than any coffee withdrawal he'd ever endured.

It was gone. All of it.

~

29

about the author

Jane Peden *is a multi-published Award Winning Author, Collector of Rescue Dogs, and Vegetarian Foodie.*

Jane writes sexy contemporary romances, thrillers set in exotic locales, and short stories including romantic capers, YA horror, paranormal, and literary fiction. Her ongoing serialized fiction project, SEX AND THE BILLIONAIRE CRIME BOSS, is available exclusively on Wattpad.

Jane is proud to be a Wattpad Creator and an author on YONDER, and is published with Entangled Publishing and Mr. Media Books. Her book LAW, LIES, AND LOVE AFFAIRS has over 3 million views on Wattpad. When she's not writing, Jane is at work as a trial lawyer.

THE WILDERNESS

by Jane Peden

DENALI NATIONAL PARK, ALASKA, USA
AUGUST 2, 1:00 PM

"I should have stayed at the base camp." Emily is staring at Jacob, who just slipped on a rock and fell, banging his elbow and twisting his ankle. She is unsympathetic. We are two weeks into our six-week grand Alaskan wilderness adventure, but it's been enough time for me to get a feel for who the others are. And how well everyone is coping without cell phones, since there's no reception here anyway.

"Don't take your boot off," Aidan warns. "You might not get it back on again."

"Shit," Jacob says, and I know what he's thinking. We only have a couple more hours to go today to reach the base camp and the rest of the group—but double that if he can't walk without help.

We broke camp at five a.m. Just as the sun came up. But even exhausted from a full day's hike, I didn't get much sleep. I'm not used to the long daylight hours, with sunset not happening until eleven p.m. It will be a while before the days get shorter, and winter comes.

By then, I'll have gone back to my hometown in Western Pennsylvania, in the hills where my love of hiking was born. But only for a few days before I leave for good. After that, my life will never be the same again.

There are eight of us altogether, plus our tour guide, Marcel. There were supposed to be two guides, but Liuna tested positive for COVID the day we were to fly from Fairbanks to our drop-off point at Denali National Park, and there was no time to get a replacement. Since Aidan has spent his life in Alaska, the tour company reluctantly decided we could go ahead, as long as everyone signed waivers. All of us are over 18 - just barely.

It took a week to hike to the area that will serve as our initial base camp. We all thought we were in good shape, but it turned out to be some more than others. Which is why half the group voted to stay at camp, rest up a little, and practice their wilderness skills with Marcel, while the other half of us were determined to head north, hoping to get a spectacular view of Denali—the highest mountain peak in North America—before our group moves further southwest along the Alaska Range.

"Emily," Jacob says, "for five minutes can you not be a bitch?"

She just stares at him, then turns and starts back down the trail. I lean down and give him a hand up.

"Thanks, Madison."

"Can you walk?"

"Yeah, I'm fine," he says, but he's clearly not. I hand him the trek poles he should have been using before and maybe he wouldn't have fallen. Aidan insisted we bring them, although both Jacob and Emily protested it was just one more unnecessary thing adding weight to their backpacks. Aidan won, because that's what Aidan does, in his quiet way.

Jacob manages, despite the injury, and I'm optimistic that maybe he just strained it. A sprain would be bad news, since we have some pretty aggressive hiking to do tomorrow. And while the four of us are already tired, the others have had five days to rest up.

But oh god it was worth it. With Marcel's directions and Aidan's skills, we reached the perfect spot to view the majesty of Denali, and what seemed like the whole of Alaska spread out in front of us. Then I spotted a moose, standing solitary and majestic. It seemed to look right at us, take our measure and then, deciding we were no threat, returned to grazing for twigs from low branches at the edge of the grassy field. All of it—the towering face of Denali, the wilderness stretching out forever, and the lone moose—took my breath away.

The only thing I imagine will top it on this trip is when we finally get to see the northern lights. Aurora borealis. Those stunning bands of color that fill the sky. I'm told no photograph even comes close to seeing them in person. They aren't visible now, because it doesn't get dark enough. But by late August we'll see them. It makes me think of new beginnings.

We stop for lunch at a small fast-moving stream that cascades over rocks in small waterfalls. The water is icy and clear, but I don't trust it. I get out my bottle filter and purifier. Aidan shakes his head and lies down by the stream, scooping handfuls of water to drink directly from the source. He tells us again that this deep in backcountry—the water is pure and safe to drink.

I'm not taking any chances. I fill my bottle using the filter, then insert the pen-like purifier, push the button and swirl it. In about sixty seconds the UV light goes off, and I take a long drink and then pass the bottle to Emily for her and Jacob to share.

Meanwhile, Aidan actually dunks his head under the running water, then shakes himself off like a dog, his wild hair flying. The time he spends outdoors in the long daylight of summer has streaked his hair with blond, and he looks incongruously like a California surfer. He grins at me, then digs out the bear-proof canister from his pack and passes out energy bars.

Emily and Jacob are sitting next to each other on a slanted boulder, his arm slung casually around her shoulders. She has the first aid kit open beside them and just finished cleaning and bandaging his scraped elbow. He protested that she was making a big deal about it, but seemed to be enjoying the attention.

In the week we've been together, I can't remember a time when they weren't either sniping insults at each other, or cuddling up and kissing. They've been a couple since middle school, and are the only two of the eight of us who knew each other before we all met up at the airport in Fairbanks. The rest of us come from various places around the country, the only thing in common being that for some reason we all wanted to spend the last six weeks before heading off to college or wherever making this once-in-a-lifetime trip.

Well, we also are privileged enough to be able to do this, because the price was not cheap, plus all the gear we had to either rent or buy.

For this whole mini excursion Emily and Jacob have been reminding us that they live in Orlando, Florida, and have amazing endurance hiking on flat terrain in the heat, but that it just doesn't translate well to hiking in the mountains. If they say it one more time I'm tempted to scream *it does not matter no one is judging you.*

Cole, Morgan, and Liam are all from the West Coast—Seattle, L.A., and San Francisco. Parker is the only one I've really connected with so far, but they didn't want to come on the extra hike. Didn't want to is perhaps putting it too mildly. *Hell no and I'm already wondering why I thought this would be fun* was Parker's reaction after the grueling week-long hike that got us this far into the backcountry. When we sat around the campfire the very first night, Parker shared that they recently came out as nonbinary, and that their parents in their small midwestern town were not so much non-accepting as simply baffled. "I just had to get away for awhile," Parker explained, "and this is about as far away as I could get."

I definitely relate to being from a small town and feeling like an outsider. I don't think I will ever really go home again. A flourishing coal and steel town a few generations ago, the area is now economically depressed. There's a branch campus of one of the state universities there, but it's not like people go there because they want to stay. They go there because of the vicinity to ski areas and because it's scenic. The only industries that flourish are illegal meth labs, and hospitals. Old men sit in corner bars drinking boilermakers and talking about the good old days. And how strip mining would revive the economy if it weren't for "those damn environmentalists."

Which is ironic, considering that the only other quasi-successful industry is hospitality, providing a destination for hikers drawn by the same forests those guys would like to strip mine away.

Aidan gets us moving again. Jacob doesn't complain, although he's limping more now than he was before. I think he realizes his ankle is going to get worse before it gets better, and wants to get back as quickly as possible.

It takes another two hours before we come out of a dense area of trees to the base camp. We all stand there, in shock.

Everything is chaos. Tents are shredded, equipment strewn everywhere. I recognize a sweatshirt that has literally been ripped apart. It's Parker's.

"Grizzly," Aidan says.

"Parker!" I scream, and run into the campsite. Aidan reaches out to stop me, but I pull away and he lets me go, probably realizing that if the bear was still here we'd know it already.

I can't breathe. I have this horrible picture in my mind of them all being dragged off into the underbrush. Do grizzlies eat people? Or do they just maul them to death? I don't even know.

Emily is crying and Jacob has his arms around her.

"Ok, everybody, just calm down," Aidan says.

Are you serious?" I ask him. "*Calm down*?"

Aidan has been walking through the campsite.

"Look," he says, "there's no sign of anyone getting hurt here. No blood." And I'm thinking, *no body parts*, but I don't say it out loud.

"And this isn't even half the gear we had," Aidan continues.

"But Parker and Liam and Morgan and Cole," Emily sobs. "And fucking Marcel, who was supposed to protect everybody."

"Emily," Aidan says, "nothing happened to them. Nothing like that."

"Then where are they?" I ask.

"They must have left for some reason," Aidan says. "I don't know. Maybe someone got sick, or there was a serious enough accident to need medical attention."

"So they just abandoned us?" Jacob says, in this kind of incredulous voice that completely echoes my own thoughts.

"I imagine Marcel left us a note, but"—he gestures at the destroyed base camp—"it looks like a grizzly got in here later and did all this, so good luck finding it now."

We all stare at each other. Then we hear a rustling in the brush on the other side of the camp site.

"Oh god," Emily says, "it's coming back,"

Aidan has the bear spray in his hand in seconds and we're all in position to jump up and down and scream and hopefully scare it away. There's a dented pot lying on the ground and I pick it up and look for something to bang against it, then drop it.

"Parker!" I yell, and I'm running toward them so fast I almost knock them over.

"Oh my god I'm so glad to see you all." Parker looks like they haven't slept in two days. "I've been checking a couple times a day, watching for you."

"What the hell happened?" Aidan asks.

"Can we get out of here?" Parker looks around nervously. "I'm still worried it will come back. The bear. I set up camp on a ridge about a mile that way."

"Wait," Emily says, "you set up camp? As in just you? Where's the rest of the group?"

"They're gone," Parker says, then sees the horrified look on my face. "No, not dead. They headed back down the trail. I stayed behind to wait for you. And then this happened." Parker gestures toward the ravaged camp.

"Parker," Aidan says, "can you just tell us what's going on."

"I will, but you're not going to believe it. Just—let's just get back to where I've got my tent and stuff and I'll explain everything."

Parker turns and heads back into the trees and we have no option but to follow.

By the time we hike the mile or so of uneven terrain and reach the ridge Parker described, Aidan is almost carrying Jacob.

"Oh crap," Aidan says, and shakes his head once Jacob is sitting on the ground. "I should go back and get the other bear canister. If Marcel and the others didn't take it." He looks over at Parker.

"Don't bother. The bear got it. Marcel was in such a hurry to leave, he didn't fasten the lid properly and that's what the grizzly got into first. Then it must have figured there'd be more food at the campsite."

"So what happened," I ask as we all sit down. There's a log Parker must have dragged over to where I see ashes from their fire, and a rock opposite it that Aidan sits on. The rest of us sit on the log except Parker, who is pacing back and forth.

"They all decided to leave—I'll get to why in a minute—but I stayed behind. It was night, but still bright out, obviously, and I was in my tent when I heard the bear. I started yelling so it would know I was here—that's what Marcel told us to do, remember?"

We all nod.

"Then I opened the tent flap and looked out. It was so much larger than I expected. It saw me and started walking toward the tent, like lumbering, with its shoulder muscles rippling. and I have never been so terrified of anything."

"What did you do?" Emily asks, transfixed.

"I tried to yell again but no sound came out. Then I remembered the air horn. I grabbed it and I just keep blasting it, and the bear turned around and ran back into the trees. But I was afraid I'd just startled it and it would be back again, so I packed up what I could as fast as I could and I kept walking until I was far enough away and found a spot on this ridge, then I set up my tent."

"When was this?" Jacob asked.

"It was just yesterday. God, but it feels longer."

"You said you were going to explain why they all left but you," Aiden prompted.

"What happened, Parker?" I ask.

"It's just... it's really crazy."

"Just tell us," Emily says.

"Ok, so a few days ago Marcel used the satellite phone to check in with the office in Fairbanks, and when he got off he said that it's all over the news and the internet that there's this huge UFO hovering over an entire section of the Eastern U.S., and I mean huge. Like they think it's a thousand miles wide. It's covering Pennsylvania, New York, DC, down as low as South Carolina and as far west as Kentucky."

Jacob looks up. "Come on, that's got to be, like a hoax."

"Yeah, that's what we thought, but Marcel called his wife and she was freaking out. They live in Vermont and he just comes up here for the summer for work, and they've got two little kids, but she was saying he needed to come home now, and crazy stuff like the world might end."

"Oh, come on," Emily says. "Seriously? This has to be some kind of hoax."

"Yeah," Jacob says, "like remember that thing from back in the 1930's? Some radio broadcast about Martians invading and people thought it was real and panicked?"

"Orson Welles," Aidan says. "It was a broadcast of H.G. Wells' science fiction story, War of the Worlds."

"Yeah, that's right," Jacob said. "It was a big hoax and I'm betting this is, too. Somebody must have been having Marcel on, and his wife was in on it."

"No," Parker insists, "you're wrong. There's something weird going on. The president has left Washington D.C. They're saying he's in some secret bunker. This is real."

"Wait," I say, "so you all learned about this a few days ago? Why did they leave yesterday? They couldn't wait for us to get back?"

"We weren't sure if you'd be back today or tomorrow, and Marcel talked to his wife again and everything has gotten insane. Yesterday this eerie blue number 30 appeared in the sky and it showed up on every screen at the same time. I mean, like every screen in the world." Parker shivers. "Phones, laptops, TV's. People are panicking. They think it might be some kind of a doomsday countdown."

I'm still trying to get my head around this. It's not a hoax. This is real.

"I wouldn't leave without you guys," Parker says. "But Marcel and the rest wouldn't wait. He wants to get to his wife and kids while he still can."

"My parents," I say. "My parents live in Pennsylvania. They're under it." Suddenly I can't stop my body from shaking.

"Cole and Morgan and Liam are all from the West Coast," Parker says. "They just wanted to get home in case the 30 days is, well, you know."

"I can't get to my parents," I say. "They might never even know."

"Know what?" Aidan asks.

"Know that I'm pregnant." My voice comes out in a whisper.

Everyone just stares at me. They don't know what to say.

Finally, Jacob breaks the silence. "So. I guess we start hiking back to the drop-off point tomorrow morning."

"You can't even walk," Emily says.

"Why?" Aiden asks suddenly, his voice quiet.

"Well, because he's got a sprained ankle," Emily explains. "It might even be broken."

"No," Aidan says patiently. "Why are we going back?"

Everyone sits in a kind of stunned silence.

"You're right," I finally say. "I can't get to my parents." I look at Emily and Jacob. "I know your families are in Florida, but people are going to panic and there will be mass evacuations. You probably can't even travel to Florida anyway."

"We'll run out of food," Jacob points out.

"Not if we follow the original plan, hike southwest, and catch the salmon run."

We all continue to stare at each other until Parker breaks the silence. "I think we should stay."

"Isn't there someone you want to get back to or at least be able to call?" Aidan asks me. For a moment I don't get what he's driving at, then suddenly I do.

"No." And then I feel like I have to tell somebody, so why not these people? After all, they might be the people I die with.

"I started going to these parties at the college my senior year in high school. I met a guy."

"A college student?" Emily asks.

"No. A professor."

"Oh." Emily's face fills with sympathy.

"He acted like I was special. I might have even stayed, gone to school there, because of him. When I found out I was pregnant I thought he'd be angry, hoped he'd be happy. What he was, was indifferent. Once he confirmed that yes, I really was 18."

"A little late to ask," Aidan says sardonically.

"Yeah."

"Madison?"

I turn my head and look over at Aidan.

"What?"

"You *are* special."

"Yeah, well." I just shrug.

"So, what are your plans?" Emily says. "I mean, if you don't mind me asking."

"That's what I came here to figure out."

"Then that's what you should do."

"Yeah," Parker says. "We'll all help you figure it out."

Aidan stands up, reaches for my hand. "Come on." He pulls me up then jerks his head over to the edge of the rim. "All of you."

We follow Aidan and sit down, a little back from where the ground drops off.

"I know things are crazy down in the Lower 48 right now, but here? It's the same as it's always been."

"Maybe I'll never go back." I picture myself keeping my baby and staying here in Alaska, making a life for us. And I realize I can be anywhere.

"The world will either end or it won't," Aidan says. "And if there's only 29 days left, at least we'll see the northern lights together."

"Yeah," I say, and he puts his arm around my shoulders. Then I put my arm around Parker's. And then Jacob and Emily join in. We are sitting in a line along the top of the rock face, all connected, looking out across the Alaskan wilderness.

"So, let's just say for now that it's not going to end," Emily suggests.

And we all agree, there in the vast silence of the bright sun at night, that it's our choice to believe the world will go on forever.

~

28

about the author

A.B. Channing *is an accidental horror author with too many books, too many works-in-progress, and just enough cats to cover all of the above. He writes part-time professionally, with a preference for speculative fiction of the dark and queer varieties. Typically combined.*

When not wrangling words, he can most often be found buried under notebooks, teaching himself graphic design, or playing in a pond.

He's an adult, if anyone asks. Please ignore the raccoon skull sitting on the table.

THE AIRPORT
by A.B. Channing

PEARSON INTERNATIONAL AIRPORT
TORONTO, ONTARIO, CANADA
AUGUST 2, 11:32 PM

The girl beside me checks her dead phone for the thirteenth time since the turn of the hour. I didn't mean to start counting. I assumed she actually had a signal at first, but that was always more hope than rational observation. Hope that *anyone* had a signal here. That the wifi outage was just a tech glitch on the airport's side. That the massive, blinking brick in the sky that's wiped out all communications for the last eight days decided it was done with us, and just up and disappeared.

I check my watch. It reads the time like it should, and I want so badly to lean over and tell the girl half-past eleven just so she'll stop checking. Her phone screen is blank. It has been since day two of her arrival, and she's been stranded like the rest of us for the better part of seven days. Or maybe she just moved here from a different terminal. The lineup at this gate's unofficial charging station has got so long, someone's started monitoring the outlets, kicking each new batch of people off when they exhaust their quarter-hour. It's enough to put a phone on life support, but I haven't even seen this girl try.

She's not looking for the time. I know that. But admitting it means admitting to hypocrisy, because I haven't stopped checking my living watch or dead phone either.

Gate D35, Terminal 1 is a study in exhausted travelers. I haven't talked to many, but I recognize the woman with the anxious toddler from my flight from Portage la Prairie. I feel for that kid. The old man who sat beside them on the airplane seems to have bonded with her, and has kept her busy with anything from nursery rhymes to origami boxes since our two-hour layover in Toronto saved our lives. The little bay around the gate is carpeted with makeshift beds, but there's a gap beside the window where you could still see smoke off the runway's end until yesterday. Nobody wants to be reminded that our plane would have been among the next to leave.

I pull my jacket tighter. It doesn't matter anyway. The wind that downed a jet and swatted two small aircraft off the tarmac when the alien craft appeared hasn't left us. Not really. There's a lull when the sun peeks between our ground and sky horizons for a half-hour twice a day. For the remaining twenty-three, you could convince me Toronto sat above the Arctic Circle. That it was natural for the sun to make such a fleeting appearance, and that December—not August—was responsible for blasting us with single-digit temperatures and that relentless, frigid wind.

The girl checks her lifeless phone again. It's 11:43.

My bedtime was an hour ago, but though I've slept less than a college student for the last eight days, my body refuses to feel tired. Probably because I can't shut my brain up any more than I can stop my heart from beating. Maybe tonight's the night they'll start allowing stranded passengers onto the planes. I still see them leaving every quarter hour, blinking lights like inverse shooting stars off to make friends with the spacecraft overhead. I know they won't get up to that altitude. They're being careful. They must be, if they're still allowing planes to fly at all, carrying billionaires or injured people out to safer cities where the sky still remembers what color it's supposed to be.

I'd try to catch a plane to Edmonton, if I could get on one at all. I can list a hundred people I'd prefer over my uncle Jim and aunt Mabel; it's been six years since our falling-out, and I'd still sooner gouge my eye out with a rusty spoon than entertain another conversation on Albertan secession. I'm also no more binary now than I was back then, but that's another matter. Jim and Mabel are family and Canadian, two things that'd make it tough for them to shut the door on me. Especially when all my uncle's siblings are—or hopefully are no longer—out of contact somewhere in the midnight zone.

A phone alarm goes off. People jump like cottontails, and someone shoots a glare across the room. The anxious toddler begins to cry. I check my watch again. 11:59 now. Someone wanted to make sure they were looking at their phone when *it* happened.

I'm packed. It's that stupid hope again, but I can't *not* hope. I never thought I'd see a day where I'm this desperate to get back on a plane.

My heart is working its way up my windpipe, displacing half of every breath I take. I'm going to choke on it at this rate. I swallow hard to push it back where it belongs, but it just starts beating up the rest of my internal organs.

My watch beeps the hour. Then its screen goes blank. A half-breath later, the glowing blue number appears.

28

It's a countdown.

I could deny it yesterday. I could hope. That stupid hope. Could still cling to the possibility that we're not trapped beneath a time bomb big enough to annihilate the eastern seaboard if it so much as dropped out of the sky. The number lingers. It's pasted over every screen. The gate display that once held our boarding information mocks us with it. For a moment, the world seems to hover with that floating blue, a weightlessness like reality itself has come unmoored.

It lands again. Crashes, really, as my stomach takes issue with the momentary lift and threatens to return my meager lunch all over the floor. The food court didn't have enough for dinner. When the ringing in my ears subsides, it's replaced by a sound I don't even realize is a sound at first. The whole room has broken out in manifested restlessness. People grip phones, bags, and loved ones, some halfway through packing up. People look at one another, ready to found their own reactions on how everyone else reacts.

The first person to get up tests the door to the jet bridge. It's locked. There's no plane at its end—in eight days, I don't think I've ever questioned where they're leaving from. Before I can ask the nearest person, the rumble of a crowd swells into existence somewhere down the hallway. My knuckles whiten on the handle of my backpack. I swing it on and buckle it. I flew to Manitoba and halfway back with nothing but a carry-on, and I don't want to be separated from it in the chaos if they've started boarding planes.

People pour up the hallway. I didn't realize just how quiet the gates get when everyone's just waiting. In an instant, I can't see the one across from us. A message ripples through the crowd. "Terminal three," hisses the girl beside me, eyes suddenly alight. She grabs her suitcase. It's the trigger everyone's been waiting for. Or maybe it already started; in an instant, gate D35 is hemorrhaging people into the human river coursing up the terminal. A child wails. Her mother clutches her as others all around them scramble for their belongings, most not even bothering to pack their bags.

If they're boarding planes, I want to be there. I dodge people to the hallway and am sucked into the flood. I've seen a river burst its banks before. I've watched it heave with ice blocks that stripped bark from trees and trees from ground, but I never imagined it could be this easy for a single water molecule in all that raging chaos. I ride the flow and don't even need to think of where I'm going. Someone else knows the way to terminal three. Everyone else will follow.

I don't remember there being a ground route to terminal three.

I grip my backpack's shoulder straps. This river's going *somewhere.* If it's not the right direction, I'll find out when we get there. I'll just turn around and come back to my gate. Then the signs begin to welcome us. My heart unclenches, and relief cools my sweaty palms. The charcoal-and-magenta signage points us to this airport's other terminal, the same way we're already going. There's something reassuring about being the opposite of alone. The people all around me move as one, an entity too powerful for crowd controls. Security guards stand back at the first checkpoint we encounter. They all look nervous as we stream past the gates.

One lifts his walkie-talkie. "Security point 17 to central. Are the planes accepting uninjured civilians? We're getting mixed messages over here."

It's my turn through the gate. I let the crowd's flow carry me, but not before the walkie-talkie crackles in reply. *"Central to point 17,"* says the voice on the other end. *"Nothing has changed. Please continue to manage the checkpoint as before."*

The doors are wide. They won't be stopping anyone. I try to slow, to turn, but it's like stepping into traffic; I'm propelled forward from behind, and then we're in another hallway. I've got no choice except to follow now, and hope this crowd will dissipate.

It doesn't dissipate. Ten minutes or more later, it begins to slow.

I slow with it. Then I jerk back as someone bumps me roughly from the front, not watching who they're running into. "Hey," I say, but they don't respond. They volley into me again, propelled by a mass of other people. I dodge sideways and run smack into another wall. Someone else runs into me. For a moment, I'm compressed, air driven from my lungs before the wave retreats. I stumble two steps after it. It's time to leave. But when I turn, there's no way back the way I came.

All I see are people. A mass of people, packed tight already, but more are still arriving. More who don't realize we've hit a dead end. "Go back!" someone bellows, voice shot through with hints of fear. Nobody responds.

I'm trapped. Already, there are people closing in on every side, so dense, I only turn halfway before I'm pinned too tight to pivot. Low, panicked voices flood the crowd. Another shockwave passes through it. I grip my bag-straps tighter, elbows sharp against the surge of other bodies. My arms ache with it. There's glass less than three feet away. A whole wall of windows, but no opening among them. I gasp as another wave pins bodies closer in around me. It's getting hard to breathe.

Someone's screaming now. Shouts roll across the human bottleneck, and the buzz of fear rises towards fever pitch. Something in my backpack breaks. I'm closer to the windows now. Close enough to see they're sliding doors, all shut—doors are supposed to open under pressure. The crowd's waves drive me further every second. I'm going to get stuck. I can't fight, can't push back against the pressure of a hundred bodies, packed into a dead end with two walls of concrete and one of glass. If that doesn't break, people will.

The glass cracks.

One window shatters with a sound like gunshot. Glass knives burst outwards, and the first surge of people lurches through the gap…

And disappears.

The second wave piles after them. All scream and fall into the darkness, sprawled across a metal lattice or dropped into the ground. Only there *is* no ground. I'm up against the windows now. We're four stories up, with nothing but a monorail outside, strung through space on gravity-defying pillars.

There's no ground route to terminal three.

The crowd has lost control of itself. Waves of human bodies are sucked into the gap like someone pulled a bathtub plug, unable to resist the forces of the crush. People spill across the steel rails. More spill across those people. Even as I watch, the newest set are pressed clean over the monorail, to vanish screaming off the other side.

Others climb along the rails. Desperate to escape the crush, they scatter like an ants' nest up and down the metal tracks. I'm almost at the hole now. I can make it to the rails. I can't control my exit, but the first drop is bridged by bodies now, and I can wriggle sideways before I go off the other side. I unlock my hands and ready for the moment. Seconds later, a surge propels me out the hole.

With the flow and sideways. I can breathe again. I gasp like someone drowning.

With the flow and sideways. My arms release. I reach.

With the flow and sideways. The drop is here. Yawning down to concrete already corpse-strewn, red-stained in the light that spills from the airport's lower windows. I look away. I catch the rails. There's no way out except along this steel lattice. Darkness swallows it past the platform's end, but even as I find purchase on the cable-wheels, another wall of glass gives way. The train platform purges human bodies across another stretch of metal and empty space.

The intact glass beside me won't hold. People press against the other side of it, screaming, gaping, dying, dead. Faces blue. Limbs twisted at odd angles. I see the whites of rolling eyes. I drag my gaze back to the gushing hole ahead. I can make it over if that flow of people hesitates.

Glass cracks.

I leap forward as the wall beside me shatters. My foot plunges off a cable-wheel, and I grab hold just in time. My hands chafe against the cable. The new breach relieves the pressure on the one ahead. There's just a mound of bodies now, some still squirming, most immobile. I scramble over them. They're warm. Something grabs my ankle, and I kick on reflex. It lets go.

Hand over hand. Step and grab. I grip the cable like a lifeline and imagine I'm a monorail, drawn along by steel wires. Monorails don't think. They just keep moving. I can't stop moving, or I'll never move again. Another section of the wall gives way. I almost don't hear the screams now, like my mind has wiped all background noise to focus on my own stilted breathing. I didn't know airport air could taste this good.

The darkness never fully closes down. Echoes of light from the train platform glance off the rails a hundred meters after I've escaped the carnage. I keep going. Light spills across a highway, a walkway, a parking lot. Streetlights glow below me. My eyes adjust as my muscle memory clings to the rails as tightly as I do, telling me where to find each cable wheel, each subsequent step and handhold that will keep me suspended over forty feet of death below.

That's when I see the runway.

Ambulances flicker up and down a line of blinking, waiting planes. That's who they're flying out. We're still camped here because we're not priorities: we're sheltered from the elements, mostly fed, and safe until we started panicking. People from the lower airport levels swarm across the tarmac. Already, an incoming plane circles, unable to land. A military jet docked close with a refueling truck beside it is surrounded. People block it. People climb onto its wings. The truck blares its horn, but it does about as much as shouting at piranhas.

I've stopped moving. That's a bad call. I can't see the train tracks' end yet, and I've got nothing but a hoodie to shield me from the blasting, icy wind. Only now do I realize I'm shaking uncontrollably. My hands can't feel the cable anymore. I risk a glance behind me. I can't see that track-end either.

There's nowhere out but forward. I force myself into motion again, hand over hand, step and grab. It's an eternity later that I spot lights ahead. Another bank of sliding glass peeks around the monorail, parked dark and silent at its station outside terminal three.

I'm not the first one here. My vision blurs from shaking, but my approach reveals a human chain hauling someone off the tracks ahead of me. I'm swarmed by hands and help before I even reach the train. Someone knots a rope around me. Others grip my arms or call encouragement, sweeping me around the train's front corner and then finally, inside. My legs give out from under me. Someone plies me with a blanket as two more move me to an empty corner. I clutch the fabric like a life raft. My helpers leave to bring in other people, and it's the better part of half an hour before I find the strength to sit up and look around.

The train is emptier than the terminal I left behind. The station it sits at is the same: people press against the windows, but it's not a crowd crush, and they're just shouting to each other as others mob the planes. I see tears, anger, and fear raw enough to bleed. The disconnect of shock makes it difficult to even remember what else I'm supposed to be afraid of.

The countdown.

Right.

Nobody here stampeded. Maybe because there aren't enough of them, or maybe because there's nowhere else to go. Even the train door they've just hauled another person through looks broken, jacked open to match a single aperture in the glass wall outside. I struggle out of my backpack. My headphones are shot, but my phone screen is miraculously intact, cushioned by the spare clothes that probably saved my spine or ribcage, too. I take comfort in its blank screen. Then I check my watch. It's broken. Smashed against the rails or windows, another casualty of my brush with death.

"Do yourself a favor and don't check," says a voice beside me.

I look up to find a woman here, a mirror to the one I sat beside back in the airport's other terminal. This one looks a lot more tired.

"I'm serious," she says. I'm not sure what expression daubs my face. I grimace.

"You're not trying to get out?" I say. My voice is wrecked.

"Out? Not a chance. I can name *maybe* thirty people in this airport who're looking out for us right now." She waves around this little enclave, where children sleep on chairs and someone's rigged up curtains in an attempt to insulate the windows. An infant cries. A man with haunted eyes rocks himself in another corner. Two old women teach a group of teenagers how to knit. The woman finishes, "You're watching every one of them."

~

27

about the author

Eliza Solares *comes from the cold prairies of Canada where she spends most of her time with her children, her cup of tea, and a good book. She enjoys movies, junk journals, and crocheting way too many blankets.*

Eliza's feel-good stories are fun, energetic and only-occasionally-chaotic tales to escape into, complete with snappy dialogue, quirky characters, and a little angst piled on top of a whole lot of humour. Not to mention characters who really like to get into situations they can't get out of. But they always find a way in the end.

THE ADVENTURE

by Eliza Solares

NEAR DRUMHELLER, ALBERTA, CANADA
AUGUST 4TH, AFTERNOON

I've never been on the run before. And I don't think I like it.

But I've been doing it since that blasted object first arrived overhead.

Didn't have much choice when the government was scrambling like ants in the rain and everyone was busy pretending they knew how to prepare for the worst. My scientist mother and former military father picked our whole family up and walked us away from anything I'd ever known.

Which is sort of how I ended up here, in this nearly-abandoned gas station in somewhat rural Alberta, clutching the two most important items in the world: my mother's favourite necklace and a letter I received mere hours before we had to evacuate.

The young woman behind the counter wears a red polo shirt, a tight ponytail and a ridiculously large smile. "May I interest you in a selection of our artisan corn products?"

"Those are *corn nuts*." I balance my borrowed blue bike against one of the walls of the small confectionary.

"Yes they are," she replies, completely ignoring my dishevelled clothing, my illegally parked bicycle, and the aisles of nearly empty merchandise behind me. "But they are a lovely treat for such a warm day as this."

"I'm just here for some water and a map."

"Maps are at the back."

I follow her directions to a small wire rack in the corner and spin the display, wondering why they still carry so many paper maps in this day of cell phones at everyone's fingertips. But I guess I should be glad of it, now that my cell phone is no more than a glorified paper weight.

And, given how I'm only here right now because my old map flew out of the basket of my bike somewhere on highway nine, it isn't even very useful as a paper weight, if I'm being honest.

My fingers find the pendant of my mother's necklace as I spin the display, the impossible task of finding my own way taunting me as I do. *You can do anything you put your mind to, mija*, she would say if she was here. *Never forget that you can.*

I'm annoyed at myself because I wish she were here. I'm supposed to be finally making my own way in the world and I'm clinging to my mother's necklace like it's life support.

"Can I help you find something?" the bright young girl asks, startling me back to the task at hand.

"Uhh—"

"Oh don't you worry, I know maps. Where are you off to?"

Where am I off to? I'm off to meet a man I've only ever met in letters and emails and text messages.

"Near here," I reply.

"Oh that's so exciting. You don't look like you're from around here." She steps in front of me and spins the display, picking out a perfect, pristinely folded copy of 'Central and Southern Alberta' and placing it in my calloused hands.

"I'm not." I don't look at the map too closely, accepting the peace offering for what it is.

"Oh I wish I could travel the world. Have you travelled the world?" She doesn't even give me a second to answer before she adds, "You just look like you're on an adventure!"

Well, that's one way of looking at it.

"Yes, you're right. I'm on an adventure," I reply, trying to convince myself as much as her. I'm not on the run from a huge alien spacecraft or the crushing weight of my mundanity, I'm just on an adventure.

I follow her through to a bathroom door while she talks my ear off about all the places she wants to go and how much she admires me for going off on my own.

"Have you seen the alien ship?" she asks. "Now *that* would be an adventure!"

"A little," I admit, "from far off."

"What was it like? Was it majestic and magical?"

"It was more humongous and terrifying," I answer, but she shrugs it off like it's nothing.

"It still sounds like an awesome adventure."

Maybe she should go see it, then. This conversation is getting awkward.

"You mind if I–?" I gesture to the bathroom.

"Of course! I'll get out of your way."

Finally, she leaves me alone to fill the old canteen Papa had given me the day the lights first began to flicker. And there, as the cold water overflows the narrow spout and runs down my shaking fingers, the weight of everything I'm doing crashes into me.

In my twenty-two years of life I'd never even been camping. And now I'm here biking across a province and a half to meet a young man I've only ever written to.

"You doing alright in there?" the young woman calls from down the hall. "I can grab you something else if you need."

"No. No, I'm good." I shut the water off and dry my hands, stowing my canteen in one of the oversized pockets on my dress. "I'll be out in a minute."

"Take your time!"

I push the door closed and take a few steadying breaths to ground myself. My fingers are still shaking when I pull Alejandro's last letter out of the tattered envelope it arrived in, unfolding the cream paper and tracing my fingers over the curling marks of my name in his hand. Beautiful and curly and ornate, like someone had walked straight out of the 1700s and taught him to write with a feather.

Even though I've memorized his words, I read them again. I let myself absorb the excitement and reverence he has for this place. And I remember why it shot right to the top of my bucket list. Which, right now, is looking like it might be on a time limit much shorter than I once believed it would be.

It's time to go. I tuck his letter and my mother's necklace safely into my pocket and pull my fingers through my messy black hair. I'm going to find Alejandro. Even if I only have a bike and my own two feet to get me there.

Even if the thought of me leaving had made my dad's head pop off his shoulders in a column of steam.

Even if I have to do it on my own.

* * *

I've been biking for an hour and twenty minutes and still not reached town. I think. Wait, did I? No, I didn't. And I definitely should have by now.

I slow to a stop at the side of the highway and turn the map over in my hands, trying to orient myself. The thing they don't tell you about paper maps is that they don't turn when you turn. They just stay however you choose to hold them, whether it is right or not.

Evidently, the situation at present was… not right.

"Excuse me," a voice says from behind me.

I grip the map and wield it in front of my chest like a shield, turning to face the sound and sweeping my eyes up and down the shoulder of the near-deserted highway. "Who said that?"

But there's no one here.

"Great. Now the barley's started talking to me. That's *definitely* not a good sign."

I spin around again, disoriented as the fear and anxiety form a nice little lump in my throat. My nearly empty water canteen laughs at me from the rusty basket of my borrowed bicycle.

I've just about calmed myself down when an incomprehensible string of words rings out behind me in a language I've never heard before. Then, a pop.

"Sorry about that," the voice says again. "I umm... sometimes a guy gets a little nervous."

Slowly this time, map gripped loosely in my fingers, I turn to face the voice. It belongs to a small compact figure of a man who can't be much older than me. "How did you do that? Where did you come from?" I ask him.

His dark hair is short, sticking up at all angles, and he's holding nothing but a small bag and a water canteen. But he doesn't answer me.

"How did you do that?" I demand. How did he just appear out of thin air?

His cute little smile has me distracted. He's about as threatening as a stuffed animal. Or the giant friendly dinosaur the town of Drumheller is so famous for. I can still see how his large green mouth smiled down at me as I cycled past.

The dinosaur, not this guy.

"Well?" I demand again when he still doesn't talk. "What do you want?" The can of expired bear mace burns a hole in one of the patchwork pockets of my mostly denim dress, but I don't make any moves. There's no need to give away all my secrets to this stranger unless it's absolutely necessary.

"I'm just here as a tourist," he answers, taking a slow, cautious step toward me. "I've always wanted to see the area. Especially the hoodoos. We don't have anything like that back home."

"Who does?" I blurt. "I mean, I've never particularly wanted to visit the area, but what else is there to do when your parents take you across the country and absolutely everyone has run out of gas? There isn't really anywhere to go. This seemed better than sitting on the porch and listening to an old guy tell stories of the alien ship that once landed in St. Paul as if there's actual truth in that story."

"I love St. Paul. I believe there's a UFO landing pad there to this day." The young man's lips curl up at the edges and he takes another small step, edging slightly closer. A little ping of electricity shoots straight through me.

What the heck, body? We don't need this nonsense today. Shake it off.

"Yes, well, it's just a tourist gimmick. When's the last time you heard of an actual alien using it?"

Instead of backing down, the mysterious dark-haired man lets out a bark of a laugh, and then has the audacity to attempt to cover it with a cough.

Maybe he's snapped, too. I mean, the world ending does weird stuff to people.

Not that I would know what *that's* like.

"So if you aren't a fan of the aliens, and you don't want to be here," the man asks, "why *are* you?"

"I told you—"

"Yes. To get away from the old man's tales. But surely you could have gone anywhere. Why here?"

Why is he staring at me so intensely? "It's a place we used to come when I was younger. I assumed I wouldn't get lost if I was in a familiar place."

He raises a perfectly arched eyebrow impossibly high into his hairline and a small smirk pulls at the corner of his lips.

"Obviously it's working," I continue dryly when he doesn't say anything.

"So your plan is to just… wander around?" he asks, stepping closer still and resting his hand on the basket of my bike.

He's too close. I can feel his breath on my face.

"Yes," I insist, pulling my bike out of his hands and jerking myself away from him. "I'm just checking out the area before I head back."

"Would you like some help finding your way? I'm sure I could—"

"No," I insist, pushing my foot into the pedal and propelling the bike forward as fast as I can muster.

Racing away from a man who got too close is totally rational, of course. But wasting at least thirteen minutes worth of energy before remembering I have no idea where I am? Not my finest moment.

I coast to a stop and hop off my bike, keeping one leg on either side in case I need a quick getaway again. I can't waste any more time if I want to get there this afternoon. And I have to get there this afternoon or he'll be gone and this will all be for nothing. I don't have a clock, but it doesn't take a genius to tell that the sun is getting lower in the sky and 'afternoon' is quickly approaching its end.

Twirling the now wrinkled map in my hands, one thing is clear: I have no idea where I am or where I'm going. I can't even find the town I'm supposed to be in.

I never knew a person could actually be frozen by fear, but here I am just… stuck. *Afraid.* Maybe of the man I just met, or the pen-pal turned maybe more who I was supposed to meet, or the fact that a giant spaceship is covering half the continent in darkness.

Even without touching us, it touches us.

The sun shines into my eyes, making it hard to see anything and even harder to think. I'd come way too far to give up now, but everything in me says I'm not strong enough to carry on. Maybe it's just best to find a place to camp and cut my losses. Maybe all of this is a sign.

Maybe this was my adventure and this is all there is for me.

"You sure you don't want some help?" The dark-haired man from before returns out of thin air. The shock of his arrival sends me falling backwards into the dirt.

"Will you *stop* doing that?" I ask with a huff, picking myself and my bike up off the ground, brushing off my dress. "You make it a habit of popping out of nowhere to scare women you've never met before?"

"Not usually," he admits with a smile. "But I do have something that can help you."

Out of his bag, he pulls a small, grey device.

"But, the satellites." I begin. "They're not working. How is that still—?"

"I must be in range," he says with a shrug. "You want to find this place or not?"

I want to lie. I want to tell him I know exactly where I'm going. But I don't know where I'm going. And I'm running dangerously low on options, water, and time. My phone remains a dead battery brick atop the crumpled map in my basket. If he knows where I'm going, well, he might be my only chance to meet Alejandro.

With a deep breath and shaky hands, I nod. "Okay. I'll let you help me."

"Alright, then," he says, slinging his bag over his shoulder and across his chest. "Let's get going before we run out of daylight."

He takes off on a light jog and I scramble to get back onto my bike, pulling my skirt around my legs to keep it free of the chain and then racing after him.

We travel like that for a long while, me riding slowly and him jogging along beside me with suspiciously little heavy breathing. Who is this guy, some kind of Olympic marathon runner?

"So, are you heading anywhere near where I'm heading?" I ask after nearly thirty minutes.

"Yes," he says in reply. Maybe he's more out of breath than he looks?

"What's your name?" I ask, several minutes later. I'm going to blame the nervous energy for why I'm incapable of keeping my darn mouth shut.

"People here usually can't pronounce it," he says simply. "So I go by Alex."

"Well, Alex, do you live around here?"

"No."

"What brings you to these parts then?"

"You ask an awful lot of questions for someone unwilling to tell me anything true."

I almost fall off my bike with the force of that comment knocking into my side. "I—" I stutter.

"It's okay," he says without looking at me. "You don't have to tell me anything. We're nearly there. Turn right up ahead."

Had I really been that close? I kind of regret caving and asking for help, now. My mother's voice rings through my head. *There is no shame in help, mija. You can do this.* Her necklace, still safely in my pocket, gives me strength to press on despite the growing winds and slowly setting sun. I can do this. For her.

"I'll wait for you around the corner," I shout over the wind.

Alex shakes his head and smiles, gesturing for me to go ahead of him. "See you there."

A twinge pulls in my belly. I'd never been good at lying, but these last four days of biking across a distance heretofore unknown to me had led me to many things I was less than proud of. Not the least of which was wearing the same dress for as many days, washing it in whatever moving water I could find.

Sometimes a lie is necessary.

The wind blows my knotted hair back and I race around the corner, triumphant in the knowledge that I've finally arrived at my destination. Except I haven't. It's just another stretch of dirt road with farmland along one side and a line of trees along the other. No viewpoint.

I skid to a stop and let my foot down onto the ground to balance myself.

Where is he leading me?

A hundred possibilities are racing through my head about the impossibly fit dark-haired man who calls himself Alex.

My thoughts must conjure him because he rounds the corner at the exact same pace he'd been keeping since we started this journey.

"Why did you lie?" I blurt before I can think too hard about whether or not that is a good idea.

"Lie?" He stops a few feet away and stares at me.

"You said it was just one more right," I accuse, heat rising in my body along with the shame and the fear and whatever other cocktail of emotions my stupid brain had cooked up. "And here we are, having taken the right. Do you see the lookout?"

"I said you needed to take a right, not that we were done."

I want to protest, but I'm mesmerised by the glint of the little silver device from before as he pulls it out of his pocket and hands it out to me.

"I wondered if you wanted to try navigating for a bit," he starts. "Just so you know you have control over where we're going and I'm not leading you somewhere you don't want to go."

Heat crawls up my neck and settles in my cheeks. Had I been that obvious?

I smooth my dress down, though the wrinkles just pop back in full force the second my hands are removed. "Yes, thank you. I would like that."

He holds it out again like a little tease, so I climb off my bike and walk it over to him, standing at the farthest distance where it is still possible to snatch the little rectangular device from his hands.

It's surprisingly light and no matter how many times I turn it over, I cannot find a place where it opens for repair or where a battery might be housed.

"What is this?" I whisper to myself.

"I believe you tend to call them navigation systems or geopositioning devices."

"This is a GPS? It must have cost a fortune."

"It is rather rare, I'll admit," Alex says before launching into the explanation of how to use it. Which is actually quite simple. I just type where I'm going and the device brings up a path. Exactly like a GPS should.

I get it right on my first try, and before he has a chance to ask me any more questions I'm back on my bike, following the little purple line.

Past a gigantic farm with at least three grain silos.

Around the bend that turns sharply downward.

Onto a bright open road with a truck with Ontario plates parked on the shoulder, full of men wearing suits and cowboy hats arguing about which way it is to Twin Butte. Bright red fabric drapes out the back of the tailgate emblazoned with some kind of Alberta Freedom slogan.

Even that doesn't slow me down. I keep moving forward, picking up the pace the closer I get. Mama was right, I am going to get my adventure.

Finally, I make the last turn off the paved road and into the wilderness. The beautiful lookout comes into view before me with the setting sun falling down behind it into the Alberta Badlands. The red-grey stripes of rock are accentuated by the purples and pinks dancing across the sky.

"It's beautiful," I whisper to myself.

"It is," Alex agrees, reaching his hand out to stop my bike. "Let's walk from here. There's stairs."

There's something about the way he speaks that makes me want to do whatever he asks. Plus, who am I to disagree about whether there are stairs?

I follow where he leads, placing my toes on the footholds he uses and taking careful, measured breaths as we climb the stairs to the platform with the little plaque explaining the history of the area.

I did it.

I made it.

I'm *here*.

But Alejandro is not.

"Is it everything he said it would be?" Alex asks, facing the edge of the platform and shoving his hands into his pockets.

"It is," I breathe. "Everything and more."

I must be hypnotised by the fresh air because it takes me several seconds to realize I never told him anything about Alejandro. "Hey, how did you—?"

"I can't stay long," he says, looking over both shoulders, pulling his bottom lip between his teeth.

"But how did you—? Why did—?"

"You just seemed like the kind of girl who longed for an adventure," he replies, reaching out to hold my hand in his. "I'm glad you get to have one."

"Are you… I mean."

"I have to go," he says again, pulling back and turning away.

But in a second he's turned back to face me, dark eyes staring intensely into mine, left arm reaching out for me.

Instinctively, I take a step forward and give him what I assume he wants. I place his lighter-than-air GPS into his hand.

He pushes it back to me. "Keep it," he says with a smile. "Have some adventures until you find a way to use your own device again. It was a pleasure to meet you."

And then he turns on his heel and races down the stairs we just climbed, reaching the bottom in no more than a blink of an eye. I must be delirious from the heat because when he gets to the bottom, I swear he disappears into thin air.

He must have gone behind one of the sharp jutting rocks so quickly I missed it. Or maybe it was all a dream?

The device in my hand beeps, the screen flashes and then a gigantic number '26' appears in the centre.

It must be ten o'clock. The sun has set and the aliens have sent us the first message of the new day. Twenty-six more days to go.

A breeze picks up my skirt and blows it right into my face. When I manage to wrestle it down, the flutter of paper catches my eye at the top of the stairs.

Tentative, gentle steps carry me to the edge of the platform and I sit down, picking up the familiar floral paper and unfolding it. It's the last letter I ever sent Alejandro.

So he *was* here.

And so was I.

That had to mean something.

The device in my hand buzzes and beeps and then stills, the number disappearing and being replaced by a map, this time with a new destination highlighted. One I didn't put in.

"Castle Falls," I muse. It's not a short trip, and it would definitely not be easy. I push to my feet and look out over the scene one last time.

Only then do I notice a scrawled note on the back of the envelope in my hands, unmistakably in Alejandro's elaborate script: *You deserve your adventure. Take it.*

A glint of the disappearing sun catches my eye and I know I need to make a choice: head east and back to my family or west to a place I've only ever seen in pictures.

Alejandro's message burns in my hand, so I shove it into my dress pocket where it can't hurt or influence me. My hand brushes the unmistakable cold metal of my mother's necklace.

I pull the delicate heart-shaped pendant out of my pocket and turn it over to read the inscription, even though I've had it memorized since before I could read.

Tú puedes. You can.

I gather all of my courage and secure Mama's pendant around my narrow neck, pulling my knotted black hair up into a ponytail.

I'm not sure where this journey will lead, but I'm going west. I'm going to see a waterfall that might well be the last gift anyone ever gives me.

No matter what happens from this point forward, it's going to be for me.

"This is an adventure," I say aloud, looking out over the quiet desert landscape. "Even if it is the end of the world."

~

26

about the author

Jinn Tiole *is a part-time writer living in rural Switzerland. She started inventing stories to satisfy her younger sister's desire for new bedtime adventures. Her works in English and German cover the genres of fantasy, science fiction, paranormal mystery, and children's fiction.*

Most of her stories can be found on Wattpad where she was part of the former Wattpad stars program.

Jinn believes in the importance of strong, independent characters and believable world-building.

When she isn't working her day job, you'll find her tending to her garden, sailing, travelling, or dreaming up a story with a cup of coffee.

THE REUNION

by Jinn Tiole

KANDERSTEG, SWITZERLAND
AUGUST 5, 7:39 AM

A tentative sunbeam kissed the meadows, promising a glorious day. As the train rolled to a stop, I shouldered my backpack, careful to protect my wrist. Still unsure I was prepared for the reunion, I stepped onto the platform. A trip down memory lane might help me forget that thing in the sky and chase off my morose mood—or it might become a disaster.

"May?" a voice called out, and I turned to see Dan's familiar face. "I should have looked for you on the train."

He hadn't changed. Less hair, a few kilos more around the waist, but his gentle smile was still ready to melt a woman's heart. Not as terrific as Jacques' smile, but it was good to see him.

"Hey, it's been forever. How's the family?"

The shadow of a cloud drifted across his features, but it blew away when a cheerful soprano voice saved him from an answer.

"Maya, Daniel, so glad to see you." Lily kissed him on the cheeks—three times, following the Swiss custom. I'd been abroad for so long it surprised me. Then she wrapped me in an enthusiastic embrace—my arm caught between our bodies.

"Ouch."

"What happened?" Her finger brushed over my cast. "Should you even go hiking like this?"

"Don't worry, my legs are fine."

She shook her head in mock desperation. "I'd never doubt your expertise, Miss Daredevil. Where are Thomas and Stefanie?"

"Knowing Tom, he took the car and picked her up."

As if on cue, a sleek black convertible turned into the parking lot and our friends climbed out. Tom bent to wrangle their packs from the tiny backseat, offering me a chance to admire his fashionable outdoor gear. Were these pants tailored to outline his crisp bottom? His trademark tan and stylish haircut fit the neat appearance of a successful lawyer.

Steff seemed pale in comparison. She had cropped her once-long blonde mane and dyed it crimson. The colour clashed with her green anorak but suited her, and her smile was warm as ever.

Lily checked her watch amidst the greetings. "Sorry to rush, but our bus is about to leave."

We piled into the yellow coach, and the doors closed behind me, their characteristic hiss signalling there was no way back. I was in for the ride. From my seat in the row behind the others, I contemplated my friends. Steff, Lily and I had kept in touch and texted each other on birthdays and New Year's Eve, but the men had dropped out of my life when I'd made the world my home.

Dan whispered something into Steff's ear, making her chuckle. Inseparable since school days, it had come as a shock to us all when he walked out of the relationship a decade ago to marry meek Ruth. Steff had taken the separation to heart, and it split our group, but today, she seemed happy to chat with her old flame.

Lily and Tom were another case. Despite his persistent courting, she'd never returned his feelings. To judge by his smouldering glances, nothing had changed. I sighed. Why had I agreed to reunite with the gang? Out of a nostalgic wish for normality?

I zoned out, watching the landscape while the driver mastered the winding road with enviable ease. When Lily contacted me last month, she convinced me a weekend with the old gang would be fun. Hiking in the mountains instead of worrying about corral bleach—or my relationship with Jacques.

But then the blasted aliens appeared and turned the world upside down. My thoughts drifted back to my horrible flight. What if another ship appeared and blew us from the road?

***

Half an hour later, the bus stopped at the beginning of the path to the Lötschenpass cabin, with no sudden alien appearances.

As expected, Lily took the lead. "Isn't it wonderful to unite for another mountain adventure after all those years?"

The woman was in denial if she wasn't ignoring our obvious lack of enthusiasm. I plastered a smile on my face. "Right, we're here now, so do we talk or attack the mountain?"

Steff shook her head. "Snarky as ever. What was your mountaineer motto?"

"'God created mountains for us to climb?'"

Tom snorted, but adjusted the straps of his pack. "As if god were real. Off we go."

I followed him, fighting the temptation to call off the hike. What would I do instead? Mope about my inaptitude to handle my relationship or the impending end of the world?

The path zigzagging upward on the southern slope offered a glorious view along the valley. I saved my breath while the others exchanged old memories. Even without seeing the spaceship, I sensed its oppressive presence.

Around noon, Dan stopped at the summit of the moraine wall and pointed at the glacier's tongue. "Wow. Last time I was here, the ice still filled this valley."

"Must have been before global warming became real." Steff dropped her pack. "Let's have lunch. I'm starving."

I wasn't, but my arm troubled me more than I'd expected. Glad for the break, I shrugged off my backpack and sat down on a boulder. Dan joined Steff on a rock across from me and pointed at my cast.

"How did this happen?"

"It's a long story." And it involved a topic everyone had been dancing around so far.

"Aren't we here to swap stories?" Tom unscrewed his lightweight drinking bottle. "Lily mentioned you were in the Caribbean when we talked a few weeks ago."

"I was, but when the tourists leave and the hurricanes arrive, I always look forward to coming home. On the flight from Pointe-à-Pitre to Paris, I woke up to the plane shaking as if about to disintegrate."

"Ugh. That's why I hate flying." Steff shuddered. Dan placed a supportive arm around her shoulders, but she shrugged it off. The renewed affection seemed one-sided.

"Crossing the Atlantic by boat is worse." I had tried, and it hadn't been my best experience.

Steff chewed on her sandwich. "And what about your wrist?"

"Right. First, it was as if the plane were hurled upward, and I braced against the seat in front. When the movement stopped, all went silent for a moment. I think we were in free fall until gravity hit—or in my case, a suitcase tumbling from a locker across the aisle."

The captain's stoic announcement had been the last thing to cut through the haze of pain clouding my mind. *We are crossing a zone of turbulence. Please remain seated and keep your seatbelt fastened.* Smart-ass.

"Sue the company." Tom's dry remark brought back the story of his dad suing the school for poor grades.

I shook my head. "Gee, when I found out what else went down on July 27th, I felt blessed I was alive. Other planes just dropped from the sky. I don't even want to think about the ones who had to land on the surface of that thing."

Dan's eyes widened. "You were airborne when the ship arrived?"

I lifted my cast. "Believe me."

"I bet this was just another turbulence." A crease had formed between Tom's squinted eyes.

"No, it was exactly the right time, three fourteen EST, or four fourteen Caribbean. We only survived because we were more than halfway across the Atlantic when it appeared over the American coast."

Tom crossed his arms, the frown deepening. "Little green men don't exist. The whole thing is a hoax from the US government—or Elon Musk."

Steff and Dan exchanged a knowing glance. Tom could be stubborn once his opinion was made. Like in the old days, Lily attempted to straighten things.

"Come on, Tom. No one said the aliens were green. But you can't ignore the pictures from the ISS. That ship is too big to be a hoax, and while an alien visit may be improbable, it's not impossible."

Dan swallowed the last bite of his sandwich and cut in before Tom could. "I wish they'd go home. We barely recovered from the pandemic and don't need aliens to complicate things. There's war in Ukraine, and the world is drowning in a recession. Not to mention climate change and another handful of minor issues."

"Perhaps the aliens mean to help?" Lily offered. I envied her starry-eyed positivity.

"Then it would be nice if they started helping instead of frightening us out of our socks with their countdown-numbers in the sky. What do they even count down to? Humanity's extinction? The salvation of our souls? Birthday of their captain?" Steff stuffed her half-eaten lunch back into her backpack. "Shall we move? This discussion is depressing. I came here to forget about all this for a day."

***

The wooden cabin basked in the afternoon sun when we spotted our destination. I quickened my steps, longing to set down my pack and get a decent drink. Lily caught up with me and touched my arm.

"Maya, something's wrong."

I stumbled over a rock while I studied the place. Then the penny dropped—the door and windows were shuttered. On a Saturday evening, it should be teeming with a dozen or more tourists.

"Don't tell me they are closed. Didn't you book us in?"

"I did, and they confirmed my reservation two weeks ago."

"Two weeks? That was before the ship arrived."

Her eyes widened. "Why would they abandon the place?"

"Because of aliens in the sky?"

The low occupation of the train and bus on the way here had been a hint not everyone went on with their lives as usual. America might be far away, but the arrival had thrown a metaphorical shadow over the world. We hurried on in silence, leaving the others behind.

Lily had been right. The heavy wooden door was closed, but when I pressed the handle, it opened. We grinned at each other in relief, waiting for the others.

"What's wrong? Why don't you go in?" Steff dumped her backpack and wriggled her shoulders. "I could do with a drink."

"Might be a problem, but let's check."

The entry hall was pitch dark, and I pushed the door wide. The empty shoe and luggage racks left no doubt the cabin was abandoned. I opened the door to the common room and flipped the light switch—in vain.

"Power is down." Somehow, I had expected this.

Dan dug in his pack and handed me a flashlight.

"Thanks." I switched it on and shone it over the empty room. The chairs sat upturned on the tables. "They didn't leave in a hurry."

"Why leave at all?" Steff checked a door to the left. It led into a tidy kitchen. "Everything is clean and ready for visitors."

"Perhaps the warden will be back later." Lily opened one closet after the other. "There is enough food to cook dinner on our own."

After a brief discussion of our options, Dan and I volunteered to find the diesel engine while the others whipped up dinner. The ancient monster squatted in a shed behind the cabin. My experience with boat engines and dive compressors helped to coax the old-timer to life.

Dan clapped my shoulder. "Well done. I doubt I'd have succeeded."

"Thanks. The perks of living at the end of the world." Jacques called me his 'guardian mechanic,' saving him from relying on external help. The thought of him made me smile. "Let's see what the others chased up. I'm hungry."

Outside, the evening sun turned the landscape into a magical scenery of coloured rock, snow, and azure sky. I stopped to take it in. "Beautiful, isn't it?"

"Yes. All the unpleasant stuff seems unreal up here."

The shadow was back, and I had a feeling it wasn't the aliens troubling his mind. "Something wrong between Ruth and you?"

"It's complicated."

Relationships always were—mine included.

I stifled a sigh. "I've time."

He took a deep breath. "We drifted apart over the last few years. Nothing grave, just different interests. But for the girls, we kept things together. Until she met a guy and had a fling. I think I knew from the beginning. To cut it short, he asked her to divorce me and marry him. She refused."

Well, that was a twist. "Good for you, I'd say."

"I'm not sure. She insists she loves me more, but somehow, I can't forget about it. I told her I'd need a weekend off to think things through. And here I am, none the wiser."

"Is that why you tried to rekindle the romance with Steff?"

"Did I?" His eyes widened, and I felt a twang of sympathy.

"C'mon, Dan, I'm not blind. If you didn't realise, she's uninterested."

"She told me she broke up with her macho boyfriend years ago, and how happy she is to be single." He ran a hand over his eyes. "What a mess, and the end of the world lurking doesn't help."

I bit back a bitter laugh. "Right, but some aliens lurking might help us make up our minds. Do you still love Ruth?"

A small smile tugged at his lips. "I do—not the way I did when I first met her, but I love her for everything she is and went through. Did you know she had breast cancer five years ago? How she handled it, and with the kids, was amazing. I admire her strength, and…"

He trailed off and checked the time on his phone. "It's only six thirty. Daylight will last two and a half hours, enough to get back." He strode towards the cabin.

"Dan, don't. You will be past the glacier, but the descent in the darkness is lethal."

"Don't worry, I have a flashlight. Thanks for prompting me in the right direction, May. If we survive, you must drop by and meet the girls."

Minutes later, he had shouldered his pack and was gone.

***

When I returned to the kitchen, golden light filled the room through an open window. Lily looked up from a steaming pot.

"Thanks for fixing the power. Where's Dan?"

"Gone. He wants to spend the remaining time with his family."

Steff took four plates from a cupboard and placed them on the wooden kitchen table. "It's for the best. His girls deserve to have their father around in such troubled times."

"Perhaps they're better off without him." Tom leaned against a counter, his face dark and a frown chiselled into his brow. "Can't you see this is just one big lie? Why does everyone accept what they're doing to us?"

He pushed himself forward and stomped out, slamming the door behind him.

"What was that about?" I knew Tom had a temper, but couldn't imagine why he was so upset.

Lily shrugged and emptied a package of pasta into the boiling water. "He worked himself into a state over the money he lost on the stock market."

"Oh, did he?"

As a dive instructor, I didn't earn that kind of money and hadn't followed the financial side effects of the ship's arrival. But the news talked about millions evacuated in the US and Canada, about riots, broken delivery chains, and random weather patterns. No wonder the stock market was affected.

"He'll calm down." Steff continued setting the table. "It's just that he likes to be in charge, which is difficult when a gigantic ship takes the world hostage."

I collected the tins Lily had opened to improvise a tomato sauce and washed them. We might be doomed, but I had no intention of leaving the place in disorder. What if Lily was right, and the aliens were here to teach humans how to behave? An intriguing idea.

Lily poured the pasta into a sieve. "Wish we had salad, or just something not from a tin. But I guess we're lucky we get dinner at all."

Steph chuckled. "True, and I'm starving. Would you fetch Tom, May? You've always been the one handling his moods best."

This was news to me, but I let it drop. I found Tom sitting on the bench in front of the cabin, watching the sun set behind a peak in the west, both hands buried in the pockets of his anorak.

"Such a peaceful sight. And so deceiving."

"Well, you can't blame the sun for what's happening. Dinner is ready. Lily did her best under the circumstances, so I suggest we avoid talking about aliens and enjoy. Deal?"

To my surprise, he laughed. "No-nonsense like in the good old times. I should have dated you all those years ago."

"Perhaps. Let's go."

This wasn't the moment to tell him about my past crush on him.

***

After a quiet dinner, Lily and Steff checked the sleeping rooms while I helped Tom with the dishes. Muttering something under his breath, he sifted through cupboards and cabinets.

"What are you looking for?"

"The booze. We came here to celebrate our reunion, right?"

"It would be shut away."

"I bet, and this is the only locked cupboard." He chose a solid carving knife from a drawer to attack the lock.

"Uh, isn't this a criminal offence?"

"We booked this accommodation, including dinner. Also, if the world is about to end, better go down with a firework. So—"

The lock snapped open. As Tom had suspected, the cupboard contained a collection of bottles. He studied the labels and lined them up on the counter.

"What's your choice?"

I hadn't planned on getting drunk, but couldn't deny the appeal of a bottle of Vieux Rhum. Tom poured me a glass, chose a whiskey for himself, and slumped down in a chair. The rum was fine, but not as good as the bottle Jacques kept for special celebrations. It hadn't been fair to leave without giving him a proper answer. I'd asked for time and promised I'd be back before Christmas, but that had been before the alien ship started its eerie countdown.

We were on the second round when Steff peeked in. "Here you are. Lily and I are going for a walk. Want to come?"

"I've walked enough today." Tom lifted his glass. "Join us for a drink when you're back?"

"Sure, see you later." She turned, shaking her head.

Tom sent me a devilish grin. "So, it's only the two of us for the party." He downed his glass and refilled it. "To the world's end!"

If only his rakish looks wouldn't send my heartbeat soaring. Would a one-night stand solve anything or just become another worry haunting my mind?

Tom reached over and placed his hand on mine. "Tell me about your Caribbean adventures."

Wrong topic. "I'd rather not—it was messy. What about you? How's life treating you?"

He emptied his drink and chose another bottle for a refill. "Nasty. Let's talk about something nice instead." Tom pushed his chair closer to mine. "Or not talk at all."

He leaned over, the alcohol on his breath a pungent cloud.

"Sorry, Tom. You're a decade late. I'll check on the others."

He sneaked an arm around my shoulders, but I moved away and placed my half-empty glass on the table.

"It's a no, so hold your breath. The world may end, but this doesn't mean we have to behave like animals."

Tom jumped up, toppling over his chair, and reached for the kitchen knife. I stepped around the table, trying to put distance between us.

Before his fumbling fingers closed around the knife's heft, he wobbled and collapsed. Appalled, I hesitated for a moment before I checked on him and found him already snoring. So I picked up a bottle of wine and went to search for the girls.

***

I found them outside, sitting on a rock slab side by side, the waning moon outlining their silhouettes in silver. Lily leaned her head against Steff's shoulder, and the other woman had an arm around her. I didn't dare to disturb their moment and returned to the cabin.

Back in the kitchen, I stepped over the sleeping Tom to stow the bottles in the closet and pick up my backpack. I raided a sleeping room for bedspreads and found a sheltered spot outside, where I built a nest from the blankets in the moonlight. Then I switched on my phone. The connection was weak, but I still had power.

Prices for outgoing flights from the Caribbean had gone through the roof after the spaceship's arrival and were still outrageous. I'd heard Americans fled to the islands by boat in the thousands. From there, the wealthy evacuated to Europe and Australia by plane despite increased hurricane warnings. The airliners returned empty to pick up a new load of evacuees. My Jacques was rooted on the island, though, and wouldn't leave his family behind.

I knew what I had to do.

When the booking confirmation lit up, I checked the time. It was early evening in Guadeloupe, and he would be at the dive centre, doing paperwork. I dialled his number.

"May, how are you?" He sounded surprised.

"Fine. Listen, Jacques, I'd like to apologise."

His silence sent a shiver down my spine. Was I too late? Then I heard him inhale.

"You don't need to. It's alright if you aren't ready."

How had I earned someone like him?

"No, I have a flight on Wednesday, and my answer is yes."

The cheering in the background was loud enough to make me hold the phone away from my ear. "Who's there?"

He laughed. *"Everyone. I bet you're the only person in the world flying towards the alien ship instead of away from it, May. And I love you for it."*

A beep announced my battery was about to die.

"Love you too, Jacques."

~

25

about the author

Hidden in a remote town in northern Canada, **Crystal Scherer** *often spends her free time writing during the snowy winter. She started writing various fantasy and zombie stories on Wattpad in 2016, gathering over 22 million reads within 6 years.*

Her passion for reading and learning inspires some unusual stories, and despite her cats' best attempts to walk on her keyboard, her books are free of swear words.

Her favorite hobbies include things like gardening and trying to figure out which snowbank her car is buried under this time. Her life is pretty boring and uneventful, unlike many of her characters.

THE CATSITTERS

by Crystal Scherer

GREENWOOD, MISSISSIPPI, USA

AUGUST 6, 12:00 PM

I carried a box into the garage and frowned at the window. The spaceship filled the eastern sky in a fashion only a 2000-mile-wide object could. It hung in the exact same spot that it had for the past eleven days. The five cats on the windowsill ignored it, watching the traffic that streamed through the back alleys as a result of the main roads being clogged with abandoned vehicles.

I stepped over another cat that wound around my ankles, meowing around a tinfoil ball in its mouth. I set the box on the pile as a large white cargo van pulled into the driveway and honked the horn. I hit the garage door switch to let Nixon in; the noise had the cats fleeing through the doorway connecting the garage to the house. I closed the garage door as soon as the van was inside.

My husband got out and opened the side door, letting three cats jump out. "Rescue mission accomplished!" He gave two thumbs up. "I used the key Mrs. Anderson left us the last time we housesat and got her cats out safe and sound. She'll text us when she finds a place to stay."

The three cats looked at each other, at us, then sauntered into the house, side by side, with their tails in the air.

I glanced at Nixon. "Did you see that? The other cats have been acting rather odd lately."

"Yeah… Those three even got into the van without me having to catch them. Weird."

I shrugged it off. Cats would be cats, and each one had a different personality. The floor vibrated under my feet. I paused, tilting my head as I noted a distant sound. "What's that rumbling noise?"

"There are a couple of bulldozers coming down the street with the military behind them. They're pushing all those abandoned vehicles out of the way."

"Are they just clearing the roads or door-knocking?"

"Both. They aren't moving fast, but they'll be here soon enough."

I began passing him the boxes I'd packed during his absence. "Let's pack up the last few boxes and get out of here before they show up, the looters break in, or–"

"Or the crazies try to sacrifice the cats to the aliens?"

"Exactly! Aliens are *not* ancient Egyptian kings with a fetish for dead felines! Who came up with that theory anyway?"

Nixon shrugged. "Probably some 'history buff' on social media." With a smirk, he added, "I bet they had their tinfoil hat strapped on too tight."

"I doubt the aliens are trying to read their minds. We're in more danger if that spaceship drops out of the sky."

We stopped and looked out the window; we were just far enough west in Mississippi that it wouldn't hit us directly, but the wind gusts and pressure waves would probably flatten everything. We couldn't see the glowing blue countdown from here, but the pictures circulating on social media could only be described as ominous.

Those images were doing more to clear out the population than the government could have ever hoped to achieve on its own. Yet, even with the threat of an alien spaceship overhead, quite a few people were hunkering down and planning to stay, which was probably why the military had finally shown up in our small town. The rumbling of the dozers was getting louder, a reminder that we were on borrowed time.

I set the three cat carriers to the side for later. The four cats in the doorway took one look at the jail cells and disappeared back inside the house. We didn't have enough carriers for our cats, let alone the number of felines our neighbors had left with us. Despite catsitting them frequently, a couple of the furballs couldn't abide each other's presence, so they were going to ride in style.

We worked in perfect synchronization to load the van. Heavy boxes of kitty litter went on the bottom, with boxes of clothing, camping gear, and bags of cat food piled on top. Then we shoved in enough toilet paper to build a mattress, because you could never have enough toilet paper, and you'd certainly miss it on your first bathroom trip without it. There was enough room on top for the cats.

As I loaded the last box, I said, "There's just some food and cat supplies to pack up, and we're ready to go!"

"Ha! Wait until you see the roads! If you thought California traffic was bad, you ain't seen nothing."

I groaned as we carried the empty bins down the hallway. A dozen curious cats followed us into the kitchen. I grabbed an armful of boxes out of the cupboard, automatically stepping over Hikari, who was underfoot as per usual. Jack was already climbing into the cupboard, and he knocked two rolls of tinfoil to the floor.

"We can take one," I told Nixon as he bent down to pick them up. "I'm not sure how much Uncle Herbert has in the way of cooking supplies. He's way out in the mountains."

"I wonder how much tinfoil hats sell for?" he mused, putting one roll back in the cupboard and fishing out the tabby cat. He pulled a sheet of tinfoil free and folded it a few times. "Are they supposed to be twisted into a point like a gnome's or folded like a sailor's hat? Is one design more effective against the aliens?"

"No idea. I'm more concerned about what Uncle is going to say when we show up with twenty cats." I arranged the food in the tote bin, trying to organize it so I could fit more in.

"Who knows? At least there won't be a rodent problem once this crew settles in!" He crumpled up the tinfoil, and the crinkling had several furry heads turning his way as he tossed it over his shoulder.

Three cats immediately leaped after the tinfoil ball. Sabi—that sly fox—gave a bird-watching chitter to make all the cats look at the window, grabbed it, and took off running. Lambo followed in hot pursuit as they raced down the hallway. Alpha jumped off the chair and trotted after them.

Nixon gestured at the kitty antics. "Ta-da! Now *that's* a worthy use for tinfoil. Forget the hat idea!"

"You won't be saying that when you put on your shoes and find five tinfoil balls stashed inside. Again."

"I still blame Click for that. You can take the cat out of Florida, but you can't take the Florida out of the cat."

I pointed out the window at a passing feline. "Did the Stevenson's forget Dianne?"

"They left yesterday. I'll go get her." Nixon grabbed a bag of treats as he ran for the front door.

I peered out the window as he lured the cat inside. The silver tabby followed him into the kitchen doorway and looked at all the activity and cats with a blank expression. We'd boarded her before, so our house wasn't exactly a novelty to her. The screech of metal down the street made us glance toward the street. Several cats stood up with poofed-up, fluffy tails as they stared at the window.

"Those dozers are getting closer," he said, frowning at the cracked glass.

"Let them clear the streets," I said as I grabbed more food. "I have no issue with that as long as they give us half an hour to get out of here." When Nixon grabbed a handful of bags off a shelf, I warned him, "Don't pack that many beans."

"Why not? They're good protein."

"One, the cats can't eat them. Two, Uncle Herbert loves them."

"Huh? Oh." He made a face. "If he gets into them, the greenhouse gases could end the world without alien assistance."

Growling came from under the table when Titan entered the kitchen. I knocked on the counter. "Enough of that, Felix. You'll have plenty of room once we reach the mountains."

"Even if they had five acres, it still wouldn't be enough for those two," Nixon commented.

"I know. Leave the cans of cat food there for now," I told Nixon, who started to reach for them. "We can feed the fuzz-butts before we leave."

"That's everything except for the stuff in the fridge."

The crashing of metal got louder as two bulldozers went down the main road, side by side, as they shoved their way through the abandoned vehicles. A convoy of military vehicles followed them. The windows and dishes rattled as a jet blasted overhead, so loud I wondered if it was going to hit the house.

Soldiers' distant voices could be heard as they checked houses farther up the street. It wouldn't be long before they were knocking at our door. We exchanged a weighted glance and carried the half-full bins into the living room. When two cats began chasing Nixon's shoelaces, he made a few more tinfoil balls and rolled them across the floor. The distraction worked, and four cats triumphantly carried off the new toys.

I pointed to the front window. "Look, it's Mary."

We headed to the door as the flustered-looking woman rushed up our sidewalk with two cat carriers. She kept casting frantic glances up the street. I slipped outside while Nixon stopped our door dashers from escaping.

"Alli, I'm terribly sorry, but can you please look after Zuko, Blossom, and Pheonix for me? Now that the road is open, we're going to my sister's place, and she's deathly allergic to cats."

"Certainly!" I said, taking the cat carriers. "Are you still using the 769 number? I can send you updates once things settle down."

"Yes! Thank you so much!" She gave me a quick hug.

Gunfire and shouting erupted down the street. With a strangled squeak, Mary covered her head with her hands and scurried down the sidewalk to the waiting car.

I ran back inside with the carriers and slammed the door behind me. "Some idiot is shooting at the soldiers and yelling something about refusing to serve the alien overlords."

"It's not anybody we know, right?" Nixon asked.

I shook my head.

"Well, it was bound to happen sooner or later. Please tell me that he was wearing a tinfoil hat."

"Give the tinfoil hat people some credit. They're usually smarter than that." I glanced nervously at the door before bending down to open the cat carriers and let the trio out. Zuko immediately spotted his nemesis, a chubby Persian who liked to torment Blossom. He started hissing, more than ready to defend his sister.

Nixon raised his voice. "Cut it out, or we're leaving you here for the aliens."

Zuko slinked under the table and sat in the corner, glaring at the crowded house. I tossed a couple of cat beds and some toys into a bin. Three cats jumped in after them; Chloe grabbed the ribbon and took off running.

"Hey! You're going to want that later!"

The cat ignored me as she tore down the hallway with four more cats chasing the fluttering end of the long ribbon. I shook my head and asked Nixon, "Do you mind rolling a few more tinfoil balls? These cats are unpacking the bin faster than we can fill it."

"Sure."

I tossed a couple of cat harnesses into the bin, which had the cats inside promptly leaping out and making themselves scarce. A thud came from the door, and the handle jiggled as someone fought to force it open in a very unmilitary-like fashion.

"We're still here!" I called. With ten states issuing mandatory evacuation alerts, there were a dozen break-in attempts every hour. So far, they'd always left when they realized the house was occupied.

With a bang, the door was kicked in, revealing the nutcase who'd been shooting at the police. Gulping down a panicked scream, I grabbed the nearest object—which happened to be a small scratching post—and threw it at the intruder.

The intruder dodged the wayward missile as he entered the house. At the same time, Nixon pulled a silver cylinder out of his pocket and pointed it at him. With a click, a red dot appeared on his shirt.

"Sarge! Sic 'em!" Nixon shouted.

The mound of orange fur on the armchair blasted forward with a battle scream that should have made the spaceship immediately pack up and hightail it back home. Even the nutcase backed up a step. A black shadow, Luna, followed like a missile with her own call-to-arms.

The cats launched themselves at the wide-eyed man. He stumbled back with a yell, trying to ward off the cats, only to receive deep gouges on his arms. Two more rallying cries echoed down the hallway as black rockets skidded across the linoleum in their haste to come to their companions' aid.

The man tripped over the welcome mat and fell onto the porch outside, trying to scramble away from the hell he'd just blundered into. The cats were relentless, biting and clawing him like ferals taken to the vet for the first time. Nixon and I ran forward to help the cats, but didn't reach the door before two men in military uniforms appeared and dragged him away from the doorway.

"Sarge, Luna! Get the light!" Nixon called aiming the laser pointer at a tinfoil ball in his hand, making the red light glitter like a dazzling disco display.

Four sets of bright eyes locked onto the object as he tossed it down the hallway with the laser pointer following it. The cats blasted back inside and chased the red dot down the hallway. More military personnel arrived and handcuffed the intruder, who was looking rather worse for wear.

One of them addressed us, "He won't bother you again."

"Were those dogs?" another soldier asked incredulously as he came over, peering past us into the house.

"Just our guard cats, Sir."

"Pretty impressive."

"Best trick we ever taught them," Nixon said smugly.

"The mailman would disagree," I replied with a grin, pulling the door closed behind me in case one of the felines inside made a dash for freedom.

"You've probably already heard this, but this area is now under a mandatory evacuation order."

"We were just packing up," I assured them, relieved that he wasn't demanding us to leave this instant.

"Another group will be coming through in an hour," he said before jogging after his companions.

We quickly retreated inside.

"Are the cats okay?" I asked, scurrying down the hallway.

The four cats were busy shredding the offending tinfoil ball into tiny pieces, almost as if it had been responsible for the earlier disruption. I knelt down and crooned over our brave felines while I checked them for any injuries. None were limping or seemed to be in pain, and once the tin foil ball was reduced to confetti, all the cats looked at me expectantly.

"What good kitties you were. Let's go get you some treats!" I went back to the living room and grabbed a bag of treats for the cats proudly sauntering back with their tails in the air now that the intruder, tinfoil ball, and red dot had been vanquished.

Nixon used a kitchen chair to prop the door shut. "I doubt we'll see any more cats. Those roads won't remain empty for long, so let's finish packing and get going."

I nodded; the crackling of the plastic bag had over a dozen cats warily edging into the room. I smirked when I saw that over half of them carried a tinfoil ball. I had never seen them go this crazy for the shiny toys before. I gave each cat a couple of treats. It was a different brand of cat food, but they didn't know that and eagerly wolfed down the morsels. Three furballs followed and tried to beg for more.

"You already had your treats," I gently chided them. "Don't pretend otherwise."

"Should we grab them now and put them in the van?" Nixon asked when he noticed that all but three cats were currently in the room.

"Nah. Let's pack the van first. They'll come running when they hear the can opener."

"That'll also be a good way to make sure they eat before we leave," he said as we resumed our interrupted packing.

As I gathered the cat brushes, I pondered aloud, "I wonder if aliens are allergic to cat hair?"

"Oh, that's a cool theory! Maybe it's our new secret weapon, and we can use cat hair to chase that spaceship back to wherever it came from!"

I rolled my eyes in good humor. "With that kind of planning, you might as well roll a few more tinfoil balls and use them as slingshot ammo once the cats finish playing with them."

"Hey, *War of the Worlds* would have gone very differently if Sarge and the shadow brigade had been present!"

Two cats wound around my ankles, almost tripping me. I told them, "You guys aren't conducive to us getting out of here quickly."

Nixon helpfully began tearing more sheets free and rolling them into balls, much to the delight of the cats who began batting them all over the place. All of our furniture was—of course—the sort cats could get under, so no toys were ever lost. Such a thing was a tragedy for any feline.

Nixon's voice jolted me out of my thoughts. "There's Cathy! Mrs. Moon couldn't find her when she left last night!" He jogged to the door, jumping over a grey cat that ran in front of him. He had excellent reflexes after so many years with a houseful of cats.

It took him a moment to unblock the door and slip outside. I closed it behind him, peeking through the gap as he cradled the cream-colored beauty in his arms. When he came back inside, I wedged the chair under the handle as the cat stared at the tinfoil ball chaos currently taking place.

Nixon managed to find an empty spot to set her down and continued packing. Cathy looked around for a few minutes, then joined the fray, stealing a tinfoil ball and running off. Nixon had to stop and make more tinfoil balls to keep the peace.

"Transporting twenty-five cats is going to make this an interesting trip," I observed as I packed a couple of the cat litter trays. The number of cats, ironically, matched the glowing blue countdown on the underside of the spaceship. I wasn't sure if that was a good omen or not.

"I can't wait to see your uncle's expression when we open the doors."

I cast a grin at him. "I dare you to put a tinfoil hat on before you get out."

"Ha! He'll be certain the aliens got me!"

"I'll have my phone out for a picture," I promised, knowing he'd never wear such a hat. I waved my cell phone in the air before setting it on the floor beside me. "It would be priceless."

"As entertaining as it would be, I'll have to pass in case he thinks someone brainwashed me." He stood up. "This bin is full."

"So is mine."

My cellphone screen flashed, displaying a single number: 25. Nixon pulled out his phone, and even though it was turned off, it showed the same countdown that glowed underneath the spaceship.

"How are those aliens hacking our phones?" Nixon asked incredulously. "It's even turned off!"

"No idea," I murmured, frowning at the phone on the carpet beside me.

The cats likewise stared at the phones. Nymph snuck up behind me and batted my cell phone under the couch. I didn't particularly feel like picking it up until the screen stopped glowing.

"I'll get that later," I said, getting up. "My bin is full."

"Mine too."

Leaving our phones, whose screens were still lit up, we carried the bins into the garage and strapped them onto the roof. The house rumbled as another jet flew overhead, and somewhere in the house, something fell over with a thud. The power flickered, threatening to go out like it had in most places under the spaceship.

I ran to the kitchen. "I'll feed the furballs if you want to pack up whatever is left in the fridge."

I skidded in front of the counter and tossed cans of wet cat food onto our three can openers. It would only be a matter of seconds until the cats heard the whirring and descended in full force. After sticking the next set of cans on the openers, I paused.

"Where are the cats?" I asked slowly, completely dumbfounded by their absence.

There wasn't a single cat in the kitchen—a feat I hadn't witnessed since we bought this house. Alpha wasn't on her chair, and Scout and Hikari weren't underfoot. This was the first time in months I wasn't shooing Click off the counters. Misain wasn't paw-whacking a cat food tin across the floor to prove it was empty, and Medley wasn't crying from the doorway in hopes of being fed first.

Nixon leaned around the fridge door to examine the kitchen. We exchanged a worried look and headed for the hallway. The front door was still closed, but the living room was empty. Not a single cat was in our bedroom. I even checked the shelves in the bathroom to no avail.

"Where are they?" I asked, growing frantic. "How did we just lose twenty-five cats?"

"The only place we haven't checked is the garage," Nixon said, running down the hallway to the open door.

We raced into the garage and stopped dead in our tracks. The cats were all in the van. Felix and Titan—the two grumps who could never get along—were sitting amiably side by side on the center console while the rest were in the back. Twenty-five pairs of eyes stared at us in a manner only cats could manage. Each cat had a tinfoil ball sitting by their paw.

"Coincidence?" he whispered, staring.

"I think the shit just hit the fan," I replied equally as quietly. I glanced at him as he turned around. "Where are you going?"

He disappeared through the doorway. "To fetch that other roll of tinfoil. We're going to need those hats."

~

24

about the author

***Cayleigh G. Kennedy** is a Wattpad Creator and Paid Stories/YONDER author who really needs to stop buying more tea than she can drink.*

With over 15+ million reads online, Cayleigh loves diving into new and exciting worlds filled with fantasy and the paranormal.

Residing in Illinois, she spends her time with her three siblings and her cat who thinks 4 A.M. is a great time to party.

THE DARE

by Cayleigh Kennedy

SPARTA, WISCONSIN, USA
AUGUST 6, 10:43 P.M. CDT

"*Darien,* truth or dare?"

"Why is it always me?" Darien asked across their makeshift circle. The four friends sat clustered beside the back tire of Jacob's truck.

"Truth or dare," Jacob repeated, wrapping an arm around Katherine.

"Dare."

Nova settled back into the grass next to Perch Lake and stared at the stars.

Her mother would've loved this: the night sky, the stars, the warm, humid breeze sweeping through the area. Her mother would've—

Chest aching, Nova sat up, her fingers automatically going to her collarbone. But there was nothing there.

And there never will be. The reminder made her eyes sting.

Around them, the summer air was sticky and humid in a way that hollowed out her chest. This weather, the water, it all felt familiar, even though it wasn't home. Instead, Sparta, Wisconsin, was closer to the border of Minnesota and where their families had evacuated to three days ago.

Three days. Nova glanced out over the water again. Three days since she'd left all her favorite places, her *mother's* favorite places, behind.

Her fingers found her collarbone again. *I shouldn't have given it to Dad to hold.* But she'd been so scared to lose it.

And now she'd lost it, anyway.

Jacob grinned. "I dare you to kiss Nova."

Nova jolted back to the present. What? Her gaze shot to Darien.

And Darien… only watched her. Wasn't he supposed to hesitate? Or put up a fight?

"Well, a dare is a dare." Darien wiped his hands on his sweatpants and stood. "Nova—"

Each of their phones lit up simultaneously. Nova's stomach dropped as a blue "24" appeared on the screen.

Midnight. Eastern Time.

They sat in silence, staring at their devices.

Nova sucked in a breath as, after thirty seconds, it finally disappeared.

Darien coughed. "Okay, group dare!"

"What?" Katherine and Jacob echoed. Nova bit back a smile.

"Group dare," Darien said again. "Come on."

"You're so—" Katherine cut herself off. "Whatever. Fine."

"Jacob?"

"Sure."

"Nova?"

Nova only shrugged.

"I dare us to go back towards the spaceship."

He said it so nonchalantly that for a moment, Nova thought she misheard.

"You want us to do *what*?" Jacob's arm fell off Katherine's shoulder as she leaned forward.

Back towards the spaceship. Maybe then Nova could—

Could she?

Hope lightened her chest.

Dizzying fear crashed in behind it.

"You always do this," Katherine told Darien. "Dares are supposed to be small. Something you can do right now."

"A dare is a dare." Darien crossed his arms over his chest. "Unless you're scared, Ms. Rule Follower."

Katherine all but growled at him. "You know what? I'm in."

"Jacob?"

Jacob jerked back at the glare Katherine shot him. He cleared his throat. "Um…"

"You have my back, don't you babe?" Katherine asked sweetly.

"Y-yes. Yes." Jacob worried a hand through his blonde hair. "I'm in."

"Excellent." Darien grinned. "Nova?"

"Don't push Nova," Katherine defended her. "If she doesn't want to go, she doesn't have—"

"I'll do it." Nova said.

Darien's white teeth flashed in the dark night. "Hell yeah, Nov." He raised a fist. She rolled her eyes and tapped her knuckles against his.

"I have a condition, though," Nova said. "If we get under it, we have to stop somewhere."

"Deal!" Darien grinned at her.

"This is stupid," Jacob said, leaning back against his truck tire.

"You agreed to the group dare," Darien reminded him.

"We thought you'd say something dumb like, '*I dare you to skinny dip in the lake*'," Katherine changed her tone to mimic Darien. "Not go near the spaceship."

"Come on, you guys," Darien picked up a stone from the gravel beneath Josh's truck and launched it across the dark, stagnant lake. The stone hit the water with a dim splash. "This is the coolest thing to happen in our lifetime. Don't you want to say you got close to the ship?"

The hair on the back of Nova's neck stood as she glanced up at the wide craft expanding across the distant horizon. Even with how far they'd evacuated, she could still see the dark mass of the ship. Only when they'd made their way out of what people were now calling the Twilight Zone had she seen the stars again.

Their small group quieted.

"It's alright to be afraid," her mother's voice echoed in her mind. *"But don't let the fear stop you from living your life."*

Nova swallowed past the sudden ache in her throat. "When are we doing this?"

Darien shrugged. "Why not now?"

"*Now?*" Katherine ripped out a handful of grass and threw it in Darien's direction. "Are you kidding me?"

Darien glanced down at the tangled clump. "No. Better to do it before we think too hard about it, right?"

"How are we going to get there?" Nova asked.

Darien pointed at Jacob. "Jacob can drive us."

Jacob frowned at Darien. "Says who?"

"Come on, man, you have the most gas."

"Only enough to get us there, maybe!"

"There are a couple of gas stations I saw open on my way in," Darien said. "We can top you off and then fill a few extra gas cans just in case. I've got two in my trunk."

Jacob scoffed. "And who's paying for this gas? Have you seen the prices?"

"Don't worry, we'll figure it out." Darien stood, brushing off the back of his pants. "Let's go, kiddos."

"We're going to regret this, aren't we?" Katherine asked Nova under her breath as they all piled into Jacob's truck.

"Maybe," Nova replied.

***

MADISON, WISCONSIN, USA
AUGUST 7, 1:33 A.M. CDT

Jacob drove them down I-90 towards Madison. Occasionally, they spotted the dim lights of bonfires among packed tents. *Tent cities*, the news had called them. On the other side of the highway, unrelenting traffic headed the opposite way, headlights illuminating the dark. Once or twice, they spotted small groups of people on foot—with nothing more than the road and brake lights to guide them.

All the cars on the other side made her stomach churn. They were one of very few people traveling *towards* the ship. Their truck stuck out on this side of the road.

This was a bad idea. It was. And yet… Nova's hand went to her collarbone. The ache in her chest grew.

Jacob swore low.

"What?" Katherine wrapped her arms around Jacob's headrest and leaned forward.

Nova glanced out the window behind them, expecting a cop car.

"You better pray we find gas soon," Jacob muttered.

"Are we almost out?" Darien asked.

"We're getting pretty damn close," Jacob replied. "I *knew* we should've stopped at that first station."

Nova crossed her fingers and tucked them under her legs. What if they got stuck on the side of the highway? What if they never made it?

She worried her lip. They couldn't run out of gas. She *couldn't* lose this opportunity to go back.

Please, please let us make it to the gas station.

"Look! There's a gas station at the next exit." Katherine pointed out the blue sign as it passed them.

"Yeah, in *fifteen miles*."

Silence coated the next ten minutes of their trip. For every moment that passed, Nova sent prayers up to anyone who would listen.

As they hit the exit, Jacob's truck rumbled onto a quiet one-lane road. Only the lights from the gas station a mile or so ahead advised of any sign of life. Soft curses filled the cab as the truck sputtered into the lot.

Nova frowned. The gas station's lights were on, but the attendant's station was boarded up. A large beige humvee sat in the back corner, just past the overhang. A soldier leaned against the front of the vehicle, smoke wafting from his cigarette and into the warm summer night. His gaze drilled into their truck as they pulled in.

"Are they… open?"

Jacob parked at the closest spot. "The pump is on."

"Looks like they're not taking cards," Darien pointed at the handwritten sign on the pump.

"Holy crap, look at the price! *One hundred dollars a gallon*?" Katherine said.

"My mom said this morning the stock market crashed," Jacob mumbled. "Bet that didn't help."

"Where are you going?" Katherine asked Darien as he snagged something from the center console and hopped out of the vehicle.

Darien jerked a thumb towards the store. "The lights are on. I'll pay for gas. And, of course, snacks."

Katherine rolled her eyes. "Oh, my—"

"I'll go with him," Nova offered.

"Be careful," Katherine cautioned.

Nova stepped out and smiled at the worry on her best friend's face. "I'll make sure Darien doesn't add B and E to his growing rap sheet."

"Knowing Darien, he'd think a rap sheet was a list of songs he could—"

Nova shut the door.

When Darien spotted her approaching, he grinned. "Nova Campbell, I didn't know you were a foodie."

"Foodie? No. Babysitter? Yes."

Darien snorted. "Mother-hen Katherine at it again, huh?"

Nova shrugged, brushing a bit of her long brown hair behind her shoulder. She'd left her favorite and very last hair tie in her father's sedan.

"I guess being captain of the poms team *would* teach you to mother everyone," Darien added.

Nova ignored that comment. Instead, she jerked her chin towards the store. "How are you going to get in?"

Darien pointed at the outline of the doors. "See the door handles? The glass is covered, but those doors still open."

"And you're going to…?"

Darien strode over to the doors and knocked hard on the wood.

After three loud knocks, Nova said, "They must not be—"

"What do you want?" A voice shouted through the wood.

Darien grinned at Nova. Then said, "We're here for gas."

"You got cash?"

Darien tugged a handful of bills from his pocket. "I do."

Nora raised a brow at the small stack.

"Don't ask," Darien mumbled to her. To the attendant, he said, "I've got more to cover the rest."

"Yeah? Like what?"

"Vape pen and spare pods," Darien told him. "But I want seven gallons for it."

With a loud click and a slight rattle, the door opened an inch. Darien held up the blue vape pen and a small box.

The attendant eyed it. "Four."

"Are you kidding? This thing alone is an entire pack of cigs. Five." Darien countered. "And this swiss army knife for another two gallons."

"Fine."

"I'll throw in this one too," Darien said, holding up another red vape pen. "For another five."

"I don't think we should give—" Nova cut herself off as Darien slid the cash and his bartered items through the crack in the door.

There was a pause. Then, "Alright. You're good."

The door locked.

"Wait!" Darien called through the wood. "Do you have any snacks?"

"Snacks?" A loud stream of curses erupted, then, "What kind?"

"Candy, pretzels, pop," Darien suggested. "We're not picky, sir."

A few minutes later, the door opened again. A plastic bag came out. "Here. Grab your gas and get out of here, kid."

Darien snatched it up. "Thanks, man."

Back in the truck, Darien whistled low at the contents. "Store guy really set us up." He held out a plastic-wrapped stick. "Beef Jerky?"

Nova took it, unwrapping it just as Jacob got back in the truck.

"Tanks' full," Jacob said a few minutes later. "Let's get going."

Back on the highway, Darien opened the window, letting the warm summer night air sweep in. Nova's hair whipped around, hitting her painfully in the face. She quickly collected it and tucked it under the collar of her shirt.

Darien twisted in the seat and smirked at all of them. "Come on, you guys, this is supposed to be fun!"

He fiddled with Jacob's phone, connecting it to the radio, and set it blasting. The heavy beat of drums and riffing guitar of a rock song shook the speakers.

Nova didn't recognize the song. Still, she took a breath, soaking in the loud music, the night air, and the feeling of being with her friends. For one blessed moment, she felt like a normal teenager again. As if in the last few days she hadn't had to pack everything she could in a duffle bag and abandon her home, her life, and everything she knew.

The closer they got, the more Nova's stomach churned. On the other side of the highway, traffic was at a crawl, horns honking, as people fled.

The sour taste of fear settled on her tongue. In the distance, the dark mass of the ship swallowed the sky, the red and blue lights underneath it expanding across the horizon.

Panic squeezed her lungs.

She could only see the edge. The rest of the ship disappeared into the distance.

Don't let that fear stop you from living your life.

Just outside of Madison, Jacob brought the truck to a stop. Ahead of them was a well-lit section of highway. Cones, white-topped tents, and various heavy military vehicles blocked their side of the roadway.

"Shit."

"It's fine," Darien said. "We'll just tell them we have to pick up a grandparent or something. They'll let us through."

Jacob turned down the music, the rock song barely a whisper over the speakers as they approached the bright, busy area.

The officer, a middle-aged woman in a beige uniform, tapped on the window. "Folks. I need licenses or forms of identification from each of you."

As they handed them over, the officer grunted. "Naperville. Seems you kids are headed back home."

"My grandma is still there," Darien told the officer, leaning towards the open window. His black hair drifted over his forehead. "My family is worried, so we volunteered to go back and get her."

The flat expression on the officer's face never moved. "Do your parents know about this?"

"Of course."

The walkie on the officer's hip activated as a static voice rattled off a status update. "Bit early in the morning to visit grandma," the officer pointed out.

"Gram wakes early," Darien supplied. A lie paired with an easy, confident smile. "We told her we'd be there by six to pick her up."

"You kids sure are brave." The walkie chirped again. The officer set her forearm on the window and leaned in. "Turn around now before I think harder about calling your parents. I have millions of people to evacuate, and I'm not wasting my time with a group of kids on a convoluted version of a joy-ride."

Shit.

Katherine leaned forward and pinched Jacob on the shoulder. "Turn around," she whispered.

Jacob cleared his throat. "We'll turn around. Thank you, officer."

The officer pointed at the emergency U-turn lane. "Head out that way."

MONONA, WISCONSIN, USA
AUGUST 7, 1:59 A.M. CDT

"This is *stupid*, Darien!" Katherine hissed.

"It's not," Darien said. He slumped down further in his seat. "Jacob, lights off."

Jacob flipped off the headlights, sitting down further in his own chair.

Their truck ambled down a gravel back road a few miles from the military checkpoint.

"They can't put blocks on every road," Darien had said.

Darien had been right. The truck slowly crawled over the uneven gravel road. Nova held onto Katherine's arm as the two of them ducked down in the backseat. From here, the odds of anyone spotting them in the darkness were low.

Five minutes. They all held their breath as another car's headlights filled the truck cab. After it passed, Nova ran a sweaty hand over her jeans.

"Another car," Jacob warned them a few minutes later.

"Shit." Katherine scooted impossibly closer to Nova.

Every muscle in Nova's body locked up as gravel crunched under another passing vehicle's tires.

The other car slowed. Lights flashed.

"Shit, he flashed his brights at me."

"Don't stop," Darien ordered.

"Just go around him," Katherine said. "Wave and pretend nothing's wrong."

Jacob rolled down his window and kept his slow but steady speed. Nova did not know if he waved. She didn't dare move. Her hip and knees ached as another minute passed. Two minutes.

Finally, Jacob said, "I think we're good."

They rose from their seats with sighs and groans.

Nova leaned forward, scoping out the surrounding area. They were alone out here in the dark, quiet Midwest fields.

Darien scrolled through his maps app on his phone. "We can take the back roads from here and avoid the highways, just in case."

On the edge of the Twilight Zone, Darien rolled down his window again. They held their breath as they stared up at the ship above them.

Nova waited for her ears to pop or for weapons to be fired at them. But as they crossed back under the spaceship, nothing happened.

Nova exhaled an unsteady breath.

Darien cleared his throat. "Well, we're alive."

"Let's hope it stays that way," Jacob muttered, swerving to avoid a pothole.

"Nova, you never told us where you wanted to stop," Katherine said into the oddly quiet cabin. Now that they were actually under the spaceship, a building tension electrified the air. Like a kettle about to whistle.

"My place," Nova said. "I left something behind that I need to grab."

NAPERVILLE, ILLINOIS, USA
AUGUST 7, 4:38 A.M. CDT

It took them three hours on twisted, uneven back roads until familiar landmarks appeared. All too soon, they drove down IL-59 towards Naperville. The streetlights and traffic lights were on, adding a layer of normalcy that felt eerie among the quiet, abandoned town.

"Do you see that?" Jacob pointed at a grocery store, its lights out. Glass from the front window was blown out, and carts were scattered across the parking lot.

Across the street, a bank was in similar condition. In big green letters, the word *Aliens* had been spray painted across the brick, with a vision of someone being beamed up into a U.F.O. next to it.

"They looted the businesses." Katherine pointed out her window. "Look, there's Celia's father's hardware store. It's all boarded up."

"There's my mom's chiropractor." Darien gestured out his own window to an office building with papers scattered across the parking lot.

At her apartment building, the entry door's window was also busted, with only the dark frame remaining. One hand at her collarbone, Nova used her key to open the door, wincing at the scrape of glass against the concrete.

"She can't go in alone," Katherine said behind her. "What if someone is in there?"

Nova wiped her hands on her jeans and glanced back. All three of her friends stood on the front step.

"Go ahead," Jacob said. "We'll keep an eye out."

She blew out a breath and attempted a smile. "Thanks."

Taking the wide, carpeted steps up, she stopped at the door labeled 2B.

When she turned her key, the lock twisted easily. Nova's heart stuttered at the broken wood along the doorframe.

No.

No.

She shoved the door open—

And walked into chaos.

Whoever ransacked their apartment had strewn their clothes over the off-white carpet in their living room. Her mother's favorite pots and pans dotted the linoleum tile in the kitchen. The drawers were open and upended; the coupons, twist ties, and pens from their junk drawer lined the floor and flooded the sink.

Heart in her throat, Nova raced down their tiny hallway to her parents' room, and froze at the sight before her. Her father's work ties hung over the lampshades. The bed sheets and mattress were ripped, with long slashes through the material. Her mother's shoes lined the walls, one of them resting next to the broken flat screen on her parents' dresser.

Her eyes ached as she moved woodenly through the room. "It's only been three days," she said, unevenly.

"Nova?" Katherine's gentle voice came from the open doorway.

"We were supposed to come back," she told Katherine. "Dad said we would come back."

But they couldn't come back. Not to *this*.

Nova's breath stuttered as she remembered the safe. They wouldn't've—

No. Nononono—

Nova shot towards her parent's closet, her sneakers catching on the lip of the carpet in the doorway. She stumbled, caught herself, and rooted through the pile of half-hung, half-discarded clothes and belts.

The safe, normally hidden behind her father's work shirts, was gone.

"Nova?" Katherine had followed her into the walk-in closet.

"It's not here," Nova's eyes scanned the rest of the closet, unseeing.

"What's not here?"

"The safe," Nova pushed aside jeans, baseball hats, and shoes. "My dad's safe is gone."

"He didn't take everything?" Katherine's voice was gentle.

"He did," Nova said. "But he couldn't find my mom's necklace. He said he accidentally left it." Her father had cried as he'd told her.

Hushed whispers came from the bedroom, but Nova didn't try to make sense of them. The world around her spiraled. They'd taken the safe with the necklace.

Her mother's favorite necklace. One of the few memories of her mother she could physically take with her. Gone.

She choked on a suppressed sob.

Hands on her shoulders had her straightening. "Come on, Nova."

Numbly, she returned to Jacob's truck. No one spoke as he maneuvered them through the familiar streets.

"I'm sorry, Nov," Darien eventually said.

NAPERVILLE, ILLINOIS, USA
AUGUST 7, 5:28 A.M. CDT

Jacob parked by the football stadium of their high school. Big red banners lined the back of the bleachers. Near the street was a sign advertising the summer school program and another sign congratulating this year's graduates.

They got out, walking to the football field. The fake turf was stiff but soft beneath her sneakers.

Katherine and Jacob stopped on the metal bleachers, wrapped up in themselves.

Darien strolled to the center of the field. Nova followed him, her heart still a jagged mass in her chest. The air was cool and crisp around them—a bit of a breeze tickled the hair on Nova's neck.

"It would've been nice to graduate," Darien said eventually.

Nova said nothing. Instead, she laid on her back in the middle of the field, the artificial grass digging into the skin of her arms as she gazed up at the glowing blue twenty-four hovering in the sky below the alien craft. Darien settled down next to her. Neither spoke.

Then, finally, Darien murmured, "I'm sorry about what happened to your mom, Nova."

More times than not, those words seemed hollow—nothing more than what people felt they *needed* to say, rather than what they actually felt.

Darien, at least in this moment, felt them. She heard it in his tone. "Thanks."

"I'll never drink and drive," he promised her.

Nova resisted the urge to point out they might never get a chance to drink legally, let alone have the temptation to drink and drive. "Yeah," she said instead.

Silence. Then, "You're pretty brave, Nova Campbell."

At that, Nova raised an eyebrow, turning her head to Darien. He grinned next to her, his white teeth bright in the eerie dawn.

"You sit out of a lot of things," Darien said, staring back up at the spaceship. "Junior prom, homecoming, football games. I just—I don't want us to have regrets in our life, you know?"

"I don't think I'd have regretted staying away from the spaceship," she told him.

"Maybe not," he shrugged again. "I wanted to see you do something that scared you. I wanted to see you be brave. Just once."

Something in her chest gave an unsteady thump.

"What do we really have when that clock hits zero?" Darien asked.

"Our demise, probably."

He snorted. "Maybe." Then he turned to look at her again, and for the first time, she noted the way his dark eyes fit his face well. His nose was crooked, having been broken in a football practice. It suited him. As did his black hair.

"Will you have any regrets, Nov?" he asked. "When the timer stops?"

Nova blinked. Would she?

No. She wouldn't. She had come back to get her mother's necklace. Even if she hadn't been able to rescue it.

Don't let the fear stop you from living your life.

She hadn't. She hadn't let that fear win. For that, despite the danger the four of them put themselves in, her mother would have been proud.

"No," she told Darien. "I won't."

The words felt right. As true as they could be at this moment.

"You guys are missing it!" Katherine said as she and Jacob joined them. "Look!"

Darien and Nova sat up, looking in the direction Katherine pointed.

Below the edge of the ship, through a slight break above the trees, the golden yellow and molten orange beams of the sun climbed the horizon.

For a blissful moment, perhaps one of her last, Nova sat with her friends and watched the sunrise.

~

23

about the author

CC Starfield *has been dreaming of made-up worlds for as long as they can remember. They are a* ***Watty Award****-winning author and* ***Wattpad Creator*** *who usually writes flawed, fabulous queer people chasing their happy endings but sometimes writes goofy stories like this.*

CC was born at the roots of the mountains and lives now on the shores of a lake, which they find much more agreeable. When they're not writing, they drink too much tea, play wacky tabletop roleplaying adventures, and try out new sports.

THE REPUBLIC

by C.C Starfield

THE FREE REPUBLIC OF THE ROCKIES, AKA THE FOOTHILLS AUTONOMOUS STATE
NEAR TWIN BUTTE, ALBERTA, CANADA
AUGUST 8, 9:30 AM MDT

Jim missed newspapers. He would never admit this to anyone in the Free Republic of the Rockies, of course. No one with sense trusted the media anymore. You'd have to be pretty foolish to trust anything a mainstream reporter said while they were all parroting the government line about the mysterious "craft" that supposedly popped out of nowhere over eastern North America nearly two weeks ago. No, Jim didn't trust the lamestream news, but privately, he had always thought that nothing could beat a good, old-fashioned newspaper to keep you occupied while you did your morning business in the outhouse.

Since newspapers didn't deliver to the Free Republic, or maybe at all anymore with the world going nuts, he grabbed the Bathroom Reader that Mabel had given him for his birthday. He'd turned sixty-five the very day the "craft" arrived. Jim wasn't superstitious. That mighty big coincidence didn't worry him. And he was most certainly not thinking about what might happen today, exactly thirteen days after he'd watched the obviously fake newsreels of the "craft" popping into the sky and The Chief had put out the call that it was time to secede. The alien hoax was the perfect distraction. No better time for them to set up their own nation.

He swung open the trailer door. It was a bright, hot morning, and he had to squint against the blazing sun as he jumped down to the ground. That's probably why he didn't notice the little brown piles in the field until one of them went *squish* under his left boot.

He lifted his foot and watched the gooey, greenish-brown substance plop back to the ground. "Aw, nuts." He'd stepped right in a cow patty.

He peered up the trampled track that wound between trailers and tents towards The Chief's dilapidated ranch house on the hill: cow patties. He looked down it towards the narrow creek: more cow patties. It was cow patties as far as the eye could see. Real impressive patties, too, gloopy brown puddles as wide across as the serving dish Mabel only brought out for the turkey at Thanksgiving. The grassy-rotting odour was almost a pleasant change from the lingering stink of underwashed bodies in the August heat. Too many people and too little water did that to a place, he had learned.

"Alright there, Jim?" Isabel waved from her camp chair, set up out front of her trailer across the way.

"Morning, Isabel." Jim tipped his crisp felt cowboy hat. He'd worn it every day he'd lived in the Free Republic, chuffed to finally get to prove to Mabel that it wasn't just a costume put on for his corporate Stampede parties. "You see these cows come through?"

"Sure did. Ugliest cows I've ever seen."

"They're still down by the creek." This was Isabel's large adult son, Avery. Sprawled on his stomach on a picnic blanket in the dirt, he scratched at his sketchbook with a nub of pencil.

Isabel laughed heartily. "They're just havin' a drink like the rest of us." She raised a mason jar of fizzy yellow homebrew that Jim knew tasted more like piss than beer. He'd get used to it, he supposed. No stores in the Free Republic, either. That meant no Big Rock beer.

"Little early for a drink, isn't it?"

"What's time when you're livin' free? No jobs, no problems."

When you're living free, or when the world might end in twenty-three days.

Jim shook himself like a wet dog. The world wasn't ending. The "craft" wasn't real, and neither were those darn numbers on the screens. It was a hoax. A false flag, a reason to finally round them all up and put them in camps, just like The Chief had been warning for years. The why of it did seem a little fuzzy, but it felt true.

"You scoop out that outhouse, Avery?" Jim hitched up his belt, feeling the rumble in his guts. "It was getting awful full yesterday."

Isabel answered for her large son. "Everyone and their dog's over there droppin' a deuce right now. He'll get to it when it ain't busy."

Avery just kept pencilling his drawing: a girl in a patchwork dress, her hair flying behind her as she cruised across the page on a bicycle.

"She looks familiar," Jim said, pointing at the page. "That the young lady who came through yesterday?"

His eyes going misty, Avery stuck the pencil nub between his teeth. "Do you think she'll come back, Mr. Jim?"

Jim scratched his stubbly chin. "I doubt it. She flew out of here like a bolt as soon as she'd filled up her water bottle. Seemed like she had somewhere to be."

Sighing out the saddest sigh Jim had ever heard, Avery scribbled flowers into the basket on the front of the girl's bike. "I think I love her," he said dreamily.

Jim mulled this over as he glumpfed down the road, avoiding the cow patties, and shuffled into line at the outhouse behind four others, his Bathroom Reader still tucked under his arm. The meadow muffins didn't stink much, just clean grass moving through those bovine bowels, but the outhouse sure did. It was a rickety affair, a slapped-together hut over a pit they'd dug the first day, but no one had stepped up to build a nicer one, and it had been a hell of an affair even convincing Avery to clean it out in exchange for a brand-new sketchbook. Jim was still a little unclear on what the whole *economy* situation was going to be in the Free Republic. He just hoped that would be sorted out before Mabel ran out of coffee.

An unbearable stench followed Carter out of the outhouse; the woman who hurried in after pinched her nose. Three more people left in line ahead of Jim. He thought he could hold it that long.

Still buckling his pants, Carter frowned at the line of would-be poopers until his eyes settled on Jim.

"Morning, Jim." Carter held out his hand and his pants slipped halfway to his knees. He scrambled to scoop them back up. "Whole place is gone to shit," he said. "Watch your danglers in there. Chocolate logs almost to the seat." He made a motion like he was lifting his balls and laughed. "And someone's gotta clean this up," he added, kicking at one of the meadow muffins in the road, scattering drying dung through the trampled grass. "You got a shovel?"

Yes, Jim supposed, you could shovel up cow poop just as easily as human poop, couldn't you? But he certainly wasn't about to volunteer to do it. "No, I don't. But where would you shovel it all to, anyway?"

Carter considered this, his thumbs on his ornate belt buckle that read *Johnson Well Services*. Cowboy costume, just like Jim's hat.

"I got it." Carter's eyes lit up. "We should dump it all in a box and mail it to Ottawa. Show that pretty boy Prime Minster that the Foothills Autonomous State isn't messing around."

"It's the Free Republic of the Rockies, Carter. We voted on it."

Carter spat out a laugh. "You can't oppress me with your *voting*. We're free here. No rules. No bosses. Just doing whatever we want, all day, every day."

"Right. I guess we don't all have to call it the same thing." Jim shifted from one foot to the other, his belly grumbling. "Didn't the Prime Minister hunker down in some bunker in the mountains? I don't think he's in Ottawa."

"Oh. Huh. Coward didn't even want to stay and watch the chaos he created?" Carter thumbed his buckle again. "Well, we should mail it to Edmonton, then. Down with all governments! I'm gonna tell The Chief to find someone to shovel these cow turds into a box and mail 'em to the Premier."

He loped off towards the ranch house, his chest puffed out, but he hadn't made it three steps before a low rumble sent him scrambling for the ditch. An ATV roared around the corner of the nearest trailer, engine growling, buffalo chips flying behind its tires. On top sat The Chief, majestic feathered headdress rippling above his long blond hair. Jim had never been able to get a straight answer about which First Nation it was, exactly, that had adopted The Chief.

The Chief reared the ATV to a stop, spraying droppings all over Carter, and slung his shotgun off his chest. Slamming one boot up on the handlebars so hard the shiny silver spurs on his heel whizzed, he cocked the gun. "Heard there was some good hunting today."

Carter rolled out of the ditch with a groan and wiped grassy turds from his face. "Hunting?"

The Chief gestured wildly with his shotgun at the meadow muffins littering the trail. "Cows! Our sweet, stupid, bovine friends have been shitting all over my Free Republic."

"Autonomous State!" Leaping to his feet, Carter jammed a wad of tobacco in his mouth and chewed furiously. "It's the Autonomous State. Sir."

"Right. That. My Free Republic slash Autonomous State is covered in cow scat and you know how that makes me feel?"

Carter gazed up at him adoringly. "How?"

"Makes me feel like eating steak for dinner!" The Chief cackled wildly.

All this talk of poop was making it hard for Jim to forget how much he needed to set his own backdoor trout free. "Don't those cows belong to someone?" he ventured.

The shotgun cracked. Jim ducked with a yelp, but The Chief had fired into the air, his laughter maniacal.

"Those cows crossed our borders, Jim! They may have woken up as Alberta beef, but they're Free Autonomous cattle now. We can do whatever the hell we want with them. And right now I've got a mind to shoot one of their dumb little heads off."

"Isabel said that Avery said they're still down by the river," Jim whimpered, scooping his Bathroom Reader off the ground and thanking God with all his might that he hadn't pinched a loaf in his pants when the gun went off.

The outhouse door opened, and the line shuffled forward again. Only two more people, and then Jim was home free. He blew out a breath and pressed his thighs together.

"Right." The Chief plumped back down into his ATV seat. "Who wants to join me on this glorious hunt?"

"Me! Pick me, sir!" Carter flung his hand up. "And I got ideas for what to do about these meadow muffins. See, I heard they used to burn 'em for fuel. Could be real valuable for trade once winter hits."

"Cow nuggets as currency, huh? You might be on to something there, my friend." The Chief offered his hand. Carter settled onto the ATV behind him, wrapping his arms tight around The Chief's middle, and spat a wad of brown gunk beside Jim's toes. Then they thundered off towards the creek.

As the sound of the ATV faded, the shotgun pellets that The Chief had fired wildly into the sky fell back to earth, splintering into the roof of the outhouse. The current pooper screamed and tumbled out the door with his pants still around his ankles. The next person in line leapt over him and slammed the door in his face.

Jim sighed with relief. He was next in line. Thank goodness. His bowels were about to burst.

The person laying on the ground with his balls to the breeze was still screaming. Jim didn't want to look too closely, but he didn't see any blood. Then he realized the man was staring at his phone.

Jim lifted his wrist, heavy with dread. There, flashing on the screen of his digital watch, was a blue number.

23

The number faded back to his normal watch face. It was 10 AM and twenty-three days to the end of the world.

Every time that number jumped down and punched him in the face, Jim knew it was true. He had family out east. Under the craft. His brother, and his brother's kid. He hadn't spoken to Misha in six years. Or was it eight? Maybe longer? He hadn't heard from any of them, didn't know if they'd made it out okay.

And the real insult was that even those damn aliens used Eastern time.

A strange wailing sound jerked him out of his head and back to reality. Back to his quivering colon and the stench of the outhouse. Back to day thirteen in the Free Republic.

The wailing sound was Isabel's large adult son, Avery. He trundled down the track towards them, barefoot, that eerie, keening screech pouring from his mouth as he leaped meadow muffin after meadow muffin like an Olympic hurdler.

"Avery-" Alarmed, Jim reached out to catch his sleeve but Avery slipped through his fingers as though he were a much smaller, nimbler man.

"You can't keep me here! I'm a free citizen!" he bellowed, as he sank his toes deep into a gooey puddle of doo doo. "Free to chase love if I want to! The world's ending, people! Fall in love!"

He dashed out of sight behind a tent that leaned as drunkenly as its owners, who were still facedown in the grass after what must have been a very good night.

"He has a point," Jim said to the pantsless man at his feet. "He is free to leave. It would have been nice if he'd shovelled out the outhouse first, though."

The man just kept on screaming, but it seemed rude to acknowledge that.

At last, the outhouse door swung open like the gates of heaven. But as the woman stepped down, the ground shook once, then again, and then it didn't stop shaking.

The rickety outhouse swayed. The cow patties liquified. The shaking resolved into a rumble, then a thunder.

Just as the noise rose to a nearly deafening din, the ATV came roaring back, tires flattening the drunk tent and maybe the people sleeping in front, it was hard to tell. Atop the ATV rode not The Chief but Avery, eyes wild and a scream in his throat like some ancient god of war. And behind him, rolling over the Free Republic like a terrible, brown wave, came a stampede.

Enormous brown bodies jostled and tumbled. Heads as big as a man's torso, nostrils snorting and squat, curved horns tossing. Even Jim in his panic could see that these weren't ugly cows. They were goddamn bison, and they were galloping straight at him, enormous hooves squashing everything in their way, two-ton bodies shouldering trailers aside like Lego bricks.

Jim let out the loudest, shrillest sound he'd ever heard come out of his mouth and vaulted into the outhouse, his cowboy hat toppling into the dirt as he flung the woman out of the way and locked the door behind him. The front edge of the stampede slammed into the outhouse, a wall of roaring and shaking that made Jim want to curl up into a ball and cry for his mother. A bison smashed into the back wall, nearly caving it in. Jim shivered and wept.

The stampede drummed around him. It kept coming and coming. But the walls held. This slapshod shed was now the single most beautiful structure he had ever seen in his life. More beautiful than his own home. He could have kissed the walls. In fact, he tried to, but the minute he opened his mouth the stench of the outhouse poured down his throat and a little bit of his breakfast came back up. Oatmeal. Chunky. It dribbled down his chin.

With a final rattle, the hoofbeats began to fade. Then they were gone. There was nothing but the chuckle of the wind through the gaps in the boards.

He was alive.

Jim wiped his chin and patted himself down to be sure, but yes, everything was in one piece. His Bathroom Reader had even made it through, although he did have to pry his fingers off it one by one. And the biggest miracle of all?

He hadn't crapped his pants.

The silence in the wake of the stampede was spooky. Jim was a little worried about what he might find when he stepped outside. The world was ending in twenty-three days, but the Free Republic might have ended on day thirteen.

Right now, though, Jim was okay, it was his turn in the outhouse, and he had his Bathroom Reader. Thank goodness, because he was about to explode.

He unbuckled his belt and dropped his pants. Then, with the biggest sigh he'd ever sighed, he plopped onto the seat, and all his dangly bits sloshed right into the mountain of waste that filled the outhouse pit right up to the seat.

~

22

about the author

*She's known as **NovaNicalynn** on Wattpad, but you can call her Jen. She deems myself a recreational writer out of necessity to curb the daydreaming. She does a lot of genre hopping but all her stories are infused with a healthy dose of romance.*

On her profile you will find girly humor, fight scenes, horror and a bunch of lyrical short stories.

THE KRUGER

by Nova Nicalynn

THE KRUGER NATIONAL PARK, SOUTH AFRICA

AUGUST 9, 9:50 AM

I heard the loud splintering of trees breaking before I saw them. A wall of gray and ivory crashed through the thick brush, and I could all but feel the earth shudder under their combined weight.

A jolt of adrenaline coursed through my body.

Fight or flight—I had no chance at either.

"Brace yourselves," I managed to yell.

The last thing I saw before tucking my head between my knees was the massive tusk sliding under the cruiser. The elephant's massive body slammed into the side of the vehicle. Glass shattered, and cold fragments fell into my collar and scraped down my back.

My stomach churned at the sensation of tumbling as the cruiser flipped.

I dropped from my seat and landed on the roof at an awkward angle. A searing pain spread like wildfire through my shoulder and down my arm.

Moans and grunts sounded next to me, but they were drowned out by heavy feet stomping by. The dust they kicked up made it hard to see if there was an end to the parade. The cruiser jerked as each passing body bumped it further off the road. All I could do was brace and pray. I was one jolt away from falling out of the cruiser and being trampled.

Finally, it quieted. The trumpeting faded, and the dust settled.

I lay motionless. My eyes stung, but I kept them shut. I was hyper-aware of my breathing, and as I inhaled and exhaled, I took inventory of my body.

"Everyone alive?" Bongani groaned from the driver's seat.

Next to me, Vusi grunted as he twisted his body upright.

"Freaking elephants," Hendrik grumbled and he kicked out the shattered windshield. "Out of their minds," he mumbled while hoisting himself from the cruiser.

"Johan?" Vusi touched my arm.

"Yeah," I managed.

Bongani reached through my broken window and pulled me out.

I held my breath as my body was dragged over the glass shards.

"Johan?" Bongani waved his hand in front of my face.

"Just give me a second." I slowly sat up and touched my shoulder.

"We don't have a second." Hendrik kicked my boot. "Get up."

"Shut up, Hendrik, the elephant slammed into his side. Look at the door." Bongani scoffed.

I glanced up at the crushed door. My shoulder must have taken the hit. "I'm fine." I rolled the joint. Movement was good. Pain was tolerable. The nerves and tissue were intact. "I think it's just a strain, a sprain at most."

Bongani raised his eyebrows at me. "You're bleeding."

"Small cuts from the glass, nothing too deep. It will stop in a minute." I wiped my bloody palms on my pants.

Hendrik huffed and knelt by the cruiser. He reached in and started pulling things out.

"Asshole." Shaking his head, Bongani bent down and offered me a hand.

I gave him a grim smile and allowed him to draw me to my feet. My world blurred but came back into focus quickly, and I waited for a wave of nausea to settle. I must be concussed.

"The radio's dead." Vusi let the mic of the CB radio drop.

"What do you mean, dead? Did you check if the battery is still connected?" Hendrik slung his Remington over his shoulder.

Vusi frowned. "There is power, but it's scrambled. So is this." He held up the GPS tracker. "It's glitching."

"Motherfucking spaceship." Hendrik dragged a hand down his bearded face.

Nerves coiled around my windpipe. "The GPS tracker isn't working?"

Vusi shook his head and smacked his palm against it for good measure.

Bongani sucked in a breath between clenched teeth. "That could become a problem."

I pulled my cell phone from my pants. The screen was cracked, but it was still on. "No signal."

Bongani handed Vusi a rucksack and slung the other onto his own back. "We can't stay here. The animals are behaving strangely. It's dangerous."

"I say we head to the nearest camp and get the hell out of the bush before dusk." Hendrik pointed his finger at me. "I refuse to be mauled by a bunch of deranged cats because of your bleeding veterinarian heart."

I stepped closer, meeting his gaze directly. Hendrik's bark was worse than his bite. "That pride has already killed people, so it's in everyone's best interest if we tranquilize and relocate them to quarantine."

"Quarantine?" Hendrik narrowed his eyes. "Those lions should be shot for what they did to that couple last night."

"That couple shouldn't have been in the park. We warned the board to close the Kruger's gates days ago. The animals are unpredictable, and it all started after that UFO appeared. We have no idea what we're up against. Putting them in quarantine ensures the safety of both us and the lions."

An angry hiss made us jump.

My heart pounded against my bruised ribs.

A banded mongoose emerged, walking stiff-legged onto the road with its back arched and its sharp teeth exposed.

"It could be worse." Vusi shrugged.

The grass on the roadside rustled, and a dozen more mongooses appeared. Their hissing and movements seemed strangely synchronized as they approached.

"They look rabid," Bongani whispered.

I stared at the troop and would have found the situation comical if I didn't know how effectively those tiny, razor-sharp teeth could tear flesh.

Their hissing escalated into a squeal, and then they scattered. The CB radio screeched in agreement.

I wiggled my jaw, attempting to relieve the pressure and high-pitched ringing in my ears.

"Eish." Vusi cupped his ears. "What's happening?"

I shook my head, trying to equalize the pressure in my ears once more.

"At least the mongooses are gone. Nasty little creatures." Hendrik glanced around. "We need to get going as well."

Bongani gazed silently at the ground, his knees bending as he knelt towards the gravel road.

"Bongani?" I crouched down beside him.

Wide-eyed, he looked at me and pointed to the road. "The aliens' space magic has reached Africa."

"Impossible." Hendrik shook his head in disbelief.

I followed his gaze and gasped. Small fragments of dirt, leaves, and twigs were suspended mid-air, hovering about four fingers above the earth.

My mouth opened and closed several times before I could find the words. "I saw it on the news this morning. Gravity fluctuations, along with pockets of low air pressure and electromagnetic pulses. They mentioned two planes that crashed yesterday. That's why flying is now restricted."

The tiny particles of matter trembled slightly before falling back to the ground. The ringing in my ears ceased, and the CB radio stopped its static wailing.

If it weren't for the shocked expressions on everyone's faces, I would have doubted what had just happened. Goosebumps spread across my skin, and an unsettling feeling crawled down my spine.

The unknown stared us in the face.

A loud roar shattered the silence.

Instinctively, I flinched. I felt exposed in the wilderness. With neither fang nor claw, I was unequipped to face any of the big five the Kruger National housed. We had already encountered the mighty elephant. One down and four more to contend with.

Hendrik fumbled a few cartridges into his Remington. A man who often boasted with words now displayed visible humility in the face of nature's superiority. That rifle was his only lifeline, his feeble attempt to remain atop the food chain. Yet I doubted his accuracy in such a state. Humans were not apex predators, and a pride of bloodthirsty lionesses would render that rifle meaningless.

Vusi smacked the GPS tracker in frustration. "It's not the lions!" He smacked it again.

"Aziza's signal is still stationary a few kilometers northwest of the Satara campsite."

The roar reverberated once more.

Bongani grinned. "It's the booming call of an ostrich."

I exhaled slowly. "Satara is the closest campsite to us, right?"

"We're halfway between Roodewal and Satara." Bongani shrugged.

I glanced at my watch—it was ten-fifteen in the morning. The predators would likely seek shade during the heat of the day. Walking over to the cruiser, I checked the CB radio again. Still nothing but static. I reached into the back and retrieved the two dart guns and tranquilizer canisters.

"Radio still down?" Hendrik frowned.

I nodded.

"The pride is between us and Satara, so I suggest we head back to Roodewal. It'll be safer."

Hendrick crossed his arms over his chest, and I stared at him with a blank expression. It pained me to agree with him.

"Fine, let's head back."

We gathered our essentials from the cruiser and followed the road toward Roodewal. The rhythmic crunch of gravel under our boots eased my apprehension. I had traversed the bush countless times.

Looking up, I saw gray overcast skies, but no sign of a UFO. My mind wandered back to the morning news. Today, the countdown stood at twenty-two. I had to resist slipping into a nihilistic mindset. What if the sun still rose after day zero?

I glanced at my watch again—it was eleven-thirty-two in the morning. Dark clouds were swiftly rolling in from the horizon. We were walking straight into the approaching storm. Flashes of lightning lit the darkening sky accompanied by rumbling thunder.

"We were lucky," Vusi mumbled out of the blue. "I don't understand why the elephants charged at us. None of the animals make sense anymore."

Bongani nodded. "We must thank the ancestors for their protection."

Hendrik huffed, but wisely kept his mouth shut.

I replayed the memory in my head and shuddered. "We were fortunate, but I believe they were spooked, and we were just in their way. It happened so fast. I don't recall them being aggressive. They seemed more interested in moving past us."

We continued walking in silence.

"Yesterday, a kudu broke its leg running in circles for no reason. Last night, a herd of zebras got entangled in the security fence. And this morning, the elephants went for a jog," Vusi mused, staring down at his boots and kicking pebbles along the path. "If you ask me, something has them spooked, and it's triggering their flight response."

Bongani huffed. "I think whatever is happening is affecting herbivores differently than carnivores. What those lions did to the couple and how those mongooses behaved were the opposite of flight—"

"More like fight," I interrupted.

Bongani nodded. "Exactly."

I scratched my chin, grasping at straws. "I wonder if what's happening to the animals is stress-induced, like an adrenal reaction to their heightened sixth sense."

"You're using big words, Doc." Hendrik spat out a piece of grass root he had been chewing on.

"Just keep your eyes open and your gun ready, hunter, and leave the thinking to me," I scoffed.

Hendrik mumbled something under his breath, but it was likely of little value.

"I haven't seen a single snake in the last week, not one." Vusi shrugged. "I'm not complaining. Can you imagine an even more aggressive black mamba or puff adder? It gives me chills."

"One less thing to worry about during our stroll through the wilderness," Hendrik offered.

I glanced at my watch—it was twelve-thirty-eight in the morning. The sky grew darker, and the thunder roared louder. Frequent flashes of lightning streaked through the somber sky.

I waited for the next flash, then silently counted. One. Two. Three. Four. Five. Six. Seven. Eight. Nine. And then, I heard the thunder. It was just nine kilometers away, uncomfortably close.

My trepidation ebbed and flowed like the tides, and right now, it was high. Taking a deliberate breath through my nose, I held it for four seconds and released it slowly. I repeated this exercise a few times.

"Do you hear that?" Bongani abruptly stopped walking.

My gut twisted, and I froze, straining my ears. Nothing.

"What? I don't hear anything," I whispered.

Bongani frowned. "Neither do I."

"For God's sake, why then—"

"Shh." Bongani dismissed Hendrik with a wave of his hand. "Listen." He gestured to the surrounding bushes. "There are no sounds. No insects. No birds. Nothing. The wilderness is silent. Something is wrong."

I tilted my head, listening intently. He was right. It was eerily quiet. "It's unusual, yes, but there's also an alien spacecraft sharing their atmosphere, so I don't know what's considered normal anymore."

Vusi's GPS tracker beeped in his pocket, and we all jumped simultaneously at the artificial sound.

Vusi fumbled to retrieve it and stared at the screen.

He gasped, and his face paled.

"What is it?" Bongani grabbed the tracker from his hands.

Bongani stared at it for a moment, then released a shaky breath. "It's picking up Aziza. She's on the move."

Hendrik ran a hand down his beard. "Where's that bloody lioness heading? Is she getting closer?"

Bongani nodded.

My breath caught, and a chill ran down my spine, settling heavily in my gut. "How much closer?"

Bongani squinted at the screen. He gave the device a smack. "It's glitching. Johan, bring your phone."

I quickly pulled out my phone and rushed over to him.

"When the screen comes back on, take a photo because it's not staying focused long enough for me to see the distance," Bongani instructed, tapping the device.

I nodded and stood ready with the camera app open.

"Now!" Bongani handed me the tracker.

I snapped a series of photos in rapid succession as the tracker glitched and turned off.

Scrolling through the pictures, I found the clearest one and handed it to Bongani.

"They were here." Vusi pointed at the screen over Bongani's shoulder.

Bongani nodded. "According to this, she's moving towards us. She's halfway to the cruiser from her original location."

"And wherever Aziza goes, her pride follows." I ran a hand through my hair.

Hendrik pointed at me. "We need to move because your blood is in and around that cruiser. If she smells it, she'll want to hunt."

I sucked in a sharp breath and swallowed the lump in my throat.

Bongani grabbed my wrist and pointed. "Hyena."

A manic laugh echoed from the tall grass to our immediate left.

Hendrik aimed his rifle at the rustling grass.

A brown spotted hyena emerged, drool dripping from its snarling mouth. More laughter followed as two additional hyenas burst out, fighting over a half-eaten warthog carcass. They dropped the carcass and froze, their hungry eyes fixed on us.

A loud bang startled me, leaving my ears ringing.

Hendrik quickly reloaded, but he wasn't fast enough. The hyena lunged at Vusi, sinking its teeth into his ankle.

Bloodcurdling screams filled the air as Vusi writhed in pain.

The hyena clamped down, and I could have sworn I heard teeth hitting bone and tearing through flesh as it violently shook its head, tearing off a gruesome snack.

A second bang rang out, and the hyena dropped to the ground. Blood spurted from the bullet wound in its neck. It convulsed a few times before going still.

The third hyena let out a final laugh, grabbed the warthog, and trotted off.

I immediately retrieved the first aid kit from Vusi's rucksack and knelt beside him. Blood gushed from his gaping wounds, pooling in the dirt. The wound would undoubtedly become infected, but there was no time to address that now. We needed to return to camp. I pressed a wad of gauze down to staunch the bleeding.

"Bongani, hand me a bandage," I requested.

Bongani assisted bandaging Vusi and helped him up.

Hendrik scanned the surrounding bush, rifle in hand.

"Vusi, can you put weight on it?" I asked, steadying him with my arm.

Vusi grimaced, but gingerly shifted his weight onto his injured ankle. "Yes, but I'll slow you down."

Glancing at my watch, it was five minutes to two in the afternoon. "We still have a few hours before dusk. We'll make it in time."

Cold drops splashed against my skin. The rain had finally reached us.

"Could this day get any worse!" Hendrik vented, kicking a nearby anthill in frustration.

The rain intensified, turning into freezing pellets.

Bongani shielded his eyes with his arm. "Run for that tree!" he yelled over the downpour.

We assisted Vusi in hobbling as quickly as he could toward the meager shelter.

Hendrik thrust his rifle into my hands. "Hold this." He hoisted Vusi onto his shoulder and started jogging.

I gripped the rifle tightly against my body and jogged after them, focusing on keeping my footing as we ventured off the road onto rough terrain.

It felt as though the heavens were playing a game of dodgeball, with hailstones the size of golf balls pelting us from above.

We huddled under the tree, arms over our heads.

The branches partially absorbed the impact of the hail, but I still received an occasional sucker punch.

After a few minutes, the hail and rain suddenly ceased.

I grimaced at the sloshing emanating from my boots. Both of my feet were soaked. No doubt the chaffing would cause blisters. I wiped the droplets from my watch—eight past two in the afternoon. "Right, let's hope that deterred Aziza's advance."

Now cold and drenched, we resumed our walk. The sun remained hidden behind thick clouds, and my spirits mirrored the gloomy atmosphere.

My eyes darted from side to side. Every rustle in the grass and every snap of a twig made my heart skip a beat.

Vusi's breathing grew labored. He didn't utter a word, but he winced with each step.

My confidence in his ability to make it back to camp on foot wavered. "Vusi, if you need to rest—"

"No." He shook his head. "The sooner we reach safety, the better."

I nodded. We had to keep moving forward, together.

My thoughts wandered to the people fleeing the twilight zone. It must be terrifying to flee from the shadow of something so extraterrestrial. They had endured nine consecutive days of hell. Here I was, feeling defeated after just half a day.

I glanced at my watch again, as I had done a hundred times during this never-ending day—three-eighteen in the afternoon.

Suddenly, my ears picked up on something. I strained to listen, but all I could hear was the crunching of gravel under our boots.

I halted, and the other three immediately stopped, their eyes widening as they looked at me.

In the distance, there was a droning noise.

"Listen," I whispered.

Bongani met my gaze. "Sounds like—"

"A cruiser," Hendrik interjected.

I spotted a cluster of boulders up ahead and decided it would provide the best vantage point. I jogged toward it and began to climb.

My jaw dropped.

There, in the distance, a cruiser approached on the road. But that paled compared to the scene before me.

A massive congregation of animals from various species stood huddled together in a clearing. Zebras, antelope, elephants, warthogs, cheetahs, buffalo, rhinos, ostriches, mongoose, baboons, and even lions. They all stood in eerie silence, gazing up into the sky.

The sight chilled me to the core.

Terrified, I looked up, unsure of what I might see. Yet there was nothing but clouds.

"What are they looking at?" Bongani joined me on the boulder.

I shrugged. "Who knows what lies beyond those clouds?"

"The animals know."

~

21

about the author

Published romance writer with City Owl Press, **Leigh W. Stuart** *can be found on Wattpad as @LeighWStuart and @BindingTies, where she is in the Paid Program and is a former Star and Ambassador.*

Favorite tropes include mistaken identities, strong heroines, "oh no there's only one bed", and nerdy, virgin heroes.

You can find Leigh currently stuck in a love triangle with reading and munching salty snacks on the sofa.

THE ANTI-HEIST

by Leigh W. Stuart

CHICAGO, ILLINOIS, USA
AUGUST 10, AROUND 9:30 AM

Three days ago, my ex—no longer the lanky-legged blonde I hooked up with for a few months thirteen years ago, but a brunette in a baseball cap, yammering on about government conspiracies—dropped off our daughter at the boss's door. Smudged overalls, hair in a curly, wild mess, Azalea leaned forward until she was on her toes. Luckily, I was there to let her in. My daughter, not the crazed cultist who birthed her. After saying she was my problem now, my ex took off, jumping into a military-grade jeep with a group of men carrying enough firepower to make Republican Jesus weep.

Jerome took one look at her and muttered, "You've got three hours to get rid of her. The boss needs us to make a pick-up."

Azalea, in the narrow hallway of the Chicago townhouse, heard him and dropped her backpack and long duffle bag on the shining parquet. She had my mother's eyes, a strange mix of brown and light green in the middle. She locked those eyes, just a touch too wide, on mine. "We've got two and a half weeks until the end of the world. Do you think you can handle me?"

She could have been one of the crusty, sixty-year-old docks workers, asking a fresh-faced summer hand if he could handle a little bit of real work for a few days. It would be a challenge. I didn't have any room to screw it up, and I had twelve years on me of pretending she didn't exist except for late birthday cards, a few phone calls, and showing up at one dance recital. *One*. When she was eight. But the way she ignored Jerome, a greasy-haired, murdering prick who chews his own fingernails? She was my girl through and through.

"I can handle you," I had said at the time. It took me two hours to get rid of Jerome permanently and pin it on a rival family, easy peasy. The boss lost his mind and trashed his office. Not that there was much left to trash since that floating monstrosity appeared in the sky and the Twilight

Zone took over the city. You'd think the aliens had popped over just to mess up all of Lorenzo "the Angel's" plans, like they had some personal vendetta against him. I wish. He shoved a pistol in his belt and rushed off with the other boys into the city—also trashed—telling me to watch the place.

That was three days ago. We've had the house to ourselves since then. Easy peasy.

Me and Azalea have been living off cold, canned raviolis, green beans, and tuna since then, except for the Captain Crunch I found on the floor of the nearby bodega, under a tipped shelf. I don't care for Captain Crunch. Raviolis, however, are a perfectly rounded meal. Plus some vegetables and extra protein? I'm finally a father.

Except we have a problem.

"I'm not waiting any longer," she says. It's morning, but from the haze outside, it could be a winter's late afternoon. I rub my hand over my bald scalp, trying to wake up. A tomato-sauce-encrusted bowl falls off my lap, and the sofa I fell asleep on has put a crick in my neck fit to make my nonna summon a priest for an exorcism.

"We're not talking about this again. The house is safe—it's the boss's *safe house*," I grumble. She must get this from her mother. "Going outside is bad. No, it's worse. It's too dangerous for little girls, so we are going to stay here until the world ends. Finito."

"I'm doing it, Marco," she says, teeth clenched. "I'll do it without you. I'm not afraid." Her trembling lower lip tells a different story.

"No."

"Yes."

"I said no. So it's no."

"No, it's not. I said yes."

"Go to your room." I point, vaguely.

"I don't have a room and besides, all the rooms in this safe house stink like old men and cigars! I'm *going*."

I hop up from the sofa, choking back the string of curse words I'm not supposed to say in front of a little girl. Between the actual pain in my neck and the one she's giving me, I groan louder than Enzo when we put his hand in a grinder. But I don't curse. I might be a useless father, but I know a few of the rules: no cussing, and I'm in charge because I'm the father.

"Your mother left you here for me to take care of you. I'm taking care of you, right? You have movies, raviolis, there's toilet paper in the bathrooms, *and* I taught you how to play poker. Hey—" She marches out of the room and I hurry to catch her arm. "I haven't taught you how to hustle when you play poker, yet. That's a good time."

"Who would I hustle?" she asks, yanking free. "The world is going to end. I have one dream. I told my mom to bring me to you because I knew she wouldn't help me, but you might. You've never been there for me before, and if you won't help me, you're no use to me now."

She stomps off.

Ouch.

How the hell did a twelve-year-old kid know how to be so mean? I massage my neck, trying to work the kinks out, but failing. Nothing cures a cricked neck but that extra-strong sports cream in the boss's bathroom. I shuffle down the hallway but stop at the door... There's a weird scuffling noise coming from his room.

I push open the door and my daughter whirls to face me, tears streaming down her cheeks and eyes puffy red.

All right. So I'm a sucker for tears. There are worse things to be.

"Tell me about your dream, Azalea," I say and sit on a leather armchair, just like when Lorenzo wanted to talk about the day first thing, him still in his silk pyjamas, cigar lit, whiskey poured. All I know is that she has some dream, something she wants to do or have before she dies.

"Why?" She crosses her arms. "You said you wouldn't take me."

"Maybe I changed my mind. Maybe. Tell me your plan. What's the job?"

She squinches up her face, studying me like I'm a twelve-year-old rookie. "You know the museum, the Art Institute?"

"Where they got paintings and statues of naked people and stuff?"

"Yeah. That one. There's something I want there."

***

"No guns," she says.

I roll my eyes.

"Hey," she says. "We don't roll eyes in this family. I said no guns; we're going to the museum, not to hold up a bank."

"I wish we were holding up a bank," I mutter.

"What did you say, Marco Guiseppe De Luca?" she asks.

I show her the gun with it pointed carefully at the floor. "Remember that car full of men and automatic rifles that your mother rode away in? We have to cross half of Chicago overflowing with those friends and neighbors, and a lot of them are business acquaintances, so to say, who didn't exactly follow police orders to evacuate. Or any police orders. If you want me to take you, I take the gun."

"I said no guns." She crosses her arms. It's as if my mother has been reincarnated and has come back to make me pay for all my crimes...

"Fine. No guns." I put it on the table, then hide it in my back holster the second she turns around.

Her dream, apparently, can't wait. We've been prepping since this morning, but it will be a total hack. I'm not proud. While Lorenzo might have run off the second he got his tighty-whities in a tizzy, I prefer to plan every step of the way. This kid, though…

"You say it's a safe house, but the government might nuke that thing in the sky any day now. Is the house safe enough to survive nuclear fallout?"

"Did your mother teach you that kind of language?"

"And have you been to the museum since that thing arrived?" she asks, packing tools in her backpack—hammer, wire-cutters, flash-light, super-glue. Super-glue?

"I didn't go to the museum *before* that thing arrived," I say.

"Exactly. How long do you think it's going to last? This is my dream. My one dream before I die. If we don't do it tonight—" She shakes her head, lips in a frown, and I swear by all that's holy, I can see my mother's disapproval shining through her.

"Fine. Tonight." It is an easy thing to say at ten a.m. Twelve hours later, with the sky like pitch and the streets about to boil over with lunatics, it is another thing altogether.

I fasten her bullet-proof vest—it bulges at the sides and hangs from her scrawny shoulders—knowing there are a thousand and one ways this thing could go south.

"Tell me the plan," I say, gathering my gear to avoid thinking of her needing that vest.

"We find an unlighted path to the museum. We check the doors and windows before we go in. We go in the safest way, and only if the place isn't overrun, we go straight to the Modern Wing on the second floor. I get what I'm going for, and we get out."

"Good. What do you do if something happens to me?"

"I run until I'm safe. Then I come straight back here, not anywhere else like the Modern Wing of the Art museum, and I have enough raviolis to eat until the world ends. I don't trust anyone. I shoot first and don't bother to ask questions."

"That's my girl."

"But no guns to the museum. I'll only use one if you die," she states.

"I'm blaming your heartlessness about my possible death on your mother," I mutter.

"Well, maybe if you'd come to a few more dance recitals, Marco, we'd get along better."

Worse than a knife to the belly, and I know what I'm talking about too well. "All right. You have everything?"

"Wait!" She disappears to the boss's room and when she returns, a tall, cardboard poster tube sticks out of the top of her backpack. "Ready."

***

I have to admit it, Azalea is a real trooper. I don't know how long her mother was with that group of gun-loving psycho-survivalists, but Azalea has genuine skills. Light on her feet, not a peep of surprise or complaining. Just the occasional, strange crunching noise from her backpack, but it's faint enough to not be a problem. I have no idea what she's got in there, or what painting we're grabbing, and I don't care.

We make it to the museum undetected and in one piece. "So far, so good."

She nods, solemn as a nun on Christmas.

We circle the museum twice, checking all the entrances and windows for break-ins. I can't quite believe it, but it seems intact. In a world that has lost its mind, no one busted any windows here for the fun of it. I tap my crowbar against one palm, going over the possible scenarios for what is going on in there, not liking any that I come up with.

"What are you doing with that?" Azalea asks, trying to take my crowbar.

"I'm going to break open a door with it. How else are we getting in?"

"Well, we could go and just—" She waves like she has an invisible magic wand at the huge building. "I mean, don't you have some rappel wires, and we could climb up to the roof and pick a lock or—"

I stop her there. "I don't know which *Mission Impossible* you've been watching, but I'm not a spy, I'm a hit—" And I stop myself there. I can't tell my baby girl I'm a hitman. She might suspect, hell she might know, but I won't say it.

I heft the crowbar. "In real life, this is how you break into buildings. You stay behind me. If I say run, you run and don't look back. Don't go anywhere but home, capisce?"

She clamps her lips together, but when I turn to go, she latches onto the strap of my bag. A hack job. I'm risking her life for a tween-age dream by doing a hack job. We make our way to a side entrance. I brace the crowbar in the crack to pry the doors open.

"Wait," she breathes. "What if the alarms are on?"

I exhale, fingers pinching the bridge of my nose. A string of curse words lights up in my head like colored bulbs in a Bier Garten. The alarms. What if one of the other families is squatting the place and has it wired? Lorenzo the Angel never would—too many windows and not enough guns in the basement, but it's possible. I'm ready to give up. She can see it.

"Marco," her little voice says. Crushed isn't the word for what's going on with her face. Heartbroken? And for what?

"Which painting is it?" I ask.

"Which?"

"Which one? Which painting could possibly be so amazingly valuable to a twelve-year-old girl—"

Her hand strays to that tube poking out of her backpack and I realize I'm an ass.

"All right. We're getting in. But carefully." I'd been a hitman for the Angelo family since I was fifteen—I picked up a few tricks besides making grown men cry before the end. Ignoring her protests, I wedge the crowbar between the two doors and bust it wide open.

Right on cue, an alarm blares. Either no one comes and we go in, or someone from inside comes. The police aren't coming. I grab Azalea and get us both behind the shell of a burned-out truck nearby. We wait.

A figure moves in the dark of the museum—I get an outline only from the faint glow of windows behind him. The city is in a partial blackout, saving electricity, but there are some streetlights in the distance. It's a male, nearly six feet, wide shoulders, slight pooch, fitted, button-up shirt, slacks. And a heavy belt, baton in hand.

Security guard? Those guys are still showing up to work? But only one. No communications with anyone else, inside or out. He must know his line of work and have balls of Damascus steel to be on his own. If he's here, running the place, then no one is squatting in the museum. Hopefully. I motion for Azalea to stay where she is.

The alarm stops, and the door starts to close. I jump forward, and in the same movement, shove the door open and point my gun at his head.

"Not a sound. Not one false move. We aren't here to hurt anyone, so you can turn around and go back to your office for the next hour. Got it?"

That's when I see what's pointing at my stomach.

Not a baton—not a fucking baton. A sawed-off shotgun. I'm fucked.

"Marco!" Azalea shouts. And against every rule we talked about, my little girl comes running in, and jumps right between us, in the line of fire. She wavers, suddenly noticing first my pistol and then his shotgun.

"Hey," the guard says, hitching his chin at my daughter, "you all right? Do you need help?"

She ducks behind me. Finally. Better late than never, am I right? His shells would shred me like tissue paper, but I feel better knowing she's back there instead of in front of me.

"I'm fine," she calls. "This is my father, Marco Guiseppe de Luca, and he promised to bring me to the museum before the world ends."

"Father, huh?" I can see his mouth working, like he's looking for the words to say, making a decision. But I already know he'll make the right one.

He lowers the shotgun. He's a good guy—not the kind who would risk shooting little girls.

"Yeah, her father. And we're just here for a little visit, nothing else."

Holstering the shotgun, he starts to walk backwards, slowly, hands in the air like he actually paid attention to his training.

"Excuse me, sir?" Azalea's sweet voice floats through the air. "Before you go, could you please direct me to the Modern Wing on the second floor?"

"You said you knew exactly where it was," I mutter.

"I've never been in this hallway," she says through clenched teeth. "And I told you, *no guns*."

The security guard, hands still in the air, hesitates, then points over our heads. "Down this hall until you reach the stairs, go up, and follow the signs to your left. The Modern Wing is clearly marked."

"Thank you!"

"No problem, miss," he says. Then adds, "Enjoy your visit."

He disappears in another hallway, and I escort Azalea to the stairs as fast as I can in the near darkness. Now that he knows we're here and where we're going, I might as well use the flashlight. I flick it on and we go up to the second floor. The signs point the way and we rush down wide, clean halls lined with paintings in heavy frames and random, naked-people statues. I have to keep prodding her to make her go faster. Where did she get that from? This stopping to look at art? What kind of twelve-year-old likes old art stuff?

The night crawlers are going to be out and thick if we don't get out of here soon.

We reach the Modern Wing, clearly marked just as Mr. Security Guard said.

Now, she knows exactly where we are. Head down, she marches forward, leading the way through several rooms, and on to the end, to the last room. There are two entrances, no windows, one wooden bench in the middle, and some statues on rectangular stands.

I swing my flashlight, checking for danger. "Clear. Do what you came to do."

She nods silently, neither the crusty dock worker nor the polite museum visitor, but a new creature entirely. Only twelve and so many sides to her. I shake my head in wonder. Who would she be—what could she become if the world doesn't end in twenty days?

Moving faster than Lorenzo's accountant when he found out the feds were coming, she flings her backpack to the floor near the wall, between two large paintings of funny-shaped people, and unloads her tools, lining them up, nice and neat on the floor. She gets that from me.

In one, two, and three, she pulls out a rolled picture from the tube, uses four tiny nails to fix it to the wall, lines the wall around it with superglue, and then sticks four individual sides of a wooden frame to it so it looks as if it is hanging. Then, she pulls out a rustling plastic bag of yellow and pink cereal from her backpack and clutches it to her chest.

"Done," she whispers. "Easy peasy."

I haul the bench from its spot in the middle of the room closer to the wall, wincing at the screech it makes. Finally, I prop up the flashlight on it so I can come closer and see what she's fixed to the wall.

I can't breathe, not even a little. It's a painting, obviously done by a kid, but also brutally honest and pure. It's divided down the middle by the dark edge of a wall. On one side, a bunch of little girls in frilly skirts are dancing on a bright stage, and on the other side, one little girl in a frilly skirt is crouched in darkness, her hands over her face. Probably crying.

Tears sting in the backs of my eyes and I clench my jaw, refusing to let them flow. I'm stronger than this. I popped off four guys in one night for the boss over some stolen diamonds and got knifed in the belly before crawling home on my own. This picture won't make me cry.

"What's it called?"

"Self-portrait at *nine*," Azalea says. "This was the moment I realized I didn't want to be a dancer, I wanted to be an artist." I swear that butcher knife is jabbed right through my heart, but she's not done. "And I wanted my art in a museum before I died."

I hold out my arms, and she rushes into them. And dammit, I'm crying.

We sit on the bench, admiring her work, not saying much for a long time. She lifts up the plastic bag that crunches. "Want a bite?"

I reach in and get a handful of Captain Crunch to snack on, like we're at the movies.

"Can we come back tomorrow?" she asks. "Or better yet, just stay here?"

"I don't know, Azalea."

"Azzie," she says. "Everyone calls me Azzie."

"Well, everyone calls me Marco, but if you want, you can call me Dad."

"I don't know if I'm ready for that, Marco. You've still got twenty days to mess this up."

"All right." I toss a cereal square in my mouth. I've got twenty days to show her I'm not going to mess this up. Twenty days to be a real dad.

~

20

about the author

Franklin Barnes *is a lifelong California resident who's written a few books on Wattpad. He thinks they aren't half-bad, and would be most pleased if you were to take a look. In his spare time, he enjoys playing piano, cooking, and reminiscing about his younger and more vulnerable years.*

THE CAPITALIST

by Franklin Barnes

NAPA, CALIFORNIA, USA - 9:00 AM PST

There was no worse news Cole Chasseur could have heard in the middle of an apocalypse than that things were getting better and that he couldn't take credit for it.

He'd had a rough few days: he had moved from his San Francisco penthouse to his summer retreat in Napa, a converted vineyard, to avoid the vagaries of city life—the tear gas, the Molotov cocktails, the demands for multi-billionaire CEOs like himself to donate their wealth to help the common man. And now, if his Twitter homepage was to be believed (and the government memos), the spacecraft was cleaning the air?

"Someone get me another mimosa!" Cole called out, placing his glass back on the coffee table with a clink. Thirty seconds later, his chef placed another in front of him, and took all the empty champagne flutes in his meaty hands back to the kitchen. Cole chugged half of the new mimosa before deciding it was too early in the morning to drink away his sorrows. He put it back down—he'd come back for it later—and moved to the terrace.

Cole had bought the vineyard and the attached faux-Tuscan villa as the architectural equivalent of a juice cleanse: his doctor had told him that fresh air was healthy, and instead of opening the windows in his office, he had bought an estate. The dull blue sky and patches of green among the gravel reminded him of a Renoir painting he had seen at the Met once, *A Road in Louveciennes*. He had a higher vantage point here, and there were no people in sight, just how he liked it. He had heard that people were fleeing en masse from the Southeast, but the United States was a big country and the roads would only take them so far. It would be a long time before any caravan of dusty travelers despoiled his estate.

Cole's silent meditations on the landscape and the fragility of beauty were interrupted by a shout from inside: "Cole, President Underwood's chief of staff is calling!"

"Tell him I'll be right there, Colette!" Cole shouted back, and returned to the lounge. Colette silently handed him the phone and his half-finished mimosa, and went to stand in the corner, supervising from afar. She wrote something down on her notepad.

"Hey Chuck, how's it going over there?" Cole said, and gargled the remainder of his mimosa before swallowing it.

"There's no time for comedy, Cole. You know how bad it is. We have a humanitarian crisis on our hands."

"So I've heard. Where are you right now?"

"I'm in the War Room. We've been calling all the shipping company CEOs to coordinate with FEMA and deliver relief to affected areas. Time is of the essence here."

"'Gentlemen, you can't fight in here, this is the War Room!' Sorry. I know it's not the time. What can I do?"

"We need all your staff and logistical networks on our side. We need food, water, and clothing going into the Twilight and Midnight Zones. We need your people to work with the boots on the ground and get this stuff to the people who need it most. Most of all, we need public-facing leadership. There are protests on the street in San Francisco calling for your head. They think you're out-of-touch. If you don't do something, they're going to storm your Bastille, and we'll see then how much your wealth can insulate you from this crisis. Capisce?"

Cole cleared his throat. "Capisce. Colette will connect you to my chief of operations. He'll know what to do. You have my full support, and my company is fully at your disposal."

"Very well. Talk to you soon, Cole."

"See ya, Chuck," Cole said, and he passed the phone to a waiting Colette.

Cole returned to the terrace. That call was too tense—he needed some fresh air. It was the start of harvest season, but his workers had been sluggish lately. Probably the existential dread. They looked like ants, meandering up and down the rows of grapevines. It would make a great scene to paint, but he didn't know how, and he wasn't in the right headspace to upskill. The mimosas were starting to kick in, but they were only making him more anxious, especially after that call; he felt his hamstrings tighten, like he were a jackrabbit about to spring into the air. He rationalized the feeling as a flight-or-flight response, and since he was in idyllic Napa and not the hazy, smoke-filled streets of San Francisco, he had chosen flight. Maybe they could bring that giant air purifier over to San Francisco to clean up afterward.

His first reaction had been, when the spacecraft appeared, to herald it as the harbinger of a new era. Spaceflight had been a dream of his ever since he had discovered *Star Trek* as a kid, and Project Icarus was one of his most dear projects out of all his projects, and one of the few that did not lose its *joie de vivre* as soon as it became corporate and profitable. He had always believed in transhumanism, that the human mind was a limitless power source only constrained by the flesh it was bound to—but this promised enlightenment had not yet come. Maybe it was a test of their patience, and they'd be rewarded with the spacecraft's technological secrets at the end. Or maybe only the worthiest would be invited to join them and explore the stars. Cole wasn't sure who would be most deserving out of humanity to join the aliens, but he thought he had a fair shot.

When Cole had told some of his employees to clandestinely reach out to the ship, offering any earthly pleasure in exchange for its secrets, they had received no response on any communication frequency. It couldn't have been that Cole was undeserving—who better than a Silicon Valley entrepreneur to turn the world into an utopia? So the aliens were clearly stingy, and so Cole's dreams of a brave new world unencumbered by mortal woes remained dreams. He went to get his laptop, and returned to the terrace, ready to finally get some real work done. But first, some more doom-scrolling through the pictures of destruction and despair from the rest of the country.

The skies had turned to shadow and the grassy fields had been trampled, everywhere but sunny California; kids with sunken eyes and hollow frames walked along crowded roads, begging for scraps, everywhere but sunny California. There were a few trending local pictures, protesters clad in multicolored bandanas marching for a revolution or a secession movement that was surprisingly gaining traction, but they did little but tug at Cole's sentimentality. One picture from the Twilight Zone especially haunted Cole: children, children that should have been in school learning to be model citizens, scrabbling through the roadside looking for dandelions to eat. It reminded him of another Renoir painting he had always had his eyes on, *The Harvesters*, but instead of a straw-colored expanse, all he saw was gray, a few flashes of yellow and green from the dandelions aside. The picture would also make a great painting.

Cole realized suddenly he needed to show some executive leadership. He opened Twitter and wrote, "Working with FEMA to solve crisis! Stay strong!." One click later and it was sent—not masterful oratory, but it got the job done. It was almost lunch time, and he decided that he would invite Colette and his chef to dine with him on the terrace. While ordinarily he'd never eat with his staff, while they were on this retreat he had surprisingly found it more comforting to see them as people rather than sentient furniture. People with their own worries, people who might have families affected by the spaceship, people who could use a bit of wine and charcuterie. The vineyard workers continued their work, either unaware or uncaring of the world around them.

Cole knocked twice on Colette's office door and let himself in, standing in the doorway over her.

"Would you care to join us for lunch today? It's lovely weather out."

"Of course, Mr. Chasseur."

"You know it's fine to call me Cole."

"Of course, Mr. Chasseur," Colette said, and she closed her laptop and followed Cole out.

The chef (Cole never could remember his name) naturally said yes too, and even deigned to let Cole help out in the kitchen and make the Caprese salad, and the three of them went out to the terrace and set up the table. They laid out the pasta alla Norma, the salad, and a bottle of Chardonnay the chef had brought from the cellar, and began eating. Cole broke the ice after a few minutes of silence:

"How's everyone doing today?" he asked.

"I've felt better," Colette said sharply. "Things are bad out there. People are reacting to your tweet, saying you aren't doing enough. They want you to donate your personal wealth for charity efforts—"

"That's the government's job! Maybe if they didn't spend so much on the military, they wouldn't need to rely on the private sector to do their jobs."

"That may be true, Mr. Chasseur, but on a more personal note, if I may speak freely, this has been stressing me out. Every night, I sleep not knowing what news I'll wake up to, or if I'll even wake up at all. It's hard to focus. What do we do when the disaster comes here?"

"Enjoy our good fortune while we can, Colette," Cole smiled in between mouthfuls. "This is great pasta, by the way."

"I was thinking, too," the chef began, "how unfortunate it is that we're enjoying this picturesque meal when there are children scrounging for weeds on the other side of the country. I heard that one family was murdered, in cold blood, all because there were rumors they had an extra food stockpile. It was something straight out of a Truman Capote novel: murdered in their own beds, and all to raid their cupboards."

"So what? There are children starving in Africa, and yet we don't all donate our extra income to help them. It's not like they need me on the front lines handing out sandwiches, either—they have people to do that for them. If they need people to hand out sandwiches, I'll give them money to hire minimum wage workers to hand out sandwiches."

"I have a cousin in Houston who's said that the supermarkets are empty now because so many refugees are coming," the chef continued. "He's scared they're going to break into his house. All day and night he and his family take shifts guarding the house with a shotgun. Like it's the Wild West all over again. What has this done to us?"

"Your cousin's being paranoid," Colette said. "People are desperate, but not that desperate. There's this fundamental sense of compassion we all have: all of us have a family member, or a college friend, or somebody affected by this. How could anyone ever betray another in a time of crisis knowing that we're all in the same boat?"

"I literally just told you about how people are being murdered over food, Colette."

"Fine," she said, and took another sip of wine—Cole's phone rang, and he left the table before he could hear the rest of her retort.

"This is Chuck again."

"Long time no see! How are things going?"

"I wanted to call and personally congratulate you on how quickly you were able to mobilize your team into action. As we speak, our disaster management teams are making full use of your delivery vehicles, your warehouses, everything. If I may speak frankly, you were the fastest to say yes to helping us: most in your position decided this was a great time to take a vacation to international waters, but you were able to snap your fingers and say to make it so, and so it happened. The country owes you a great debt of gratitude."

"I really appreciate it, Chuck. Anything else I can do to help?"

"Your team is doing plenty. We've made a tweet praising your swift response specifically. How is it up there in Napa, anyway? Still sunny?"

"Still sunny, like always. We're in the middle of lunch here."

"I won't keep you. Wish I could be there. That salad looked delicious."

"Next time, Chuck. After this is all over."

"Bye-bye."

Cole returned to the table with a triumphant air, and resumed eating as if nothing had happened. It wasn't every day that the government praised him and his heroism, but he'd take it when he got it.

"That was Chuck calling me again to praise me for my fine leadership. We're doing good work out there. We're saving lives."

"We were talking and I came up with a thought exercise," the chef said. "What if he had called you and said that he wanted you, personally, to fly out there and work on the front lines, as a publicity gesture—a gesture of goodwill, whatever you want to call it. Would you?"

"Of course I would. Who am I to deny him?"

"And would you do it, even if people called it a publicity gesture, saying it's a distraction from how you aren't donating to charity. Or if people started screaming in your face, blaming you for this spacecraft like some of the conspiracy theories out there—you've surely seen that a lot of the more creative sectors of the Internet have accused this spacecraft of coming from Project Icarus. Would you still do it?"

"You're trying to make me say no, aren't you. I still would. They know better than I do how to help best. My job is to innovate; their job is to execute. It's why I'm letting my team handle things and not trying to step in myself. You think the president is sitting around researching policy or writing reports? He has his people bring him info, and then he acts how they tell him to. And here, if they in their infinite wisdom have decided I can help the relief effort best by handing out sandwiches, I'm going to be the best sandwich deliverer there ever was."

"I'm starting to see why I like you as a boss so much," the chef laughed, and they switched topics to lighter things, having done their part to save the world.

After lunch, Cole returned to his previous seat overlooking the vineyard. No plumes of smoke had yet rolled in like the Bay Area fog, and Cole was confident that they never would, and that the less he looked at his phone and social media, the more easily he could convince himself that there was nothing wrong in the world. He closed his eyes and imagined himself walking through Louveciennes, in a world without pain and with a lot more paint.

Cole was abruptly roused from his well-earned nap by *The Stars and Stripes Forever*, Chuck's ringtone, playing from his pocket.

"Hey, Chuck. What's up?"

"I just had a meeting with President Underwood, and I was telling him about our lovely chat earlier—he's been really pleased with all you've done to support the aid effort. And he had the marvelous idea that there's an overnight aid convoy flying from SFO to Minneapolis tonight, another result of your cooperation, and that it would be just peachy if you could go with them."

"That would be a splendiferous idea, Chuck."

"So is that a yes?"

Cole paused.

"So this isn't a rhetorical question?"

"President Underwood wants you to come. He asked you because he thinks you're the most likely to come. We aren't asking for much, just a few hours on the bread lines. Then maybe a few photos with displaced persons, a speech about how you're doing all you can to support the government, and you're done: your hands are clean."

"I'll call you back, Chuck."

"Talk to you later."

So Colette and the chef had been setting him up the entire time! He knew they couldn't be trusted: their state-school grins had always been portents of betrayal. They probably had him bugged, too, the government. He checked inside a potted plant—nothing. Were they reading his thoughts?

His instinctual reaction of panic had led him to the kitchen, and after scouring the cabinets for tinfoil and fashioning a rather fashionable helmet, he realized he wasn't healthily confronting his feelings. He poured himself a glass of water and leaned against the counter by the window, imagining himself in an endless queue with other refugees waiting to replenish their precious bodily fluids. Being the one giving them the water was better, but it was only one degree of separation away. A different roll of the dice and they'd be trading places.

"Mr. Chasseur, are you all right?" the chef called out. Cole had forgotten to remove his helmet.

"Oh, I'm fine, I'm really fine. Just got another call from Chuck."

"And he told you to wear that?" the chef asked, and opened the cabinet to pull out the tinfoil.

"Not at all. He made me, how do I phrase it, an offer I can't refuse. The president wants me to fly to Minneapolis tonight and help the refugees."

"That's great. Will you?"

"I don't know," Cole sighed. "The ethics of it all are very complicated. If I'm only one person there in Minneapolis, why not hire ten people to do my job? According to a strictly utilitarian school of thought, one advocated by the likes of John Stuart Mill, I should—"

"An hour ago you said that if the president summoned you, you'd go. What gives?"

"He's been under a lot of stress lately, and you know how under stress we aren't always of sound mind, and we make suboptimal decisions…"

"I scared you earlier, didn't I?"

Cole nodded.

"This would look great if you ran for president, I'm just saying. Don't tell me you haven't imagined your name in lights, or on a magazine cover—maybe even on a baseball cap."

"I already have all those things."

"But there's one thing you don't have: the respect of the people. Or the access to the spaceship's technology the government certainly has."

Cole chugged the rest of his glass and held it ready to slam on the counter, but reconsidered the materials science involved and delicately set it down instead.

"You're right. I don't have that. Will they like me after this?"

"When someone, red-eyed and dehydrated after driving all night with their family and worldly possessions in tow, walks into that refugee center, Satan himself could hand him his morning coffee and he'd take it with a smile."

"I know why I haven't fired you yet," Cole laughed, and he left the kitchen. "Get my suitcase!" he shouted down a hallway, and received a muffled "Yes, Mr. Chasseur!" in return. When he reached his bedroom, he called back Chuck, who picked up immediately.

"You're going?"

"I'm going. The people want me."

"They need you, at least. We'll have a car at your place at seven. Thank you once again for your generosity."

"*Dulce et decorum est pro patria mori*," Cole joked. "But it's really nothing at all."

"Bye-bye, Cole," Chuck said, and there Cole was, having eaten his words against his will. Colette knocked on the door, and opened it with his suitcase in hand.

"I heard you're going to Minneapolis. Whatever Colin said must have made your heart grow a few sizes."

"Is that his name, now?"

"Always has been. Pack light—leave the suit."

"Silicon Valley business casual then?"

"I have your jeans and monochrome T-shirts already folded and ready to go. *Bon voyage*, Mr. Chasseur," Colette said, closing the door and leaving him with his thoughts once more. He pulled out his laptop and doom-scrolled more, his eyes once again resting on those weed-harvesters, and imagined them silently mouthing "Thank you."

"You're welcome," he said, as he typed out a tweet: "See you soon, Minneapolis," before deleting the tab. He'd come as a surprise. Everyone loved surprises.

A few hours of packing and emails later, it was almost the fateful hour. Cole took his suitcase and backpack to the front driveway, where Colette and Colin waited like proud parents seeing their child off to summer camp.

"You think I'm doing the best I can do?" Cole asked them.

"The absolute best you can, Mr. Chasseur," Colette said. The black van pulled up, exactly on cue.

"Don't miss me too much," Cole said as he boarded the van, and they drove down the grapevine-lined road into the cooling twilight.

~

19

about the author

Mags Lorang *is a grammar-obsessed writer with 12 years of experience. An amateur editor. A reader of all formats.*

Writes dark and hopeful stories that exude themes like "everyone belongs" and "life isn't precious without death." Love of literature has caused an obsession so great she won't stop reading even for a slice of cake.

THE WAY HOME

by Mags Lorang

JEFFERSON CITY, MISSOURI, USA
AUGUST 12, 6:20 AM

Chadwick Wilkins' heart burned. It burned for *her*, his life, his everything, his wife.

Ingrid.

It had been twenty days since he'd seen her. She was supposed to be back home fourteen days ago. This time was the longest Chad had been without her, ever since the day they'd met.

As he looked at the empty Walmart shelves, he couldn't recall why the groceries were so sparse. All he remembered was that his wife was lost in total darkness under the vast cloud.

His daughter said it wasn't a cloud, but he forgot the real word for whatever it was.

Chad motored his scooter cart away from the aisle and to the checking area, all while his heart squeezed.

The kind young woman he'd seen at this same time, every day for the last ten days, stood behind the checkout counter. She wore her blue and yellow Walgreens pullover with a badge that said "Maine" pinned to her. They were the only people in the store, as usual. Everyone else was home watching their televisions, most likely the 24/7 news coverage of the big, constant cloud.

Maine showed all her pearly white teeth. "Chad! You're later than usual."

Chad tried to smile back. He really did. But it turned into a grimace as his chest tightened.

She moved to the other side of the counter to help him unload his groceries, her big black curly hair bouncing every time she leaned down. She arched her bushy black eyebrow at his cart, which only consisted of one thing. "Still using napkins as toilet paper?"

Toilet paper was the first to go when the cloud appeared. Then the fruit, meat, and corn. Then everything else. So rapidly, most local businesses were out of business or steadily crashing, including Chad's favorite bakery in town. His wife loved their scones.

Ingrid.

As Maine checked through the numerous, extra-soft napkins, Chad tried to catch his breath. But he couldn't. Sweat broke out in visible droplets over his body, and began leaking from his red flannel button-up, creating dark spots. And yet he shivered in his scooter. He was so cold. It reminded him of running, like the good old days when he and Ingrid were still young and able-bodied.

But no, he just sat in his scooter cart in Walmart with pain stealing the air from his lungs. Chad knew the symptoms of a heart attack. He'd had many before. His heart had become increasingly cantankerous the longer he lived. It was worth it when Ingrid was around—less so now. Not with the cloud, a shade on Earth, a shade on Ingrid.

He wanted to see her again. He *needed* to.

To do that, he needed help. He couldn't die yet.

He stood from his cart, one hand on his chest and the other carrying him. The burn intensified. He gasped, mouth open like a fish out of water, desperately trying to draw air into his oxygen-starved body. He doubled over, clutching his heart like it was his lover.

Ingrid.

Finally, Maine noticed something was off. "Oh, my god! Are you okay, Chad?"

He fell to one knee and groaned, still grasping his heart. His fingernails dug through his shirt and into his skin. The sting was a slight distraction from the pain invading his body.

Something pressed between his shoulder blades. Maine's panicked voice returned. "I'm calling the police. Don't worry."

His knees weakened, and he fell to his stomach.

As if from a great distance, the kind woman said, "My friend. I think he's having a heart attack."

Darkness.

Then, light.

A pure white that scorched Chad's eyes, skin, and heart. It was like a promise that his wife was close.

The more his gaze focused on his surroundings, the more the light blessed him. Blue skies and fun, puffy clouds—his favorite.

Is this Heaven? Chad spun, basking in the perfection until another thought occurred. *If there was a sky, then there must be a ground, right?*

He angled his sight downward. Like puzzle pieces, his favorite locations were sown together in a landscape tapestry below him—his very first home, his university, the church he and Ingrid married in, their first home together, the second where their daughter was born, and the third where their son was. And then there was his favorite thing of all: the garden he and Ingrid had built and groomed in their current retirement home. All the places he cherished so.

Yes, this must be Heaven.

But something nagged at his contentment.

Although the garden was there, the home it belonged to was not. He looked to his left. Nothing. Then, to his right.

Instead, in the distance, a shade of darkness loomed endlessly. Still in the blinding light but directly in front of the shadow's edge, stood their retirement home, lonely and meek amid the great phantom.

Chad gazed up, up, up, and found the source of the dark. A great edge of something out of place, its size inconceivable, hovered.

He suddenly remembered the name of the dark, dark cloud his wife was trapped under. A ship. An *alien* ship. A spacecraft. A shade on Earth.

There was only one speck of light under the ship.

Ingrid.

A young Ingrid with blonde curly locks and flawless skin floated under the craft at the same height as Chad. As soon as her wide eyes caught his, she plummeted.

Chad watched her, frozen despite his attempts to thrash his arms and legs. He couldn't reach her. He couldn't catch her. How was she so calm?

His quavering voice found itself. "Ingrid!"

He fell, too. But, unlike his wife, he screamed like some bastard was trespassing on his lawn.

He tumbled to the garden made beautiful only by Ingrid's presence and was inhaled by a whirlwind of color and no color.

And, again, he was blinded by an unpleasant white light and an overwhelming smell of antiseptics.

A hospital.

He wasn't dead. Not yet, anyway.

A familiar beeping sound and murmuring voices greeted him.

He knew this charade. The doctor—or nurse, maybe—was speaking with his daughter about his heart condition. And, soon enough, Lizbet would be in there chewing him out like *she* was the parent. Best perhaps, to keep his eyes closed and listen. After that light, they needed more rest anyway.

He caught the doctor's words mid-sentence. "—short on supplies, but we'll work him into the list as soon as possible."

"What can I do for him in the meantime? He doesn't listen to me. He goes out when he's not supposed to, he argues all the time, gets his heart rate up real easily. And it's all gotten worse with this U.F.O."

She didn't mention Chad's wife, her mom.

The doctor's professional monotone answered, "Ma'am, the best you can do is make him comfortable and keep an eagle's eye on him." A pause. "At this point, he's so weak, you have nothing to worry about." Another pause and more hesitance and grimness. "If push comes to shove, there are always nursing homes. I can give you a list. But there might be some long waits because of the influx of elderly coming out from the east. Might have to go with a cross-country option."

Chad would rather go to Hell than a nursing home. Probably the same thing. And Lizbet knew his feelings on that choice.

Lizbet sighed. "Thought you might say that."

Her soft yet strong tone reminded Chad of his wife.

Ingrid.

He tuned out the voices at the reminder of his wife. She was trapped in the dark, apart from him. He wanted her. No, he *needed* her. But she was almost gone. Certainty grew in his chest. Sometimes, dreams were real. Sometimes, they were destiny.

Chad sat up abruptly and purple stars swam around his vision. Through the haze, Lizbet's wide frame ran towards him. "Dad!"

She was streaked with purple and red until she forcefully laid him down. Her hair shifted and bled to gray. How strange, especially since her mother was still blonde. Then, he remembered he was close to bald himself and Ingrid was out there somewhere, with a mop of white and a bald spot of her own.

Ingrid.

He cried and struggled, but Lizbet held him down firmly, cooing words of comfort.

"Calm down, Dad. It's okay. I'm trying to help, Dad."

His body went limp without his brain's consent.

Then, a female nurse wearing blue scrubs took over. No doctor, of course. What doctor wants to bother with any of his "elderly" patients? His tears were dry now.

Chad clenched his fists till he couldn't anymore. Weakness betrayed him and left him at the mercy of the nurse's soothing voice while she wrote on her clipboard.

"How are you feeling, Mr. Wilkins?"

He didn't answer.

After a long pause, the nurse continued. "Are you in any pain?"

Chad took inventory of his desperate body and nodded.

"Alright, I'll give you some aspirin, and that should tide you over for a few hours."

She left the room for a bit.

Lizbet turned to Chad, red in the face. "Dad, you can't do that to me! When I say don't leave your house, I *mean* no leaving your house!"

"Napkins," was all Chad got out before his daughter exploded in his face.

"Especially not with a fucking *spaceship* floating over half the U.S.!"

Lizbet didn't curse. *Ever.*

The nurse returned with a tray of two white pills and a plastic water cup. After holding the cup to Chad's mouth to help him drink, she turned to Lizbet.

She'd clearly heard the outburst because she pulled her to a corner and whispered to her. Lizbet's face contorted into a look of guilt, and she nodded.

They walked back to Chad, a smile on the nurse's face. "I hope that aspirin helps. Call for me if you ever need me. The name's Tammi. Take care, Mr. Wilkins."

And she left him to the less-than-calm Lizbet.

Nostrils flared, she sat on the chair next to Chad's bed. "Dad, I have to tell you something…" She rubbed her nose. "It's about your health."

Chad just stared at her, already knowing what was coming.

After another nose-rub, she got to the point. "The stents aren't helping." A pause and no response. "You're gonna have to get a heart transplant since your heart's so weak. The doc said they'd get you on the list, but it might be a long wait." She took a tiny breath and plunged into her duty of mothering her father. "That means you gotta stay safe. I'll go to Walmart for you. I'll do everything you did for yourself before now. But you just gotta stay indoors and give yourself time to breathe." Another breath. "I know you're not gonna like this, but I'll also have to help administer your medications. I know you sometimes forget, especially since Mom's gone, but it's super important now, 'kay? So you gotta work with me, yeah?"

Chad still didn't answer. He could take care of himself. He'd been doing it for years. The only difference now was there was no Ingrid to motivate him. He had to drive himself forward. And it just wasn't working.

"Ingrid."

Lizbet frowned and brought her eyebrows closer to her cheekbones. "I know it's hard without her, Dad, I really do. But we still gotta go on and trust that she'll get home. She and John both."

"Why?" Chad moaned, tears silently dripping again.

"Because, that's life, Dad. People disappear sometimes."

"No! Why?"

"You mean why'd she leave?"

No response, just more tears.

"You know how much she loves her sister. Auntie Tiana didn't have much time left."

He groaned again.

Lizbet's sorrowful eyes were on him. "Just… try to sleep. Okay, Dad?"

So he did. And it wasn't difficult. Darkness enveloped him and he saw the young Ingrid again.

Sunshine and haloes and… something more. Something divine.

He wanted to join her. But, this time, *he* was in darkness under the ship. And she was his only light.

Ingrid smiled and spoke softly. "Chad. I've missed you. But—"

A beeping noise intruded her speech, along with a familiar voice saying, "Hey, Mama. How's Pops doing?"

Ingrid bit her lip. "You've got more strings to tie." Then, she waved bye and faded as the hospital lights and a baby's tiny head replaced her.

"Ba!" the baby said.

"What's up, Han?"

The baby pointed directly at Chad. "Ba!"

"Holy shit, he's awake Ma!"

Her strong and soft voice was just like Ingrid's.

"Ingrid?" But when Chad looked away from the baby, he saw the woman carrying her. Not Ingrid. She had dark hair and a honey-brown complexion, the same vase looks as the baby, and was wearing military camouflage.

They both looked like Ingrid.

Vikki, Chad's granddaughter. He'd never met her baby girl.

He held out shaky hands, somehow managing through the weakness. "Baby."

Vikki's face lit up. "I thought you'd want to meet her, Pops." She looked at her mother to give a sense of reassurance. "Want to hold her?"

He patted his lap twice. And then there was a toddler sitting on his legs. Her hands waved in the air, and her mouth rounded into a silent *oh*. She looked up at her mom, then pointed at Chad. "Baba!"

Then she crawled into Chad's arms. Although he couldn't even remember her name, his despondent expression shifted to a bright smile.

And there she stayed, speaking her baby language, many *bas* and *ahs* and other noises that didn't make any linguistic sense. She was happy and wonderful where she was. And so was Chad.

"I almost forgot how friendly she is," Lizbet quipped.

Vikki ignored her and faced her grandfather, sorrow apparent. "Hey, Pops… I'm sorry for not visiting after we evacuated." She rubbed the back of her neck. "I just… Well, we're dealing with a lot right now, and—"

"Evacuated?" Chad didn't remember an evacuation.

Vikki eyed her mother again. "Yeah, remember the ship? Little Hannah and I evacuated from my military base several days ago." She rubbed her nose. "And I didn't visit you till now."

Oh, Hannah. That was his great-granddaughter's name.

Suddenly, the television in the corner of the room turned on. The only thing on the screen was a bright blue number eighteeen.

"Shit," Vikki said, looking at her watch. "It's already eleven." She rapidly looked between her daughter and Chad, then at Lizbet. "You got Hannah, Mama?"

Something else to do with the ship, Chad imagined.

"Yeah, I got her. Where are you off to?"

"I gotta get back to my duty station and bust some boneheads for thinking it'd be a good idea to shoot down a two thousand mile spaceship out of the sky. Fucking world-ending's what it is." She sighed and recovered herself. "And Pops… I'll bring Gran home, okay? Uncle John, too."

John. His son. He was stuck with Ingrid. But Ingrid was gone. So where was John?

"Gone," Chad said. "She's gone."

Vikki ignored him, instead grabbing a blue and grey chevron-patterned bag from the floor. "This has got everything you need for Hannah. She'll wanna read her favorite book. *Goodnight Moon*. A classic. And—"

"I know my grandbaby's favorite book, Vik." Lizbet glared at her from above her glasses. "Now, don't you got somewhere to be?"

Vikki was at the doorway when she paused to look back at Chad. "I'll bring her home. Count on it."

She took one deep breath and marched into the hallway, nodded to a passing pink-clad nurse.

Then, Hannah was taken from Chad.

He glanced back at the television. The glowing eighteen had been replaced with a black screen.

He squeezed his eyes shut. "Ingrid."

Lizbet turned to stone, clutching onto Hannah.

Then, the baby chimed, "Boo—ah!" It was as if she worked so hard to add the 'k' that it became frustrating.

Chad smiled slowly as Lizbet sat down on the bench by the window and rummaged through the diaper bag. Out came the bright green cover of *Goodnight Moon*.

Chad stared out the window at the pouring rain and listened to his daughter say goodnight to so much. He fell asleep after she said, "And goodnight to the old lady whispering 'hush,'" for the third time.

Goodnight, Lizbet.

Goodnight, Hannah.

Goodnight, Vikki.

Goodnight, John.

His eyes opened to Ingrid, an old woman again.

The love of his life. His light and salvation. His everything.

"Ingrid."

He did not fall this time. Instead, he floated toward her, toward the divine light surrounding her, and away from the shade on Earth.

He was being saved.

Ingrid.

She was so beautiful. He couldn't wait to join her.

But he was stopped right before reaching her. Powerless to move, he couldn't control anything or even reach for her.

"Chad, before you join me, think about those you love."

Suddenly, clouds of visions appeared around the couple.

One hosted a sleeping Hannah resting on Lizbet's shoulder who stared at something—probably Chad's sleeping body. He knew that she wouldn't be as peaceful once she heard the constant beep of a heart stopping.

Then, it switched to Vikki standing at attention with several other soldiers. He hoped she succeeded in her mission to bust some heads, if not for the safety of John, then for the world.

As if on cue, John entered the vision, leaning over Ingrid's body. No. Chad's poor boy. His well-loved son. Seeming so distant, but so loving. *I'm sorry, John.*

Then, for some reason, another vision showed Maine shaking her knee in a hospital waiting room. Friend. She'd called him friend. His first friend since… forever.

"Is this my imagination?" His voice cracked.

"Does it really matter?" Ingrid asked. "Chad… Are you prepared?"

Lizbet and Vikki were grown women; they could take care of themselves and Hannah. Maine probably had so many friends; she'd get over him quickly.

But, John.

John.

John.

Vikki.

She was going after him. She would get him and bring him home.

Chad closed his eyes and smiled. "I'm ready."

Then, Ingrid's hand was in his.

Husband and wife, together again.

~

18

about the author

Evelyn Hail *is an writer and a holder of PhDs in English Literature & Latin American Literature.*

She is also philosopher-ish, lover of butterflies, Harry Potter die-hard fan, Nikola Tesla admirer, Beauty and the Beast 2 in 1, bacon cheese fries devourer, white chocolate adorer and illustrator.

Having always been passionate about storytelling, she's a curious writer who loves exploring different themes.

As an author, Evelyn has forged works based on fantasy, science fiction and magical realism, as well as literary fiction with a dash of satirical elements and humour. She has recently tried her hand in romance and found out she quite liked it!

THE WORSHIP

by Evelyn Hail

SUMMITVILLE, COFFEE COUNTY, TENNESSEE, USA
AUGUST 13, 6:30 PM

The alien ship hangs above our heads, akin to a colossal, dark spectre. Its metallic bulk suffocates the last rays of sunset like a cosmic umbrella. It's as if the sky itself had birthed a behemoth from another realm.

The deserted suburban neighborhood stretches before us, a haunting reminder of the world we once knew.

"Almost everyone evacuated," whispers Aadila, placing a protective palm on her tiny baby bump.

She's right. Rows of empty homes stand as silent witness to the exodus. We'll be leaving as well, right after we pick up Aadila's phone.

Soon enough, these boarded-up windows and overgrown gardens might create a post-apocalyptic scene straight out of *The Walking Dead*.

"Mick… The man on the phone—you sure he said Clark Road, fourteen?"

"I'm sure." I take out my cell phone from my pocket, placing my other arm reassuringly around her shoulder.

The address pointed us to a house like any other in this town—a dim and dusty wooden relic with its windows shuttered and curtains drawn, and a rusty circular handle looming at the door. This place stands as a mirage of the quintessential American dream home. Complete with a manicured garden and white picket fence, it whispers promises of suburban bliss. I half-expect a playful puppy to bound through the yard, adding a touch of warmth and companionship to the illusion.

Not so different from the place Aadila and I were looking to buy, for when baby Josh comes into this world.

With no bell to ring, the house stands in quiet anticipation, as if hugging its secrets close.

Knock, knock. The sound reverberates through the empty halls, unanswered.

The silence is deafening, and I can't help but wonder what story lies behind the door wide-shut.

"Should we head on inside?"

Before she can answer, I already have one sneaker on a lacquered, inviting threshold. It creaks underfoot, protesting my intrusion. The wood is splintered and rough to the touch, its grain raised and curling in places. The recently applied white coat of paint is fresh, camouflaging the remnants of the peeling and faded wood.

The door opens slowly. Its hinges squeak like the whispers of a secret, and the warm light that spills forth beckons me inside like a siren's song.

From the outside, the well-kept yard and fresh paint suggested a degree of upkeep to the house, but once we step inside, the illusion fades, revealing a different story altogether.

The air in the hallway is thick with the musty smell of decay, as though the place has been abandoned for quite some time. Cobwebs cling to the corners of the ceiling, while layers of dust cover every surface.

As I make my way through the fading light, I can't help but feel like I'm trespassing on some forgotten secret.

Aadila's bark-like cough startles me from my thoughts.

"If you want to stay outside, I'll go get your iPhone," I suggest.

"Er, I wish none of us had to go inside and get it." She hugs herself.

"Baby Josh's ultrasound photos are on it," I gently remind her.

"And all my family contact phone numbers," she huffs. "Without it, we… we might not have a chance to reach them in all of this chaos. But no way I'm staying outside this place *alone.*" Aadila gulps and accentuates the last word, clearing her throat.

A door slams shut in the distance. The sound reverberates, a sudden punctuation to our whispery silence.

Aadila claps my hand, and I relish in her hold. This place is certainly macabre.

"*Hello?*" I dare a whisper-shout, my words echoing through the empty hallway.

A moment passes.

"Enter," a deep and creepy voice whispers from the poorly lit bowels of the house.

My hairs stand on the back of my neck. What lurks beyond is unknown, and the thought of stepping into the semi-darkness makes my heart race with fear.

But as the seconds tick by, curiosity and a sense of morbid fascination overtake me.

Plus, we're here to retrieve Aadila's phone, then leave.

Taking a deep breath, we step forth together. The door clicks shut behind us.

The air is thick with silence and the unknown.

Aadila and I tread carefully, stepping over crumbled ornaments, cracked lamps, and piled bits of crushed furniture, covered by fabrics, rugs, and carpets.

"I don't understand how anyone can live like this, Mick," Aadila whispers close to my ear.

I barely have the time to shush her when a haunting creak echoes around, the sound of rolling wheels announcing a presence before a man comes into view.

A wave of compassion washes over me as I behold the wheelchair and the stranger's countenance conveying a profound sense of helplessness.

Up close, he has wrinkles and his square jaw is covered by a scraggly beard that surely hasn't seen a razor in many weeks. He looks like he hasn't eaten in days, with sunken eyes and sharp cheekbones. His muscled arms are tanned and weather-beaten, as though he's spent a lifetime outdoors, and it doesn't quite add up to the picture in my mind.

"You Aadila?" The cripple shifts in his rickety seat, and a peculiar hungry expression flashes on his face, like a wolf on the prowl. He bares his teeth, crooked and yellowed from what might be years of toothbrush-toothpaste neglect.

"Yes, um, and this is my boyfriend, Mick? You called him earlier today to tell him you found my phone," Aadila says, introducing me. "Nice to meet you," she adds with a deeply ingrained civil whisper, even as I know her words couldn't be further from the truth.

After a moment of silence, because there is no point in politely chatting about the weather, I point at a short, dusty bookshelf topped by an ornate mantelpiece and ask, "Is that Aadila's phone?"

The man nods wordlessly, sizing us up.

Wanting to get the hell out of here, we hurry through the piles of books scattered on the floor until we reach the wooden shelves. They must never use the fireplace barely visible behind it.

The mantelpiece is cluttered with a collection of photographs and the absence of the old man's image awakens my curiosity. Next to Aadila's phone, there are two new unlit candles, their light blue wax clumsily molded into crude numerical shapes of one and eight.

As the taller of the two of us, I reach for the phone, touching a layer of dust and maybe some dead bugs, before finally, it's between my fingers.

The screen appears damaged—probably from hitting the ground when it fell unnoticed from her jacket pocket during her bike ride—but it still opens to an app with personal emergency data.

Just as I hand it to her, a slam echoes through the adjacent room like a gunshot, rattling the nearby window.

For a moment, I stand frozen, stunned. What could possibly have caused such a clamor?

My fiancee's eyes are directed toward what I imagine is the kitchen door. Her face shows an expression I had only seen when she learned that her grandmother had died.

I've no idea what she saw, but there's no point in causing her and the baby further discomfort.

"Love, look, the phone's working fine... How much do we owe you, sir?" I ask, trying to leave this mournful home as fast as possible.

"Nothing," the man growls.

Aadila's face morphs into a weakly grateful smile, but she can't hold it for long. An uncontrollable sneeze escapes her, and she merely manages a courteous nod.

"Well then. We won't bother you anymore. Thank you for letting us know you found it," I add hastily.

At my words, the screen of an ancient tube-style TV set flickers and jumps, the picture warping and distorting like a black and white desert Fata Morgana. The unintelligible sound is tinny and muffled, as if coming from somewhere deep within the bowels of the machine.

Aadila's phone screen flashes to life.

A glowing blue number eighteen appears on both devices. Seconds pass, and eventually, the ominous countdown is replaced with a WKRN Nashville channel news reporter.

The journalist's face is a flurry of agitation and eagerness. His puffy cheeks and straw-blond hair give him the air of an anxious canary trapped behind cage bars. His black-beetle irises dart back and forth, and his mouth moves rapidly, spewing a stream of rapid-fire commentary.

"Our 24-hour news coverage of the craft continues. Some reporters have dared to venture into the Midnight Zone itself. The government has established a task force to coordinate a response to the alien object…"

"Ugh," Aadila huffs incredulously, her eyes rolling in exasperation.

The on-screen canary resumes his shrieky chirping. "Conspiracy theories abound, with some claiming the government is hiding the truth about the aliens. Protests have broken out as people demand answers. Some fear the spaceship will just drop from the sky. So there you have it, folks. This is Jack Thompson, reporting live from the Twilight Zone, Nashville, Tennessee."

"Of course we demand answers," I add. "What's the government gonna do about the craft? If anything? No one's telling us anything."

"Yeah," Aadila adds, squeezing my hand. "I think they know more than they're telling us. Can't wait to get to that protest meeting in Nashville tomorrow." She plants a sound kiss on my cheek.

"Urcula, dear, are those guests I'm hearing?" A sudden raspy, low female voice echoes from the kitchen.

"They are indeed, Esmerelda darling," Urcula replies, and before we can utter a polite *we were just leaving*, the kitchen door swings open.

A bizarre woman half stands, half crouches before us, her icy-blue gaze gleaming with a feral calm. Her greasy black hair is wild and unkempt, and her crusty and rugged overalls tattered and marked with blotchy red stains. Clutching a bloodied cleaver in her left hand, she stares at Aadila and me with greed and malice, akin to a child who's just found the last piece of candy.

The rotten meat smell emanating from the kitchen hits me like a punch to the gut, sharp and acrid. It writhes in the air like a living thing, filling my senses with putrid decay. It clings to everything, permeating the very fabric of the room. I can almost feel it sticking to my clothes, clinging like a second skin.

It's a smell that won't let go, leaving me feeling violated and dirty.

"Aadila! Run!" I scream, but it's too late. She sways on the spot, her body twisting and turning like on a carnival ride. With a sickening lurch, I realize she is going down, and she hits the ground with a dull thud.

I scoop her up in my arms, my face contorted, my cheeks puffing out as I struggle not to breathe, to keep my stomach contents down.

Sweat beads bloom on my forehead, every muscle in my body tense. It's a losing battle, I know it. Still, I miraculously regain control and rush towards the exit door. The waves of nausea subside like a receding tide the further I am from the kitchen.

"Stop them, you idiot!" Esmerelda screeches somewhere behind me.

A *swiish* pierces in the air and a pain I've never known before shoots through my shoulder like a lightning bolt. My muscles tense and knot, my breath escaping in ragged gasps.

My steps slowing, I catch my reflection in the dusty hallway mirror. Holy shit! That maniac threw a cleaver at me!

The fricking thing is embedded in my shoulder blade. Blood flows down my back in a gruesome crimson waterfall stream.

With each heartbeat, the pain intensifies. "Eustace! Get him!" Esmeralda sounds positively livid.

I don't dare turn to see who the heck "Eustace" is. I advance firmly forward, clutching Aadila's unmoving, limp body in my arms, my eyes fixed on the door.

Only… two… more… steps.

If I could just get to that rusty knob, I could escape outside… Then surely, someone would come? Someone would hear me yell and save us from this nightmare.

I stretch and grasp the cool iron handle.

The door creaks open and I take a deep breath, inhaling the crisp evening air—a welcome respite from that putrid stench behind me. The scent of freshly cut grass and garden flowers wraps around Aadila and me like a cozy, calming embrace. It's a peaceful, almost otherworldly experience, one that reminds me how beautiful nature can truly be.

How beautiful *life* can be.

Alas, before I can open the door all the way and flee with my precious cargo, something sharp sinks into my calf like a hot knife through the butter.

I gasp, my breath coming in short ragged bursts, as I drop to the floor next to Aadila's unconscious body.

I stare at a pencil jabbed deeply into my leg, as my blood pools on the ground beneath me.

A dark stain spreads outward like a macabre painting.

With each passing moment, the pain and shock intensify, overwhelming me like a tidal wave.

I lean my forehead against the cool hallway wall and press the touch screen of Aadila's cell phone, with my trembling fingers fully intending to call 911.

My droopy eyelids flicker anxiously over the device, desperate for a signal, any sign of life. But the screen remains stubbornly blank, the bars of her network coverage non-existent.

I can't get it to work.

Panic rises in my throat—the realization of our fate hitting me like a sledgehammer.

We are alone.

The lights flicker in the hallway and as my heartbeat deafens my ears, I glimpse a silhouette of a boy of no more than ten years old.

He's crawling towards me on all fours, blond hair matted with gore, his baby teeth bared in a feral grin. With the stealth of a hunter, he stalks me, his moves eerily animalistic. He grinds the pencil into my leg and snaps it off. Blood spurts onto the kid's freckled face, and he smears it around his cheeks in glee.

The last thing I see before I lose my consciousness is hunger in his eyes.

***

"Eustace," Esmeralda coos, as if from a great distance from me. "Do wash your hands before dinner, will you, darling?"

"Yes, momma," a sweet childlike voice replies and tiny footsteps resonate eerily on steps that seem to lead to a floor above me.

My eyes snap open in a burst of sudden awareness, my heart pounding as I'm unable to move my wrists.

I'm tied to a chair!

Panic floods my system, my mind racing as I try to piece together what's happening.

My hands move instinctively to try and free myself, but the binds are too tight, cutting into my skin like razor wire.

The scene unfolding before me is a nightmare: a waking horror I can't escape.

The living room window is wide open, the curtains drawn back, and the man kneels on an azure mat, the wheelchair forgotten in the corner.

He looks up with a sneer. "Took you long enough, didn't it?" Urcula grins like a child who'd just pulled off the greatest trick. "It belonged to the previous owner. Not a bad chap. His legs were a bit stringy though, tough to chew if you catch my drift."

Then he turns his face away from me and bows reverently to the light-blue number eighteen hovering in the night.

The alien craft floats silently, encompassing the sky in every direction. It seems almost surreal, a figment of my imagination rather than a real object.

If I just close my eyes, I can pretend it isn't even there. That none of this is happening.

And yet, there it is, hovering ominously above us like a dark cloud.

The air around us seems to hum with energy, a palpable static charge.

I can't help but feel a sense of unease, as if the craft is watching us, waiting for something.

Its otherworldly calmness is more unnerving than any overt aggression would be.

It's as if it knows something that we don't, and is content to simply purr in the sky like a giant black cat, biding its time.

A dark alien God demanding sacrifice from his loyal earthly vassals.

Esmeralda passes me as she joins Urcula on the mat.

Her gaze caresses my exposed flesh, and I sense the hunger, the need to consume, radiating off her like a palpable force.

"He's B-positive, isn't he? We'll just have him for supper tomorrow," she says in a light, conversational tone of a pleased hostess.

"He is, indeed. What a good nose you have, my love!" exclaims Urcula with loving admiration.

The delicious aroma of roasted meat fills the air, tantalizing my senses with its savory scent. It makes my mouth water, and my stomach growls in anticipation.

"You sure she's O-negative?" Esmerelda wrinkles her nose, pointing at the kitchen.

"I'm sure. Saw it on her cell phone blood donor app. Don't worry so much, my love," Urcula reassures her in a sugar-coated tone of voice, placing an affectionate smooch on the cheek, not unlike the one Aadila gave me mere minutes ago.

"I hope you're not wrong and that it's not going to be like last time. I can't believe you let me serve that O-positive bitch to our son. You know how delicate Eustace is. He can't eat that. It gives him tummy aches!"

A slew of trepidation roils in my gut. I stare on through the ajar kitchen door Esmeralda had pointed to, trying to get a glimpse of Aadila.

What I see both startles and comforts me. Her body slumps in the chair, her limbs bound tightly by ropes.

Deep gashes mar her fragile flesh, but she's alive!

She's okay. The baby's okay.

They're okay.

I repeat the mantra until a wave of relief and absolute calm washes over me.

It's that image of the future me—Aadila hugging in front of that quintessential American dream house, kid Josh running after the golden retriever puppy—that spurs me on.

I move my thumb and forefinger ever so slightly and find the blade of the Swiss knife in my pocket.

If I can reach it and cut my binds before they notice what I am doing… I eye the broken lamp close by. After I free myself, incapacitating Urcula from behind should be a piece of cake.

Then, I will run to Aadila, free her, and our dream of suburban bliss will come true.

My hands tremble, but I manipulate the blade into position. With each meticulous incision, the bindings yield, thread by thread.

It's a battle of patience, as the invisible chains holding me captive fall away, one slice at a time.

The tiny footsteps resonate on the steps once more, and a sensation of dread accompanied by the trembling pain in my leg announces Eustace's return.

I freeze, stopping my fingers. I can't risk him discovering me.

The monster child moans at his mother. "Mommy, I'm hungry!"

Esmeralda kisses the top of his head with tenderness.

"That's alright, sweetie. Dinner is ready."

She swooshes past, ignoring me, and strolls into the kitchen.

The door whooshes wide open and my eyes meet Aadila's. A silent understanding passes between us. I nod gently towards the Swiss knife, hoping the sight of me will assure her that everything will be alright.

Her gaze holds a kaleidoscope of emotions—love, hope, and the vibrant essence of life itself.

Life worth fighting for.

Esmeralda raises the cleaver high above her head and lowers it unceremoniously with a dull thud, like a butcher slaughtering a lamb.

My heart lodges in my throat.

Aadila's head snags for a second, still attached to her body by a strip of skin. Her warm brown eyes stare blankly at the overturned dustbin, as if she's curiously inspecting its contents.

She's gone. Josh's gone.

I am unable to move, unable to even breathe. Rage and sadness surge through me in equal measure, and I wail—a single desperate, impotent howl filled with horror and incredulity that one human could do this to another.

The future Aadila and I were meant to build together is gone. Eustace joins his father in silent prayer, as the squelchy hacks at Aadila's flesh in the kitchen continue.

The two cannibals chant words of gratitude, "*Our Craft who art in the sky, hallowed be thy name…*"

Urcula rises from the mat as he welcomes the woman back into the living room.

"*Thy numbers come, thy will be done, on Earth as it is in space. Give us this day our daily flesh…*"

Esmeralda, a sinister delight dancing in her eyes, presents the silver platter adorned with crimson-stained meat.

Aadila's meat.

"*…and forgive us our trespasses, as we forgive those who have trespassed against us. And lead us not into temptation, but deliver us from evil.*"

It's a scene of grotesque elegance, yet I can't look away. I stop struggling against my binds. The world around me is a desolate grey landscape, devoid of purpose or significance. But for the red flesh I can't unsee.

The forever-absence of Aadila echoes through every empty fiber of my being.

"A chance for redemption, perhaps?" Esmeralda cackles, deviously pressing my beloved fiancee's tender meat to my lips. "You can have the family you always wanted, here, with us. But you must worship. Eat. Or be eaten."

My eyes weep bloody tears and longing as I gaze upon what is left of the love of my life.

Desire awakens within me, fed by the luscious aroma of her skin. Hunger roils in my belly. As my tongue tentatively licks her skin, I yearn to devour her.

To become one with her irresistible sweetness.

… *And the two shall become one flesh.*
Genesis 2:24, Matthew 19:5, Mark 10:8, Ephesians 5:31 NASB

~

17

about the author

Lorraine Tramain *is a writer of paranormal/ fantasy and history, with stories dripping with excitement and drama. There is nothing she enjoys more than to put her characters through the ringer and bringing lovers together only to rip them apart. Plot twists are her forte.*

A feisty Leo and redhead who loves to read and write, bake, draw, and dress up in cosplay and vintage clothes. She enjoys exploring the world, but will always prefer the quiet peace of home.

Things she cannot live without include chocolat, musical theater and movie soundtracks, and her Flounder-hugsie.

THE SURFACE

by Lorraine Tremain

300 MILES OFF THE NORTH COAST OF PUERTO RICO
AUGUST 14, 6:40 PM

Why the hell did I agree to do this?

Eric sneered at the two people lounging on deck in the pre-evening sun. Those goddamn fools had made him turn off the engine an hour ago and were now acting like this was some luxury cruise and not an attempt to escape the frigging apocalypse. This was exactly why he practically lived a recluse's life on his boat, away from 'civilization'.

"Stop it."

Eric glanced over his shoulder to find Aaron entering the bridge. The ginger with the sparkling green eyes and perfect cheekbones threw Eric a sly grin as he approached.

"I know you don't like we picked up those stragglers in Key West, but you've gotta stop being such a sourpuss about it, Blue-Eyes," he said. "You'll get frowny wrinkles on that gorgeous face of yours."

Aaron snaked his arms around Eric's waist and planted a sweet kiss on his neck. Eric leaned back against Aaron's muscular chest, finding comfort in his touch. He still couldn't believe their relationship had grown from colleagues, to friends, to lovers. Then again, maybe it wasn't a surprise. For months on end, they'd been each other's only company. That their love had bloomed on the *Venus* seemed only fitting.

"I'm sorry," said Eric. "I can't stand them."

"I can't either. That guy's a pompous ass, and I'm pretty sure the wife has had every operation a plastic surgeon offers. The only decent one seems to be the goth fourteen-year-old, but she scares the shit out of me, walking around like some angel of death."

"Tch, we should've left them in San Salvador. I don't care about the other five hundred grand. I just want them off the *Venus*, even if we maroon them on the next patch of land we see."

"Lord, how did I ever fall for such a cruel man?" Aaron laughed and leaned his forehead against Eric's shoulder.

"I'm not cruel, I'm practical," reacted Eric. "They're an inconvenience. Besides, we might not need the money anymore. We could all be dead by the end of the month."

He regretted saying it as soon as the words left his mouth. Aaron stiffened behind him. Slowly, he unlocked Eric from his embrace and stepped away from their position at the helm. Eric turned to watch his partner sit at the monitors, his expression sullen. He groaned silently. Fan-freaking-tastic. All right, time for some damage control then.

"Aaron, I–"

"Why do you always have to be such a pessimist?" asked Aaron, looking up at him from his seat. "Can't you just, for once, believe that things might not be as bad as they seem?"

"There is a giant alien spacecraft hovering over the East Coast. How can I *not* think the likely scenario is we're all gonna die?"

"That thing has been up there for two weeks now. If they were really going to invade and kill us, they would've done it by now. Besides, didn't they say a few days ago that the air under the craft isn't as polluted as it was before the aliens arrived? Who knows, maybe they're the galaxy's clean-up crew or something."

"Oh, you've got to be kidding me." Eric dragged a hand over his face. "Aaron, this isn't a movie where we all get together with the aliens and sing songs around the campfire. Their mere presence is ruining the planet. Animal behavior is changing, the weather is topsy-turvy, and–"

"And if the craft drops from the sky, it'll probably make the Earth go boom," finished Aaron. "Yeah, I know. You told me that and every other doomsday scenario you that occurs to you. I don't care. We're about to put an entire ocean between us and ET, so quit constantly worrying. The sooner we drop these people off, the sooner we can kick back on a black sandy beach in Tenerife."

Eric released a chuckled sigh. It didn't surprise him to learn *that* motivated Aaron's agreement to sail the Nolan family across the Atlantic. The week they'd spent there four years ago had been phenomenal. And it would be a welcome change of scenery after the many years in Canada and the US.

Aaron rose to his feet and closed the distance between them. He gingerly caressed Eric's jawline and then entangled his fingers in Eric's raven shoulder-length locks. Their lips brushed against each other. The fleeting kiss stirred an all-too-familiar heat.

"*If* things go bad," whispered Aaron, "and the world really does end, I'd rather spend my last days with you in our little paradise. Let *me* be the one who shows you heaven, Blue-Eyes."

"You already do each night you're with me," Eric said lovingly.

"Get a room."

The couple pulled apart at hearing an emotionless female voice from the bridge door. The gloomy appearance of Nessa Nolan made Eric think of every vampire movie his cousin had forced him to watch during the holidays when they were teens. He completely understood why she scared the bejesus out of Aaron. Her lace clothes and high-heeled boots were black, her hair was black, her make-up was black, even her eyes were black. Honestly, Wednesday Addams had nothing on this porcelain-skinned girl.

"Is there something we can do for you, Miss Nolan?" Aaron mustered a smile while Eric imagined pushing her and the rest of her family overboard.

"There's something in the water," said Nessa.

"Yeah, they're called fish," deadpanned Eric.

He grunted when Aaron elbowed him in his side. His partner had a soft spot for kids, but to Eric, they were just another reason to avoid dry land.

"What did you see?" asked Aaron.

"A body."

They stared at her, flabbergasted by her reply. She said it with such calm, like it was a common sight out in the ocean. Eric was the first to regain his senses.

"Hilarious, kid. Gold star." He turned to Aaron, scoffing at the teen's attempt at a joke. "Can you believe–hey, where are you going?"

"Checking it out," said Aaron as he made his way to the door.

"Oh, come on, you don't seriously buy this crap, do you?"

"There could've been an accident with another boat or someone who fell off a cruise ship. Wouldn't be the first time that happened. You check the radars."

Eric tsk-ed when Aaron followed Nessa toward the aft. Unbelievable. He loved Aaron dearly, but he could be so gullible sometimes. Sighing, Eric sat down at the control panels. The radio hadn't picked up any SOS calls. Nothing on sonar either–whoa, hold on.

"Son of a bitch, not again."

Eric was a skeptic, but even he had to admit, something strange happened to the electronics whenever they sailed through the Bermuda Triangle. Fortunately, he knew how to handle the glitching screens on his right. He shut the controls off, gave the primary panel a good bang with his fist, and then turned everything back on. Worked every single time.

"All right, now let's see if I can…"

He fell silent when his eyes were drawn to the flickering screen of the underwater camera they used to observe and record marine life. It showed a peculiar circular pattern on the ocean floor. Several, in fact. Their intricate design was mesmerizing.

No way. But how is it so close to the surface? Wait…

Eric jumped to his feet, took the binoculars from their hook, and scoured the water outside. That shadow, it couldn't be…

The sound of hurried footsteps echoed outside. He turned right as a very agitated Aaron entered the bridge and closed the door behind him.

"We have a problem," he said. "The Nolan girl was right about the body. I used the hook pole to bring it closer. It was a young man. His lower half was gone. Noticed some driftwood further out as well. He must've been attacked."

"Let's not jump to conclusions. His boat could've been destroyed in that storm two days ago, and scavengers probably got to him after he fell in and drowned."

"It didn't look like scavenger nibbles to me, Eric. Something ripped the flesh and bones right off him. I didn't want the kid to see it, so I pushed him back out. Did the radars pick up on anything?"

"No, nothing. But, here, look." Eric handed Aaron the binoculars and pointed toward a spot in front of them. "Tell me what you make of that."

"Is that a *sandbar*?" Aaron's voice went up a few notes in astonishment. "In this part of the ocean? How? There aren't any islands close by."

"That's not all."

Eric turned back to the controls. His fingers moved nimbly over the keyboard, and the camera screen zoomed in. Aaron leaned in over his shoulder to watch, but then recoiled.

"What the hell?" he exclaimed.

"Calm down, it's not what you think, it's–"

Suddenly, the door swung open, making them both jump. In stormed Nathaniel Nolan, for once not in a five-thousand-dollar Armani suit, but a 'simple' Ralph Lauren leisure outfit. A cutthroat businessman, through and through, he had slick brown hair combed back, beady brown eyes, eagle-like facial features, and a rotten attitude to top it off.

"Ah, there you are," he said. "Now look here, Morgan. Next time I tell you to let us relax for a while, make sure we can do it without having to smell and look at a damn blood bath!"

As a rule, Eric despised anyone who used his last name so disrespectfully. But the blood bath comment spiked his attention just enough to let it slide. He pushed past Nolan to hurry out of the bridge and peered over the railing. The sight before him was unlike anything he'd ever seen before - not one, but three great whites. Their carcasses floated amidst chunks of flesh and organs. Even with the light fading from the setting sun, Eric could still clearly discern the blood around the dead animals. No doubt about it; this was a recent kill.

"Eric, what is—oh my God!" Aaron had come out to join him but instantly drew back at the carnage. "What did that?"

"I'm not sure," said Eric. "There aren't a lot of animals capable of tearing apart a great white, let alone three. I can actually only think of one. But I haven't heard of any sightings in these parts."

"Morgan!" Nolan suddenly bellowed from the bridge.

"Ugh, great, now what?"

The couple went back inside to find the enraged businessman near the controls. His trembling finger pointed at the camera screen.

"What the fuck is this, Morgan?"

"First, don't use that kind of language on my boat," reacted Eric sternly. "Second, that is nothing."

"Don't give me that crap!" yelled Nolan. "Those are damn underwater crop circles! You've led us right into an alien ambush in the middle of the fucking Bermuda Triangle!"

"Mr. Nolan, please calm down." Aaron put himself between Eric and Nolan. "The rumors about the Triangle are wildly exaggerated. I'm sure there's a reasonable explanation for what's going on."

"Pufferfish."

The two other men looked at Eric as if he'd lost his marbles. He continued, "This is what male pufferfish do to attract a mate. I saw something similar in Japan about a decade ago."

"You expect me to believe damn *pufferfish* did this?" Nolan's face flushed scarlet. "Pufferfish don't eat sharks, boy!"

"I never said the two events are connected," Eric said, trying really hard to keep himself from punching the guy's lights out.

"Listen you–"

An ear-piercing scream instantly silenced the discussion. Only one person on board could've produced such a high-pitched sound–Mrs. Nolan. The trio ran out of the bridge to find the bleach-blond bimbo in the Barbie-pink beach dress holding her daughter at the aft. Her head snapped towards them as they approached.

"The horizon! Look at the horizon!"

Eric raised his eyes. As the last rays of daylight painted vibrant hues of orange across the darkening sky, an ethereal emerald glow shone at the very edge of the disappearing sun. The green flash pulsed with an otherworldly energy, lasting only a fleeting moment before fading into the twilight's embrace.

"It's them," said Mrs. Nolan in a panic-stricken voice. "They're coming! We're all gonna die!"

"What the hell are you two waiting for?" Nolan grabbed Aaron by his shirt. "Get us the fuck out of here!"

"Let go of him!" Eric pried the violent man off his partner. "Now listen, this has nothing to do with the craft. It's a natural phenomenon that happens regularly out at sea. There's no reason to—"

The boat jolted. Everyone held their breaths, hoping the carcasses in the water had bumped into them because of a wave. Then it happened again, much stronger this time. Eric spread his feet to steady himself.

"Aaron, get the light," he said.

Just as the singular lamp at the stern flicked on, Eric heard the distinct sound of a blowhole. He peered over the water. A faint ripple broke the surface. And another further ahead. He looked at Aaron, seeing a streak of cautious apprehension on his partner's face. They'd both been sailing the seven seas for long enough to know that it harbored ferocious predators. Yet none had ever attacked their boat so brazenly.

"God almighty."

Mrs. Nolan's awed whisper drew their attention. They followed her gaze, eyes settling on a radiance flickering across the water. The dark ocean was transformed into a breathtaking yet ghostly tapestry of light. With each stroke of the waves against the hull, the brilliant blue and green luminescence drew closer.

All were quiet, entranced by the enchanting glow. Then Nessa pulled out of her mother's protective embrace. She stepped onto the casting deck, sat on her knees, and trailed her fingers through the water.

"Miss Nolan, step back, please." Aaron carefully came up behind her.

She glanced over her shoulder. The usually straight-faced girl noticed how everyone held their breath and rose to her feet. Just then, something collided against the hull from below. The boat rocked, and Nessa lost her balance. She plunged into the water, setting off an explosion of shimmering sparks around her. Her mother cried in terror as Aaron jumped onto the casting deck and reached out for Nessa.

"Give me your hand!"

Nessa stretched out. The tip of their fingers touched when, suddenly, she was pulled under. Eric lunged toward Aaron to prevent him from falling in as well. His eyes widened when a dark shadow passed underneath the boat.

"Oh my God!" Mrs. Nolan sped to the railing. "Nessa!"

All remained silent until the teen broke through the surface, screaming at the top of her lungs, "Help me!"

"Hold on!" yelled Aaron.

"What are you—Aaron, no!"

But Eric was too late to stop Aaron from diving into the water. Cursing, he opened the side latch containing the emergency kit and pulled out the neatly packed yellow rescue raft. He yanked the red tag and threw it out into the water. It inflated instantly.

Aaron was almost within reach when something pushed itself between them, driving her further away. Her desperate cries echoed through the night until, suddenly, they stopped. Mrs. Nolan clutched the rail with her perfectly manicured fingers, shouting her daughter's name.

Eric ignored her and searched fervently for his partner. Where did he go? He was there just a moment ago! And where was the raft?

"Aaron!"

There was no reply. Nothing broke through the heavy silence except the sloshing of water and Mrs. Nolan's weeping sobs.

"You bastards!"

Eric was rowdily pushed aside by an enraged Nolan. He hit the deck and groaned as pain shot through his shoulder. The sudden sound of gunfire roared through the air. To his dismay, Eric realized Nolan had snuck a Glock on board with him. When had he gone to the cabin to get it?

"Are you crazy?" Eric stared in horror as the mad gunman released another shot in the water. "They could still be alive out there!"

"Open your goddamn eyes, boy! My girl and your buddy are dead, and we're next! Well, I don't plan on making it easy for these alien freaks! They messed with the wrong planet, and they messed with the wrong human!"

Nolan aimed again, ready to fire. Eric scrambled up and jumped at him. As they fell to the deck, the gun went off, taking out the only light they had, thus plunging them into haunting half-darkness. They struggled and rolled, fighting for control over the weapon. Another shot barked. The moment they heard the body drop, they froze.

Audrey Nolan's head was turned toward them. The life drained from her hazel eyes. Blood spilled from the wound in her chest, staining the usually spotless deck. The bullet had pierced her already shattered heart.

Crying in anguish, Nolan disentangled himself from Eric's hold and crawled over to her. Eric saw his chance and ran. He went into the bridge and sent out an SOS. It was too late for Mrs. Nolan, but there might still be hope for the kid. And Aaron.

You can't be dead. You just can't! I'll find you, dammit!

Eric took out the flare gun, hoping other ships might be nearby. But before he could go outside, the starboard side of the *Venus* tilted up, and Eric stumbled, landing on his ass. The controls flickered as the collisions against the hull continued. Crashing sounds rose from the kitchen below.

The water splashed as everything not secured outside fell in. A chilling scream that abruptly cut off told Eric that Nolan was one of those things.

With one hand on the helm and the other grasping the flare gun, he tried to get back on his feet. The boat tipped over. Eric lost his grip and slid away, right into the open entrance of the cabin below. He tumbled down the stairs and landed in the kitchen with a hard smack. Water poured in as it broke through the windows of the bridge.

Eric pulled himself up by the bolted table. The water was quickly rising. There was no way he could climb back up the stairs. And there was no other way out. He was trapped.

"Aaron," Eric whispered, tears rolling down his cheeks. "I'm sorry."

Short clicks made his head jerk up. Whatever had attacked the Venus, whatever had killed Aaron, was waiting for him. The hell he would give in to those monsters outside! If he was going down with his boat, he was damn well going to take them with him!

Eric found his footing on the leg of the table and reached for the stove to turn it on, dialing the buttons to the max. He jumped back into the water and aimed his flare gun up. His eyes locked on to the cascading water and the open door. A black tip poked through.

"End of the line, ET. From me to you. Choke on it."

He shot. A supernova burst within the cabin, and in less than a second, the *Venus* blew to smithereens, taking along everyone and everything near it. The blazing inferno cast away the darkness and luminescent waves, leaving the only witness to the event paralyzed in shock.

As the ocean slowly devoured the flames, the broken-hearted man's harrowing cries drowned out the wails that echoed under the surface.

~

16

THE EVENT

6AM EST

about the author

With a lifelong love for the art of writing, Fiora Voss began her publishing adventures with her debut novella, The Fate of Kane, which shortlisted in the 2023 Open Novella Contest.

A founding member of Melkat Indie Solutions, she strives to unite writers with their readers. When she isn't writing or editing, she can usually be found tending her beloved gardens.

THE LIAR

by Fiora Voss

MILAM, WEST VIRGINIA, USA
AUGUST 15, 6:00 AM

Be-beep.

Be-beep.

The device looked like a watch, but within this apocalyptic scenario, power and communication had been reserved only for those deemed the most important, and this was obviously more than just a smartwatch.

"Agent Donovan." Upon engaging the device, the caller didn't waste any time on pleasantries. "Your report is late. Again."

"Shhhh…"

"What? I'm your Commander. You can't shush me."

Agent Donovan crouched in a corner of the kitchen, head cocked to one side as he pressed the communicator to his ear and tried to maintain listening beyond it.

"He'll hear you," he whispered.

"He? Who? Donovan, you're alone!" The commander's tone descended from anger to contempt, "Light has been reported as emanating from the center of the craft and what do I hear from you? Crickets!"

You didn't have to look out the window to know the light was there, eerie and synthetic. As if the darkness wasn't enough of a mind-fuck, the light was worse. It didn't glow; the shadows hadn't lost their density. The room wasn't bright, even though everything outside was bathed in the light's euphoric glow.

Donovan didn't answer. Maybe he was too scared to feel the rhapsodic flare. Maybe he had been alone in the dark for too long.

"Donovan!" The Commander was yelling now, a tinny-sounding anger through the tiny speaker.

Donovan's gaze flitted aimlessly around the room, what could he possibly say?

He closed his eyes, "Trying to survive."

Cryptic, seemingly lucid. Of all the possibilities, that was a pretty good choice, but there was no way this pompous Commander would infer the plea within his words.

"I have no interest in your ramblings and hallucinations. I want to know what's going on up there."

Donovan began nodding, though the action was out of sync with the conversation.

"The chickens."

"Jesus, Donovan." The Commander let loose a strained sigh. "I have no choice but to extract you. You're not the first, everyone out there is falling apart."

Enough of this. Listening to the Commander fret about weaklings.

Donovan looked up in surprise, "No!" Backing into the corner, his spastic finger cut the call short.

Perfect.

* * *

"Ninety-seven."

He hovered so near to the ground his nose brushed the dingy carpet, and Donovan paused. Pushing a steady breath through his taut lips, he held his body rigid; in, out, he breathed. Pressing his palms into the floor, he straightened his arms, his back ram-rod straight.

"Ninety-eight."

This is so boring.

It was now the fifteenth day since the massive, stolid blue numbers had appeared in the sky – when the bona fide hysteria had begun.

Donovan let his body sink again, then pressed himself up with conviction.

"Ninety-nine."

The repetition of his motions, a structure, kept Donovan afloat. The darkness and the silence had been all consuming and he was employing every tactic in the book to preserve his faculties. Sounds, apart from the ones he made himself, were all but nonexistent, and he had taken up talking to himself as a tether to reality. In all honesty, that was probably one of his less effective tactics; does talking to yourself really divert insanity? But still, saying the words aloud seemed to give him reassurance.

He had been counting everything.

"One hundred."

Time moves more slowly in the darkness of isolation.

He slid his knees beneath himself, and, wiping his face with the hem of his shirt, he compulsively checked his watch. Shaking his head, he stood and strode to the kitchen with surprising ease, like he had memorized the darkened maze of this shabby, desolate little house.

But there were chickens. Nestled in their coop, none the wiser. The original allure of this property had been the fields which surrounded it and the coop full of chickens in the backyard.

What a fools errand that had been.

The center of the Midnight Zone was dark.

And cold.

In some of his more coherent ramblings, Donovan had lamented both the loss of the crops as the mercury fell within the unrelenting darkness, and his bitter realization that without light, chickens didn't lay eggs.

"Today," he spoke aloud, between gulps of water, "Today, I will roast one of those chickens."

Fool. He'll never hurt a feather on their backs.

Some part of that enormous "16" in the sky stretched directly over the house. The countdown. But the countdown to what?

With the exception of disruptions in normal Earth functions as a result of the physical presence of the craft, nothing had actually *happened.*

Nothing.

At this point, annihilation seemed a better option than remaining here, holed up in the spectral emptiness of Appalachia. Waiting.

Donovan turned to the window, for no reason, really, because there was nothing for him to see; the foreboding countdown failed to cast even a moonlight twinkle on the land beneath it. Life had become undetectable. The Eastern seaboard was rapidly achieving Atacama status - completely devoid of all life.

But not here. No, here he was. Agent Donovan, stationed as close to the center of the craft as the Agency had deemed safe for a long-term assignment, ready to serve his country valiantly. Donovan had talked about all of this: of his Hollywood-induced dreams of acting as a secret agent. Only he had become, instead, a stupid man following orders, slowly drifting away on the coattails of his own crumbling mind.

The glass in his hand shattered as he slammed it on the counter. Startled, but unscathed, Donovan flicked the shards into the sink; it was the third glass that had fallen victim to his frustrations, and if he wasn't careful, he'd be left drinking from a bowl.

Isolation and darkness can play cruel tricks on the human brain: desperate for stimuli, it loses its ability to differentiate between thoughts and reality, conjuring any matter of entertainment to maintain sanity.

His descent had begun with flickers of light, faint flashes in his peripheral vision, whipping his head from side to side, trying to discern their origins.

Maybe if he knew I was here, that he wasn't alone, it would help?

I chuckled to myself at the thought. Knowing I was here would definitely *not* quell his disquietude.

Admittedly, though, part of me feels the need to be thankful for Donovan; without him, *I* would be alone.

Cock-a-doodle-dooooo!

Donovan scrunched his eyes, peering out the window. "What's up, buddy?"

He's talking to the chickens.

Cock-a-doodle-dooooo!

I watched as Donovan strode through the door and into the backyard, peering briefly above him at the craft. It always loomed up there, somehow out of sight; dark, invisible, but entirely present. I took the opportunity to slip out the front door and into the overgrown bushes surrounding the house. Mere sticks, I had no idea what sort of plant they had been, but in the insurmountable darkness, their defoliation didn't matter anyhow.

All of the chickens were cackling, responding to their rooster, and the cacophony around him was clearly making it difficult for Donovan to focus. You have no choice but to rely on your hearing in the absence of sight, and without the monotonous din of civilization, these chickens and their squawking seemed to echo through the fields.

But that was for Donovan to worry about.

This was coal country, and the landscape would have been breathtaking, had Donovan been able to see it. Perched on the precipice of a mountain, the town had arisen as the summit of the ridge had been flattened. This backyard faced due West, and he should have been able to look over the valley at the surrounding mountains. He couldn't stop himself from straining to see into the darkness, however futile the effort.

As he gazed into the empty wilderness, the nothingness that had come to surround us, I picked up on the faint rustle of leaves. Donovan heard it, too.

He narrowed his eyes, trying to zero-in on the sound, but the chickens had become so frantic in their coop, he couldn't tell where it was coming from and instead moved haphazardly closer to the treeline.

Growing louder, it was a scrape and a pause; like something limping, someone struggling, and my heart began to race.

Wasn't the town, maybe even the entire state, abandoned? Save for Donovan, I hadn't seen a single soul after crossing the West Virginia border.

This couldn't be another person? But whatever it was, it was definitely alive.

Appreciable excitement rose in Donovan's movements; maybe this was an animal he could eat, something large enough and hot enough to warm him. To quell the constant ache that went along with the constant cold.

Maybe Donovan would start a fire, roast the meat right here in the backyard.

Why hadn't he started a fire? That was certainly an oversight.

"Light," a tiny, shrill voice rasped.

Donovan wheeled around, but no one was there.

This would be entertaining.

There must be someone there, but Donovan had no hope of seeing whomever it was.

"Who's there?" he shouted.

"Light!" the voice repeated, more forceful this time. "Behind you."

Slowly, Donovan turned, and so did I; in a moment of equality, we all three peered up and over the roof of the house.

And indeed.

There was light.

A single beam, emanating from what must be the center of the ship.

I could do nothing but stare.

Light.

"Light," Donovan whispered.

"It nearly brings tears to my eyes." The effeminate voice was gravelly, thirsty, and very nearby.

Unable to tear his eyes from the light, Donovan walked around the house, vaguely aware of the shallow footsteps that followed behind him, but seemingly completely unaware of me. There, with the house to his back, he could see the beam more clearly, illuminating everything in its path, from the center of the ship to the ground. *Only* everything in its path.

"It's a shaft of light?" the voice had become hesitant, still dry, but losing some of its softness. "It isn't right."

"It's over," Donovan stated emphatically. Finally looking over his shoulder, assessing the woman standing behind him, "Insanity," he concluded. "I've finally lost my mind."

If only Donovan knew I could see her, too.

She shifted her wary eyes between him and the column of light, growing wider as we stood watching. Sweeping over the trees and rocky crags, the land encompassed by this new light was rapidly increasing.

"Maybe we should go inside." Her suggestion fell on deaf ears as Donovan spread his arms wide and I stifled a laugh.

"No," he adjusted his stance and threw back his head. "I'm going to stand right here and soak up every ray."

Ray? Those didn't look like rays of sunshine. The woman was correct - something was off. For all of its brightness, my body should have been instinctively delighted.

I should have been elated, but I, the hunter, was petrified.

Coursing wider still, the light had nearly reached us.

"The edges," the woman observed, "it isn't glowing. The periphery is chiseled."

"Don't ruin this for me, Figgy."

"Figgy?" the woman scoffed.

"I know you're not real; you're a figment of my ailing brain." Donovan shook his head, "I should probably be concerned that you're talking to me, that's a new development, but I'm not."

She snorted.

"My delusions are laughing at me, and I don't even care." Donovan stood stock still. "The sun is about to shine on me."

And with those words, the light came.

A torrent through the landscape, the devastation of unseasonable cold and prolonged darkness festered in my view just before the beam wooshed over us.

Palpable and unnervingly stagnant, the light felt as wrong as it looked; it crawled over us, tingling like heat on my skin without delivering any warmth, but somehow bringing calm. Euphoria. A growing strength of confidence.

Donovan sighed, a smile spreading across his face as he basked in the glory of hope. Finality.

Righting his position, he turned to the woman, a happy grin plastered to his pallid visage.

It was dismaying. And creepy.

Rubbing his hands together, Donovan advanced towards the chicken coop, "Shall we eat?" he called over his shoulder.

I call bluff on this.

"Eat?" Looking between Donovan and the coop, "I'm going inside," the woman gestured towards the house.

Donovan paused just outside the coop door, looking back towards the house and pursed his lips, thinking. Finally, he nodded, traipsing to where the woman stood holding open the door.

"There's a man in the bushes," he leaned in close like he was whispering, but I could hear him clear as day.The woman scrunched her face in confusion. "He thinks I can't see him," Donovan winked and jerked his head towards where I was standing, "but I can see *everything*."

Her eyes widened, irises flicking around the now-illuminated yard. It looked like another planet.

"Should I check it out?"

"Suit yourself," Donovan shrugged and stepped through the door. "Since you're in my head, I bet you can see him, too."

Eyes perusing the withered garden and the hedge of sticks where I stood, her gaze passed over me. None the wiser.

"MRE's! Huevos rancheros," squinting at a silvery package in his hand, Donovan struggled to read the smudged ink as he leaned out the door, "or bacon and eggs?"

"Bacon and eggs?"

"Coming right up!" Donovan chirped happily, smiling at the sky once more.

Hesitating on the porch, the woman eased the door shut after Donovan had retreated inside to make breakfast. Lithe on her feet, she silently descended the steps, inspecting the ground as she made her way around the circumference of the house.

As she passed me, she whispered into the watch on her own wrist, but I could only make out a few fragments of what she said, "confused… no footprints… leave…" Holding the device briefly to her ear and nodding, she dropped her hand and I noted my nearly spotless shoes, despite skulking around this unkempt place for the last two weeks.

Slipping back inside, the woman's footsteps echoed towards the kitchen, and I followed silently.

Donovan had set only one place at the table.

"How will I eat?"

She was prodding Donovan and he looked up at her as he set the steaming plate of gloppy, re-hydrated bacon and eggs between the fork and knife. He didn't answer.

"And the other man?" She waved a hand around the room, "Didn't you say there was another man here, too?"

With an eye roll, Donovan sat down, "How can you eat? You're not real." He dug the fork into the mess before him.

Pulling out a chair,she sank down into it and crossed her arms. "Why didn't you set a place for him?"

"Him?" Flicking his eyes to where I was watching their interaction through a crack in the living room door, Donovan whispered, "He has never eaten."

As he scraped the last of the egg substance into his mouth, wiping the corners with a neatly folded napkin, the woman stared at him.

"Why haven't you left?" she asked.

"This is my home," robotic and monotone, I had heard him

practice this speech. "I'm not leaving the farm my family has worked for generations because of some apparition in the sky." His inflection towards the end almost sounded like a question - would she believe him?

She glanced at the watch on his wrist and back at her own.

"My name is Marcy. My family left, but I didn't want to. I've been wandering these hills for days, maybe weeks, but without the sun, moon, or stars, I can't find my way back to the light. To wherever civilization still exists."

Hmm. Equally as prepared as Donovan.

Donovan tapped his temple knowingly. "You're welcome to stay here, there are chickens. But, it's over." Emphatic, he swept his hand towards the light outside.

Outside. It was only outside. The shadows were still dark, dense and impenetrable inside the house; there was no reflective quality to the light.

"Over?" Standing, she pointed out the window. "It's still there."

"Probably not," Donovan pushed his chair away from the table, "the sun is shining." Wiping the plate and fork with a sponge at the sink, he turned towards the woman, but she was gone.

Looking about the room haphazardly, like he doubted he'd see her anyhow, he shoved back the living room door where I was hiding and trooped up the stairs two at a time, whistling as he went.

I stood, waiting. He would be back.

Sure enough, a short time later, he bounded back down the stairs, bulging suitcase in hand. Still whistling, he whipped open the front door, slamming it against the hinges as he jumped back in alarm.

In all of her blond-haired, blue-eyed bombshell glory, the woman was there. Outside, on the porch.

Looking back to the kitchen, Donovan pinched the bridge of his nose for a moment and dropped to the ground.

"One."

He pressed himself into the floor, then rose again.

"Two."

Ten times he repeated the motion.

He was too far gone for this type of grounding, I could see it in the jerky motions of his arms, no longer the fluid, easy strength I had seen when he first arrived.

Hopping up, he brushed himself off.

Maybe it was time.

Stepping out from behind the door, I cleared my throat.

Donovan spun around, crouching like a cat ready to spring.

"I thought you could see everything," I chided.

"You!" he sputtered.

"Me," I drawled.

"Me?" the woman cooed, now standing at the foot of the stairs, directly behind Donovan.

Be-beep.

6:15 the clock on the wall read.

Be-beep.

Usually dark, the device on Donovan's wrist lit up like it had around this time for the last few days.

"Fuck!" he screeched.

Running out the front door and around the house, I could hear him crashing through the back door into the kitchen, the clatter of chairs ringing through the house as he barreled around the room.

"Agent Donovan," a voice rang out, "Your report…" it faded as Donovan must have turned down the volume. Unintelligible whispers followed and I slunk across the room, purposefully slapping the soles of my shoes against the wooden planks. Manufactured, ominous footsteps.

The woman cackled.

Close enough to hear again, "...everyone is falling apart."

And here we are. Me, staring down at the broken man. Her, somewhere in the bowels of the house, laughing for all the weaknesses of humanity. And him, huddled in a corner beneath the kitchen table.

"No!" Donovan yelled, pointing at me. Frantically backing further into the corner, his spastic movements swiped the communication device, ending the call.

Perfect.

Advancing towards him, the frightened look in his eyes is what I lived for.

The fear.

The condemnation.

The unknown.

Should he run? Because he definitely wasn't hiding.

Exploding from beneath the table, whapping his communicator on the counter, Donovan ran through me towards the back door, hands pressed against his ears.

Out, into the meaningless light, the unrequited hope of empty relief.

Crashing through the crumpled scrub edging the fields, Donvan ran.

It didn't take long for the silence to, once again, settle over this wasteland.

"Hey, chicky, chicky," I chirred, approaching the chicken coop Donovan had just blown past.

Leaning against the wire enclosure, the chickens scattered to the far corner, their earlier bustle quelled once again into silence.

The woman slipped down beside me.

"Do you think he'll be back?"

I shrugged.

Time was meaningless to me, I could wait.

When, finally, the drone of a motor made its way up the hillside, rounding the fields we were observing, a black Explorer came to a stop in front of the house.

Leaning over the dash, two men surveyed the smashed front door and upended kitchen chair laying haphazardly on the porch. The driver nodded, and both men stepped out of the car.

Handing a small, electronic device to the passenger, who cinched it around his wrist, the driver retrieved a suitcase from the trunk. Handing it to the passenger, he patted him encouragingly on the back.

"Where is he?" the passenger asked, a wary look lingering on the house.

"Fuck if I know."

"What do I do if I find him?"

The driver tapped the communicator on his own wrist. "Call it in."

Call it in, I smirked.

Slamming the car door, the driver peeled erratically down the driveway, drunk on simulated sunshine. We all watched as the vehicle rounded the fields, its beams distinct from the pseudo-light of the craft, illuminating the desolate landscape.

Righting the chair and carefully closing the cracked door behind him, the passenger, a new agent, settled into the beshadowed disarray of the house.

Let the games begin.

1PM EST

about the author

J. A. Jumphol is a queer Thai Canadian that loves writing fiction with intersectional diversity to match. From coming-of-age contemporaries to disaster teens with powers to Thai-inspired high fantasy, there is no genre ze is unwilling to write. You can find her current and latest works on Tapas and Wattpad under the username JJJoooYYY.

During the day, xe works at the largest book chain in Canada and enjoys recommending books to booklovers and friends. In between writing and work, he is either watching movies or is attempting to tame their forever growing collection of books.

THE READER

by J.A. Jumphol

TORONTO, ONTARIO, CANADA
AUGUST 15, 1:00 PM

Nothing beats the feeling of a book. The smell of the paper with each page flip and the sensation of pinching the pages softly between her fingers both add to the reading experience for Preeda.

Usually, just holding a book brings Preeda comfort, but the constant movement of her family's preparations deepen her conflicted spiral as a single thought dominates the forefront of her mind:

How is she going to finish all of her unread books?

She stares at her bookshelves and instead of her usual glee, she only feels dread. For months, while living with her now-ex, Jett, Preeda wasn't able to see her full book collection, and now that she's here, it only adds more pain instead of the excitement she had hoped for. There must be over two hundred books she has to read.

Where should she start? The unfinished series? But she didn't like the main character. There's a romantasy featuring a war between demons and angels, but will she be able to keep track of all the worldbuilding and lexicon? What about the contemporary story of a young teenager finding a ghost in her apartment? No, that would be too sad. There can't be a happy ending for a human and a ghost. She could reread an old favourite, but that would put her even more behind in her goal.

Finish as many unread books as possible before the mysterious countdown ends.

She felt a deep ache looking at all these books. Every single one has some form of exciting new romantic relationship, which is Preeda's favourite part of reading. At least, it used to be. This new feeling could only be described as "off". Weird.

Maybe it's because she and Jett aren't talking anymore. She doesn't find herself missing his touch or his affection like break-ups in the books she reads, but she still misses talking to him. They used to spend hours talking about stories. He's a writer and she's a reader, so it was a match made in heaven; at least, that was what Preeda thought.

Slapping one side of her face in resolve, her eyes flick to the bookcase once again. If she can't decide for herself, fate will.

"Preeda?"

Kosum lingered in the door frame with towels in her arms. Sweat dotted her forehead as she handed Preeda a towel. She must've been running around with their parents, trying to protect and secure the house.

"Mae said to stuff these at the base of the windows. She's worried about the spacecraft and thinks blocking most of the air from outside will help."

"Don't we need to breathe?"

Their mom always has some strange advice from the Thai side of social media, and Preeda can't be sure if this is her mother's own idea or if she's just doing what the internet told her to do. She wouldn't let the family evacuate because of the horror stories she had read, and with the reports of the sudden light in the Midnight Zone, she'd probably never consider it again.

"She's still keeping the door wide open, so I don't understand either," she says with a shrug. "She's anxious. We can't do anything else really."

"Er, we could convince her to evacuate." Preeda could feel her mouth getting dry and Kosum shook her head in response.

"Pa has lung issues and a bad leg. I know you've been away for a while, but I thought you knew." Kosum looked behind her and pursed her lips. "Mae is standing on a chair. I have to see what she's trying to do. If you're not going to help out, at least stuff the window with a towel like Mae wants."

"Um, Kosum."

"Yeah?"

Preeda looked down in embarrassment. The words, half-formed in Preeda's mind, could barely make their way out of her mouth. Her older sister waited for her to speak, her eyebrows slowly furrowing together.

"Are you not feeling good or…?"

"I don't know what book to start with," Preeda cut her off in a rush.

Kosum blinked, staring at Preeda blankly.

"Book?" Trying to process what her sister just said, she rubbed the heel of her hand on her forehead. "Didn't you say you were going to read all of Jett's stuff?"

"We… we broke up. Remember?"

Kosum stiffened and glanced at Preeda's bookshelf. Her hand hovering for a second, she pointed to a spine. "How about that one?"

Her eyes focusing on the book Kosum suggested, Preeda frowned. "Why that book?"

Shrugging, "I bought it for your birthday, you could at least not waste the money I spent on you," Kosum reasoned.

Preeda's face went slack. "Just get out of my room."

Normally, Preeda would have thrown the closest thing she could get her hands on at her sister, but only books surrounded her. It's a hard decision, but Preeda would rather let her sister go free than risk damaging a book. Kosum rolled her eyes, stepping out of the room.

"Also, close the door properly!"

With Kosum finally gone, Preeda hesitantly picked up the book her sister suggested, examining the cover. Bright purple, it showed a girl sitting, her head hung low, hiding her expression. Preeda could only sigh. This book isn't her type at all.

After the book is safely stowed in her closet, out of the way and off the list of contenders, she returned to the task at hand. Making her way to the window, she stuffed the towel Kosum left behind into the bottom of the windowsill, as instructed.

Maybe she should finish a book that she put down and forgot to pick back up?

The world could possibly end at any second, and the only thing she cared to think about was all of the unread books in her possession.

She picks one from the top of her in-progress pile, neatly stacked on her bedroom floor. The book in her hands was beautiful. With a gold foil title and artfully painted characters on the front cover, it would be hard for any dedicated reader not to stop and stare at the artwork. The edges of the book were stenciled with a scenic garden; blue, pink, and purple hydrangeas.

Cracking it open, Preeda began where she last left off:

"How could you do this to me? You had your lips pressed against hers!"

Claudia wiped her eyes with her sleeve. The hem of her dress caught on the bushes and Alrick followed after her.

"I had no choice in the matter," he cried. "I was forced into this arrangement."

She harrumphed as she tugged her skirt which she failed to break free from the brambles. "But you didn't have to kiss her. You're betrothed to her, you two aren't being forced to act like a true pair."

Shoving her bookmark back into the novel, Preeda let out a ragged sigh. The book is physically beautiful, but she doesn't feel any connection to the story. Why not?

She could feel a gnawing in her stomach as she stared at the book, remembering how Jett would get jealous whenever other guys talked to her. She had never thought people actually got jealous. Maybe she just wasn't the jealous type? She had trusted Jett, but when they began to drift apart…

She slammed the novel shut.

Another book. She needed to try another book.

Maybe a new read would help.

Walking to her bookshelf, she looked it over again. Maybe she needed a light-and-fluffy read. A nice contemporary romance.

Plucking a paperback from the shelf, she shook it by the spine. The pages wobbled effortlessly and she smiled to herself. A good start. She could read under these conditions. Who doesn't need an escape from the real world right now?

Her thumb flipping open the pages, and her eyes skimmed over the first few sentences. She waited to feel that familiar rush of excitement, the oncoming giddiness. Just something. Anything.

Anxiety rose in her throat and she forced herself to take a few deep breaths. Maybe she needed to get familiar with the story before she could be fully invested. She could read the last few pages and see how it ends. She's just experiencing a little reader's anxiety and the easy remedy is seeing how the story turns out. Preeda nods to herself and shakily turns the text over to open the back cover.

Mila's heart pounded as Dean brushed a strand of hair behind her ear. Their eyes were locked onto each other, neither of them willing to look away. Dean's chiseled jaw was still bruised from the baseball earlier and Mila wasn't able to stop herself. She stood on her toes, her lips grazing the tender spot, causing Dean to flinch.

"Oh my god, are you okay?" Mila asked him.

His eyes shone. "I'm more than okay."

His face dipped down to meet hers. Their lips were locked—

A squeal bubbles out of her throat and Preeda quickly slaps a hand over her mouth. Staring at her door, expecting her family to barge in demanding to know what was wrong. When she's sure her family didn't hear her, she glares daggers at the book.

The hollow feeling inside her chest grows more prominent. Is that how she's supposed to feel when she kisses someone? Whenever she kissed Jett, she didn't feel anything. It was always a hollow feeling that now feels like a giant void. She likes him. She enjoys talking to him and she misses him, but she doesn't like kissing him.

Shaking her head, maybe he was just a bad kisser? She's still new to dating.A late bloomer, she's young and still has lots of time to date. She's only in her early twenties.

Yet… how many stories are about teenagers finding their true love? Especially their first crushes being their one and only partner for life.

Preeda struggled as she tried to think back to her first crush. She swears she had crushes before; at least, she thinks she did. She remembers the one guy from her class in high school, but only lists him as a past crush because of her friends. They had asked her who she liked. Preeda had been frustrated when they asked her if she had to choose any guy, who she would date. Preeda recalled she ended up choosing the first guy her eyes landed on and feeling confused for the rest of the day as her friends went around saying that she had a crush on said boy. She never even passed the first step outlined by the books.

The shelves loomed menacingly. Preeda could feel her throat closing up as she struggled to think of any positive romantic interaction in her own life.

She liked going on dates with Jett. She didn't mind hugs.

Judgment radiated off her collection of books. Every book has some kind of romantic plot, everything she should have loved in a story, but they all seem to lead her thoughts to her own failed first relationship.

Is she broken?

Her knees wobbled as she stood. She shouldn't be having an identity crisis, she should be reading. She has all these books, and, yet, none of them feel anything like her own experiences.

"Hoy."

Kosum, again.

Scanning her sister from head to toe, wrinkles of concern formed on Kosum's face.

"Your room looks messier than it did earlier. Are you reorganizing your bookshelves again?"

"No, I just," Preeda took a shaky breath. "I don't know what I'm doing anymore."

"Weren't you reading?"

"Yeah, but I can't seem to read." Preeda's voice was quiet, so quiet that Kosum leaned forward to hear what Preeda was saying.

"You just open a book, then you let your eyes look at the words."

"I know *how* to read," Preeda waves her hands frantically. "Everything reminds me of Jett and I don't even know if I ever really liked him in the first place. I don't understand why I'm feeling like this."

"You don't know if you liked a stupid boy?"

"I don't know if I like any stupid boys. Will I even get married or have any kids or—"

"Preeda!"

Reeling herself back, Preeda looked to Kosum. The look of judgment she expected wasn't there; instead, Kosum's expression was empathetic. Her older sister gently placed a hand on Preeda's arm, giving it a reassuring pat.

"We might not even live through the end of the countdown. There are more important things to worry about than romance."

Preeda remained silent, waiting for Kosum to continue, but a loud shout echoed from the hallway and Kosum sighed.

"Mae needs me," she winced to herself. "We can talk more once everything is settled."

As Kosum left the room once more, Preeda was left alone, digesting what her sister just said. She shouldn't be worrying about romance?

Her head hurt.

She couldn't look at the books anymore and her chest still ached from her existential crises.

Maybe she wouldn't be able to read her whole collection after all.

Before she realized what she was doing, she found herself sitting on the floor of her closet, the clothes hanging from the rod above her head brushing against her shoulders. With the door partially closed, her bookshelves out of sight, there was still just enough light in the small space to see. On another shaky breath, she shut her eyes.

She now has so many more issues than she had at the start of the day, and none of them seem to have a solution. It isn't even close to evening, so she can't just sleep this off, either.

Leaning back, a sharp edge jabbed into her side and she grabbed at the thing poking her. The book Kosum gifted to her, tossed aside earlier, she had forgotten she left the book in here. Out of curiosity, she flipped the book to read the summary on the back, but her hopes were low.

Ayesha doesn't know if she ever had a crush on anyone, and she has never been in a relationship. All of her friends are now in happy marriages with children, yet she's left wondering if she's missing something fundamental. Or worse, if she's broken. Now that she's in the workforce, more family members are asking when Ayesha will find that special someone, but she doesn't have an answer for them.

Follow Ayesha in this riveting coming-of-age story about aromanticism and asexuality and finding your place in the world as an adult.

Preeda paused. The book touched a part of her heart she had never been aware she could feel. Slowly, Preeda opened the first page and began to read.

Maybe this book had the words to vocalize what she felt.

~

3PM EST

about the author

Bethany Swafford, known on Wattpad as thequietwriter, has loved reading books for as long as she can remember. That love of words extended to writing as she grew older and she became determined to write her own books.

She has written eight historical fiction novels and three novellas. THE LIBRARIAN *is her first contemporary/ sci-fi short story.*

THE LIBRARIAN

by Bethany Swafford

PERU, INDIANA (THE FRINGE) - 3:16 PM CST

> *Any reports from inside the zone are the same: residents are experiencing a euphoric sensation. While no one appears to be harmed by what is happening, there are concerns about what the long-term effect will be. All attempts to venture into the zone to make further analysis have failed. We will continue to keep you updated on this event…*

The closed captioning of the news report was enough to make my heart climb into my throat. Across the room, the usual local conspirators were huddled around the computers, sharing headphones as they watched news reports and the video feed of one of the rebel streamers who were in the zone. They were muttering their disagreements about what they were seeing, debating whether it was all really happening or not.

The worry that had become a constant stone in my stomach had shifted to an ivy squeezing my heart.

"It's a hoax!" Mr. Calum, the library's most frequent conspiracy theorist, declared for what had to be the tenth time in the last hour. "The government just wants us to think something is happening."

"I can't believe the government I voted for isn't doing anything!" was Mr. Friedson's reply. "You can be sure I'm not going to reelect any of them!"

"Gentlemen, please keep your voices down!" I reminded them. "This is still a library after all!"

They didn't even glance at me as they began to discuss which political party was more to blame. Maybe it was too strict to cling to the rules of the library. After all, it wasn't as though they were bothering anyone. They had been the only visitors to the library all day.

But the rules existed for a reason and as much as I could, I was going to adhere to them.

My gaze drifted up to the second floor above me. I knew all too well how easily raised voices could be heard between the floors. Hopefully, Mr. Calum and Mr. Friedson hadn't been too loud.

Convincing myself that one of them would let me know if there was any change, I forced myself to look away from the computer. My cart was full of books that needed to be cleaned. It wasn't a terribly important task, but it gave my hands something to do.

Unfortunately, even though my hands were busy, my mind kept racing. What did it all mean? Was something worse going to happen? Were the aliens going to go away? Attack?

It was hard to believe it had been just over two weeks since the… Well, the Unidentified Flying Object had appeared in the sky. Since then, nothing had been learned about the object or what it was doing on our planet.

Or, as Mr. Calum insisted, nothing was learned that had been shared with the general public.

Life was suddenly a science fiction adventure that I hadn't asked to be part of. Sci-fi wasn't even a genre I enjoyed reading. I relied on my fellow librarians to make recommendations to patrons.

I ran my cloth over the cover of the book in my hand, being careful not to use too much cleaner. It would never do to get the pages wet and accidentally ruin them.

"I hope Emma appreciates this when she gets back," I muttered under my breath. "She's always complaining that she gets the dirtiest books to clean."

Where were my coworkers? They had all evacuated the minute the governor had made the order. I didn't blame them. They had to do what they had to do for their families. But it would have been nice to hear they had made it to safety.

The sound of the door opening made me lift my head. Oh, dear. "Hello, Mikayla," I said, greeting the twelve-year-old girl who came in. I'd hoped she would stay upstairs today. "Is there something you need?"

"I'm bored," she declared. "Liam is watching YouTube. Can I help you?"

Somehow, it didn't surprise me that her younger brother was glued to the tablet. "Did you finish your book?" I asked.

"Yes, I did," the girl said promptly. "Can I put another star on the wall?"

With a nod, I handed her a pen and a large gold star. She scrawled her name on the star and then took it to the wall. Going on the tips of her toes, Mikayla stuck the star as high as she could.

It was something the children's librarian had done several years ago before we used an app to keep track of summer reading programs. How excited the children had been to get their star first on the wall!

Since Mikayla and Liam were at the library all the time, I proposed that they put a star on the wall every time they finished reading a book. Mikayla loved the idea. She was highly competitive when it came to the summer reading program. Her brother, on the other hand, was not as eager to read.

"Now can I help?" Mikayla asked, turning back to me.

"Alright." I set one of our complete series of *Harry Potter* on the desk. "You can put these back on the shelf for me."

With a serious expression of concentration, Mikayla picked up the entire stack and carried it to the right shelf. I watched her carefully put each book in place, taking care to align the books neatly against the edge of the shelf.

It had been the third day after the UFO's appearance that the two children had walked into the library with a stack of books. I'd been grateful that someone was returning their library books before leaving town. That was before I realized that their mom had driven off without waiting for her children.

During summer reading programs, there was invariably one parent who ignored the direction that children needed to be accompanied by an adult. I'd lost count of how many times we'd been forced to call the police when the program ended and we were left with unaccompanied minors and no way of contacting parents.

Had this been an act of desperation? A mental breakdown? Why abandon your children at a library when you were evacuating?

No calls to the woman's cell phone were answered. I'd searched online for other family members but they hadn't responded to any messages. With the police handling evacuation and trying to keep riots from getting out of hand, Mikayla and Liam had stayed at the library with me.

The second story of the building, the children's section, had been taken over as our bedroom. I'd brought my cat, Shakespeare, from my apartment, and we had all been living in the library since then.

On the one hand, I was grateful not to be alone during... whatever you called this thing that was happening to the United States. At the same time, having the responsibility of two children on my hands and being at my place of work twenty-four-seven was something that had never entered my mind. Staying behind to keep the library open was one thing. Living there was another!

"Miss Anderson, do you have any more books?" Mikayla asked when she returned to the desk.

"Not yet, but you can start bringing me every book by James Patterson," I told her. That would keep her busy for a while. Popular series and authors were the priority of my cleaning efforts. Sometimes it was difficult to clean them since they were often checked out.

"Why doesn't someone go out there?" Mr. Calum exclaimed. "All we're getting is speculation!"

"Mr. Calum, please!" I reprimanded. I did not need his pessimistic opinion affecting Mikayla.

"Miss Anderson?" the girl called out at the same time. The uneasy tone of her voice made me turn toward her. "I see smoke."

Alarmed, I ran to the window. If there was smoke, there was fire, and fire was a librarian's worst nightmare. Mikayla was right. There was smoke so thick and dark it had to be very close.

It took a moment for me to find my voice. "Fire!" I called out. "Everyone evacuate the building!"

When I spun around, no one at the computers had made a move. Their focus was glued to the continuing broadcast. Groaning, I rushed to the wall where the fire extinguisher was waiting.

"Mikayla, get your brother and Shakespeare and get out!" I snapped. "Everyone! Evacuate the building. Please!"

While Mikayla ran for the stairs, I dragged the fire extinguisher to the front door. None of the men even glanced over. "Idiots," I muttered under my breath. Working with the public had always revealed the stupidity of some people, but never as much as in the last two weeks.

I ran down the marble steps to the door. There were three teenagers standing just outside. "The library is closed!" I said without pausing. I charged around the corner of the building. If something happened to this one-hundred-year-old Carnegie Library on my watch, I would never forgive myself!

It might be a stone building but fire was sure to cause some damage!

In the back corner, I saw the source of the fire. The garbage bin had been dumped over and now flames were consuming the bags of trash. Next to the garbage were branches that had definitely not been there before.

Putting that detail aside, I pulled the pin on the fire extinguisher. With any luck, I would be able to put out this thing. Who knew if there were any firefighters still in town? I aimed the nozzle at the fire and braced myself. I'd never actually had to do this before. Praying, I squeezed the trigger.

The contents sprayed out and after a moment, I remembered to sweep it from side to side. The smoke seemed to grow darker and thicker as the powder hit the pile. After a few minutes, I didn't see any flames and I let go of the trigger. There was still smoke coming from the pile, and it smelled awful.

Uncertain, I nudged the pile with the toe of my shoe. I knew it was all too easy for a fire to flare up after a person thought it had been put out. Breathing out, I thought the danger was past but decided to wait just in case.

As I stood there, the silence that had become normal in the last two weeks made me uneasy. There were supposed to be birds singing in the trees and insects humming in the grass. Instead, there was only the occasional bark of a dog in the distance.

How strange it was for it to be so gloomy outside and yet not raining! It was August, a time when it was usually bright and sunny and hot. Instead, the temperature was at least twenty degrees colder than what it should be.

Glancing around, I tried to figure out how this fire had begun. I was sure I had closed the bin when I took out the trash. Had an animal knocked the bin over? Even that would have been an unlikely reason for a fire to start.

It wasn't as though this was one of the big cities where there had been rioting and looting. What was there to gain from trying to burn down a library? Destruction for the sake of destruction?

There was a laugh from the front of the building. Were those teenagers still there? Were they waiting for something or someone? Curious, I carried the used fire extinguisher with me to the front.

"Stop it! Those aren't yours! Miss Anderson! Miss Anderson!" I heard Mikayla shriek.

I rounded the corner and the tallest boy called out, "Run!"

Just as I realized he was holding the door open with his foot, his two friends came running out the door. They both had backpacks in their hands and out of one fell a CD case.

A CD case that I knew well and had a library barcode on the side.

"Thief!" I screeched, outraged. Everything clicked into place. They'd set a fire to draw me out just to steal some CDs? Or had they pilfered some of the DVDs as well? "Stop!

All three of them took off at a run.

"You-You hooligans!" It was the least threatening thing I could have said but the only thing that came to mind. "Stop! I'll-I'll call the police on you! You'll be banned from the library for life!"

Their laughter seemed to float on the air, taunting me. How I wished I had a copy of ***Les Misérables*** by ***Victor Hugo*** to throw at their fleeing backs. It was thick enough to knock some sense into their stupid heads.

In fact, the hand holding the fire extinguisher started to rise. It might be empty, but it was sure to slow them down.

But, instead, I lowered my hand. What was the point? They knew as well as I did that the police were busy elsewhere and it was highly unlikely anyone would come over stolen DVDs. And I would never risk harming a book when I had the worst throwing arm ever.

Suddenly, the extinguisher was too heavy to keep holding and I let it fall to the ground. I landed on my knees next to it a moment later. Tears filled my eyes. How was I supposed to report this? How would the library recover from such a theft?

"Stupid. Stupid. Stupid," I muttered. Not just those thieves but myself. I should have known better than to leave my post. Leaving the library unattended was the last thing I should have done.

I brushed my eyes, but the tears would not stop. The patrons at the computers hadn't come. They must have heard. Not just when I called for the building to be evacuated but just now when I was shouting. How could they not have heard those thieves rifling through things?

They didn't care. All they were worried about was their conspiracies and theories.

"Why am I even here?"

The governor of the state had ordered a mandatory evacuation and the mayor had added his command to do the same. Within hours, the roads had been choked with people headed west. Everyone who could leave abandoned everything to get beyond the shadow.

My gaze drifted to the library sign. *Reading gives us someplace to go when we have nowhere to go.*

All of my coworkers had said I was crazy to stay behind. My family had begged me not to be stupid. "Let other people risk their lives. It's just books," they had said.

But it hadn't been about the books, though I did consider them important. It had been about being the unchanging source of information. If technology failed, the library could still stand and provide information from books that had stood the test of time.

Where had that idealism gotten me? Covered in smoke, nearly deaf from conspiracy theories, and...alone. I had been carrying the burdens of the library on my shoulders with no one else's help.

"Miss Anderson! Are you alright?"

Mikayla.

Hastily, I wiped my eyes and took a deep breath. "I'm fine," I answered, my voice. I cleared my throat. "The fire is out. Everything is fine."

Or as fine as it could be.

"I tried to stop them," Mikayla said, "but they wouldn't listen to me. I even kicked his ankle, but he just pushed me down. They took a lot of the DVDs."

Brave girl!

"Shakespeare is hiding somewhere," Mikayla continued. "Liam is trying to find him but I don't know if he will."

"I found him!" Liam called out. "Miss Anderson, Shakespeare is hiding under a shelf and he won't come out for me."

No doubt the shouting had upset my cat. At least there was no more threat of fire. "Alright," I answered, pushing myself up from the ground. "Thank you, Liam. We'll leave him be and hope he comes out when he is hungry."

When I turned around, the seven-year-old boy was leaning out the door. "It smells bad out here," he complained, his face scrunched up in disgust.

"It's not that bad," Mikayla immediately contradicted.

It actually was. There had been no sign of a trash truck in weeks, which was not unexpected given the evacuation. However, there were still trash cans on the curb filled with trash. Today the smell was compounded by the smoke from the fire the teenagers set, that disgusting scent of burning plastic and trash.

"Miss Anderson, the guys at the computers are getting loud," Liam complained. "I think they're going to fight."

Why was I not surprised? Every time I turned my back, those grown men completely forgot the rules. I was tempted to unplug the router and put them in time-out!

"Thank you, Liam. Why don't you run in and remind them of the rules? I'll be right behind you."

With a grin, the towheaded boy pulled his head back into the library. Mikayla reached down and picked up the fire extinguisher for me. "Do you need me to keep watch at the window?" she asked. "I can let you know if they try to come back."

"No, I don't think they will be back." At least, I hoped they wouldn't. What else of value was left?

Mikayla slipped her free hand into mine as we walked to the front door. "No one else is going to hurt the library while we are here, right?" she asked.

My heart warmed as I smiled down at her. No. I wasn't alone. "Right," I told her. "In fact, why don't you help me find a place to put the rest of the DVDs so no one tries again."

Her eyes lit up. "Yeah!"

As we walked through the door, I heard Mr. Calum exclaim, "Why doesn't someone do something already? It's been all day and we don't know a dam—"

"Shh!" Mikayla and Liam said at the same time.

"Did you just try to hush me?" Mr. Calum demanded. He jumped up from his chair and shook a finger at the children. "Children do not shush adults, do you hear me? I am your elder and that means you have to respect me. Do you understand? I can say whatever I like, however I like, *when* I like!"

How dare he? Who did he think he was?

"Mr. Calum, that is quite enough!" I said sharply. "There are children present and this is a library. You will keep your voice down or I will have to ask you to leave."

He turned towards me, his mouth open to argue.

"No," I continued, putting my hands on my hips. Every instance of the man trying to sidestep the rules flashed through my mind. "This is not up for debate. If you cannot abide by the rules of this library, you are not welcome here. This is not *your* library and you do not make the rules. I do. You will keep your voice down and be respectful of the other people who are present."

His eyes were wide. "They are just children! They shouldn't even be–"

"I shouldn't have to remind you that none of us 'should be here'," I interrupted. "We were all ordered to leave. I *chose* to stay and keep the library open. Everyone I knew told me to leave, to think of myself first, and I didn't because I have always believed that the library was the one constant source for people to turn to for facts and information. No matter what happens in the world, the library doesn't falter or fail. Because of me. I will continue to make sure the library remains open and that means that I will ensure the rules of the library are obeyed. If you have a problem with that, I can just as easily choose to leave and close the library. That means no more internet connection and no more computer access. Is that what you want?"

Color flooding his face, Mr. Calum shook his head and sat down. The other three men stared at me with wide eyes. I glared right back at them. "My library. My rules. Is that understood, gentlemen?"

As one, the four men nodded. They all turned back to their computers with sheepish expressions and began whispering together.

The kids turned to me with triumphant expressions and I grinned at them. "Now. Liam, help your sister find a hiding place for the DVDs. It is important for us to protect library property. I'll keep an eye on these miscreants and make sure they follow the rules."

With matching nods, the pair bolted to make a thorough search. I settled onto my seat. I closed the tab on the computer that had the broadcast. What was the sense in worrying about what would happen? If something changed, I would deal with it like everything else.

Come what may, the library was a safe zone and I was its protector.

~

5PM EST

about the author

Jamie is an illustrator, graphic designer and author from India.

You can find them either munching on a snack and daydreaming about exquisite new worlds or drawing queer characters.

They are currently working on THREE'S NOT A CROWD, a sapphic polyamory rom-com.

THE CONNECTION

by Jamie Lemon

WASHINGTON D.C, USA - 5:23 PM EST

Raazi felt tired, more so today. She checked her watch, though she knew it would be futile. It was past 5 p.m. It would have been tea time if she could go home. If there were any semblance of it left.

She sighed, closing her eyes, trying to envision what she would be having if it were a normal day. Chai and hot samosas. Or if she felt better, perhaps she would scour the neighbourhood for pani puris. She would know.

Food always made her better. Laughing with her mom as she rolled the dough for aloo parathas always made her heart feel feathery.

Lost.

She felt like she was floating and peeked a look outside. It was as dark as the depths of the sea. Who knew what lay above in the clouds?

Well, you could tell she lost her hope in heaven. There was definitely none of that if the sky had been dark since…

13? How many days had it been? Her phone read August 15th. 15 days since a ship had landed over them and never left. Every day as she tried to fall asleep, her phone would blink rapidly with a number. It started with 30 and now declined to 15. She didn't know what would happen when the number read 1 and she didn't want to find out. A visceral fear would take over her now and then but she would push it away.

It started with a huge ship hovering over them and then coming to rest almost as if it refused to land and it refused to move up any further, with it blinking a number every day in the sky like a ticking time bomb.

There was a tiny part of her that simply wished she had someone to lean on.

Anyone. It felt lonely and empty inside after evenings. While mornings contained of Philia moving about and asking how she felt, and the fact that perhaps it was better to stay here than elsewhere, the evenings were pallid and dark. Lights didn't function anymore unless emergencies called for it. Raazi had no clue about the other severe patients, or if there were any. It had also been long. Five days since the evacuation started and not many were really left. The nurse, whose name tag read Philia, looked at her with a frown.

She wanted to go home. Raazi knew. But she couldn't be here for the money after businesses had nearly shut down and most of the prestigious doctors left town.

Raazi knew. And she didn't give two flying fudges about it. Because after 54 years you learn to take it a little more easy.

Or you would be lying in the hospital, all alone like her. Nobody wanted old people after all, but she had hoped she would outlive her cat.

And she did.

She just didn't expect heartbreak to get her here.

She had no children, her mom had just fled the city and her cat was her sole comfort. He passed away two weeks ago.

Heart aches came in different forms. Raazi had primarily two major heartaches in her entire life and the second one was the reason she was even here in the first place. Her cats meant the world to her and she had chosen them fourteen years back when she moved from India to Washington D.C.

She hadn't been meaning to look for cats the day she moved into the city. She did love plants though and she went out one gloomy morning with a heavy heart.

That was the day she felt the impact of her first heartbreak.

She missed her. The laugh that sounded like the universe had reached into itself and plucked every bit of oblivious happiness and put it in her. Her best friend.

Or rather her ex best friend now. Who knew?

She hunted the nursery for a succulent or any juicy plant that called out to her. Maybe something that was low maintenance? She had grown fruits but never flowering plants and she just wanted something pretty to look at as her heart grew thorns.

And then she wandered into the cat café next door which was littered with cats as she slumped into a chair and had a stare down with a persian cat after which she closed her eyes and tried to relax but felt something heavy plop onto her lap.

She jolted and looked at the furball in her lap who meowed with delight. She was unsure, because she was generally a dog person and cats never blended well with her.

It purred happily and scrunched up its butt towards her.

She petted it a little awkwardly first and then couldn't remember when she had fallen asleep and the persian cat was trying to scratch at a fish tank and then jumping into it before yelping and scrambling back out. She heartily laughed at that for a long time.

She took it home and named it *Meen*, the Malayalam word for fish as it kept getting into hilarious situations involving fish. And then she lost him fourteen years later.

It didn't feel like enough time. It never felt like enough.

Sometimes, she wished she could…end it. After all, if her closest pals were gone, did it make any sense to be here?

She had switched on the T.V. in the morning and saw the news reporter wildly point above and then giggle hysterically.

"This is so cool, guys! Over here," she giggled some more and went and side hugged another reporter who looked so out of his mind. "We have the biggest hole ever! WE HAVE LIGHT. JOY TO THE WORLD!"

The male reporter nodded and looked at his fingers for a while before pointing them with finger guns. "You guys rock!" he screamed to the ship above.

And she felt even more depressed. She was so far away that not an inch of light fell where she lived. Bitterness coursed through her veins though she was repeatedly told not to stress about grave things.

Couldn't an old woman enjoy her final stage in peace? She switched it on again to see the same reporters crying and agonizing over the loss of light as evening hit. Sunlight would be gone in a few hours and they'd have to wait.

The door burst open and Raazi thought it would be Philia to tell her off for playing the T.V so loud or something but instead it was a woman in fifties with bright purple and pink hair that contrasted her black and gray hairs and her dark nut brown skin.

She immediately knew.

Niloufer.

Her throat constricted as various shades of emotions crossed her face.

"Nilou…fer?" she whispered and her lungs ached with a million thorns piercing into it.

Niloufer looked pale in comparison to her hair. It stood out oddly against the unspoken feelings between them and the white hospital walls.

Raazi looked away and then blinked again. "Fourteen years…"

"I know."

"You didn't–"

Niloufer didn't say anything but sat down on a nearby chair and dragged herself closer to the bed. She reached out, her fingers a hair's breadth away from Raazi's.

Raazi stared at her hand mid-air but didn't say anything. "You left me."

She seemed to be staring into nothingness as she said those words, as if she were recollecting a memory. She didn't have to recollect it much. Raazi saw her everywhere, in the laughs of strangers, in the tilted hat her cousin wore, the mismatched socks her nephews wore, in the neon signs that shone bright in darkness.

She could never wipe her–not that she had tried much, to begin with.

"I know," Niloufer let her hand drop. "I-I made you cookies. And they're the peanut butter chocolate kind with a hint of hazelnut just like you like it when you would come over and well, I kinda ran out of peanut butter, because supermarkets were closing you know, but then I found this secret stash my grandma kept?? Can you believe that–"

Raazi raised an eyebrow. *Did she really think Niloufer could get cookies and bribe her?*

You're damn right about that.

The delicious scent of chocolate chip and peanut butter oozed out as she opened a tin can and passed it to her.

"Don't think I'm forgiving you because of cookies."

"You are speaking to me because of cookies, though," she giggled a little and then stopped, looking embarrassed all of a sudden.

She felt lost and hurt. The dark hovered between them and clasped fourteen years' worth of lost secrets in its arms. Neither dare to speak anymore. Raazi hunted for the emergency light. She reserved them for purposes like this. Or unlike this because she never thought it would come in handy for broken hearts and a friend who broke it.

"You were the one who moved, you know…" Niloufer muttered, hugging herself tight. Her shock of purple hair was the only thing keeping Raazi sane; she was real. Niloufer would always dye her hair randomly but electric purple had stuck more often. Raazi would joke that Niloufer was like purple itself. She knew it and carried herself royally.

Yet now, she seemed so unsure. Either too quiet or delirious.

"Yeah and I did call you every night. Or at least during your day," she pointed out. She paused for a while. "Until you stopped picking up and texting me so frequently."

It hurt to say the next few words so she kept it in. *Did life really get in the way for so many years? Or did she just get bored and leave?*"I see there isn't power here either. Well, guess it's evening so that doesn't matter does it? In my—" she stopped midway and then looked away. "Your mom said you just recovered from a bypass surgery. A heart attack."

Raazi looked stunned and munched on a cookie and then another and another. She stared into the tin can and ran her thumb over the dented edges. "You could call her and not me?"

"I—I got busy yes,"

"Please don't give me your petty excuses. Are you here to say goodbye to me for real? Or because you're feeling guilty?" Raazi swallowed hard.

It sucked that she still cared. After all these years they had been through, all it took was Raazi moving to another place to call it quits? Was the foundation that shaky?

The lights in the room flickered on and off and then went back to off. Hospitals were trying to conserve energy and direct it to their most severe patients. Some of it was futile.

She heard a racket outside and looked through her window. There was a group of people all dressed in white chanting with slogans. "Punishment for your sins! Repent and get saved before the aliens get us!" They seemed to be marching and stomping loudly from the looks of it.

The past week she saw people on T.V. wearing black and green and excitedly telling people if they wanted to see aliens they had to pay to get to see them. And some of them were even selling custom alien merchandize

Raazi snorted. Every other day she would witness something bizarre like this. Not that she didn't have her own theories, but propaganda seemed to unite people in tough times too. "Would you look at that? People seem to be getting hyped about this."

"Looks like everyone is looking for their quick fix to heal their soul from not having seen the light in fifteen days."

"You would know, wouldn't you? Have you been here the entire time?" Raazi bit back, one hand clutching the blanket.

She was letting her irrational side take over. She was supposed to not give two fudges at this age.

"I came to Washington a year back."

"Oh, what gave it away again? Was it my mother?" her voice dripped with sarcasm, as she huffed.

Niloufer shrugged. "She's pretty active on Facebook. But I left for India a month later."

"Hmm," Raazi mused as her world spun a little around her.

Raazi slid down under her covers. She needed to breathe under her blankets where it was warm and she didn't have to face the world ending or whatever the space ship would do in fifteen more days.

She remembered her life as a kid when she would be scared of the dark in college days and Niloufer, her then roommate would curl up beside her, pulling the blanket above their heads and making a cozy little space. She would light it up with her giggles and fun stories and read them out to her until Raazi fell asleep.

Those were some of Raazi's best days. The little things.

"Mama says she used scented candles when she felt alone," Niloufer's voice hung heavy.

"Sometimes you talk the most random shit," Raazi muttered, curling into a furry ball and then turning around.

Niloufer was silent for quite a long time.

"Raazi...I-" she started after about ten minutes of pondering what would be best to say. Was there really an apology for when your closest pal leaves you in the dust for fourteen years?

Her voice sounded distant and muffled because Raazi had tried to pull some of the blanket close to her ears too. She was safe. She was okay. Under the blanket, not even spaceships and friendships and broken hearts could get to her.

A sob ripped through her as she tried to hold it down. Her vision blurred and felt like a teen all over again. She missed her mom. Just yesterday she was lying on her mom's lap, eating piping hot bowls of rice and fish curry and now her mother had left for safer spaces.

It was on Raazi's insistence, yes. But she still wished her mom was here. To pat her head and massage her hair with coconut oil and say she would be okay.

"I'm sorry, Raazi. I am so sorry I didn't...call or text you back. But mostly..."

Niloufer took a deep breath in. The room felt smaller.

"I was a coward."

Raazi didn't say anything for a long time. She just let her tears flow. Why Niloufer had to pop in during a world crisis situation was beyond her understanding and how the universe worked.

"We–" her body wracked with sobs. Raazi pulled the blanket over her head as Philia came rushing in.

"Ma'am, I must ask you to not stress the patient. She has just recovered from a surgery."

Niloufer nodded apologetically.

"Did you see? A 100 mile hole opened up in the spacecraft. And people look out of their minds. I mean...I guess if you see light after many days...who knows, what's real and not anymore?" Niloufer mused.

"I didn't even get to see the goddamn light," Raazi muttered, wiping her eyes. "Could you get me a tissue from there?"

Niloufer passed her the kleenex and then turned around. "Raazi...I know it's the end of the world. And you have no reason to even want me here, but I...I wanted my last moments to be with you. I don't know when we would go with this huge spacecraft over us and when it's been two weeks since I saw the sun. But can we..."

Raazi was only able to make out Niloufer gesturing wildly in the emergency light that cast harsh shadows across her face. She hugged herself, felt very small and under scrutiny.

"I tried so hard to reach you."

Raazi was silent after saying that. If it was the end of the world, who cared? She leaned over to the other side and reached for her cassette player. Every day she would just play one song to let the charge last. This was one of the few antique devices she fought for to be allowed in the hospital and promised she wouldn't blast it.

Removing the old cassette, she plugged in a new one and switched it on and patted the space beside her. Niloufer got in without a word. Perhaps words were too much, they hung around like wet clothes in the monsoon, heavy and hard to bear.

It started playing the song *If the world was ending* by JP Saxe and Julia Michaels.

Niloufer looked guilty, most of all. She glanced up at Raazi.

Raazi smiled a little sadly and then held her hand out. "I know we have a lot to make up for and there's so much to speak about but…I can't lose you again."

Her eyes were wet and she rubbed them as Niloufer clasped her hand, laying her head on Raazi's shoulder. Perhaps nothing would ever be the same, if the crisis was averted. But perhaps, just for now, maybe they could pretend it would be and be with each other. Raazi reached out to hug her and they held each other for a long time.

No words were needed as Raazi switched off the light and the dark enveloped them.

~

7PM EST

about the author

Mittu Ravi is a poet and experimental long-form writer.

They are currently working on their paranormal dark comedy, All Hell's Broken Loose, and have written adult contemporary works such as A Little Love for Pennies and Life, On Hold.

Mittu hails from South-East Asia and is dedicated to BIPOC and queer representation in their arts.

THE CIRCLE

by Mittu Ravi

LYNCHBURG, VIRGINIA, USA
AUGUST 15, 7:00 PM

When I returned home and flung the flashlight off my Mini2Go scooter, I didn't expect it to tumble to the ground and land at the feet of Maheri Mikhaylov.

Half-slouched against the stairs leading to his doorstep, Maheri turned away to puff off the smoke from his vape. "What's that?" he asked, motioning to my scooter.

"How do you expect me to get to work, eh?" I replied, taking a seat on his front porch and nestling the flashlight in my pocket. "Catch the Amtrak?"

He snickered. "You should ask the alien overlords," he pointed up,"to bless you a ride."

I snorted and glanced at the towering spaceship: it was a magnificent monstrosity glimmering in the darkened sky, a searing light streaming down from the middle. Just a day before, ink-black darkness shrouded Lynchburg — but now, the blinding brightness bounced off windows, basking us within a dim, haunting glow.

Maheri straightened his back. "Fucked up shit."

"It's like an SNL rendition of an UFO skit. In what world does a giant turd show up to block the sun?"

"It's pretty circular," he noted.

"Never had a circular shit? Or if you're me, you haven't because I'm scared shitless," I said. "I also haven't seen you since everything went down, so..."

"Well, I…" he waved his hands in the air. "Stocked up on my vapes, biscuits, ramen, and chilled in a dark corner."

"You, chill? You're telling me you —"

"Okay! Okay, I was freaking the fuck out, all right?" He sighed. "Thank fuck there's some light now. And whatever that is, you saw the news, yes?"

"Electricity gone kaput."

"Rigged the dynamo. Maybe I'd get you some supply, but it doesn't do much," he said. "Apparently that heavenly UFO light-bulb has this ionizing… air. Thing." He shrugged. "Happy particles. They sent in a reporter who acted like he downed a whole bottle of Edibles."

"He was… high?"

"Yep."

"Do you really trust the government saying that, Maheri?" I pursed my lips. "Maybe they'd wanna bait us to the centre so they could force us to evacuate."

"They weren't wrong," he said, taking another drag of his grape-flavoured nicotine. "It's on us if any shit goes down, you know. God knows what that floating timer is for."

"Countdown, in minutes, to my next mental breakdown," I retorted.

He snorted and pushed his dark-brown locks away from his forehead. His hair had grown into a messy mullet — paired with his lack of shaving, Maheri looked like he had aged from 24 to 30 in the span of days. Unzipping his winter coat, he stuffed the vape into his pocket and entwined his palms around one knee.

"Vini," he started, "I wanna go there."

"There?" I glanced at the light, and then over to him. "Why?"

He frowned. "It's not like I have Edibles or the patience to spend my unemployed time jerking myself off."

That evoked a very specific memory, which I immediately shoved to the back of my mind, and then let out a sigh. "I don't have great ways to spend my unemployed time, either."

"Hm?"

"Got fired today."

"Oh. Fuck."

"And" — I suppressed a laugh — "they offered me the Ultimate Detox For The Ultimate Lady package, after I'd cursed out my boss for ignoring every one of my marketing suggestions."

"Generous!" he remarked. "The school just sent me home with my Kool-Aid costume, and then I didn't see daylight for a week."

I sighed, shook my head and held out my hand. "Lend me a puff?"

"Nope. Last canister."

I sulked, and we sat staring at the saucer. God's prophecy, some called it. The Second Coming, the End of the World. And in the half-darkness peppered with a ghostly aura, it simultaneously felt like those words were both bogus and the greatest truths. Maheri, meanwhile, unzipped his coat and pulled out a scrunchie to tie back his hair (which could have been mine), and then got up to his feet.

Throwing me a glance, he asked: "How fast does your toddler scooty go?"

"Yeah, no —"

"— you could come along."

"You… do know how most of our trips end, eh?" I crossed my arms. "Spare us from it. I have wine, and my couch isn't half bad."

"Fuck that." I had never seen him reject any offer with that much conviction. "We have fifteen days before that thing detonates or some shit. I've vaped myself out of my mind, Vini." He buried his hands into his pockets, still staring at the light. "Sit around or die trying."

I rested my hands on my hips, biting my lips, and then shrugged. "I'd go grab another scooter."

"More of that Mini2Go?" he asked as I kicked it to him. "Good, god."

***

"Holy hell, it's burning into the ground."

Maheri scuttled over, hauling my scooter in one hand. It was a shorter ride than we expected — 15 minutes, I said when we first got on, but it proved itself to be a sweet seven-minute ride.

It was a chilling descent into the light. With every metre, the darkness around us slipped away in tendrils, the light sharpening soft edges, contouring Maheri's cheekbones and flooding his dark-brown eyes. The silence that strung around us now, near to the halo, was different. Not eerie, just peaceful.

We stared at the pavement now cut through by the halo, leaving a thick, black radius.

"Wanna become a roasted duck, lovely boy?"

Maheri shook his head, pointing into the halo — just at our vision's edge, a group of people were sitting together, laughing. "I don't think so, cynical Vini."

Name suits me. "Look, I don't have a death wish."

"I don't think that matters." He pointed to the countdown. "The Gods are already doing it for us."

"How you do know —"

Maheri pushed the scooter away and walked towards the halo.

"Stop."

He took off his coat and tied it around his waist.

"Maheri!" I yanked his elbow. His gaze met mine and it was unwavering — and subtly firm. I let go and he straightened his back.

"Vini," he started, eyes fixated on mine. "Look. I want to be a carefree, just for a little while."

"You cannot trust—"

"Trust for what? Just, look around..." his voice trailed before he caught it. "You're seeing this, right? A fucking spaceship, ticking down from 30. Fucking barren lands, and" — he waved his hands — "we're still here because, hey! My boyfriend's gone and I hate the world; and, your dad's gone and you hate the world; and, the soldiers who came to evacuate are gone, and... We hate the world." He exhaled and buried his hands in his pockets. "Let's be real, too. We've seen worse."

"Heri," I whispered. "We can't just..."

"Just what?" He inched away. "Unless you've got a stash somewhere, I won't survive."

"But it's burning into the ground!"

He tilted his head — the light slowly kissed the tip of his curls. I backed away, biting my lip, my throat winding tight.

He stumbled into the light, staring up.

Silence. I tore my gaze away and squeezed my eyes shut, until I heard his voice again — slow, steady, and in a breathless whisper, almost like his words were a sigh of relief.

"Vini. I'm here, still."

My eyes grazed him — fleeting and in fear — before I took another look, and yes, he was there. Still standing. I expected his skin to start searing, but no, he was there still. I stared. He was there. I walked up to him, and he was there still. I was almost waiting for everything to combust spontaneously, but he was there, still.

With shaky hands, I touched his shoulder. He was there, still, and he smiled. Not like his good morning! smile or a throwaway smirk, but he smiled. He stared again at the radius of the streaming halo, I did too — and now, I was feeling the pressure and the shivering dissipate from my hands. I grabbed his shoulder with both my hands, and a small beat of pure joy nestled itself in the corner of my heart. He grasped my wrists.

Breathing in, I leaned closer and stumbled into the radiance.

It took me in, like a warm embrace. My body eased, ever so slightly, with my knots relieving as I took another step. And another. I was gliding with a tinge of giddiness until I stopped and took the deepest, most satisfying breath.

"Wow," I mustered. "What the hell."

"Heaven," Maheri corrected. He had his hands in mine, and I ran my finger along his knuckles. He nodded to a nearby shop nestled between two ghosted office buildings, where an old woman sat singing. "Heaven, and ice cream."

And there we were, moments later, sitting on a bench with two butterscotch cones in hand — for free. In this economy, darling? the woman asked, digging up the biggest scoops I've seen. Who knows what dollar bills are, haha! Enjoy!

"Some did stay, eh?" I asked, taking a lick. "There's a person every 500 metres, and some families."

"Why wouldn't they?" Maheri replied. "It feels like being high, but it's not. It's strangely beautiful."

He smiled through ice-cream stained lips, and I laughed. I hadn't seen him this happy — or even happy — and I couldn't look away, because… maybe I wanted this Maheri. Not the Maheri who smelled like the lovechild of grape and marijuana. Not the Maheri who was enough with a barebone routine in bed, just there for barely a hit of pleasure.

"Not really a bad idea," I said. He licked a small stream of butterscotch that had run amok along his wrist. "You're even better than when you're high."

He chuckled. "What am I like when I'm high?"

"You deadpan at the ceiling."

"That's boring." He bit into the last of his cone, a mess of ice cream sticking on his scraggly beard. Cautiously, I tugged at the hem of my plaid, waiting for him to lean ever so slightly — and then I wiped his lips with my sleeve.

"Oh," he said with a tinge of surprise. "Thanks."

I tilted my head. "That's it?"

He threw me a questioning glance. "Hm?"

"Just thanks?" I asked, confused. "You always say 'Liwei's gone, I wish I had someone who'd hug me' — and that one time I kissed your forehead, you acted like you'd never experienced that before in your life."

He shook his head and laughed. "Of course I have."

"Yeah, but…" I shifted closer to him and our shoulders grazed. "Is it just me, or am I feeling this wave of so many different things?"

He furrowed his eyebrows. "Huh?"

Silence. I stared at his golden-brown eyes, his pupils dilated.

"Damn," I remarked. "You're just zoinked out."

"Right?"

"I mean…" I waved my hands. "You're happy, yes."

We had now started to wander around the neighbourhood, where ten-o-clock flowers had once bloomed in now-barren gardens. A slight breeze blew along and playfully burrowed itself beneath my shoulder-length locks. Stray cats and dogs stalked the barely-inhabited lands. My chest felt like a tethered helium balloon — filled to the brim and aching to float, and at that moment, all I wanted to do was let myself feel free. But as I looked up again at the blinding halo and then at the silent carcass of a neighbourhood, that swelling feeling slowly abated. It was beautiful, but that was about it — we were still alone, very alone.

So, I did the next best thing: I intertwined my fingers with Maheri's.

He squeezed my hand back slowly as we strolled along ghosted roads. Nothing more — just an acknowledgment of my existence. It was strange to me. Does your chest feel jumpy, I asked him. Does it feel full? How does it feel?

"Nothing," he said, staring straight ahead.

"You always tell me you feel like nothing, but you're feeling everything."

We turned around the corner — he thought of my words in the silence, and then nodded. The walkway ahead of us was filled with dustbins that no one had the time to clear when the state of emergency was declared. And as we passed building after building, the waste started morphing. It started morphing from unshredded paper documents to uneaten food, to the remains of a bird smeared against the road pavement, to a dead husky in the middle of our path — eyes half-open, fleas crawling over its body.

I could only smell traces of flowers and fresh-cut grass — jarring to my senses. As we looked down at the pretty creature gone too soon, I grasped Maheri's wrist.

"No…" I whispered. "He looks so much like your Bailey."

All Maheri replied was with an "mhmm". I paused, a twinge of uneasiness threatening to take root.

"Heri, he's… dead."

"Poor thing," he said.

"No, you — this…" I let go of his hand. "You can't just — stare at nothing. You pet every damn dog you see on the street. Heri. Do you hear me?"

His eyes, though fixated on me, held a far-away gaze. He was entranced, in apathetic silence, entrenched in peace so deep that nothing mattered any longer.

"So, you feel nothing, huh?" I clutched his shoulders. "I'm here, feeling everything. You're the one supposed to feel that, you."

His eyebrows furrowed before he returned to a melancholic smile.

"You're the one drunk-crying in my bed and then claiming that you were absolutely fine in the morning. But I feel nothing" — I took a deep breath — "because I deny it and it all goes away, and I'm all okay."

Silence. Maheri's blank stare turned to one of confusion, and he ran his hand through his hair. "You shouldn't do that."

"And you shouldn't be this lifeless, but…" I let my voice trail off. "It makes us feel good. I'm bursting with everything because I never do, and you've got nothing because you never shut up about feeling something."

I saw a flicker of something in his eyes. His lips parted in subtle silence — he looked down at the dead husky, and then caught my eyes again. And then, while still wearing a smile, he said, "I don't — understand the feeling."

"I don't, either," I admitted. "Because, you're you, but you're not you. I'm not me." I stared up at the halo, and then at him. "It feels illegal, Heri. I was the girl who just took a half day off to cremate Pa, signed off with 'Vinitha Deshpande', and then went well, another Deshpande down." My words gave me a strange sense of relief, not pain. "I told you 'He'll be back' when you were unbuttoning your shirt in my hallway and asked where he was."

"I saw the urn."

"I know. You hovered over me until I told you," I said. "Because you know what it's like to feel, and you stayed for me. I didn't know what it was to feel, so I just offered myself as a rebound girl when Liwei broke up with you."

His smile wasn't as bright anymore.

"I don't know why you dragged me here," I continued, "But I want you to be happy, because…" my voice struggled as I stared at him.

"Because?" he asked.

"I love you."

His gaze wavered, his eyebrows furrowed. And that was it.

Compared to the giddiness seeping into my head, his reaction was nothing. I slid my hand across his shoulder, but all he did was return a painfully-peaceful stare: it was as if my heart was bursting at its seams, but so much so that it hurt — and he didn't see that.

And then it hit me.

It hit me like a slow wave, a gentle crash through my chest. I looked up, and then at him — and I started walking away, almost by instinct. But all I heard was silence from him before his slow footsteps followed, and I paused to look behind.

"Don't follow," I whispered.

"Where?" he asked.

Biting down on my lip, I turned the corner, passed the ice-cream shop with the singing lady, and then the bench we had sat on, eating our cones. And then I finally heard footsteps catch up to me.

"Where are you going?" he asked, eyes locking with mine and his reverie-ridden gaze now sobering.

I gave him a half-chuckle. "We're fucking fools, darling." I stumbled backwards, looking up. "A halo's not gonna fill any hole in our hearts. Are you happy? No, you're a zombie," I said.

"Don't," he mustered, his eyes widening at whatever was behind me.

"The darkness?" I asked, throwing a glance behind. "I'll take that."

"Don't."

"No. I see me in you now, Maheri. Nothingness doesn't make you happy, it makes you nothing," I said. "You remember — the time you stuffed the okroshka you made inside my pani puri, and I said I loved it?"

He took a step forward, but I stepped away.

"You said 'That's me! Your Russian stuffed Indian!' and then when we laughed, you asked — 'Do you love me?'" I felt the greying cold hit my back, coming closer to the partition of the halo. "I said nothing, Maheri. And I wish I had. I know how you feel now."

"No, no. It's all okay," he said, with a small trepidation in his eyes. "We'll survive this."

"We'll never know." I closed my eyes. "If we don't survive this, it's okay. The world returns to okay even if we're fucked and dead, but..." my voice trailed off. "I wish we didn't have to be."

And I stepped into the darkness.

Emptiness tore into me, as if it had always been waiting. Serenity shattering with a snap of a finger, I struggled to take a breath, tears stinging against my cheek. I'd already been crying, but under the spell of the shining halo, all I had to show was a smile. All we had to show was a smile.

I fixed my gaze on Maheri at the edge of the halo. My heart — now hollowing out into a bittersweet pit — begged for just a touch of the halo again, so the quiet ferocity of my feelings could return. But his vacant eyes said otherwise: who would love a peaceful abyss?

I toed the line, a small something flowing through my body every time the light hit my sandals. And as I glanced up, I felt him move closer, his wrist brushing against mine, a loose long lock falling against my neck. A gentle heave of my chest and I averted my eyes, straining for words.

"Who do we have but us?" I asked, grasping his hand. "We're second-class, lumped together with conspirators who didn't want to leave. Uncooperative, useless — we're nothing. Not a reporter, not a renowned spy, and hell, not even employed citizens." The number on the spaceship was now in sight again. "If we die, Heri... they wouldn't even step in here to put us in a body bag."

His gaze flickered up.

"Running into pleasure just ruins us more," I said. "Nothing has made us happy for so long, Maheri, but we made us happy."

Running my hand along his knuckles, I tugged his palms to the darkness. His fingertips grazed the grey nothingness — he instinctively moved, eyes widening as the shadows fell against his jaw. But he stayed in the light still, pooling against his cheeks and now mine as I basked in the light happiness that traced my collarbone. He angled in, face half-shrouded. His smile faded slowly, while I felt my lips stretch into one.

"Vini," he said my name breathlessly, the first time since we were there.

I cradled his face in my palms as his muddy-amber eyes finally focused on me. I traced the edge of his scraggly jaw, the nook of his earlobe. His Adam's apple bobbed as he swallowed and leaned closer, his breath warming my skin. I buried my hands in his locks. His fingers interlock behind my neck.

His lips met mine.

A cold tear of his smeared against my cheek, and he kissed the corner of my lips, the tip of my nose, and my shivering eyes. I pulled myself in as his arms wrapped around my waist.

He gingerly inched more into the darkness, and then kissed the top of my head. "I love you, Vini."

I stifled a whimper, burying my face in his shoulder.

"I love you."

Blinking away a tear, I stroked the back of his head. "I love you, Heri," I whispered. "I love you, too."

~

9PM EST

about the author

Julia is a science fiction writer originally from Trumbull, CT, with a Bachelor's degree from the University of Pennsylvania. She currently works in an administrative position while writing part-time.

Her most popular work on Wattpad, Snow, has garnered nearly a million reads and was shortlisted for the Watty's.

Julia is also a Wattpad Creator and a Wattpad Ambassador. Outside of work and writing, Julia enjoys learning about astronomy, drinking tea, and working on jigsaw puzzles.

THE BREAKUP

by Julia Esposito

HARRISONBURG, VIRGINIA, USA
AUGUST 15, 9:00 PM

Driving down the empty, potholed streets solidified that Joanie and I should have left already.

Every hefty bump in my decade-old sedan sent pain spiking up my spine. My purse sat fully on the dirty car floor of the passenger seat. On the road ahead, the familiar street lamps were dark, bulbs as dead as I should have been.

Why didn't we evacuate with the rest of this cursed town?

The overwhelming brightness of the sky filled my car with golden light, nearly blinding my tearing eyes as I took a right turn at a stop sign. Not that I needed to stop. Too busy manning checkpoints and preventing people from returning, the police had stopped monitoring local traffic as the days had progressed, and the ominous daily counter in the sky ticked down.

The next song blasted out of my radio—a crooning woman singing about a lost love. *"If only he hadn't left you after six yearssss."* Her vibrato filled my ears as she held the final note.

"A bit on the nose, isn't it?" Sydney chimed in from the backseat. Her blonde hair swayed in the rocking car as she leaned into the small opening between the passenger and driver's seats. Her eyes glowed a shocking purple, distracting me from the desolate road ahead.

"Shut up," I snapped, swiping at the salty droplets coursing down my cheeks. I turned up the heat which blasted at my face, drying them instantly.

"What? Don't wanna think about it, about him? Maaasson. Maaasson. He was so lovely," Sydney nagged. "I miss him."

"I said, *shut up*!" I swerved my car, the right side mirror crunched against a tree and broke off, falling onto the road behind me as a honk resonated in the night air.

Had I done that?

I can't do this with you anymore. It's over.

A single text and my life was in shambles. Everything we had built over the past six years. Every last memory from our earliest dates at the port, to the movie nights in our rented house with Joanie, and then the world started ending. What was he going to do now? Move out? Where was he going to go? His family lived two states over.

I turned left at the next intersection, ignoring the blaring red light. Just down the road, the gas station's green neon sign read, "REG $66.78". Good thing I had nowhere to go. Who the hell could afford those prices?

Sydney leaned her elbows on the center console. "Is buying a bunch of shit really going to make you feel better?"

I sniffed. "Yes. Yes, it will."

No. No, it won't.

Nothing could fill the gaping void fracturing my soul. Nothing could remove or hide the undeniable pain his single text had wreaked. Stupid, stupid, stupid. I was such an embarrassment. An ugly, disgusting rat. Why else was it so easy for him to do this to me?

Why else?

I parked my car, and the world shifted. The gas pumps in front of me swirled like a painter twirling a dirty paintbrush through them. Gas spurted out onto the cement, clear liquid leaking everywhere. Oh, how easy it would be to light a match and set everything aflame. Let it all burn to ash like my dreams or the future.

But I liked Glen, I couldn't do that to him.

It took me five minutes to blow my stuffed nose, exit my car, and stumble to the front door of the convenience store. Attempting to push through the glass door, I headbutted it and fell to the ground, sharp pain radiating up my arms from where my palms scraped the ground.

This was all Mason's fault.

Everything was his fault. The flying spaceship. The fifteen days remaining on that glowing blue number in the sky. The fact that Joanie would be stuck in the house with Mason and me. He was probably also the reason I'd stopped getting paid—the reason Gina's Fashion had closed, and my boss had told me there was no point in coming to work the following morning.

My bank account cried every time I swiped my card. I'd been coming here a lot lately. Glen was one of the last remaining store clerks in town, and we still needed to eat.

"Get your stupid butt up. You're wasting time. You need to hurry!" From inside the convenience store, Sydney shouted to me. How'd she get in there so fast?

I shoved to my feet, wiping off my bloody hands on my pajama bottoms. Gross. Blood stained the little designs of sheep dark red. Devilish animals.

"Nice to see ya again!" Glen yelled as I finally shoved my way into the store. "Whatcha you doin' here today, Kaitlyn?" He chirped every word, hands cheerily on his hips. Weird. Usually, he was grumpy.

"Don't worry about it," I slurred as my vision spiraled. Clutching the nearest shelf, I squeezed my eyes shut.

A hand gripped my shoulder. Sydney? After a moment, it disappeared and, finally, I opened my eyes to see the surrounding world stabilized.

Just don't throw up. Don't throw up.

I clawed my way to the freezers near the back of the store.

"Fifty percent off everything today!" Glen calls from his post at the cash register, "Today only!"

The freezer door was unreasonably heavy, but I managed to yank it open before stumbling backwards.

"Oh, come on, you're really that weak?" Sydney taunted.

I ignored her as I grabbed the two nearest pints of chocolate ice cream. Chocolatey swirl with brownie chunks. Clutching both containers to my chest, I turned toward the snack aisle and snatched a bag of M&M's. To my right was a rack of face masks and facial tissues. I grabbed three masks and a jumbo box of tissues, the tower in my arms wobbling.

"That looks expensive. Shouldn't you put some back?" Sydney leaned in behind me, droning on in my ear. Without responding, I continued on towards the front of the store, when suddenly Sydney stood in front of me. One second, behind me; the next, blocking my way to Glen and his register.

I stuck a middle finger in her face and walked past her.

"What do ya got today?" Glen excitedly cleared off the counter, wiping away piles of candy as I dumped the armfuls in front of him. "A lot, I suppose. You know what? We're already doing fifty percent off. Why don't I give ya seventy-five! As a friend, you know?"

I hadn't really considered Glen a friend, but I'd take it. "Okay," I shrugged.

Glen began scanning each item. "Beeep!" his high-pitched drawl echoed in the nearly empty store as he slid them one by one across the lightless counter and into a paper bag.

I eyed the magazines. Bold headlines bragged about massive breakups and whether or not he was cheating. Another read, "Mid-Twenties? Learn how to get back in the game post-break-up!"

I snagged it and added the magazine to the shrinking pile Glen was gradually working his way through.

"Wow, that's dumb," Sydney jeered. "What do you think you're going to learn from those ridiculous articles? How to get Mason back?" Waving her hands in the air, "He doesn't want you! He hates you. Why are you still vying for him?!"

"Shut up!"

Glen jerked his head up from the register, eyeing me suspiciously, "Beeeeep," he continued slowly, dropping the magazine into the bag.

"No, you!" Sydney sneered.

"Please," I muttered, "just stop talking!"

"I'm sorry. Did I upset you?" Glen's eyes seemed a bit glazed as he stared at the empty space beside me.

Where'd Sydney go?

"I'm fine!" I screeched, looking around me. She wasn't in the store or the car. I pointed at a five-dollar scratch-off hanging on the wall behind Glen. "I'll take that, too."

"Alright, Miss Kaitlyn, that will be... Oh! Would you look at that! Only forty-eight cents! Miraculous." He grinned, head tilting from side to side as he waited for me to swipe my card through the darkened card reader.

"Thanks, Glen."

"Before ya go, did you see the light? Did ya? It's amazing! Hank said it's finally coming. The end. It's the end!" Glen bounced on his toes again, giggling and beeping maniacally.

I fled from his frenzied glee with my overflowing bag. The empty car was hot and stuffy. As I shoved the key in the ignition, I cranked the air conditioning to maximum and let it blow in my face.

Sydney was once again in my backseat, and I scowled at her in the mirror. At least she wasn't talking.

I felt the tears sneaking back, the sobs racking my body once more. I heaved out my cries, not even trying to pull myself together.

I didn't want to go home.

Mason may have returned by now, whether to pick up his stuff and go or to berate me. He hadn't called me back. As soon as I'd read his message, I'd left at least five voicemails and a massive string of texts. What started as me telling him he was a horrible person for ending a six-year relationship over text ended in begging him to stay because I'd already planned our wedding.

"Did you actually?" Sydney crooned from the backseat. "You know? Actually plan the wedding?" She lay on her back, feet against the passenger side window.

"No," I admitted.

I checked my phone again.

Joanie had called five minutes ago, so I checked my text messages.

Joanie: Where are you??

Ugh. Couldn't she just leave me alone? Didn't she know I was going through something?

No, she did not.

Me: Don't worry about it. Went to get food.

Joanie: What kind of food? Can you get me a Sprite? Please? Pretty pretty please?

I scoffed and put my phone down. She had a car, too! She could go herself.

A few coins sat in the drink holder by the car radio. A small, dirty penny caught my eye. As Sydney leaned over my shoulder, I scraped the light covering on the scratch-off I'd bought, revealing…

Nothing.

"Argh!!" I shrieked and slammed my forehead into the car horn. It blared into the lit-up night, a cacophony disrupting the lonely gas station's peace.

"Oh, calm down, you idiot! Nobody cares that you lost." Sydney crossed her arms and pressed her forehead against the car window, leaving behind an oil mark.

Revving the engine, I cranked the music up so loud I could no longer hear Sydney. I was about to peel out when I remembered the magazine. Right. I wanted to read it.

The brightly colored cover jumped out at me as I pulled it from my bag. *Page 38. How to Get Through a Breakup.* Stupid, stupid, stupid. Useless advice. "Try to take deep breaths," it read. No. I didn't care. "Try and find a new hobby." Boring. "Find someone else to help with your burning passion."

Hmph.

Burning passion.

Burning.

Sydney appeared and tore the magazine from my grasp. Her eyes, a bright orangey-red, stared deep into my soul. "Get over yourself! Drive. Go home! Go! Go!"

She chucked the magazine onto the passenger seat.

She was right.

I had work to do.

The whole ride home loud music shook the car, and my eardrums rang. The singer wailed about how her lover had abandoned her on a date at a restaurant. How it had happened so quickly with almost no reason. How she was going to cry until her very last days of living.

Unlike her, I was finished bawling my eyes out.

I had different plans now.

Joanie's car wasn't at home. I struggled to put the pieces together; she worked at the coffee shop every other day? Maybe she was at work?

My car hit the trash can as I sped into the driveway. The house was small, a two-bedroom, one bathroom, and cheap enough for Mason, Joanie, and I to split three ways. Joanie had added a few tweaks here and there: painted the mailbox pastel pink, giant wooden letters spelling out "home" hung by the entrance with our house number, thirty-five, accentuated in gold.

I flung open my car door, rushed inside, and dumped my groceries on the kitchen counter.

Right there. The drawer.

Wrenching it open, that's what I needed.

A match.

Isopropyl alcohol.

Taking the stairs two at a time, Sydney's hurried steps followed me to the room Mason and I shared.

I bee-lined the top drawer of the dresser.

On one side were bursting piles of my underwear and his boxers. On the other, a small lockbox with gilded silver edges. I popped it open to reveal various tokens and memories I had not thought about in years.

A handful of Polaroid photos.

The dried rose I'd given him on our second date.

An empty Sprite bottle from the time we went to a movie premiere for a sequel to the one movie he actually liked, but I couldn't remember the name of either one.

A set of dice from the board game cafe we visited in the city on a spontaneous day trip.

I scooped up as much as I could possibly carry, shoving the smaller things into my pockets until they overflowed. My muscles strained as I stumbled down the stairs, my heart racing.

Breath rasping, my nose ran from the harsh, heavy sobs that escaped me with every step.

In the kitchen, I passed Sydney, conspicuously quiet, and grabbed Mason's winter coat from the closet. I'd bought it for him as a gift—the most expensive gift I'd ever given anyone.

Now, the most expensive thing I'd ever destroy.

Expertly, I crafted a circular heap at the top of the driveway, piled high with Mason's stuff and my memories of our happiness. I ran back up the stairs and made a second trip, grabbing everything that I hadn't been able to carry the first time around. Sydney watched in wicked amusement as the hill I was building grew higher and higher.

"Burn it! Burn it, Kate! Burn it!" Sydney squealed as I doused everything until the entire bottle emptied onto the paved ground.

The discordance of the broken-hearted radio song, Sydney screaming with wild excitement, and the hum of the spaceship above all blasted inside my head.

But the moment I held the match in the air, it all disappeared.

Silence.

Blissful, wonderful silence. If only for an instant.

The lit match fell, and my world blew with it.

In a blinding, fiery burst, the pile caught flame. The contrast of the orange hot heat with the weird alien glow surrounding me only added to the impact of the explosion and I jumped backward to avoid being consumed by the ravenous beast. An incendiary wave scorched against my face, and I slammed my eyes shut as it dried my tears and my muscles shook.

Standing for a moment, I let the satisfaction of heat and anger radiate across my body.

"What the hell?!"

Mason?

Wailing?

Slowly opening my eyes, the light from the ship had disappeared, every last bit of it. The darkness of the spaceship hovered above me, the fire now a burning sun in front of me.

And there was Mason.

On his knees, hands bleeding as he bent over, his car was parked haphazardly, sporting a massive dent on the front right side.

I sneered. "This is what you wanted, right? Break up?" My face contorted into a toothy grin. "Pretend six years never happened?!"

"Six years?" Mason screamed through the dancing flames. "What are you talking about?" Tears glistened on his face as he looked between me and the flames. "You did this?" He shook his head as if to shake off all the pain.

"You texted me. Broke up with me!" I snarled.

The sound of the crackling flames roared loudly between us and I turned to Sydney for support, but she was nowhere to be found.

She should be backing me up. Where did she go? Why did she leave me?

"Texted? I can't text you! And my phone finally died this morning, I told you that." His last words came out as a hopeless screech.

Fine. He was playing dumb.

I whipped out my phone, ready to swipe through the myriad of ranting texts I'd sent about how much he sucked.

Me begging him to come back to me.

But…

My screen was black and cracked down the middle.

And suddenly I remembered breaking it a week ago, around the same time electricity and internet had become restricted within the shadows of the ship.

There was nothing.

Nothing.

No texts from Joanie, either; she was already gone.

It was me who hadn't left, stubbornly holding out hope this would all end. And Mason who had foolishly stayed behind with me.

I gazed across the fire at Mason, tears streaming down his face. The fire burned in front of me, heat billowing in toward me, but the heat also assailed me from behind, blowing my shirt forward.

No.

No, no, no.

I turned around.

Everything was aflame. The white painted windowsill. The "h" in the word "home", the other letters soon to burn.

And above me, where the blinding light from the ship had been, the hope everyone had clung to since it had appeared this morning, had again darkened to endless midnight.

Highlighting the hellish glow of my former home.

I fell to my knees on the blistering pavement, not caring as it scorched my palms.

"It's over, Kate. It's over."

~

15

about the author

***Cardin Watts** is an editor who dabbles in writing every single genre under the sun (except high fantasy, never that). While his works fall all over the genre spectrum, the one constant through their stories is determination to seeing the world from a distinctly unique lens, and making his readers feel emotions they never expected.*

His paranormal novella HOUSE GHOST received the Longlister award in the 2022 Open Novella Contest.

When they're not writing, you can find Cardin nose-deep in books at the nearest library or gleaning inspiration from youtube letsplays for free worldbuilding aesthetics.

THE REPORTER

by Cardin Watts

STAUNTON, VIRGINIA, USA
AUGUST 16, 5:50 PM

> *"...As far as we know, circumstances haven't changed. Scientists are still speculating as to the cause of the mysterious artificial light that emanated from the spacecraft for eighteen hours yesterday, but first studies have shown no effects of radiation from the light or of any similar fallout. It was a pleasant surprise to be able to wear a tee shirt in the middle of summer… at least for a day." The reporter shifted in his winter coat and laughed. "But it seems we're back to our regularly scheduled weather in the Midnight Zone. Hopefully, we'll find out soon if the light plans to open up again, or if this was a one-time event. In the meantime, stay safe, stay together, and stay tuned. This is Gary Garcia with CNN."*

The red light blinked off, and the cameraman motioned from behind the camera.

"Great job, Gary. See you in thirty."

"Thanks, Chadwick." Gary gave him a weak smile and clapped him on the shoulder as he walked past into the base camp, tugging his coat closer around himself. Everywhere people scurried about, bundled in winter clothes on a summer day, each set on their path.

Looming above it all, in the darkness, was the number 15. It was at least a mile wide, a glowing blue number projected into the air under the looming darkness.

To Gary, the strangest part of it all was how quickly they'd all settled into the situation.

With a scowl, he passed the sleek elevator with several large "OUT OF ORDER" signs pasted on it and headed for the stairs. He cursed fate for making the elevator go out of order three days ago and lightly kicked the "wet floor" sign placed in front of the closed doors for good measure. Gary paused in front of the stairwell, bracing himself for the grueling climb of twelve sets of stairs ahead of him. When he reached for the handle, however, the door swung open. Another reporter stood in front of him, panting heavily. Martha Banks, an elderly black woman usually assigned the morning recaps, dragged a suitcase with one hand and carried another over her shoulder.

"Martha, are you okay?" Gary took one bag before she could protest. "How far did you bring that stuff down?"

"Oh, aren't you a sweetheart—just from level five," she huffed, letting him carry the suitcase forward a few feet before taking it back. "I'll be alright. Thank you, son."

"What are you doing with all this?" he asked.

Martha shrugged, adjusting the duffel bag on her shoulder.

"I'm leaving. Going to my grandchildren in Nevada."

Gary shifted awkwardly in his boots. "You're leaving, too?"

"After that gravity shift this morning? That light show yesterday must have done something to the area, and I don't want to stick around to find out what."

"It was only for a few seconds—"

"It was a *gravity anomaly*, Gary! Everything floated two feet off the ground. I'm an old woman. I can't take a knocking if this ship decides to disobey Newton's law at random times." She considered him for a moment. "You should leave, too."

Gary shook his head. "We don't know what the numbers in the sky *mean*. We have to just focus on the facts. This is the story of a lifetime—I'm not going to throw that away out of paranoia."

"There's been a two thousand-mile-wide object hovering above us for two weeks and you don't think the world is ending?" she scoffed gently. "Gary, you're a good reporter. You've always thrown yourself into danger to get the inside story, but this is too much. The situation is dire, son, and what happened yesterday has got everybody panicking even more."

"If we all leave, how will the world know what's happening? We're the only source of unbiased information in this situation, one that won't be encouraging fearmongering or panic."

Martha gave him a withering look that made him feel like an idiot. She had always been good at that.

"Do you have a child, Gary?"

He nodded, "A daughter, Sofia."

"How old is she?"

"Her birthday was last month; she just turned six."

Martha hesitated, then clapped a bony brown hand on his shoulder. "I'm not going to try to change your mind, Gary. I just hope you think of your family before it's too late."

"No doubt they are coming down to finish us off," I said, hunching my shoulders and wrapping my arms around my middle. "I doubt they'll blow us up. You were right, Camilla. They want the planet if they're clearing the air and disappearing things. Not only that, but we also have to run from other humans. We must hide."

How long would we be able to hide?

And what about when they found us?

We were going to have to move, to try to escape down south. I wanted our mom, dad... But I had my sisters. I took a slow breath, forcing myself to sit upright. I was going to be strong for them.

We were going to survive, no matter what.

Fear might have paralyzed me initially, but I'd helped that girl escape. Who knew what I was capable of? I'd fight for my life and theirs when the time came.

I met the gaze of my two sisters. "We'll wait for the creepy sky countdown to end and get ready to fight if necessary."

And together, we entered a path deeper into the dense forest.

~

10

about the author

Debra Goelz *(BrittanieCharmintine) is a refugee from Hollywood where she served as a financial executive for companies like Jim Henson Productions and Universal Studios.*

After garnering over 13 million online reads on Wattpad, her YA fantasy MERMAIDS AND THE VAMPIRES WHO LOVE THEM, was published by Hachette Audio and released as a Chapters game.

She lives in a magical redwood forest in rural Marin County and believes mermaids frolic nightly in her pond.

THE GRANNY VS THE MOTHERSHIP

by Debra Goelz

BLUE RIDGE MOUNTAINS, NORTH CAROLINA, USA
AUGUST 21, 4:00 PM

"Dagnabbit! Those sons of a bee sting are still there!"

The cabin door slammed in her wake, as Henrietta Bowman marched outside toting her shotgun, fed up with that damned monstrosity in the sky. Thing had to be filled to the brim with Federals fixin' to cart her off to one of those nursing homes. No one was going to inject *her* with mind-controlling drugs and turn her into a drooling zombie. Her grandson, who was always on her about livin' alone, was behind the whole thing, she was certain. There ain't nothin' worse than bein' betrayed by your own kin.

"You'll never take me alive, dammit!" She shook her fist at the metallic eyesore. "You hearin' me?"

She hesitated, waiting a breath for it to move off in surrender, but all she heard was the whistling of the wind through the trees. The interloper didn't budge one iota. Same as the past three-and-a-half-weeks, the circles of light on the black hull just blinked at her in some government code. That contraption up there was near as big as an oil spill across Alabama, and it swallowed up the sky. Twenty-six days without the sun or the stars! Her vegetable garden was sulking almost as bad as she was. And the critters were damned near as discombobulated as the plants, with owls hooting at noon and robins hunting at midnight.

For days she'd yelled at those trespassers till her throat was hoarse. She even tried shining her flashlight at 'em in Morse code, demanding they get the hell off her property, but they stayed as closed up as a coffin. Lord knows, sometimes, the only way to get your point across is with the business end of a shotgun.

Still, Henrietta planned on goin' to heaven when the Almighty took her, so she'd offer them Federals one last chance. "I'll shoot," she warned. "You'd better be flyin' south for the winter now."

She hadn't expected a reply, and she didn't get one. Some people think they don't need to pay you no mind if yer eighty-seven, but a shotgun is the Lord's equalizer. No matter how old you are, it works just as good.

Before firing, for good luck, Henrietta spat into a clump of brush, then squinted, pointing the barrel toward the underbelly of the aeroplane. At least it was a big target. No way could she miss, even being halfway blind.

Henrietta started to squeeze the trigger, when a large black jumble of feathers streaked across the sky, inches from her face.

"Arrgghh!" she cried, her old heart racing. She dropped the shotgun and windmilled her arms. Despite her efforts, she fell backward on her nether cheeks, and with such a bony keister, it smarted all to hell. "Ol' Chester, what you think you're doin', you bird brain? I could've shot you dead."

"Caw," Ol' Chester the crow said, landing on one of the rusty old antennas in the field that had been left behind by Chester, her ex, Ol' Chester's namesake. (Ol' Chester was his name because he reminded Henrietta of her ex due to his uncommunicative nature, not because he introduced himself that way). The only thing Chester ever planted was that damned antenna farm, just so he could talk to strangers on his HAM radio. Maybe the crow wasn't much of a conversationalist, but he was a better listener than the human Chester.

Oh, sure, her ex loved talking on that damned HAM radio like he was some lawman, but he didn't talk to her except when he made her sit there and listen as he talked her ear off about how the damned thing worked. For years she let him ramble on about ranges and repeaters and doohickeys and thingamabobs, but she had her limits, and eventually, whenever he brought up the subject, Henrietta's anger would flare, and she'd picture him six feet under with only a headstone to yak at.

"Caw yourself," Henrietta spat. "And no more sneaking up on me. Damn near gave me a heart attack!" She stood, brushing dirt and dried grasses off her tattered housedress. "Now shush yourself."

"Caw!"

"What about the word 'shush' ain't clear to you?"

"Caw caw."

She bit off a smile. That was another thing Ol' Chester had on his namesake—a better sense of humor. "You're just messin' with me now," she said, retrieving the shotgun, and getting in firing position. She held her breath and squeezed the trigger, bracing herself for the satisfying CHOOM!

But all she got was a disappointing click!

"Doggonnit!" She spat again, kicking at the dirt. She'd forgotten to clean the damned gun.

"Caw."

"Now yer just rubbin' it in," Henrietta said.

***

Those Federals wasn't going noplace fast, so Henrietta decided to take her sweet time cleaning her shotgun till it was good and done, rocking back and forth in her creaky old chair on her creaky old porch while Ol' Chester swooped onto the rail, his talons click click clicking on the wood. Immediately, he turned his attention to the peanuts she'd put out for him.

Peck, peck, peck.

"Sometimes I wonder if yer here for the nuts or for the nut," Henrietta teased.

"Caw." Peck, peck, peck.

"Thought so," Henrietta replied.

Henrietta emptied the barrel of the chamber and the magazine before grabbing the bore cleaner and drizzling some on the floss end of the boresnake. She sniffled at the kerosene smell, then ran the snake through the barrel. She'd cleaned her shotgun so many times over the years, she could've done it in her sleep.

Anger stung in Henrietta's gut like a sewing basket full of wasps. She ought to've known better than to let her shotgun go to all hell. Guns needed as much tending as a garden. You had to make sure when an intruder came, you were ready to clear them out.

"Caw." Ol' Chester jumped closer to the sack where she kept her supply of nuts.

"No more for you. You got to maintain your youthful figure if you're ever gonna attract a new honey," Henrietta said. Since Ol' Chester's mate had died last winter, he and Henrietta were both unattached. She made it her business to educate Ol' Chester and keep him company as she had a lot more experience with bein' alone. The real Chester flew the coop, leavin' her standin' on this very porch near thirty years ago now. Probably found himself someone else to do his laundry, cook his meals, and listen to him rambling. Bless her heart.

Good riddance, Henrietta liked to say.

Though sometimes in the cold of night, she remembered his big body lying beside hers, heating the sheets like a human bed warmer. When she shivered, he'd scoop her up in his arms and tell her, "Shimmy on over, darlin', I got enough heat for the pair of us."

"Caw."

Henrietta sniffed. "It's never too late when yer a crow. Plenty of birds in the sky, 'cept right now with that government monstrosity up there messin' with mother nature. Satisfied the shotgun was clean as a hound's tooth, she slowly hoisted herself out of the rocker, bones creaking and popping with the effort. "How's about we convince these hooligans and their flashy flying machine to move along?"

Ol' Chester cawed enthusiastically, kindred spirit that he was, and flew up to the rafters. "Caw, caw, caw."

"No way. I ain't going up on that roof."

"Caw, caw."

"Don't see hows it makes any difference a few feet closer."

"Caw!!!"

"Fine. We'll do it your way," she said, knowing the bird was right. Every little bit helped when you were communicatin' via shotgun.

She rolled some boxes of ammo in the hem of her housedress, then tucked her housedress into her panties, and slung the strap of her shotgun over her head. The strap crossed her chest, and the gun tugged up tightly against her back.

She climbed the rickety old ladder to the roof slower than usual, holding on so tight, the splintered wood bit into her wrinkled palms. The ladder wobbled with each step; the base rotted out from neglect. Her heart kicked like a steel-tipped boot against her chest. She should've found the time to build a new ladder, but that used to be Chester's job, and she hadn't felt much like it. Instead, he left her with a broken-down ladder and a broken-down heart. A rotten ladder was better than no ladder, so she climbed. Slowly. Old lady sweat, as acrid as mothballs, sprung to her brow and her dress clung to her back.

Ol' Chester was on the roof peak, hopping from foot to foot when she heaved herself over the edge, a huffing and a puffing. "Stop yer crowing, young man. You cheated with them there wings."

"Caw."

"Whatever makes you sleep at night," Henrietta said. "Criminy, this roof! I ought to've brought a broom!" It was covered edge to edge with spiderwebs, bird droppings, and dried out pine needles, thick as fleas on a farm dog. Still, there was a job to be done, so Henrietta lowered her bony behind onto the roof ridge and swung the gun back around front to load her up.

Once in shooting position, Henrietta aimed straight at that eerie blue "10" glowing at her from the center, racked the gun, and gave the intruders one last warning. "Git now," she said, "or I'll shoot." Knowing they'd ignore her, this time she just squeezed the trigger.

CHOOM! Pressure built in her ears, then for a moment, the world was as silent as a buzzard's supper.

Ol' Chester squawked and swooped off the roof. But the aeroplane? She didn't budge. Just sat there, looming like usual, not caring one bit about being shot at.

Although Henrietta couldn't tell if the slugs had hit their mark, she fired again and again, till the shotgun emptied, then she reloaded and kept at it till her butt ached, her back ached, her arms ached, and her belly ached.

Turned out tryin' to down a giant aeroplane with a shotgun was as useful as hollerin' down a well. Granny knew she was beat. Time to fire up some grub and figure up another plan.

***

Inside the cabin, light from the fireplace flickering against the smoke-blackened walls, Granny lifted the bowl to her mouth and slurped up the last of her soup. She offered a soggy carrot to Ol' Chester, who gobbled it up and flew to the mantel over the fireplace, jostling an old black-and-white photo of human Chester and Henrietta on their weddin' day. She kept the picture there, propped up against a taxidermy squirrel, as a reminder.

Of what, she wasn't sure anymore.

That she was once young with skin as smooth as boomtown silk?

That men were all cheaters who turned your life into a sorrowful country tune?

Or that maybe once someone had loved her?

It was that last one that bothered her the most. But that was a lifetime ago, and now she had bigger devils to send back to hell.

"Ol' Chester, you got any ideas?"

Ol' Chester only said, "Caw," then flew back to the table to see if there might be more scraps. She broke off a crust of bread, and he took it happily. Birds were way easier to please than men. Once he was sure there'd be nothing else comin' his way, Chester relocated to the opposite end of the cabin and perched himself atop Chester's old HAM radio.

Lord knew why he'd left it.

Henrietta slapped the table. "Well, ain't I as dumb as a box of rocks! Of course! I'll get those g-men on the horn and tell them what's what."

She blew off the thick layer of dust, and sneezed, housekeeping not being her forte. Silently, she thanked Chester for his endless ramblings about HAM radios and his logbook where his call sign and frequencies were written in the perfect penmanship of a schoolboy trained by nuns. Also, she spared a moment of gratitude for her keen memory when it came to anything prior to 1998. With the logbook on one side of the table and a tall whiskey on the other, Henrietta went to work bringing the old thing back to life.

She flipped a switch on the old transceiver. The tubes took a good five minutes to heat up, but then she heard distorted high-pitched voices yammering on like Alvin and the Chipmunks, about what she had no idea. Suddenly, the voices settled into something more humanlike. As she dialed into different frequencies, the chatter was all pretty similar:

"Does the military have a plan for alien invasions?"

"I wonder if they have tentacles?"

"I hope they have tentacles!"

"I hope them aliens beam me up!"

"They'll definitely beam you up, Arthur!"

Bunch of crazies talkin' about aliens. Henrietta dialed into a less busy frequency and pressed the button on the microphone. "C.Q. C.Q. CQ. This is WA4UDS," she said, using Chester's call sign. "Calling the Federals on that aeroplane. You'll never take me alive," Henrietta said, because this was the main point she wanted to get across.

No one replied. Crafty suckers, them Federals. They could probably hear her, but just in case they couldn't, she tried a different frequency. Henrietta cycled through, making her threat over and over.

For old time's sake, she dialed in on Chester's favorite frequency, and finally a voice answered, clear as mud, "Hensheets?" Adjusting the dial, the static cleared slightly.

"What's a damned hen sheet? Who is this?" she demanded.

"Henrietta?" the voice crackled through.

A snarl grew in her throat. They knew her name. She was right! They were after her. "I'm armed and dangerous. You better take your giant aeroplane and stick it up your—"

"Darlin'?" the voice interrupted.

A cold prickle went up her spine. She knew that voice. Holy Mother of God! "Chester? They got you?"

"What you talking about, woman?" Chester said.

"The Feds? You're up in that big aeroplane?"

"I'm in my cabin. Only two hoots and a holler away. You gone crazy? You think them aliens abducted me? I'm sure they'd find fitter humans to probe than me," Chester said.

"Aliens?" she spat. "No such thing. They're government agents come to take me to that home our grandson picked out for me."

"No one is taking you to no home," Chester said.

"How do you know? Did they tell you that?"

"Did who tell me?"

"The Feds."

"Caw," Ol' Chester interrupted.

"Shush now," Henrietta said.

"Someone there with you?" Chester said. There was an odd tone to the man's question. Like jealousy?

"Just Ol' Chester," Henrietta replied.

"You got another man named Chester?"

"Hell, no! Ol' Chester's a crow. And far better at talkin' than you ever were." It finally occurred to Henrietta that she wasn't quite used to speaking with humans after mostly talking to crows and squirrels and occasionally her plants when they weren't growin' right. And not just any human, but Chester, who never talked to anyone unless he was on this damned HAM radio.

Figured!

"You okay, darlin'? Those aliens didn't mind control you, did they?"

"No one's mind controlling me," Henrietta said, stomping her foot. She'd forgotten how damned frustrating this man was. "Where'd you come up with this alien obsession?" The line crackled, and she adjusted the dial a hair.

"You think human beings built up a ship that's two-thousand miles long?"

"How do you know how big it is?"

"I got the interweb."

The man was talking nonsense. "The interwhat?"

"The news. Look, darlin', I reckon we're livin' on borrowed time. Maybe we ought to stop arguin' and start—"

"Start what?"

"The making up part."

She remembered their "making up" interludes from long ago, and it was like lightning struck her lady parts, waking 'em up from a long winter's nap. "You think after thirty years you're gonna waltz back on into my life without even a how-de-do?"

"I'm hoping there'll be a lot of how-de-doing," he said. She could hear the smirk.

"We're near ninety years old, mister. And don't you got yourself a new woman?"

"Been no one but you, darlin'."

Against her better judgment, Henrietta's heart twisted. Such a traitorous organ. "Then why'd you leave?"

"You threw me out. Said I loved my HAM radio more than you."

"That's not how I remember it. But still, you didn't have to go just 'cause I said so."

"You had a shotgun pointed at my head."

"Does sound like me," Henrietta agreed, nodding her head.

"Caw."

"Shush, bird. I don't need the two of you teamin' up."

"Sounds like a smart bird," Chester said. "Besides, I left the HAM so you could call me back. Been waiting thirty years, and I'm not waiting a second longer. I'm headin' over."

"No, you ain't," Henrietta said. "I don't need protectin'. I got my shotgun all cleaned and ready to go."

"But *I* need protectin'. The news says this is an emergency, and I'm runnin' scared. This could be the end."

"We're old as mud. Any day could be the end."

"All the more reason to let bygones be gone."

"You come on over then," Henrietta said, eying the shotgun gleaming in the firelight, and she winked at the crow.

"I'm heading to my truck," Chester replied. "Over and out."

"Well, damn," Henrietta said to Ol' Chester. "Now alls I have to do is figure out whether to load up the shotgun again or put on another pot of soup."

She stood, bones complaining with a series of cracks, and massaged the small of her back. That old picture fluttered to the floor. She bent over, knees aching, scooped it up, and set it back in the squirrel's paws. Then she looked out the window to where the stars were supposed to be, held up her saggy arms and shouted, "Thank y'all! But now, git! I got company coming!"

Then she headed for the vegetable basket, plucked out a carrot and started chopping, a faint smile playing on her face.

~

09

about the author

Van Carley *is a co-founder of WritersConnx, and is part of Wattpad writer programs, such as Creators, Paid, and formerly Stars.*

When writing, she enjoys the freedom of bouncing between genres or mashing them together. She's best known for writing morally grey characters in chaotic settings and loves anti-heroes.

When Van isn't reading, writing, or hanging out with writer-friends on Discord, she is binging Netflix with the fam or floating on the lake.

THE DETECTIVE

by Van Carley

MEXICO CITY, MEXICO
AUGUST 22, 10:00 AM

It started with a dead body, and the number *thirty* burned into the victim's forehead.

Murder wasn't unheard of in Detective Mateo Moreno's line of work, but this was different. There didn't seem to be a rhyme or reason connecting the murders, other than the numbers, and by day five, when a fifth victim turned up with a burn, he knew a serial killer was prowling his beloved metropolis of Mexico City.

Now, it was day twenty-two, which meant another body was bound to show up. Yet, it felt like he and his partner were the only ones taking it seriously. He stood at his window, scratching the overgrown stubble on his chin while staring into the yellow haze of smog tainting the sky. While he couldn't prove it, the rapid influx of deaths had to be connected to the UFO's countdown, and there would be more if he didn't find the culprit soon.

Today had to be the day.

"Mateo." Detective Lola Espinoza knocked and stepped into his office. "They found another one."

His shoulders sagged at her words. With his palms braced against the windowsill, he blew out a breath. "Where?"

"Atras del catedral."

Of all the places to find a dead body, behind a church was the last place he would've guessed. Yesterday, one was found in a municipal bathroom at the train station and the day before in a dumpster at a construction site.

What would it be tomorrow?

"Joder!" Mateo cursed and rubbed his temples. "I refuse to have another body turn up on our watch. We have to find the killer today."

"And we will."

A migraine was on the precipice of taking a royal dump on his day, so he reached for the pain medication in his desk and tossed back a few pills. Lola watched with a clenched jaw.

"Que?" he growled.

"I'm worried about you."

"Well, stop."

"That UFO has brought out the worst in you. Look at you. You haven't shaved in days, your morning cup of coffee has turned into five, *and* you've started smoking again."

"So?"

"You've been nicotine free for ten years, and don't get me started with your temper."

"In case you haven't noticed, Lola, a serial killer is running around Mexico City."

"Oh, I know." But before she continued, she glanced over her shoulder, causing the eavesdroppers to dart their gazes and return to work. With a huff, she closed the office door and glared at Mateo. "You don't sleep. I wake up at night and find you in the living room going over autopsy reports. You're falling apart."

"Then maybe I should go back to sleeping at *my* place."

It was a low blow. Mateo knew this, but he couldn't take it back. However, Lola wasn't one to submit.

"Yeah, maybe you should. Then your wife will stop asking questions. Besides, I think it's time we cut things off, don't you?"

"Lola, I didn't mean—"

"Uh, huh. Now, how about you gulp down your billionth coffee, so we can get going?"

But she didn't wait for him to reply. Instead, she flung the office door open and walked out with hips swaying.

"Lola, wait. I need to grab my gun."

"Make it snappy!" she shouted.

And despite the many amused gazes flashing back and forth between them, Mateo couldn't help but grin.

Let the gossipers gossip.

***

The blinding sun shone onto the brick-paved piazza, where citizens loitered to watch news updates about the spaceship. Since the arrival of the UFO, most had abandoned going to work, and teenagers ran wild in the streets with alien masks, not giving a damn about school. If that wasn't bad enough, now vendors at the farmer's market were encouraging pandemonium by selling alien trinkets. So when one waved a mask in Mateo and Lola's faces, he tore it out of the man's hand and tossed it on the ground.

"Why don't you all go home?! There's a killer on the loose," he yelled, but everyone stared as if he were crazy.

"Disculpa," Lola apologized to the vendor and dragged Mateo away while scolding him. "You can't do that. Do you want everyone to panic?"

"These people piss me off. And yes, they should be terrified. Not marveling over little green men," he growled.

The latest craze was scammers claiming they had items from the Midnight Zone that contained mystical alien powers, and tourists who couldn't get back home would buy the crap. In fact, everyone was spending money as if these were their last days on Earth.

They were too occupied with extraterrestrials to care about being the killer's next victim.

Then again, how could Mateo expect anyone to take the murders seriously when even the Mayor had refused his request for a citywide lockdown? Instead, he issued a nine PM curfew, which was proving to be useless.

When they arrived at the scene, the cathedral was taped off, and a small crowd stood on tip-toes, craning their necks to catch a glimpse of what was happening. The susurrus of another body being found floated in the air like the buzzing bees, but this wasn't a playground, so Mateo shoved through them, shouting to disperse.

"Largansen!"

"Inspectores." A police officer held open the yellow tape and motioned for them to cross.

"Take us to the victim," Mateo ordered.

"Right this way."

They strode around the back of the cathedral toward the garden where rose bushes bordered a path. The coroner and forensic team were already there and dressed in white coveralls, snapping photos, while others took samples. There, amongst the thorns, was the body. Mateo took a deep breath and pushed aside a few roses to inspect the young man's face.

"Nueve…" he sighed deeply. Just like he feared, the number nine was etched into the victim's forehead.

"Tiene la misma marca?" Lola peered over his shoulder and scribbled into her notepad.

"Yes, the same mark as the others." He nodded. "Dr. Hernandez, what time would you say the victim died?"

The coroner glanced up from her note-taking and teetered her hand. "Media noche."

"You sure?" Mateo rubbed his beard.

"I'll know for certain once I get the body to my lab, but at the moment, my findings point to around midnight."

"Hm…"

"What is it?" Dr. Hernandez asked.

"It's just the times of these deaths are never around the same hour. There is no pattern here."

"Yes, I noticed the same, but you and Detective Espinoza are the best at what you do. I have full confidence you'll find this sicko soon."

"What about this?" Lola grabbed the backpack laying next to the body and removed a student ID card. According to the information, the young man was a nineteen-year-old student at the local university. "Esteban Cruz."

"Que dijiste?" Mateo whipped around and snatched the student ID card from Lola. With wide eyes, he reread the name and cursed, "Mierda."

"What?" Lola furrowed her brows.

"His father is running for twenty-twenty-four Mayor. He's the competition."

Now Lola's eyes widened. "Oh…"

"This has to be more than coincidence. Someone has a vendetta."

"Then we should go talk to the Mayor. See what he has to say. As far as I'm concerned, he's now our suspect."

"Agreed. Let's finish up here."

***

Mayor Zaragoza's hillside home with city views was the epitome of wealth, a far cry from his origins of a barrio with dirt roads and little shacks on the U.S border. When Mateo and Lola arrived, a maid dressed in the traditional black and white uniform opened the door. She escorted them across the Italian terrazzo floor and through the wall-to-wall sliding glass overlooking the expansive backyard. Mrs. Zaragoza was doing laps in the infinity pool with her bleached blonde hair tucked inside a swimming cap, while Mayor Zaragoza paced the edge of the lush green lawn, wearing loafers, white skinny pants, and a silk Versace shirt that revealed his hairy pecs.

He reeked of arrogance.

"Que ridículo," Lola said under her breath. "He thinks he's so sexy."

"Shh…" Mateo elbowed her.

Mayor Zaragoza whipped around with a cell phone pressed to his ear, muttered a goodbye, then stretched out his arms to greet them. "Inspectores. Bienvenidos a mi casa."

"Yes, thank you." Mateo shook his hand. "We've come to inform you that another body was found."

"Ah, yes. I just heard the unfortunate news." He motioned for them to follow him to the poolside cantina, where a worker mixed up drinks. "Would you like a cantaloupe cooler?"

"Sure, I'll have one." Lola reached out, then pointed at the news broadcast on the flatscreen TV above the bar. "Now what's happening?"

"It's the great bug migration!" the Mayor chuckled. "Every critter you can think of is moving away from the spacecraft in droves, but it's not only up north. I saw a video yesterday from East India, where there are so many locusts that they block out the sun. And southern Europe is getting invaded by cicadas. Can you imagine all that hissing they make? It would drive me crazy. But don't think we're lucky. Monarch butterflies are suddenly migrating this way."

"Why is that awful? Butterflies are beautiful," Lola said.

"Because it's swarms of them! There are so many, it looks like bats in the sky."

Mateo gripped the sides of his seat. "Well, it's still nothing to worry about."

"But it's not autumn, yet," the Mayor continued. "It's too early to start their migration to Mexico. This could mess up the ecosystem."

"Still, we have bigger worries. Like a serial killer, which is why we are here," Mateo huffed.

"Oh, no, dear Inspector. Our biggest worry is what'll happen when that UFO runs out of numbers."

"And in the meantime, you want us to sit back while a killer runs the streets, murdering our people?"

"If these are our last days, then let everyone enjoy them." The Mayor wagged his finger. "This is why I refused a citywide lockdown. No one should spend their last breaths stuck inside."

Mateo glanced around the well-manicured yard and smirked. What a damn hypocrite. Gardeners wiped the sweat from their sun-drenched foreheads, and somewhere inside, the maid was running the vacuum. Sure, everyone should enjoy their final days, but not his employees. No, they were still expected to keep his house pristine.

"Que pasa, mi amor?" Mrs. Zaragoza approached, a towel around her waist as she shook out her bleached blonde hair from the swim cap.

"Los Inspectores have come to give us the news about Esteban Cruz."

"What about him?" she turned to the bartender and ordered a daiquiri.

"He was found *murdered* this morning," Lola said.

"What?"

"With the number *nine* burned into his forehead."

"Dios mio…"

Tears stung Mrs. Zaragoza's eyes, so she turn away fluffing her hair with a sneaky swipe of her cheeks. She seemed to be taking the news a lot harder than the Mayor, but Mateo would scratch that curiosity later.

"Mayor Zaragoza, where were you last night around midnight?" he asked.

"*Me*? I was here."

"Sleeping?"

"No, he was up late," Mrs. Zaragoza said, which caused the Mayor to force out a laugh.

"Sí, mi amor. Because I was doing a late-night workout in our gym."

"Where is your gym?" Lola asked.

"Next to the pool house."

"I see." Lola jotted down notes. "And can anyone else attest to you being here?"

"Just talk to Fernando, my trainer. He'll confirm it."

"Your trainer provides workout sessions late at night?"

"Well, I do pay him ten grand a month to be at my beck and call, so yes."

"Noted."

"Wait a damn minute…" The Mayor held up his hand. "Am I a suspect?"

"Esteban Cruz is your competitor's son, is he not?" Mateo asked.

"So? When the countdown hits zero, it won't matter who runs for Mayor next year."

"Ah, but if nothing happens, then murdering Esteban to weaken your opponent wouldn't be out of the question."

The Mayor's mouth formed a tight line as he sucked a breath of disgust through his teeth, and if he had been an animal, his fangs would've been showing. "Get out of my house. This meeting is *over*."

"Fine." Mateo got in his face. "But I'm telling you right now, if you're the serial killer, I will be back here so fast to slap handcuffs on your wrists. You might be mayor, but this is *my* city."

"Let's go." Lola gripped his elbow, but neither man budged as they locked gazes. "Ándale, Mateo! Let's go."

Finally, Mateo dropped their ego-filled pissing contest and exited the mansion. This was the closest lead they had to finding the killer, and deep in his gut, he knew they would be back.

"Did you see how Mrs. Zaragoza reacted to the news of Esteban?" Lola said as they climbed into their car.

"I did."

"What do you think is going on there?"

"Well, based on the telenovelas my mother watches, my guess is Mrs. Zaragoza was having a torrid affair with Esteban Cruz."

"But he was only nineteen years old. Just a boy."

"But of legal age."

"True. Now what?"

"We should visit the Cruz family. Maybe some answers are waiting for us there." Mateo shifted the car into drive but paused when he noticed someone in the rearview mirror. "Is that the trainer?"

"You mean that hot buff guy walking up the driveway?"

"Yes, *him*." Mateo rolled his eyes and hopped out of the car to flag the trainer down. "Fernando, correct?"

"Yes. May I help you?"

"We need to verify where you were yesterday between ten PM and midnight."

"I was here."

"Doing?"

"Mayor Zaragoza called me for a late session. He's been very stressed with the campaign for next year's election. Plus, the UFO." Fernando pointed to the sky.

"And did the two of you go anywhere?" Lola asked.

"No. The house has everything I need to provide Mayor Zaragoza a thorough workout."

Mateo rubbed his chin in thought. "And what about Mrs. Zaragoza? Was she here?"

"Now that you mention it, I saw her car pull out of the driveway."

"What time?"

"I honestly don't know, but she likes doing yoga down at the Namaste Studio. They have late sessions."

"I see, and how long do *your* sessions run?"

"However long the Mayor wants. Last night was about two hours, and then we sat in the cantina drinking protein shakes."

"And how long did that last?"

"I think I left here around one AM." Fernando bowed his head sheepishly. "I'm going through a rough breakup, and the Mayor is a good man to talk to."

"I see." Mateo nodded. "Did you notice if Mrs. Zaragoza had returned by then?"

"She parks in the garage, so I honestly don't know."

"Thank you for your time, Fernando. You've been a great help."

As Mateo and Lola drove away, he had this itchy feeling about Mrs. Zaragoza. Hopefully, there would be more answers in Esteban's home.

***

Unlike the Mayor, Guillermo Cruz and his family lived in a highrise condo close to the city square. When Mateo and Lola arrived, police were already in the apartment, along with sniffling family members. Guillermo sat on the edge of the leather couch, his head in his hands, sobbing, while his second eldest son stared in a daze, his eyes red from crying.

"Mis condolencias," Mateo said, causing Guillermo to look up.

"Inspector Moreno, do you know who did this monstrous thing to my son?"

"We have a lead we're pursuing."

"Who?"

"We cannot say yet, but when we know for certain, you'll be the first to know."

"May we look through Esteban's room?" Lola asked. "Perhaps there are clues we can find as to who did this."

"Sure. Go right ahead. It's down the hallway and to the left."

"Excuse us." Mateo nodded.

The door was open when they reached the room, and inside was Guillermo's wife, Anabel, with their daughter Elena. They sat on the bed whispering as the little girl hugged her brother's pillow with tears streaming from her eyes.

"But why did he go?" Elena cried.

"Because Esteban has a bigger purpose, and the aliens chose him to go live on their planet."

"But why him? Why my brother!"

"Because Esteban is very smart." Anabel wiped her daughter's tears. "And the aliens picked the smartest humans to teach them about Earth, so they can use that knowledge to make their world a better place."

"But why does he have to go with them? Why can't he just tell them what they want to know and stay here?"

"It's easier if he goes to their world, but Esteban will be fine. He's on a new adventure. We should be proud of him."

"But I won't see him again."

"Let's try to be happy for him, ok?" Anabel choked back a cry and forced a smile. "No matter what, Esteban will always be in our hearts."

Mateo and Lola eyed each other. What in the hell kind of twisted fairytale were these people telling their kid?

"May we look around?" Lola stepped into the room.

"Yes, we'll get out of your way," Anabel said and turned to Elena. "Mi amor, meet me in the kitchen and I'll make you a snack."

"Ok." The little girl wiped her eyes, then walked out with her head down, still clutching the pillow.

"Interesting story," Mateo said to Anabel.

"Well, how do you propose I tell a five-year-old about her brother? When that *thing* in the sky arrived, Elena started having nightmares. She thought we were all going to die, and maybe we will, but after I told her fairytales about the UFO, the nightmares stopped. If I have to tell my daughter an *interesting story* so she doesn't live her last days in fear, then so be it. Don't you dare judge me."

"My apologies," Mateo murmured as Anabel stormed out.

"Look." Lola nodded at the photos on Esteban's dresser. "He was on the same soccer team as the Zaragoza's son. Maybe that's how Mrs. Zaragoza knew Esteban?"

"Perhaps."

Mateo rifled through the drawers, searching for clues, but aside from a stash of marijuana, he came up empty. Meanwhile, Lola flashed a light under the bed and lifted the mattress.

"What have we got here?" She slid out a folded journal. "Drawings."

However, it was more than doodles.

"Is that…" Mateo squinted. "Is that a naked Mrs. Zaragoza?"

"Yes, and she's posed like that woman from the Titanic movie."

"No kidding." Mateo turned the page, where another racy drawing stared back at them. "Wow."

"It's just page after page of this woman, and each one is sexier than the last."

"I think we have our answer. So, let's say the Mayor found out, and he confronted Esteban, they had an altercation, and—"

"But that doesn't explain the motive for the last *twenty-one* victims or the fact he has a good alibi."

"Diablos. You're right." Mateo rubbed his beard. "What if Mrs. Zaragoza didn't go out for yoga? What if she met up with Esteban? Clearly, they had a sexual relationship, and there is a power imbalance considering her age and status."

"What if Esteban wanted to go public with their relationship, and it freaked her out?"

"Many motives for murder where affairs are involved." Mateo nodded. "But it has to be more than that if she's our serial killer."

"We should visit the yoga studio to ask if she was there."

"*Also* do a stakeout in the square to keep our eyes on the cathedral and the yoga studio. Killers like revisiting the crime scene. It's an ego thing. If Mrs. Zaragoza is involved, she didn't act alone, and her accomplice could be another yogi."

"Agreed. She's too petite to fight and kill a six-foot-tall athlete alone." Lola glanced at her watch. "Let's finish up here, then get something to eat."

"Can't. I just remembered my wife is bringing dinner to the office."

"Right." Lola furrowed her brows.

"I'm sorry."

"It's fine. She's your wife, and if these are our last days, then you should spend them with her. As I said earlier, we should end things."

"Why are you saying this?"

"Maybe I don't want to die hopelessly in love with someone that doesn't belong to me." She fanned through the journal "Like Esteban."

"Lola, I—"

"You know I'm right." She left the room, and Mateo facepalmed himself.

He never imagined becoming an unfaithful man, especially not after twenty years of marriage, but he didn't know how to sever the relationship.

In truth, he was a coward, and Lola was right. There wasn't a future for them.

***

Later that evening, Mateo and Lola sat on a bench in the square next to a taco vendor. She stuffed her face with a late dinner, while he sipped horchata and kept his focus on the two buildings. Merchants were cleaning up their shops, and the local bars were bringing their tables inside, so spotting anyone suspicious would be easier with fewer people around.

"Thought about you said."

"Hm?" Lola cocked a brow, her fingers pinching a lime to squeeze juice over another taco.

"About ending things. This guilt has been eating away at me anyway."

Lola took a bite, and said with a mouthful, "Are you going to come clean to Imelda?"

"No. If we're all going to die, why break her heart? Better to die happy."

"Fair point."

"Hey, look." Mateo elbowed her. "We've got company."

There across the piazza, wearing a baseball cap and sunglasses, was a skittish Mrs. Zaragoza, looking both ways before entering the studio of the yoga guru, Diego De Rosa.

Mateo glanced at his watch. "It's almost curfew, yet she's here, miles from home. So we're definitely on to something."

"And there's only one way to find out." Lola tossed her garbage into the trash and stood. "Let's go."

Shadows bathed the inside of the yoga studio when they entered, and the place appeared empty as they tiptoed from room to room. However, a hum of voices floated from somewhere in the back. They approached a set of double doors cautiously and peered through the crack. There, standing inside a glowing circle of candles, was Mrs. Zaragoza and about ten other people.

"The police came to my house and accused my husband of killing Esteban. I told you this would happen, and that we needed to pick someone else."

"And we told *you* not to fall in love with the boy!" a woman hissed. "You're old enough to be his mother."

"How else was I supposed to gain his trust?"

"Ladies, none of that matters," rumbled Diego De Rosa. "We don't control who is selected for the sacrifice, we just carry out the plan, and the final countdown is fast approaching."

"Screw the sacrifices!" a man barked. "You heard Mrs. Zaragoza. The police are sniffing too close."

"Are you saying you're not a *believer*?" Diego asked. "You know we have to make these sacrifices or else we all die!"

"Or you could be making it all up."

"How dare you?" Mrs. Zaragoza exclaimed. "Diego performs miracles, and you question him?"

"Yeah, how dare you?" another woman said. "He's trying to save mankind. You're lucky he chose you to help."

"I'm sorry," the man muttered. "I'm just stressed."

"Hush, my child..." Diego cupped the man's face. "You are still a novice to my teachings, but you have so much potential. I will give you the honor of carrying out the next sacrifice. How does that sound?"

"You will?"

"Yes." Diego presented a branding stuck. "I spent all afternoon crafting this one. Look at how beautiful the *eight* turned out."

"Wow," the group said in unison, their fingers grazing the iron.

"However, the universe has requested a change for our sacrifice. They don't want the cashier from the grocery store anymore. They want *Imelda Moreno*."

"What?" Mrs. Zaragoza gasped. "But she's the detective's wife."

From the hallway, Mateo's blood avalanched down to his toes, causing his body to sway. There was no way in hell he would let them lay a finger on his Imelda.

"We don't have a choice," Diego continued. "That was the name they whispered to me when I meditated this afternoon. She's our next sacrifice."

"I wish the universe would talk to *me*. I wish I had the gift," a woman said somberly.

"Shhh, Maria. Once we get through all of the sacrifices, I will take you as my apprentice to deepen your meditations."

"You will?"

"Yes, you have so much potential."

"What about me?" Mrs. Zaragoza blurted. "You said I was your best student!"

"Ladies, none of that matters now. The clock is ticking, and the time has come. We must drink our peyote wine and do what the universe has asked."

Diego walked in a circle, handing them each a dagger, and pouring the hallucinogenic wine into everyone's glass. Sweat dripped from Mateo's temples, his mind racing. He clicked the safety button on his gun, his muscles tensing to take down the delusional killers that dared threaten his wife.

"We drink," Diego said.

"We drink," the others murmured.

Together, they gulped the wine and wiped the excess from their mouths.

"What do you want to do?" Lola whispered.

"We arrest these pedazos de mierda. On my count to three…" With his heart pounding, Mateo kicked the double doors wide open. "Put your hands up. You're all under arrest!"

The crazed group whipped their attention in his direction. However, their surprised expressions morphed into something sinister when Diego pointed at Mateo. "The universe has changed its mind. *He* is the new sacrifice. Kill him!"

The group charged forward, daggers in hand, and Mateo fired his weapon, wounding a man in the shoulder. Lola also shot off around, yet it didn't deter the killers as they trampled over their fallen friends, and continued running.

"Coño," Lola squeaked.

"Run! They've gone mad," Mateo shouted, urging Lola toward the exit while firing over his shoulder.

"Don't let them leave the studio," Diego ordered.

A few from the group lunged, the tips of their knives almost catching Mateo's shirt as he and Lola slid into the lobby. They pushed through the door and tumbled onto the street where citizens wandering the square gathered around to see what the commotion was. Mateo skyrocketed to his feet, yanking Lola with him as the murderous group spilled from the doorway. However, the crowd didn't dissuade Diego from diving to stab Lola. She fired her weapon, but the chamber jammed, and Mateo was out of bullets.

For a moment, it seemed helpless as citizens stood around watching, none of them helping, but then a merchant rushed forward swinging a baseball bat at Diego. Then another citizen jumped in, too, throwing a brick at one of the yogis, and like a domino effect, more people came to their aid. When some of the group attempted to flee, citizens ran after them and dragged them back. Together, they held down the killers, allowing Mateo and Lola to zip-tie them while someone else ran to the station for help.

After a few minutes, police officers ran to their aid and hauled the killers away for booking, but Mateo wanted the pleasure of one last word with the yoga guru.

"You're a fraud," he said. "You're not some savior. Why did you kill all of these innocent people?"

Diego raised his chin, still pompous and proud. "Because we're all going to die anyway when the countdown ends."

"So you thought you could play God?" Mateo tightened the zip-tie, squeezing Diego's wrists, making him yelp. "Countdown or not, you don't get to do that in *my* city. So I have a punishment for you."

Snatching the branding stick from the ground, he flicked a lighter to heat the iron, and when it glowed red, he pressed the number *eight* into Diego's forehead.

"Make sure they all get one," Mateo ordered the officers. "I need to get home to Imelda."

After twenty-two days of victims turning up dead with a countdown of numbers burned into their foreheads, Detective Moreno could finally exhale a sigh of relief, knowing that tomorrow, no one was going to show up dead with the number *eight.*

~

08

about the author

After an engineering career with over 400 patents, **Henry Scott** *now invents thrilling plotlines in his novels. He lives in metro-Detroit with his family, two lovable golden retrievers, and a turtle whose pictures are on his Instagram and TikTok feeds.*

Henry loves coffee, Detroit-style pizza, true-crime TV shows, and his Triumph motorcycle.

THE FAMILY

by Henry Scott

OLMSTEAD, KENTUCKY, USA
AUGUST 23, 5:00 AM

Madison brushed her long, dark hair from her eyes. It clung to her sweaty forehead after her two-mile hike from town. She jerked open the front door to her house and stepped inside, having timed her trip to be back before the gravity shifts. The rickety screen banged shut behind her. Michael, her fifteen-year-old brother, lay on the nailed-down couch, staring longingly at his useless phone, while their dad flipped channels on the ancient tube television. For all his efforts, he received nothing but static.

Honestly, it was a miracle they still had electricity on this remote mountain because otherwise, they'd be in the dark. Literally. Before they lost all communication with the outside world, the news said they'd need to leave Kentucky and travel west of the Mississippi River to see sunlight again. That had been six days ago—right after The Event.

But her dad wouldn't leave then, and he probably wouldn't now, either. Though Madison prayed she could convince him to go, especially after what the soldiers had told her. Or... well, she wouldn't allow her thoughts to grow as black as the sky. Damn stupid spaceship. It had ruined her life.

To keep from screaming, she quickly put the milk and eggs in the fridge and began to pace around the house. If it could be called a house—more like a shack held together with duct tape and chipped paint. Her brother and dad watched her pace. Neither one said a word. Nor did her mother, unsurprisingly, who sat slumped in the rocking chair in the corner. She was covered in a wool blanket.

Madison made it to the far wall in five steps. She turned and paced back across the uneven floorboards. The flashlight she'd used to make the journey to the grocery store banged against her thigh with each step.

"Don't break that. It's the only one we have," her dad barked.

Rolling her eyes, she said, "So?"

"So?" Her dad retreated to his recliner. The footrest went up with a loud squeak. "So, if you break it, how are we supposed to go outside?"

"And when are you going to do that? You haven't gone outside since Mom's accident."

"That's not the point."

"That's exactly the point." She set the flashlight on the counter. "We need to leave this mountain, or we'll die."

Her dad's face turned as red as a tomato. "Stop talking that nonsense. We're not leaving our land. Not again."

"How can you say that? We're right underneath the thing. It could fall out of the sky right on our damn heads. Or shoot us with lasers. We need to evacuate. You heard the warnings before the TV stations went off. They have camps for everyone in the West. The government says we'll be safe there."

"Don't cuss."

Sticking out her chin, she said, "I'm almost eighteen. I'll swear if I want to."

He glared at her long and hard. "Well, you're wrong. Nowhere is safe. Besides, how can the government protect us when those aliens stole all our nukes right from underneath our noses?"

"The military isn't the government—or at least, not the part of government you hate. And we have to trust someone if we want to survive this mess because your old truck won't make it ten miles out of town. So why not the military? They have a convoy leaving tonight, and there's room for us."

"Tonight?"

"Please, Dad. We can't stay here," Madison begged as she made another lap around the room.

"Is that what the cute soldier told you?" Michael asked with a smirk.

Her dad put down his footrest and leaned forward in his well-worn Lazy-boy. "What are you talking about?"

Michael said, "One of the soldiers hanging around town has big muscles and a chiseled chin. Maddy said he looks like Henry Cavill."

"Shut up, dork!"

"So it's true?" Her dad growled. "You've been talking to a soldier?"

"I talk to lots of people when I go into town for groceries."

"You know how I feel about the government."

"Dad, I told you. It's not the government. It's only the National Guard."

"Same difference. They'll screw you just the same as look at you."

Her dad hadn't cussed. Not really, but it wasn't something one would say in church. Not that their mother would be dragging them there anytime soon. Still, Maddy wasn't surprised by his colorful statement. Since before she could walk, he'd been telling her how the government had stolen their land from them. Their scenic parcel down by the gorge had gone back generations in his family. But today, it was Mile Marker 113 on the Interstate. Eminent domain had screwed him out of his birthright, forcing them to move to the side of this godforsaken mountain, and he would never forget it. Or forgive them, no matter how hard her mom tried to get him to love their new home.

She stopped in front of him. "Ok. I understand how you feel, but not everyone in the government is out to get us. I've talked with the soldiers in town, and if it wasn't for the National Guard protecting the Dam, we wouldn't have electricity, and then where would we be?"

"Right here in this house," her dad laughed.

"True, but we'd be sitting in the dark."

Shaking his head, her dad said, "Big deal. Electricity. How is that protecting us? They should be shooting that stupid thing out of the sky, not talking to young girls, and eating up all the food in town."

She wouldn't respond to his taunts. He was trying to get her flustered, but Madison needed to keep a cool head if she was going to get him to leave this mountain tonight.

"Dad, they brought their own food. And really, what do you expect the military to do? That spaceship is hundreds of miles wide, and the aliens must have all kinds of advanced technology to fly that thing across the universe. So keeping the electricity on is better than nothing."

He crossed his arms in front of his chest. "I'd take nothing."

"Please, Dad. Will you at least consider leaving with them?"

"Of course, Henry Cavill wants you on his truck. He can't stop staring at your butt," Michael said with a sneer.

"He did what?" her dad hissed.

Great. She could kick her brother. Just when she thought she was winning her dad over, Michael had to stick his nose into the debate and ruin everything, but she shouldn't have been surprised. Mike always took their dad's side in any argument.

"He was not staring," she insisted.

Michael said, "How do you know? Do you have eyes in the back of your head?"

Her dad shook his head. "Maybe they wouldn't stare at your butt if your shorts weren't so short. I can't believe your mother bought you clothes that don't cover your cheeks."

"It's the style. All the girls wear them like that. Can we stop talking about my freaking butt?"

"I said don't cuss. Your mother doesn't like it."

"Mom is dead!"

A hush fell over the room.

Several seconds passed before her dad pointed to the corpse hidden under the blanket and shouted, "Don't you think I know that?"

"Then what does it matter what she likes or doesn't?"

His eyes nearly bulged out of his head as he jumped from the recliner. His fists clenched and unclenched. The sinewy muscles in his arms hardened by a lifetime of manual labor stretched the sleeves of his t-shirt. "You'll respect her. Dead or alive."

Scared that he might smack her in her smart mouth, she took a step back. "You're right. I'm sorry. Can you forgive me? It's just I'm upset. I don't want to lose anyone else."

"Fine. Don't let it happen again." He fell back into his seat.

It had been over a week ago. On the day of The Event. At least, that's what all the news stations called it. After weeks of darkness, a big hole suddenly opened up in the ship, letting the sun come through. The whole family ran outside to bask in the light, even her dad. A feeling came over Madison; it was euphoric. They all felt it, punctuated by their hair standing on end. For a moment, they forgot all their troubles. The spaceship. The missing nukes. All the countries arguing. No answers from anyone. The doomsday clock counting down to an unknown future. They forgot about everything—even her dad. They closed their eyes, soaked up the sun, and danced.

But her mom also forgot to watch where she was stepping. Wandering to the edge of their property, she tumbled into the ravine. She rolled to a stop in a jagged pile of stones. Her leg snapped in two, along with a few ribs, but the broken bones were the least of their concerns. She'd hit her head on a rock, denting the side of her head. She couldn't speak, only groan... until that stopped, too. She hung on for a little while, but she slowly slipped away from them. Afterwards, their dad wouldn't let them touch her. Mother remained in her favorite chair, covered in a blanket with candles burning around her, though it wasn't for the light.

"Please, Dad." Madison got down on her knees in front of her dad's chair. She took her hand in hers and squeezed. "I don't want to die. You or Mike, either. Can we leave here in the trucks with the National Guard?"

"What about your mother?"

"We have time. We could give her a proper burial. What about we do it out back by the big oak tree she liked? We could perform a little service like they do in church and each say a prayer. She'd like that."

Through her decline, they kept her home—not bothering to take her to the closest hospital two towns over. It wouldn't have mattered.

Everyone with any smarts had left after the first evacuation order. Besides, it was better she passed in familiar surroundings amongst her family than on a metal bed in a sterile room with beeping monitors. She couldn't stay in that rocking chair. It wasn't right.

"No." He shook his head violently from side to side.

"Why not?"

Pulling his hand away, he ran it through his thinning hair. "Because it would be against her wishes. She wanted to be cremated and have her ashes spread amongst her flowers."

"That's true, but there's no one at the funeral home for the cremation. No one around for anything. Just us—and for how long?"

"We'll stick it out as long as we need to, or the government will take this house from me, too."

"The government has bigger problems. And even if they did, Mom would want us to leave, to do whatever it takes to survive."

His jaw clenched. "Don't tell me what your mother would want."

"You're not the only one who loved Mom. Mike and I loved her too." She stood up as the tears streamed down her face. "And I know she wouldn't want to be a martyr propped up in the corner, watching her family die for her. Or a silly piece of land. Right?"

Her dad didn't respond. Instead, his eyes fell into his lap as he avoided her pleading stare. Her death broke them. Her dad, most of all. Their mom was the backbone of the family and the only woman her dad had ever loved. They'd started dating at fourteen and were married a week after their high school graduation, which was not unheard of in their neck of the woods.

Continuing to play with his phone, Mike didn't say anything either. She wasn't surprised. Her brother hated confrontation, and he certainly wouldn't go against their dad.

So, without any hope of changing their minds, Madison made the toughest decision she'd ever made in her life. She turned and ran to her tiny bedroom. Dumping the books from her school bag, she filled it with clothes, some of her toiletries from the bathroom, and the small amount of money she'd managed to squirrel away from babysitting the neighbor's twins.

With the bag slung over her shoulder, she found her family exactly where she'd left them. Breathing through her mouth, she leaned over and kissed her mom on her covered forehead. She almost faltered. She almost returned her stuff to her room and stayed, but the smell of death strengthened her resolve. That wasn't her mother underneath the blanket. That was only a hollow shell. Her mother had gone on to a better place—but a tiny part of her remained in Madison's head urging her to do the tough thing. Urging her to go.

"Thank you, Mom. I'll see you soon. But hopefully not too soon."

Her dad stood up, blocking her path to the door. "Where do you think you're going?"

"I'm leaving on that truck."

"No, you're not."

"Yes! I am!"

She tried to step around him, but he moved with her.

"Dad, this is crazy. Mom wouldn't want us to fight. And she wouldn't want us to die for a freaking piece of land. Think of what you're doing to Mike. Please. You guys need to come with me."

"I said don't cuss!"

Spit flew from his lips with each word. He put both hands on her shoulders and pushed. Pushed hard. Madison flew across the room, landing on her butt. A jolt went up her spine.

Before he could hit her again, Mike jumped up from the couch and tackled him. Although smaller, he had the element of surprise. The blow knocked their dad into the far wall, stunning him as much from the hit as from the shock of Mike finally standing up to him.

"What the–" Their dad tried to climb to his feet.

Mike didn't back down. He loomed over their dad with his fists clenched. "Stop it. Madison is right, so if she wants to go, she should be able to go."

"Fine. Go." He slumped to the floor as he pointed a finger at his son. "And you can leave, too. I don't need either of you."

Full of regret, Madison took a hesitant step towards the door. "I love you, Dad. Will you please come with us?"

"No."

She sighed and forced herself to put one foot in front of the other because if she didn't leave now, she might never find the courage to try again. Mike followed her out the door, grabbing the flashlight from the counter. On the porch, he handed it to her. "Here."

"You hold it."

"I'm not going."

"You're not?" She stopped. "But you have to come."

He shook his head. "Someone has to stay here with Dad."

"B… But… You could…"

"We'll be fine."

"Mike… Mikey… No… Please, come with me."

"I said we'll be fine." He pulled her into his arms.

They hadn't hugged in years. It felt good. Too good. The gesture turned her into a sniveling little girl, drawing out a fresh set of tears. She wished she had the words to convince him to come, but he was just as stubborn as her father. Nothing she said would change his mind. But he had stood up for her, and she'd never forget it.

He kissed her on the forehead. "I'll see you when it's over. I promise."

"I'll hold you to that." Sprinting down their dirt lane, she wiped the tears from her eyes. She didn't dare look back. No. Instead, she ran into the great unknown.

~

07

about the author

Melody Grace Hicks *writes spicy science-fantasy romance with a twist of popular culture.*

She'd apologize for the increase in your lingerie replacement budget, but really, we both know it's those darn wickedly sexy males that bring you back for more, right?

Born and raised on Canada's West Coast, Melody has travelled the world and brings this diversity into her fiction.

An award-winning internationally published scientist and professor by day, by night under cloak of her pen name, she's an enthusiastic masher of mythology and tells tales of soulmates, secret identities, unknown origins, betrayals, magical powers, polyamory, and love triangles.

THE NEWTONIAN TWINS

by Melody Grace Hicks

WINDSOR, ONTARIO, CANADA
AUGUST 24, 4:50 AM

"Babe, are we going to evacuate? The traffic from the border isn't so bad now." I dragged my eyes from the computer screen displaying camera feeds of the bridge between Detroit and Windsor and rose on my knees to search for Fraser. Our eyes met and his scowl had me taking a deep breath, trying to relax the tension gripping my body.

Highway traffic had been bumper-to-bumper since the alien ship appeared twenty-nine days ago. Its enormous ebony mass blotted out the sky, turning day to permanent night, and hung overhead like an ominous doomsday poised to squash us in seven days. Even when I couldn't see it, the knowledge of the craft's oppressive presence pressed with a claustrophobic heaviness that didn't seem to bother my boyfriend or my brother. Not even the glowing countdown number in the sky worried them. If we hadn't run out of food, I'd never have gotten them to leave our apartment, despite the supposedly mandatory evacuation ordered days ago. It's not like I could have predicted gravity would start going wonky and we'd get stranded.

This wasn't my fault, damn it.

"Dylan isn't back from checking that auto shop yet. We need another wheel to get out of here. You know that," Fraser grumbled as he shoved another mattress out of the way from where it had fallen when gravity returned last night.

Anything not tied down during the twice-daily episodes tended to crash. Like our jeep into the industrial paving scrap yard nine days ago as we'd braved the barely moving log jam of vehicles, half of them stranded when they ran out of fuel. We'd been lucky it was only our tires receiving the rebar puncture make-over in that first chaotic gravity shift. Taking refuge in the abandoned furniture store had given us plenty of soft padding to cushion our ten-minute floating sessions and an office with a fibre-optic internet connection—the only kind that worked now.

His scowl deepened. "I'm not fucking walking six hundred kilometres out of the twilight zone, Charity."

I rolled my eyes and held in my snort. As if I didn't know that. "I'm just saying that we should try for Sault Ste. Marie instead of Montreal. It's half the distance and time." The ominous number seven in the sky—seven days remaining until who knew what—sent a chill through me every time I glimpsed it. I tried not to see the damn thing when we went outside, but I couldn't ignore it.

Fraser's eyes bugged out. "Hell, no." He shook his head violently and chopped his hand through the air. "We'd have to travel the entire length of Michigan. Do you have any idea how many guns, wacko militia, conspiracy theorists, and other nuts we'd have to get past?" His deep baritone voice rose into an uncharacteristic squeak.

Guns were one of the few things that disturbed the usually amiable Fraser. Understandable, given his dad killed his mom, then himself in a murder-suicide. A teenaged Fraser found the bodies when he'd returned home from the movies.

Still, this damn ship hung over my head like Sisyphus' rock waiting to smash me. I wanted out from under it. "I know, babe. But surely it's better than trying to get past Toronto." I rose from the padded corner where we'd duct-taped the computer to prevent it from damage when gravity disappeared twice a day. "All the cameras show one accident after another and tons of abandoned cars. It's completely snarled."

A crash came from the front of the store with a series of curses.

"Your oh-so-graceful twin has returned," Fraser said, smirking as he pulled me into his arms.

I snorted. Although my brother was impressive at picking locks, he was ridiculously clumsy. If there was something to trip over or knock down, he'd find it with a foot or elbow.

"Any luck getting food?" I called out. "Or another tire?"

"Even better," Dylan shouted back. "We'll be set for life, Charity!"

Fraser and I exchanged frowns.

"Did you find a tire?" Fraser asked as Dylan's lanky frame came into view.

Dylan grinned, nodded and swiped long blond bangs out of his sweaty face. "Yep! I've already swapped it out on the jeep."

In slow motion, a wrought-iron lamp that had survived days of gravity upsets toppled sideways, brought down by my brother's wayward elbow as he passed. The metallic crash rang through the building. I winced, but Dylan didn't even slow down.

"And you'll never guess what else I found." He wiggled in place like a puppy needing to go outside, not the twenty-five-year-old I knew him to be.

Fraser's frown deepened, but he waved a hand for Dylan to continue.

"There's a gold and gem depository on the next street over. The place is deserted. The doors and windows are barred, but not the roof access. We can use the next gravity shift in"—he checked the sports watch on his wrist—"an hour to get to the roof and break in from the top where the building isn't as secure." His round, brown eyes looked earnestly at first Fraser, then me. "One score and we'd be rich, no matter where we end up."

A smile grew on Fraser's face as his eyes lit and I groaned to myself. There was no way I'd be able to talk them out of the cockamamie scheme. Fraser had tried before to get rich with little to no effort, like his last solar roofing company scam, and my brother's fingers were so sticky, he already had a police record. God damn it. Did the idiot *want* to go back to jail? A prison cell wouldn't protect us when the aliens squashed us.

For fuck's sake, why did I always have to be the voice of reason? We needed to get the hell out of here. "Isn't gold heavy? How would we get it out before the cops show up?" Part of me wanted to scream, my chest tightening with a throbbing starting in my temple as I stepped out of Fraser's hold.

Dylan rolled his eyes, giving me a pitying smirk. "We'll use the time between gravity shifts to crack all the safes and package the gold and gems. Then, when the next shift hits, Fraser and I will toss it up to you on the roof and you can push it towards the jeep."

Fraser nodded, rubbing his hands. "Yeah. With everything floating, it will be easy to move, even for your meagre strength, Charity. As long as we don't trip any alarms, it should be safe enough inside."

With my arms folded over my chest, I gritted my teeth, determined to not yell at them. There was no point. They'd go forward with their plan regardless of what I said. Stubborn, idiotic asses. Why was I the only one worried about the aliens?

"Let's load up the jeep and we'll leave for Quebec right after," Fraser said, reaching out to grip my forearm. "I know you wanted to go through Michigan, but we can't cross the border and risk inspection." As Dylan moved off to stuff clothes and food he'd pilfered from nearby stores into his duffle bag, Fraser's voice dropped lower. "Dylan can't cross the border with his record, even if they aren't requiring passports."

Fuck. I'd forgotten about that. "Yeah, okay." I gave him a weak smile, then drew away to gather my own belongings.

In half an hour, we'd piled everything into the jeep's backseat, ready to be pushed on top of our loot in the cargo area to hide it. Dylan squeezed into the back and gave directions as we engaged the four-wheel drive to get us around dead cars, partially flooded streets, over curbs, landscaping, and across sidewalks. With fifteen minutes to spare, we parked the jeep against the back wall of the Precious Metals building, facing an incline with a train switching yard below us. Both the diner on one side and the oriental market on the other side of Precious Metals were quiet in the darkened street as we crept to the brick wall. A streetlight several hundred meters away flickered but failed to illuminate much in the midnight shadow of the alien craft.

And that goddamn number seven hung in the air.

I shivered, gooseflesh rising on my skin despite the temperate wind blowing in from the west. Cooler than usual for August—barely t-shirt weather, but then, we hadn't seen rain in weeks either. Who needed rain with all the flooding every time the river and lakes rose with the gravity shifts? In the distance, the droning hum of vehicles on nearby highways led further into the city and the bridge over the Detroit River. Few ventured onto choked and partly flooded side streets like the one where we waited.

Damn it, I wanted this over with. I hunched my shoulders, hating the oppressive feel of the featureless black spaceship above me and the ominous countdown. Whatever was going to happen in seven days when the massive blue numbers reached zero, I did not want to be underneath the fucking thing.

"How much longer?" I whispered, fidgeting as I placed my hands on the rough brick.

"Any minute now," Dylan answered, flashing me a wide, crooked grin that showed off his chipped left incisor from when we'd fought over chores as kids. If this worked, maybe we'd finally have the money to get it fixed.

The loss of gravity always started in my stomach first—a slightly nauseous feeling as my hair spread out and my feet lifted off the ground.

"Hang onto the building," Fraser warned as we pulled ourselves up the wall.

Reaching the top, I clung to the roof's edge as they held onto me and used the tools they'd brought to pry up the air conditioning unit. Faster than I would have expected, they had it detached and shoved it away to float over toward the closed diner. Gravity returned, and I groaned as my hip and elbow smacked down. The air conditioner smashed with ear-ringing finality on the cement below.

"Stay up here, sis, and keep a lookout. Give us a shout if you see cops approaching," Dylan said as he and Fraser crawled into the ductwork with accompanying thuds and metallic twangs.

"Fine," I grumbled, rising to my feet and rubbing my hip and elbow.

I walked across the black rooftop to sit at the roadside edge, squinting out at the stationary glow of streetlights and the moving headlights of vehicles. A few buildings had lights, but not many. Most of the houses in the distance were dark. Were people asleep there? Or had they abandoned their homes like so many others when they called for evacuations? It was barely half-past six in the morning… not that there was any dawn under this godforsaken ship.

Loud wrenching and squealing sounds echoed up from the opening an hour later and I sprang to my feet, darting over. "What the hell are you doing?" I called down as I approached. But instead of ductwork, Fraser's grinning, dirt-smudged face met me.

"Dylan is cracking the safes. There are a ton, so we'll see how many he can get into before we need to leave. I'm tearing down the ductwork so we can toss the bags up to you when it's time."

"It's really fucking loud. You're lucky no one is around right now," I grumbled, scowling at his enjoyment.

"Stop worrying. Dylan confirmed that the entrances to the building and to the safe area are barred and alarmed, but the ductwork dropped us past all of it. We're golden, baby."

I snorted. "Fine. I'm going to keep watch." With stomping steps, I moved back to the roof's edge and retook my seat, trying to not flinch as Fraser continued his destruction.

Despite the continued darkness surrounding us, more signs of life rose as the hours progressed. A breeze carried the scent of tar and smoke, and in the distance, someone laid on their horn in an angry exclamation of impatience. My eyes started to drift back to the number in the sky, but a growing rumble drew me to my feet.

Lights approached from behind and to my right, but there was no road behind me. What the hell was in that direction? As I crept towards that side of the roof, a rhythmic thumping became clear. The trains were still running? I supposed they *were* able to move food, supplies, fuel, and people more efficiently. The highways were too clogged with vehicles to get semi-trucks through. Over the noisy train on its tracks, another sound reached me.

A vehicle had turned onto this side street.

My heart leapt into my throat and I dashed to the roadside roof's edge, crouching to peer over.

Oh fuck.

A dark SUV with a red and blue light bar on top wove around abandoned cars, prowling the street. A searchlight passed back and forth as they drove. I ducked when it approached.

Each beat of my heart thundered in my ears.

I held my breath.

But the cops didn't stop. They didn't even slow down. Instead, they continued on their way, turning at the next intersection that led toward the bigger box stores.

I let out a shaky exhale, sinking back on my butt as the adrenaline left me trembling. Staring up at the impenetrable darkness above me, I vowed to change my life.

"When I get out of this mess, I am never letting those two knuckleheads convince me to do something so idiotic again."

"Charity! Yo, Charity! Wake up!"

I closed my eyes for a moment, taking the time to breathe deeply, before pushing myself to my feet. I strolled over to the opening.

"What?" I called down, seeing the top of Dylan's head as he talked with Fraser.

Dylan shot a satisfied smirk up at me. "Are you ready? It's almost time." He tossed a length of orange extension cord up. "Tie this around your ankle. I'll tether you so you don't go floating away."

"Good thinking," I agreed as I took the end and knotted it around my ankle in a clove hitch.

When Mom had enrolled us in scouts, I doubted she'd envisioned I'd use the skills like this. As much as I missed her, at least the cancer took her before she had to see aliens invade our world. Dylan's two-year incarceration had knocked the fight out of her. She'd died six months after he'd started his sentence. I rubbed a sweating hand over my face, reminded of her lingering sorrow. This had to be the last time I got sucked into one of his insane plans.

Dylan coiled the other end of the cord around his waist, tied it, and flashed me a thumbs-up.

My stomach lurched as gravity disappeared. Dylan braced himself in the opening, tossing up the first heavy grey sack Fraser handed him. It shot past me and I snatched it, letting its momentum drag me higher into the air. The tether caught, jerking me to a halt, then ricocheting me in the opposite direction. When I shoved the sack past the edge of the roof and towards the jeep, I was pushed up and away again.

"You'll have to pull me down to the roof between bags," I shouted.

Dylan nodded, quickly reeling me back to the roof. When I was above him, they tossed another bag at me. Again, it yanked me upward until I halted, then back when I thrust it at the jeep. Like a balloon on a string, I was jerked around twice more before lunging for a poorly launched sack sent me careening at an upwards angle past the edge of the roof and out over the parking lot. Unable to grasp the material for more than a brief second, the sack slipped past my fingertips, sailing up into the sky towards a dark mass far too close to be the spaceship.

"What the—"

My question was cut off by a curse below me. Flailing in the air under me, Dylan rose from the roof opening.

But if he was rising, what was holding us to the roof, to the ground?

My lungs seized, the scream trapped in my throat as the ground got farther and farther away.

"Oh, fuck… fuck… fuck!" Dylan shrieked.

I twisted and tried to swim my arms, to push us down. Yet we continued to rise.

And as we did, the dark mass resolved to a familiar shape in the gloom.

"Oh my god," I gasped.

I watched in horror as the grey sack struck the underside of a floating rust-coloured train car between massive, body-crushing steel wheels. The bag burst, gems exploding out into the air to reflect bits of light, like stars in the midnight sky.

Every moment brought the train car closer on its own upward path. The sack's weight was too slight to deflect the far greater mass—we were on a direct collision trajectory. If the impact didn't kill us, the returning gravity would crush us under the train any minute now.

"I'm sorry. Oh god, I'm so sorry, Charity. I didn't mean to kill us," Dylan babbled, the words tumbling out on top of one another like the gems raining above.

Fear was a metallic taste on my tongue as I bit back my curses. I didn't want the last thing my brother heard to be his twin's fury. Even if I was damn certain I wouldn't be in this bloody situation if it weren't for my brother's and my boyfriend's bad decisions. Using the cord between us, I dragged myself towards him with shaking hands until we hugged tightly, our flight changing to a tumbling, drunken spin with the grace of a bumblebee on alcoholic nectar.

"Whichever one of us gets close to the train first, we have to try to kick and knock us clear." It was a foolish hope. We were more than sixteen times the height of the one-story building and rising. Was that even a survivable distance to fall? The ground looked a long way down, but the train was even closer.

Only seconds away.

Dylan nodded, swiped tears from his eyes, then drew his legs in and kicked out as we neared a ridged wheel. The impact drove the breath from my lungs, and he choked out an agonized cry as his left leg snapped with a wet crack.

But he'd done it. He'd redirected our momentum towards the ground and at a right angle to the train car. Hope bloomed warm in my chest. As long as we got out from underneath it and closer to the ground, we'd make it.

Holy crap, we would actually survive this.

Gravity returned with an increase in heaviness, driving us downward faster. As our speed increased, hope turned to horror that only left time to scream. My last thought was an explosion of pain.

***

I didn't expect to wake, but when I opened my eyes, it took me a while to focus. The world was upside down and fiery agony accompanied my attempts to right myself from the tree branch I hung from. My ribs hurt with every breath, every movement, and no matter how I squinted, I saw double. Still, I had all my arms and legs.

After pushing myself up onto the branch and turning towards the trunk, pain-sweat coated my trembling body. But my twin's cold eyes froze my movement, and I barely breathed.

Below me, a shattered tree limb speared Dylan through the chest.

Unable to move, I stared at him, tears blurring my already fuzzy vision. Long minutes passed, and I finally looked beyond him to notice the further wreckage of my world. The train car had landed on the Precious Metals building, collapsing the roof and wall, but somehow missing the Jeep. Yet in the rubble, Fraser's body lay bisected by a huge steel wheel.

Dylan had saved me but killed Fraser in the process.

With shaking fingers, I untied the electrical cord from my ankle and eased my way down past my twin's body until I reached the ground. Holding my ribs, I staggered to the Jeep, ignoring the sacks of gems and gold. What use did I have for riches when my brother and boyfriend were gone? Money wouldn't replace the hole in my chest. Nothing would.

Maybe I would just sit here as the end of the world counted down. Mine was already over, after all.

~

06

about the author

David J. Thirteen *is a horror author based in Toronto. Returning to writing in 2012, he garnered over a million reads on Wattpad posting serial novels. This led to him joining the Wattpad Stars program and the publication of his novel,* ***MR. 8,*** *as well as his novella,* ***THE GARRISON PROJECT.***

His most recent work can be found on The Other Stories podcast and in various anthologies.

David is a representative of the ***Horror Writers Association's Ontario*** *chapter. His real surname is a chaotic convolution of vowels and consonants. Certain mispronunciations may summon beings from beyond the void.*

THE KILLER

by David J. Thirteen

SOMEWHERE IN PENNSYLVANIA, USA
AUGUST 25, NOON

The bodies in the trees are easy to mistake for something else. Torn sheets, plastic bags, even ragdolls. The torchlight barely penetrates the murky woods at that height. From the vantage of the forest floor, all that can be seen are the white shapeless shirts or dresses they wear.

Bartlett's the first to realise what they really are. Or at least, he's the first to speak. But he's also the youngest and likely has the best eyes.

"Ohhh!" he moans. "Good God. There's people up there. Oh, Good God Almighty!"

"There is very little good about God these days if there ever has been," Rainer says from his spot at the head of our little column of misfits. He holds the flame of his scavenged tiki torch close to his face, and his shorn head seems to float in midair while his bland green prison-issued uniform is lost to the darkness. "Keep moving, everyone. We need to find shelter before we all fly like little birdies again. Don't want to join those fellas up there now, do we?"

Cocolo stretches his back regarding the morbid sight above us. His spine makes an audible crack. "You think that's what happened to them? They got stuck up there?" The old Cuban has stripped to the waist, and the flickering light glints off the sweat that slicks his emaciated body where each individual rib stands out.

"Nah," says Marcus, taking a similar pose next to him. The contrast of the muscular young man just makes the other look all the more decrepit. "They were strung up, Cocoa. Hung."

Bartlett and I join them, trying to make sense of the scene. Three bodies are directly overhead, but more blurs of white are farther off in every direction. It's hard to say how many, but if I had to guess, I'd go with ten. Give or take.

Without raising his eyes, Rainer says, "You're both wrong. They were killed. Exsanguinated. Then tied in place like Christmas ornaments.

The ropes are around their chest, not around their necks." He runs a hand from armpit to armpit to demonstrate. "But I'll wager, it was this morning's little fun that got them caught up in the branches."

"How the hell you know all that?" Cocolo asks with a hint of insolence. It's the most I've ever heard anyone stand up to Rainer.

"I observe, friend. I look, and I observe."

"Damn. He's right." Bartlett stares up in a mixture of awe and horror. He absently scratches at the swastika tattoo emblazed on his bicep, a nervous habit he's fallen back on several times today.

I still couldn't make out much, although I probably should've gotten glasses years ago. But farsightedness never seemed important when my days were spent in a six-by-ten cell. So, I take their word for it.

"Who do you think did it?" Marcus asks.

Rainer answers, "Perhaps that is a quandary for the authorities, hmmm?"

This might be his idea of a joke. None of us have a whole lot of faith in *the authorities.* Or any interest in coming across any. I imagine the local cops ran away just as quickly as all the prison guards did. They abandoned their posts and charges—citizens or convicts—so long as it meant their safety. What did they care if chaos and barbarism filled the void they left?

"Now, now, children. Come along. Quit your dawdling. Let's keep marching down this happy trail. Valderi, Valdera!" Rainer moves on, not waiting for us, but we hurry to fall in step behind him.

He's become our de facto leader if for no better reason than he appears to have a plan. Also, everyone's terrified of him and won't challenge him for the position.

"Man, that guy gives me the creeps," Bartlett whispers.

If it was one of the others, I might say I felt the same way. But I wasn't predisposed to getting buddy-buddy with a school shooter and prison yard skinhead.

But, yeah, Rainer was something else alright.

We all earned our spots in supermax. However, his crimes should have secured him a cell in an institute for the criminally insane. Deep in a basement, behind inch-thick plexiglass, so he could be studied like a strange and terrifying new species of spider.

Yet, the crazy bastard got us out of that hellhole when we all thought we were good and dead.

He was the one to see the failure of gravity as an opportunity and not another horrible development. While everyone else bounced wildly about the yard screaming with the fear that this fresh hell brought, Rainer looked and observed.

I hovered a foot off the ground while the bloody body of Paterson threatened to float into me. Everything had become strange and fluid, as though we were all in a pool of water, buoying us up and slowing down our movements. The bonfire in the center of the yard was drawn upward into a flaming ball twenty feet around. Streams of burning debris broke away and flared over the yard adding to the mayhem.

The ship above us blocking out all the sky above, was certainly to blame. But how or why were questions for another time. The only thing that had changed from yesterday was the glowing number had dropped to six, getting closer to whatever catastrophe it had planned for us.

Marshall, one of the neo-Nazi gang's lieutenants, shoved Bartlett behind him, saving the kid from Marcus's shiv, and in the same move, lunged at the black man to add another kill to his scorecard. He might have succeeded if he'd been able to achieve any momentum. But he only floated comically away, his body stretched out like a sleeper carried to the land of nod in a cartoon.

Rainer was by himself, crouched low, one hand gripping the outer wall's bricks. His feet planted on the ground.

"Gentlemen! Gentlemen! Cease the hostilities at once."

He was ignored. We all knew the rules. Only one person would be let back into the prison. Everyone else was meat to fill the depleted pantries. No one was going to let their guard down under such stakes. It didn't matter what Rainer or anyone else said.

"Fools! You are all fools!" he screamed. "This is our chance. We just need to float up. Flap our wings and fly. Up, up and over the wall to freedom."

This got everyone's attention, and for the most part, we shifted our focus from murder to escape. Not that it went smoothly.

Some ended up in the fire adding to the flaming obstacles. Others obtained too much height and could no longer reach anything to grab. They drifted off toward the stratosphere like wayward balloons. Still others were dragged back to Earth by those hellbent on winning the morning's death match.

Of the twenty-one of us who entered the yard, five made it over the wall. It would have been six, but Diaz got caught up in the razor wire on his descent during the slow return of gravity.

Everyone celebrated Rainer as the hero of the day. But I'd noticed how he hadn't moved until he saw what tactics worked and which didn't. The son-of-a-bitch hadn't told us how to escape out of altruism. It was cold and calculating. He looked and observed, studying our clumsy attempts to scurry up the wall to ensure he would make it out okay.

***

"What's that?" Marcus waves his torch wildly in an arc as if expecting a bear to come roaring from the brush.

Everyone's nerves are beaten and bruised from days on end of terror and impending doom, but our little band rallies. We close ranks and aim the flimsy bamboo torches like weapons. Only Rainer stands apart, nonplussed by Marcus's alarm.

Something is out there. An animal, perhaps, crashing through the brittle, dead undergrowth. A grunt rings out. Then, another. This one sounding human. A groan of pain. The noise of pounding feet and foliage being crushed stops.

"Help me! Please! Help!"

We look to one another for direction until our eyes land on Rainer.

He doesn't need to speak. The hand he holds up tells us what to do. Wait. Stay still.

The scramble in the woods resumes, nearing. Of course, whoever is there will zero in on our torches. They have no light or none that I can see.

"Please! Please!" A boy breaks through into the clearing.

He's around sixteen. No older than one of Bartlett's classmates when he mowed them down. His white shirt and pants are filthy, covered in mud and a black substance that has turned crusty. Dried blood. Too much to be his. Although a fresh gash tags his forehead.

Between gasps, he says again, "Please help me."

"It's alright, son." Rainer puts a hand on the boy's hunched shoulder. "Is someone chasing you?"

He shoots a panicked look behind him. When no one appears to snatch him back into the darkness, he says, "No. But they're looking for me. We've gotta get out of here!"

"What's your name, son?" The boy tells him. "Well, Carl, that's our plan, too. Second star on the right and straight on 'til morning. Where did you come from?"

"The church."

"There's a church in these damn woods?" Cocolo asks.

The question rattles Carl, and his panting for air nears hyperventilation. "Yes… uh-huh… yes, sir… terrible… they do… it's… they're… evil."

"Cocoa, leave the boy alone. Now, Carl. Put your mind to rest. You're with a bunch of strapping fine folk. We'll protect you. Why don't you walk with me? And tell me all about it."

Rainer wraps an arm around the kid and leads him off. Cocolo gives us a look that says he doesn't like this development before hurrying to stay close to the newcomer.

"Shit's gonna get real." Marcus shakes his head and trudges along.

"What? What's going on?" Bartlett asks, walking beside him.

Nodding his head toward Rainer, he says in a quiet voice, "Him and kids. Not good. Don't you know what he did, Bart?"

"No. All I heard was that he was called Dr. Turkey."

"Dr. Turkey Day," Marcus hisses, dropping his voice even lower. "And don't you let him catch you saying that. Last guy who said it to his face was fed his own eyes." He looks nervously up the path to make sure they won't be heard. "Killed his whole family. Not in no normal way, neither. They all sat down to Thanksgiving dinner together. Wife, kids, grandkids, aunts, and goddamn uncles. All of them folk eating a nice turkey dinner. Only none of them makes it to the pumpkin pie."

"He poisoned them?"

"Nah. Just drugged them. Made them sleepy. Turkey makes me sleepy, too, but not like this. They don't wake up until he gives them a little something else. An antidote, like."

I read all about it when it was in the news. It was a shot of adrenaline he used to counter the anaesthetic.

"One by one, he wakes them. And when their eyes open, they're out in the garage strapped down to a metal table."

"Damn."

"And that ain't all. Old Dr. Reiner really was a doctor. A mortician."

He was a pathologist, but I don't correct him.

"And when they come to, they find that they're not exactly whole. He's got their chest cut open. He pulls out their hearts so they can watch them stop beating."

Bartlett looks like he's going to puke.

I smile to myself. As if what he's done is any different. They're all the same.

I used a gun. I did it quickly. They weren't family. Silly distinctions to make you feel better.

Marcus's excuse is he did it out of duty and revenge. The only pleasure was the satisfaction of payback against the foes who'd encroached on his gang's territory.

Cocolo killed three of his lovers. Knifed them in the shower like a proper Norman Bates, then buried the bodies in the basement.

All the same.

Yet, they cling to the little distinctions, so they can feel better about themselves, as though it all comes down to who was killed and how many. And how it was done.

Which is why they avoid me.

I'd like to think it's because they're afraid of coming at me in a fight. But that's a laugh. The truth is the sexual nature of my crimes makes me worse in their eyes. They act as if they don't want to get any of my filth on their blood-soaked hands.

"No! No! You're going the wrong way!" It's the kid, Carl. His voice has risen in pitch as though fear has reversed his trip through puberty, and he's squealing loud enough to alert everyone in the state to our presence. "We gotta go! Now!"

His face is an elongated mask of terror, and he's pulling against Rainer, struggling to get free of his grip. Like Rainer's family must have struggled against their restraints.

"Easy now. You're safe as houses, my boy."

"No. No. I won't go back!"

The three of us have almost caught up with the others when the boy breaks free. He's blind with fear and instantly ploughs hard into Cocolo, finding himself ensnared once more. Although this time, the hold is more gentle. The old Cuban half hugs him and coos noises of comfort. But his mothering only gets him a knife between the ribs. The sneaky kid.

We're the stupid ones for not searching him. If nothing else, prison has taught us a weapon can be hidden anywhere.

Cocolo goes down with black fluid streaking over his dark skin. The boy chooses not to come at us and turns back into the dead forest, his footfalls crunching into the distance. No one pursues him. Rainer and Marcus go to our fallen comrade.

"Cocoa, you're gonna be okay." Marcus pulls off his shirt to put pressure on the wound.

"Shit!" Bartlett says, keeping his distance. For a mass murderer, he's awfully squeamish.

And he hasn't even seen what spooked the kid yet.

A man has been tied face down on a cross. The apparatus is set at an angle as though it's in the process of slow collapse. But the angle may be intentional because it gives the body the impression of flight. Especially with his lungs pulled out through his back and his skin spread to form demonic wings.

"Let me see," our resident medical professional says. Rainer pulls away the shirt and examines the gash with his eyes and fingertips.

Cocolo flinches and releases a sharp intake of breath. "Don't hurt the boy," he says through gritted teeth. "He was just scared. It's not—" A horrible keening sound escapes him.

Rainer tuts.

"We won't," Marcus says. "Rest a moment. Then we'll get going. Find help. Medicine."

"Not sure I can walk."

"Then, we'll carry you. Like the old man said, we're all big strapping men."

But we were also starving men. Even with the daily battle royal, there was only so much yard-meat, and it made for paltry portions once it was spread around. And we've been walking all day with nothing to feed us but a can of lima beans and half a box of stale crackers. We're barely carrying ourselves. Keeping an injured man with us will kill us all, and everyone knows it.

Maybe Cocolo knows it too because he does us the favor of dying.

Marcus cradles his dead friend. His face is ashen but unmarked by tears.

***

It's an hour or so later when the first torch sputters dead.

The fuel jug contains only the horrid citrus smell and a dribble of drops.

Marcus tries lighting a fallen branch, but it goes up in a flash. With the ship blocking the rain, everything is dry and eager to catch. He flings it away before the flame can reach his hand.

We curse his stupidity and stomp out the embers so the whole forest doesn't go up around us.

I'm pretty sure we're all thinking the same thing.

We'll be dead soon.

We managed to survive the first couple of hours of our freedom in total blindness, but we had streets to follow and driveways that led to houses. None of us knew the town beyond the wall worth a damn, but there was a town. We'd gotten water and our meagre supplies.

Lost in a state forest, groping from tree to tree, we will spiral in circles, starving and praying for rain that will never come.

The flickering light of the remaining torches is the only thing keeping the hysteria of our approaching death from turning us into panicked animals. We trudge on, one foot in front of the other, telling ourselves—lying to ourselves—that we're going somewhere. Going to a place where we'll be safe.

I'm so focused on my feet and the lie that I almost run into the others who have pulled to a stop. Rainer crouches down, looking over the brown and crispy brush toward a light in the distance.

Rationally, we ought to go the other way. Everything—the bodies in the trees, the winged man, the boy's terror, all point to a place we don't want to be. But when you're drowning, you'll grab onto a knife's blade to gasp for one more breath of air. Even cold, calculating Rainer grows incautious. His only warning is to go slow and not to run. Keep quiet.

The lights are high up on posts. Great industrial beasts that glare through the withered branches and make me wonder if we've somehow looped back to the prison. But the prison hasn't had electricity for close to a month.

We crawl the last few yards to a clear break in the trees. An invisible wall that separates the wild from the tame. At one time, a wide lawn spread over a hill. The grass is all dead and flattened. If not for the desiccated brown colour, I could imagine it was recently mown. At the top of the mound, a rustic lodge sits like a bloated toad. On lower ground narrow rustic cabins form a semi-circle.

"Damn!" Bartlett says. "It's a summer camp."

"Splendid. I can't wait until we're sitting around the fire singing *Row, Row, Row Your Boat.*"

Marcus says, "We should check the cabins." When no one moves or says anything, he goes on, "Look for supplies… or people."

Rainer stares at the big lodge off on its own. Lights are in its windows. That's where people will be if there are any around. But then, it really isn't a question of *if,* is it? The electricity alone is a testament to occupation.

Rainer doesn't take his eyes from the top of the hill but nods in agreement.

I guess he's not anxious to kick the hornet's nest either.

The first and nearest cabin contains the dank odour of stale sweat and urine, as well as six bunk beds stripped of their mattresses. We're not so lucky with the next.

The mouth-souring, stomach-turning stench of rotting meat slams our sinuses before we reach the door. Inside, it's the exact layout of the first cabin, but bodies are shelved two by two on each of the bunks. The harsh spotlights glaring through the lattice windows turn their skin alabaster white.

"Jesus!" Bartlett says with a loud moan. "What the hell happened?"

Rainer doesn't move beyond his place near the entrance. "My guess would be poison."

"How the hell can you tell that, old man?" Marcus is too freaked out to mind his mouth.

"No visible wounds. They appear to be slightly malnourished but clearly didn't starve to death. And the young age of some of them makes it unlikely to be illness or natural causes."

Perhaps it's because I'm standing apart from them, still on the porch. Or maybe it's my habit of looking over my shoulder, but I'm the first to spot the men coming down the hill.

Eight of them. Their speed is due more to gravity hurrying their steps rather than a sense of urgency. There's a trudging quality to their movements. The sort expressed by men determined to complete a laborious and unpleasant task. They wear loose white shirts that are luminescent in the bright light. I spot rifles in a few hands, but I suspect all are armed.

"Time to go," I say softly but urgently, tapping Rainer's shoulder so he'll turn.

"I'm afraid the man is correct. Gentlemen, best be on our way before the welcome wagon arrives."

We dash around the side of the cabin with me in the lead.

A shot shatters the night and chews through a chunk of the cabin's pine siding. The men from the hill are no longer lumbering. They're running, letting the downward momentum propel them to sprinter speeds.

The woods are a good ten yards away, and the next cabin is at least four, so I skirt behind the makeshift morgue. We'll be sitting ducks, but that's a problem for later. Even if later is mere seconds away. Right now, finding cover is more important.

The others must think so, too, because they follow. Or maybe, they imagine I have a plan. If so, they're sadly mistaken. Scurrying behind the cabin reminds me of childhood games of hide and seek when I'd grab the nearest and most obvious spot because the It is raising his voice to show that time is nearly up.

Eyes bulge and dart from side to side, looking for the next route of escape. Sweat plasters grime to our faces, and in the shadow of the building, it's the frantic flickering of the whites of my companion's eyes that stand out.

The men from the hill come around the cabin before we can act.

They're not trained like cops or military, and they turn toward us as they skid to a halt, their speed throwing them off balance and scattering them into the open. They fail to see Marcus pressed tight to the corner of the cabin.

He fights hard. And he fights mean.

Had you asked me to lay a wager before the yard fight this morning, I would have bet against him every time. The next few moments reveal that it would have been a losing bet.

Despite his weakened state, he moves fast and puts his wiry muscles to full advantage.

He drops the man closest to him with one sharp strike, driving two fingers through the left eye socket and into the brain. Holding onto the dead man's shoulders as he falls, Marcus swings into a roundhouse kick, catching the next guy below the ribcage. He doubles over and seemingly offers Marcus his head, which gets savagely snapped back. The wet crunch of vertebrae overshadows the yelling and commotion that's broken out.

As he moves onto his third opponent, Bartlett grapples with his own. They dance close together in jerky steps, neither gaining an advantage.

Rainer has also engaged them, which is surprising because of his age and intellect. I would have thought he'd hold back like I am. These men are not only well-fed but large and armed. They're the type I avoid. I'm not ashamed to admit that my preference has always been for those weak and defenceless. Women alone at night. Families asleep in their beds.

Yet, Rainer is no easier prey than Marcus. He manages to get a revolver off his target. Although, he doesn't shoot. With calm, steady strokes, he bashes the butt into the man's face. Cartilage and bone crack. Teeth chip away. The man would crumble, but Rainer holds him up with a fistful of the man's white shirt.

For a brief, startling second, it appears we might actually get out of this.

But the cannon roar of a hunting rifle returns us to reality.

Three of the pack had split off from the rest and flanked us from the other side.

The bullet that's fired is high calibre and meant for large game. It shears Bartlett's skull apart. Blood gouts out, geysering with chunks of pink-grey flesh. But the slug of deadly lead doesn't stop. It caves through the other man’s face, punching a chasm through his cheek.

Marcus and Rainer spin to see the source, and the men they've been pummeling slink bonelessly to the ground.

The fight is four to three—or more accurately, it's even because I have my hands in the air and am pressed against the pine boards, making myself small. Still, my companions aren't dumb enough to charge this group. There’s too much distance between them, and their guns are out and aimed.

***

They bring us to the lodge, prodding us along with gun barrels to the small of our backs and boots to our backsides. The main door opens to a dimly lit mess hall that's full of the aroma of damp and mildew rather than food. But our ultimate goal is off to the right, in what was once the camp's rec room.

It's filled with dining chairs lined up like pews facing a large stone fireplace with deer antlers hanging above the mantle. A dying fire backlights an altar built from a trunk turned on end. Any doubt about it being an altar is laid to rest by the guttering pillar candles oozing vines of wax down the sides. Not to mention the woman with her throat cut. She's draped on her back across it to ease the flow of blood. It's dry now and stains a wide circle of the floorboards a dark, rusty shade of brown. Flies swarm the body in ecstasy at the rising charnel stench.

Often, I've left a home with a similar tableau, but always fresh. Ripe like summer fruit. I never linger to see death turn into a thing of revulsion. When I reluctantly depart, the body on the bed will still have the colour of vitality, and her blood will be thick, syrupy, and gloriously glossy red.

I'm so engrossed in the woman that I miss the man in black leaning by the fire.

"Kneel heathens!"

A rifle butt against my lower spine quickens my obedience. "Brother Laurence tells me you are responsible for the deaths of many of the faithful. This displeases me more than you can ever know. You are all owed painful deaths and eternity in the fiery depths of hell." His anger is overshadowed by the haughty tone of a Sunday preacher snarling about sin and brimstone.

He steps forward and strides partly into the aisle between the chairs. When he speaks again, grim resignation shapes his words. "But now, especially now that there are so few of us, I must put you to use. However unworthy you may be, you must help us."

"Kind, sir," Rainer says with no hint of mockery. "In what way can we be of assistance?"

The guard closest to him clouts him on the ear to shut him up, but the preacher raises a finger to stop the abuse.

"You will help us find a way to the great reward." He gestures upward with his eyes and a slight lift of his hands.

"Heaven?" Marcus spits out the question. Whether out of incredulity that he'll ever end up there or out of sheer disgust at the suggestion, I don't know.

But the reverend gives a wan grin of dismissal. "Oh, if only it were that simple. But, yes, that is the ultimate destination. But heaven is not a place you simply forge a path to. We must trust that to the angels." Again, his eyes go skyward. "The chariots of God have come for us, and now, it is up to the righteous to find our way to them so they may convey us to paradise."

"Christ! You think E.T. up there is sent by God? You're tripping." This earns Marcus several blows. Our captors are only too happy to prove their loyalty and correct his impudence.

The reverend, for his part, takes a few more steps toward where we're cowed at the back of the room. His tone is bemused, although a scowl adorns his face. "I assure you, the beings on that ship are the harbingers of the Almighty. If you weren't so ignorant, you would know that it has been proven beyond a doubt—scientifically—that heaven is located at the middle star of Orion's Belt. Here, God has set his throne, as it's stated in Revelations."

He paces back to the altar with his hands clasped behind his back. "Why do you think they wait? An invader or an explorer would have made their intentions known by now. These are angels, and they await the faithful. It is up to us to discover the method of ascension to their craft."

"And pray tell, my good man, how does one ascend to your awaiting chariot?"

His words grow sour. "That is a formula we have yet to strike upon. We can not do it corporally. That is clear. It is the spirit that must rise and be gathered. We have tried many things. But I believe we are close. The weakening of the Earth's pull is proof. Were one's soul set free at the right moment, it would float up to meet our guides." Now, he stalks toward us with a predatory gait. "It is your great luck that you have joined us for our experiments."

"Oh, hell no!"

Meekly, the cultist directly behind me says, "Father, we cannot send these men. Look at them." He grabs my hair and stretches me out of my slump. "They wear prison uniforms. They're criminals."

"As Matthew says, 'If you forgive men of their trespasses, God will also forgive you.' Or, more practically, beggars can't afford to be choosers. Our numbers have dwindled. Brother Isaiah and his men have not returned from the pursuit of our lost lamb, and time is running out. Bring the insolent one forward so we may begin!"

The men pause, attempting to determine who he means. They settle on Marcus, who fights and curses as they pull him up.

Rainer lunges for him, snatching him close. The cultists cuff the old bastard across the jaw, dropping him back to the floor, but not before he whispers something in Marcus's ear.

The fight seems to go out of Marcus, and he lets two of the men drag him toward the altar.

I look over at Rainer, who's crumpled on his side. He winks. His mouth shapes the words, "Get ready."

My eyes are still on him, so I don't see Marcus strike. I only hear the sudden sounds of struggle.

"Now!" Rainer barks. And for reasons I don't comprehend, my body obeys.

Maybe it's knowing there's no way of leaving here alive. In this moment, I'm a cornered animal, and the odds are meaningless. What does it matter if I die this second or an hour from now?

I spring to my feet with an agility I haven't known since my free-range days. Our remaining guard is focused on the scuffle in the aisle, and I use my momentum to drive a fist at his throat. The blow isn't strong enough to crush his windpipe, but he staggers and chokes.

I give his shotgun a sharp yank by the barrel, freeing it. The gun scuttles across the floor and seems to spin purposefully to Rainer's waiting hands.

The guard recovers and comes for me. I grab his wrists, and his punches turn into a slow, struggling reach for my neck.

My feet retreat and tangle up in a chair. It tips over along with the both of us. I'm caught between hammer and anvil. The seat bites me above my hip, digging into my right kidney.

All the air escapes my lungs and fingers squeeze around my neck so no new oxygen can enter.

Monumental booms overtake the makeshift chapel.

BOOM! Shook-chick. BOOM! Shook-chick. BOOM!

The world fades. A spotty haze of greyness blots out my eyes. My ears switch to a station containing white noise.

BOOM!

The man on top of me slackens his hold as the flesh is stripped from his face. Lacerations peel the skin back in strips while the left side of his skull caves inward. Blood and viscera spray out the other side like a Roman candle ejecting its light.

When the cordite smoke lifts, I'm still alive. So is Rainer. Everyone else has been pulverized by blasts from the 12 gauge. Including Marcus.

Rainer watches me as I limp over to the body of our former companion. He rests the shotgun on his shoulder in a pose I've seen many times around the prison.

"Couldn't be helped," he says. "He was dead anyway." With his free hand, he points to a puncture in Marcus's thigh. The frayed fabric surrounding a bullet hole. "Would have bled out. But it's not like you really care, is it?"

"I suppose not." My eyes move to the nearby reverend. His ticket to heaven has been punched. A constellation of pellets marks his chest. His tongue hangs down nearly to the floor like a dead dog.

"Didn't think so. You always struck me as a little too reptilian to concern yourself over such matters. Never saw a flicker of emotion in you. Always curious about what made you tick."

Standing, I wipe my hands on my grimy pants.

It turns out, even Rainer clings to our differences and places himself in a different category from me. All the same.

"Me, reptilian? That's rich coming from Dr. Turkey Day."

Rainer strolls over to a wall lined with low bookcases. Some shelves contain worn paperbacks, others hold board games in tattered boxes. I follow, wanting to see if he'll take the bait.

But he doesn't

He says, "Guess we should see what supplies we can gather and skedaddle before Isaiah returns, hallelujah! But we probably have some time. That wily kid is likely leading them on a merry chase." He fingers through the selection of games. "We have time to fill our bellies and maybe play a few rounds of Parcheesi. Or is there a game you prefer?"

He brushes a pile of boxes, so they tumble out onto the floor, spilling dice and cards.

My attention is caught by the haphazard mess, so by the time I focus back on Rainer, the butt of the shotgun is plummeting toward my face.

"Personally, I've always been partial to Operation."

***

I awake to pain so intense it's hallucinatory. The signals to my brain bend and twist until nothing is real except the agony.

"Ah, just in time," Rainer says close to my ear. "I was worried that shot wouldn't work. Not the best medical facilities in these parts."

His hand squirms underneath my shoulders and bends me forward with surprising ease. It's as though I would float away if not for the ropes binding me down.

"Have a gander."

My eyelids peel apart to see him hovering horizontally beside me, kicking his legs for stability, swimmer-like. A joyous grin contorts his face and changes him into a stranger. He nods for me to look down at myself.

A bloody bear trap on my chest slowly resolves itself to be my ribs spread open at an unnatural angle.

Globules of blood float from the cavity that once was my chest. They do a slow weightless ballet. From the blackness, a strange pink creature emerges, shuddering rhythmically. It tries to drift away, but thick meaty cords hold it back.

My heart! It's my heart.

Its frantic beating begins to slow.

From beside me, Rainer says, "Isn't it marvellous? What a time we live in, old boy."

If I had the strength, I'd scream.

~

05

about the author

C. S. SOLARYS *is a multi-genre, dark and erotic romance author. She crafts swoon-worthy men, and feisty women who fight their real-life flaws to earn their happy ending.*

She drinks Rooibos tea everyday, and loves bedtime routine with her two babies.

You can find her on Wattpad, Instagram, and Tiktok as kristianabooks

THE SOLDIER

by C.S. Solarys

ON A DESERT ROAD, 8 HOURS FROM DUBAI, UAE
AUGUST 26, 8:00 AM

A soldier follows orders. Obeys and executes.

I hung upside down secured by the seatbelt on the passenger seat of the Land Rover Defender.

The air was a baneful swirl of thick dust, and my mouth was full of sand. I coughed it out. Most of it stuck to my face and eyelashes. My head felt heavy, and my limbs ached with pain. A thin trickle of blood ran down my left temple, and crimson beads plopped on the roof of the rover in a *one, two*…counting. I had been knocked out cold after our car toppled over. We shouldn't have traveled with a severe weather warning, but I dared my chances. I stretched out my hand to check the driver's condition.

His seat was empty.

I crossed my right arm over my suspended torso to reach for the safety harness to unbuckle. It was a game of touch. I couldn't open my eyes and risk more sand in them. My best chance of survival and rescue was retrieving my protective eye gear from my sling bag or Tactical Rifle Case. I pushed my thumb harder on the red buckle, again and again, digging my thumb deeper until the buckle released with a soft click, and my body dropped on the roof with a thwack.

"Fuck," I gritted out.

I crouched and felt my surroundings, navigating my hands to the rear side of the car for my bag carrying the Wiley X sniper's eyewear. Before I could take cover, a ghastly wind swirled towards me. A vicious smack of grit, soil, and debris knocked me on my back and rattled the car sideways. I inhaled a lungful and coughed the choking bits out. A bottle of water would be handy to cleanse my mouth, but the sooner I got out of the car, the sooner I could search for the driver and signal for help.

I found my bearings and pulled the military green t-shirt from underneath my uniform and covered my mouth and nose. I redoubled my efforts to look for the eyewear, stretching and touching with eyes firmly shut. My knuckles smashed into a cold aluminum case. *Fuck.* It was a metallic gray Rimowa luggage case, carrying my essentials and the trophy I'd won at the 9th International Military Games hosted in Jeddah.

My request to leave base before the closing ceremony had been rejected. Instead, my superiors saluted, shook my hand, and offered a flat "congratulations" before handing me a gold-plated falcon cradled on a wooden base. My name was engraved on a golden plaque with bold black lettering: RAMI ELZAAK, United Arab Emirates Army, Sniper Frontier, Winner.

Our last name, Elzaak, was worth nothing. We were nobodies in this sandy paradise dripping with gold. My brother and Lieutenant General, Haydar, was counting on this win. The ruling family would honor our house and reward our family with fuck you cash and a rise in rank for both of us: General for him and Brigadier General for me.

Haydar breathed strategy. With every stomp of his shiny black shoes, and constant mustache-rolling between his thumb and forefinger, his black eyes moved surely like chess pieces mapping the path to victory.

Her. She was the compass of my life. The tipping point of my axis. My day began and ended with thoughts of her. I dreamt of *her*.

—Got it.

I clasped the sling bag close to my chest and felt for the mechanical lock. Snapping it open, I fished out the glasses, pulled my t-shirt up to my brows to wipe the sand, and then secured the glasses over my eyes. I dragged my lids open. Cautious. The sand attack had made me distrustful of items that were second nature to me for the last five years.

I crawled out of the car and squinted to look into the distance. It was all a blur of brown. I held the door frame, preparing to go back into the car and retrieve the satellite phone, but blinding lights and blinking orange hazards caught my attention from a distance. A rescue car was approaching at slow speed.

"Colonel."

My driver and first lieutenant, Hafeez, jumped from the moving car and stood at attention. He raised his right hand sharply, fingers and thumb extended, joined, the tip of his right forefinger touching the rim of his tactical helmet visor, slightly to the right of his right eye—a perfect salute.

"First lieutenant, Hafeez. At ease." I returned the salute, ignoring the burning pain in my right wrist.

"Colonel, you are hurt. Let me attend to you."

"No. We keep going. I need to get back to Dubai."

"But, Sir," he looked to the sky, and my eyes followed his movement. "We don't know what that is," he pointed skyward.

Odd.

The sun shone from an opening of a perfectly circular cloud that stretched for miles—a tiny dot of yellow encircled by fluffs of brilliant white with no end in sight.

"If it doesn't harm us, we drive. The alien craft still floats in the United States, and we are okay."

I marched to the trunk of the toppled Cruiser and collected my Rifle Case and personal luggage. Hafeez held the rear door of the monstrous rescue jeep ajar. I shoved the items inside and came face to face with the driver.

"You are a civilian," I pointed out.

"T-That is my cousin, Sir. He owns a garage close by. I sought help when I couldn't wake you up, Sir."

Guilt serrated my insides. I was risking another family to get to mine. Hafeez had to follow my orders to a T, his cousin shouldn't.

"What's your name, young man?" I extended my hand to greet him.

"Adeem, Sir."

"It's nice to meet you, Adeem. I wish it were under different circumstances. However, we really need your car. We can take you back home—"

"I'm the best person to drive this car, Sir. I can get you back home safely."

I cast a glance toward Hafeez. We knew our oaths. We lived to serve, protect, and defend. Uncertainty brewed in the horizons. We'd be out of cell phone range for hours, unknowing what awaited us in the city or along the way.

"It may not be safe for you." I offered no further explanations.

"Sir, I understand the risks." Adeem began, "Besides, my cousin twice failed his defensive driving course. That's why he came running to me like a little baby." Adeem grinned widely while Hafeez's eyes rounded in humorless fury.

I smiled, gave a clipped nod, and settled in the back seat. I prepared the medkit while listening to the cousins argue about the choice of music for the seven-hour trip. Adeem's playlist had six hours of Charlie Puth. That was it.

I stuck my head and shoulders out of the window and rinsed the sand off my mouth and face, then sutured the wound on my temple. Hafeez insisted I take pain medications before tuning out the music with earplugs.

Peaks and dips of creamy-white sand stretched beyond the eye. I turned off my cell when we lost connectivity and laid my head against the window, mulling over the events of the past two weeks. My stomach knotted with unease at the changes forced by the world-ending theories.

The Ministry of Economy imposed the circuit breaker to curb panic-selling and manic-buying. Parents kept their kids at home, and supermarkets limited the number of essential items purchased by one family. The government disabled automated teller machines to control money reserves, and queues outside banks wound around blocks for miles.

Adeem cruised at high speeds when we got to the smooth tarmac. The thought of seeing my wife's smile in a few hours spread a comforting warmth all over me and my leaden eyes, and I gave in to the exhaustion.

"Sir!" A voice yelped, "Sir! You need to see this!"

In a minute, I scoffed internally.

The majestic falcons and camels could wait. I was dead asleep, struggling to come to. I filled my lungs with cool, conditioned air and held it in for five seconds—a moment of calm. Hiding a yawn behind a fist and squinting at the sharp rays of the afternoon sun, I flung my arms outward and stretched, wiggling my toes for circula—

BANG!

My eyes shot open, my spine froze. Saliva dried in my throat as my gaze bounced from the unmoving traffic ahead to the carnage on my right. I was deathly dumbstruck. A sea of collided cars on the outbound road piled on top or next to each other. Teenagers leaped from car to car; some stole flares and dispensed them like it was the fourth of July, and others helped the wounded—

THUMP!

Two, tiny, bright red handprints were smeared on my window from a bleeding toddler in the arms of a terror-stricken, wailing mother.

"Here! Take my baby! Help her!"

My left hand frantically rolled down the window, and my right reached for the medical kit somewhere on the car's floor. The mother dropped the baby on my lap.

She continued shrieking, "We are all going to die! We are all going to die!"

I placed two fingers close to the child's windpipe and stilled, listening to her slackening heartbeat for fifteen seconds.

Thud…

Thud…

Thud…

"Record, seventy!" I shouted.

"Recorded! Sir." Hafeez affirmed. He was on a call badgering whoever was on at the other end of the line.

I took two white bandages and rounded the deep cuts on the child's arm. "Ma'am, is your child taking any medications?"

No answer.

I craned my neck. She sat on the heated tarmac, her eyes looking straight ahead. *What the fuck?*

"Adeem! Bring the mother inside the car. She is in shock."

No answer. No *creak* of a door opening.

I threw a gaze at the front seats while bandaging the second cut. Adeem gripped the steering with white knuckles, and Hafeez was writing instructions from whoever was on the phone. The child's breathing was strained, but her skin was warm to the touch. She had a fighting chance if they made it to the hospital in time. Given the mayhem outside, the only way into the city was on foot.

Cradling the child in my arm, I stepped out of the car and opened the driver's door. I pincered Adeem's jaw hard, tightly enough to bruise.

"You drop her, I kill you. Understand?"

He nodded and moved to the back seat, the girl securely in his arms. Hafeez ended the call, lips pressed into a thin line.

"Report." I issued the directive, stone-faced.

"Umm," his eyes avoided mine as he assisted the mother. "People are fleeing the city b-because of earth tremors. Some skyscrapers… Dubai was affec—"

NO. My heart dropped. Zahra. My heart. My love. My wife.

Our apartment was on the forty-sixth floor of the tallest building in the world.

My chest constricted. Fear barbed around my heart, shattering my ribs one by one, and a sinking feeling shot through me like a raft with holes in the floor. Yet through the terror, a grim determination pounded in my blood. Nothing would stop me from protecting her.

I reached for my bag with fumbling hands and rifled for my phone. My thumb hovered over the power button instead of pressing and holding. I stared at the black screen…waiting…hoping…praying. The damned bitten apple finally appeared but was immediately replaced by an eerie blue 5.

What in the—

"Hafeez, give me your phone. I need to make a call."

He held his Galaxy Z open, the same eerie blue number 5 front and center on its screen. What did it mean? Was the world ending in five minutes? Five hours? What the fuck was it?

I tossed my phone on the back seat and shook him for answers. "What else do you know? Which buildings were affected?"

"I-I don't know the specifics, Sir. The tides breached the shorelines, and some villas flooded. E11 is closed, and there are cases of vandalism."

How the fuck would I get home?

Thirty seconds later, the mysterious blue number vanished from our screens. My phone flooded with incoming messages and missed calls from my brother and Zahra. I called her first; it went straight to voicemail and her melting-honey voice pulled at my heartstrings:

"You missed me, and I missed you. Let's try this again. Mwaa!"

After five unsuccessful attempts, I tried the house phone.

"Beep, Beep. This line is temporarily disconnected."

Time became my enemy. For every second I didn't know if she was okay, I'd move twice as fast to get to her. My hands moved on their own accord. I snapped open my case and assembled my McMillan TAC-50 heavy caliber sniper rifle. I secured the weapon across my body.

"Turn back and go to the nearest hospital."

"Yes, Sir."

I slammed the door shut and leaped on the car's hood for a vantage point. Around me, terrified mothers rocked babies to calm, cars with partial body shells and bumpers honked and blinked amber, fathers hauled suitcases from the wreckage, and teens made smiley, end-of-the-world TikToks despite putrid air with choking exhaust fumes.

I landed on my feet and broke into a sprint toward the border. As I ran, I speed-dialed my brother. He picked up on the first ring.

"Akh, *brother*, are you safe?"

"CAR! AUH 0.33!"

"Done!"

I clutched my phone tighter and ran through the chaos like my life depended on it. I didn't stop until an immigration police officer held his palm upright to slow me down. He leaned closer to read my credentials as I flashed my badge, then saluted.

"This way. Follow me, Sir."

Highway cameras flashed bright white like they were giving me treats instead of tickets. The red, white, and blue above the car rotated in sync with the *Whamp! Whamp!* of the sirens, and my driving was more dangerous than the blinking hazards.

Forty-five minutes later, I pulled up at the headquarters. The normally pristine, quiet office environment had been transformed into an emergency base center. It was organized chaos, the air thick with tension. Menacing sirens from fire trucks, police cars, and ambulances blasted at the training grounds as they lined up and waited for orders.

Police helicopters and media choppers swarmed the skies, their powerful rotors sending vibrations through the ground and into my combat boots.

"Colonel." A junior officer held my door and gave a salute.

"Lieutenant General Haydar?"

"He is waiting for you, Sir."

We marched in urgent strides toward the command center, passing officers from Dubai Police loading water on a truck in their boring green coverall uniforms.

"Akh."

I halted in my tracks as soon as I heard his voice. With a ramrod straight spine, I executed a sharp salute. "Lieutenant General!"

Haydar gave me a once over and squinted his brows when he saw my blood-stained pants.

"As you were, brother." He squeezed my nape and brought the tip of his nose to touch mine in the traditional greeting. "I'm glad you are alright. Walk with me."

Anxiety pinpricked my skin like a caress of a thorny stem. Haydar wasn't himself. He never called me "brother" outside our homes, and our interactions mirrored the protocol handbook. For him to act this strange meant he was keeping something from me.

"I had to block Mama because she kept calling and asking about"—Haydar broke off to answer a call— "It is madness. Absolute madness, brother. We wouldn't need to move anyone if they'd stayed calm and listened. These Gen Z kids—" Another call interrupted our conversation. "You have the east wing of the American Consulate."

"What are you talking about?" I asked.

"You are watching the east wing of the consulate. The ambassador general is still there."

"Mama, Asha, are they okay?"

"Yiess," he waved his hand and responded with a bored tone as if the imminent danger was a figment of imagination in peoples' minds. "They are in a villa in Dubailand."

"Is Zahra with them?"

"She refused to leave your apartment."

My hand gripped his wrist before he could take another step. "You left her?"

Venom dripped from my voice, and my eyes searched his face for malice. But there was none.

Letting go of his hand, I stepped back and saluted. "Permission to report at 1600 hours."

I could go home and back in an hour.

Haydar twisted my wrist, grabbed my shoulder, and slammed my back into the nearest wall.

"Have. You. Gone. Mad?" He punctuated every word with a breath of fury. "You'll destroy us all because of her!"

I ignored his barking and gruffly repeated, "Permission to report at 1600hrs."

"DENIED!"

He drew his fist back and smashed it into the wall, narrowly missing me.

"Brother," His eyes misted, his lips trembled, and his knuckles dripped with blood. "You will bury both of us if you do this."

He was right.

But what options did I have? My wife's worst days could end with a check in at a mental hospital because of loud noises, abrupt movements, or weird smells. Almost anything could be a trigger. She did not "refuse" to leave the house, things had gone awry. She was in the middle of a danger zone, alone. How badly had the earthquake affected her?

Blood drained from my brother's face. His arms went limp by his side. He could feel my resolve: I had to get Zahra, and the cost would be his demotion and my arrest.

"Permi—"

His hand shot up and sliced through the air like lightning. I heeded, my breath hitching. Murderous waves rolled off his bulky frame.

He stepped back, rivulets of bitter sweat staining his crease-free grey camo shirt. Angry veins appeared across his arm as he slowly crushed the two-way radio in his right hand. My eyes trained on an object far away as I waited for his wrath. Anticipated it. Estimated the force his punch would crack my nose bridge…

I wouldn't flinch or back down. I'd stand there and take it. I deserved his anger.

Haydar clenched his eyes shut. His jaw sawed. The cords on his neck stretched to breaking point. He opened his lips to speak—and sealed them without uttering a word.

He about-turned and stormed the opposite way. The action spoke his words: he'd be on the prosecuting side tomorrow morning.

I bolted for the car park.

In dire situations, only ambulances and special license plates had access to sealed-off areas. So, I hot-wired Haydar's car.

Ten minutes later, I pulled up in front of our building. I left the engine running as I rushed upstairs. If I could get her out fast enough, maybe I'd only get hit with multiple infractions instead of a life sentence. Flinging the apartment door open, I called for my wife.

"Zahra? Zahra!"

Our bedroom door was ajar. I peeked. The drapes were closed, making the room pitch-black except for the light of a small battery-operated candle beside Zahra. She sat on the floor, knees hugged to her chest. I stepped into the room, the rubber of my shoe squeaking softly as it met the brown-tiled floor. But she didn't look up at me, her back lightly brushing the wall as she rocked herself softly.

"Baby, can I turn the lights on?" I asked.

She replied with a soft "Yes."

Our gazes met. The skin around her eyes was furrowed and dark, but her brown irises shone brightly against the bright pink. Damn, she was stunning. Perfect. Even now, eyes cried out, blotched face, disheveled hair, puffy red lips… every inch of her was mine to love. And I did. I adored her.

As I slowly approached, my hands and limbs warred with my brain. I wanted to rush to her, hug and comfort her, but experience reminded me that crowding her could worsen the situation. Taking off my boots and socks, I silently sat on the floor beside her. My knees were drawn up, and my arms rested helplessly on top of them. Our bare toes almost touched.

The heat from her body soothed my worries. *She's here, she's alive.*

I glanced at her adoringly and asked, "Tough day?"

She gave me a lopsided smile and told me everything: from the earthquake to the ruckus with the nurses. My eyes roamed her body while I listened, taking in her mauve-painted toenails, black yoga pants, a white short-sleeved…No! Her arms were covered in scratches. Sloppy red lines and crescent-shaped nail marks marred her silken skin. She'd fought to stay. Pain diced my heart knowing that she endured all this because I was away.

Then, she asked about my day. There was no time to explain.

"I came to get you, baby, then back to work."

Zahra was on her feet and across the room before I could blink. My mind raced to figure out what affrighted her, but she beat me to it.

"They sent you," she pointed an accusing finger, "did they tell you to take me outside, and they'll take it from there? Huh? Are you working with them?"

"N-no," I spread my arms wide open, palms facing her, shaking my head, "I—"

Zahra leaped for the closest bedside lamp and held it in her hands like a tennis racket. The crystal droplets on the lamp swished like a warning song as she swung it back and forth. I took a giant step and lurched for her.

Crash! She flung the lamp towards me, its droplets clinking as they shattered. Before I could react, she rolled across the bed and grasped the other lamp, ready to hurl it.

I pleaded with her, "Baby, please, trust—"

The second lamp crashed in an explosion of crystal. She had thrown it past me, toward the bedroom entrance and I turned, expecting an intruder. But there was no one; she'd distracted me so she could slip into the ensuite bathroom.

"Don't you dare come close to me!" she shouted, teary-eyed. "You asked me to trust you and gave me to them the last time they were here!"

"That was five years ago!" I clenched fists and screamed at the ceiling.

It'd happened while we were dating. One night, she found out I hid playing cards under the seat, and that's how I won Gin rummy. I thought it was funny, she obviously didn't. Things had escalated until I called for medical assistance. The results were disastrous. She feared to look me in the eye for a whole month after the incident.

But that was before I knew about self-soothing strategies, medications, and avoiding certain sensory stimuli. We purchased an apartment in this building because the dancing fountains calmed her. She watched them every night before sleeping.

Our need to be together eclipsed the naysayers. We learnt about each other: what our hearts wanted, what our souls needed. She knew my thoughts before I spoke them aloud and I knew her frustrations when she couldn't vocalize them. The twinkle in our eyes when we gazed at each other rivaled the brightest stars in the skies.

We were running out of time. With a resigned breath, I walked to her nightstand and pulled out her medication and noise-cancellation headphones. I pushed and twisted the cap and held out two capsules in my hand. Zahra glared at me, ran a tirade of profanities and locked herself in the bathroom. I threw the pills in anger. They bounced against the lilac wall then rolled under the bed.

I pounded the door, growling her name desperately. She made elaborate arguments about the building structure and weather patterns supporting her safety up here. Some of her points were valid. I thought about breaking the door and dragging her out, but she'd taught me about empathy and humanity towards those with mental health challenges. She had a goal to educate the world on the same and I vowed to keep her fire burning.

"I love you, Rami. Sorry I make life harder for you."

"Never apologize for who you are, Z. You make my life richer. I love you."

Slumped against the bathroom door, I dropped to my knees until I was sitting on the floor. I'd sleep right here if I had to, listening to her breathing as it evened out. Her feet pattered across the bathroom as she dragged a mat to the door. She loved sitting in a lotus position. Hours passed as we spoke over the door, laughing and reminiscing about our adventures. Her fingertips brushed mine from underneath the door.

"Rami, I want to come out now," she whispered, "if tonight is our last night on earth, I want to spend it with you."

I wanted that for us, too. I adored the freckles on her nose, kissed the scratches on her arms, imprinted every curve and dip into my memory and immortalized her. With every sultry whisper my mind prayed for tomorrow not to come, and with every moan she brought me back to the present, to her. I pushed aside fear, obligations, and duty. The world could end now and it'd be the perfect ending because she was mine. In our last hours together I did what I loved the most, being her husband, loving her.

~

04

about the author

H.J. Nelson *is an Idaho native who graduated from the University of Wisconsin. She began writing on Wattpad in 2015, where her story* ***THE LAST SHE*** *garnered over 12 million reads and became one of the most read Science Fiction stories on Wattpad in 2016 and 2017. Since then, The Last She has been acquired for publication as a three books series, optioned for television by Sony and translated into French and Italian.*

When not writing, Nelson has lived on a boat in the British Virgin Isles, worked in two zoos and ridden an elephant through the jungles of Laos.

You can sign up for her newsletter at hjnelsonauthor.com, or find her on Instagram at @h.j.nelson.

THE TRADE

by H.J. Nelson

SOMEWHERE IN KANSAS
AUGUST 28, 5:50 AM EDT

I snuck across the dew-damp grass, gun in one hand, bag of food in the other, dawn still an hour off. Behind me, the house was quiet. Of course it was. Nothing ever happens in Kansas town.

Want proof?

The aliens show up, literally the whole world goes insane, and my dad declares that he needs help patching the fence so the cows stop escaping. That's it. Oh, and that I probably shouldn't go shooting bullfrogs with the guys—on account of all the newcomers driving through.

Most people see the days counting down on the TV as a countdown to impending doom, but for me, it's a countdown for my last chance for adventure.

"Kip," I called softly across the lawn. "Kip, come here boy." I pulled out my dog whistle, and blew, then waited. Damn dog was probably off chasing coyotes—which was exactly why I'd trained him with the whistle. There was no way I was charging off across the country, in search of adventures, or aliens, without him.

Kip suddenly materialized behind the barn, his tongue lolling out of his mouth. I opened the creaking door of my truck—my pride and joy, besides Kip—and he launched himself into the passenger seat. Then I set my rifle in the back seat, along with my food.

The truck rumbled through the pasture, and I left the window open, breathing in the fresh air as my heart beat with the thrill of adventure. I'd felt the earthquakes shaking the land—but I wanted to see it. The ship. I want to be there when the countdown stopped and something finally *happened.* The back of my truck was already packed with spare bullets, three extra canisters of gasoline, and a pile of canned food from the cellar.

Adventure, aliens, a good dog and a working truck—what more could a guy ask for?

I roared down the highway, thinking about how I needed something more than this small town, that I needed to see the spaceship and crazy happenings for myself—

—then slammed on my brakes.

There, standing in the center of the highway, was a woman.

I'd been expecting military personnel, chaos, even green aliens with too many eyeballs, but this… this wasn't something I'd planned for. I slowed down, and cast a look at Kip. He just sat there, tongue lolling out, no opinion.

I eased the car slowly closer. The woman was youngish, maybe around sixteen. She would have been beautiful, dirty blonde hair and wide eyes, if not for the fact she looked like she'd been in a car crash, covered in scratches and scrapes. In fact, I glanced around, expecting to see a car in the ditch—but there was nothing but Kansas fields for days.

I slowed as I drew level with her. Still she stood there, unmoving. Didn't she know you weren't supposed to stand in the middle of the road? I couldn't see her hands—they were buried in the long flowing cotton dress she wore, so dirty my mother would have had an aneurysm.

"Umm, are you okay, miss?" I stopped the car beside her. "Do you need a ride?" I said when she still didn't respond.

Her eyes suddenly came up to mine—and my stomach bottomed up. They were the color of a summer Kansas storm.

"I'm sorry," she whispered. And then she pulled a trembling hand from her dress.

She was holding a pistol.

My heart beat faster as I looked at the cold weapon in her hands.

"Leave your keys in the ignition," she said, her voice shaking as much as her hands. There was a desperate, terrified look in her eyes. I was suddenly afraid she was going to shoot me without even meaning too. "I… I don't want to hurt you. All I want is your truck."

"Okay," I said slowly, my hands held in the air. Then, because I didn't think it was safe, I said, "I need to shift into park. Can I do that without being shot?"

She nodded, both hands on the pistol now—at least it made her aim a bit more level.

"Kay," I said, when I put the truck into park. "I'm going to open the door, okay?"

"Fine," she said, taking several steps back.

The door creaked open, and I stepped out, looking her dead in the eye. "My name is Ralph… Are you okay?"

"Be quiet!" she said, shaking the gun at me. "Just… go away."

"Can I take my bag?" I said. "It's in the back."

"NO!" she said, and I froze again.

"Okay," I said. "Easy. You can have my truck… Can I at least call my dog?"Her eyes shifted to the cabin of the truck and back to me and she nodded. "Yeah, fine, call him."

I hadn't planned it. I wasn't even sure why I did it.

But when her eyes went to Kip, I leapt forward. I'd meant to simply knock the gun free from her hands, but somehow I ended up with my arms wrapped around her, the gun skidding down the pavement, as I lifted her free from the ground.

It felt like trying to hold onto a rabid raccoon. She thrashed and kicked against me, literally reaching down to bite me; and then it happened.

The earth started to shake.

It happened all the time now, since the ship had appeared, the earthquakes. But somehow I went from fighting her, to our arms wrapped around each other, holding onto each other while around us the world trembled.

It felt like it lasted an eternity, but was probably only a minute or two.

When it finally stopped, even the birds were silent. The only noise was Kip, letting off a low whine from where he crouched on the pavement.

"Are you okay?" I whispered to the girl.

She nodded, and then, to my embarrassment, I realized my arms were wrapped tightly around her, holding her pressed against me.

I let her go, realizing too late I'd released her right next to the gun. But she didn't go for it. Instead, she just looked up at me with those big, sad eyes.

I cleared my throat, suddenly embarrassed. "You umm, you can take my truck," I said. "Do you know how to drive a stick shift?"

"No."

"Well, um, I could teach you," I said, feeling stupider by the minute.

She stared at me—I wished her eyes weren't so *big*. "You're going to teach me how to steal your truck?"

I blushed. "I mean, I would prefer you didn't steal it. What if I just gave you a ride?"

She thought about this, then slowly nodded. "Yeah… Yeah, I guess that would be alright."

"Okay," I said, feeling awkward. I made my way over to the pistol on the ground, and picked it up and handed it back to her, hilt first.

"Thanks," she said, her eyes darting up to mine, then back down, something both shy and curious there.

I cleared my throat. "Like I said, I'm Ralph." I nodded to Kip. "That's my dog Kip. Don't give him any sweets, or he'll never leave you alone." Kip had already made his way over to the girl, licking her fingers, not seeming to care about the gun she held.

I opened my truck door, and then watched as the girl walked around the other side, Kip trailing at her side as if he were now her dog. *Traitor.*

She opened the door and Kip shoved his way ahead of her—he always wanted to sit in the middle. She settled into the passenger seat, silence fell before us, only Kip seeming at ease.

"You can put the pistol in the glove compartment, if you want," I said. *With the safety on*! I wanted to yell, but didn't. She put it there, and because I honestly had no idea what else to say, I started to explain how to use a stick shift truck, and started off again.

"This is how you shift. It takes a bit to get the feel of it. I flooded the engines the first few times I tried, but only cuz my dad was yelling at me."

She nodded, saying nothing, and, because she'd literally given me no directions, or name, I just took off down the highway. We drove for a bit, saying nothing. Kip lowered his head into her lap, and she petted his head as he laid there.

"He's a nice dog," she said. I glanced at her for a moment, and then quickly back at the road.

"Yeah. He is." *Wow, Ralph, amazing conversation you've got going here.*

"You from around here?" she said.

"Yeah. Just down the road actually."

She frowned. "Are you going to get something?"

"No… I want to go see it. The ship."It was like I'd said something foul—she stared at me with an expression that went from shocked to angry. "You want to go into the Twilight Zone? Have you heard what's happening there?"

I had heard, but I just shrugged. "So? The countdown is almost over. What if I miss it?"

Her eyes flashed. "If you miss it? Pray to God you miss it, and after the countdown we're all still here. I saw *it*, and trust me, you don't want to be anywhere near there. I barely got out."

"What's it like?" I said, because I couldn't help it.

She looked as if she were going to yell again, but instead she shrugged, stroking Kip's fur when she said. "Just like it looks on TV… except everything's dark. And weird shit keeps happening. Honestly, the worst part isn't the ship—it's that everyone has lost their minds." She suddenly looked like she was about to cry. "My mom was too sick to leave. We had this old camper van, we were going to travel the states in it, but when things started to go crazy, she made me promise to take it and drive west as fast as I could. I made it all the way here, until this morning—"

She suddenly cut off, and when I glanced at her, I saw she was crying. Sobbing actually. I would have rather she pointed the gun at me again.

Luckily Kip seemed to know what to do, sitting up and licking her face so fervently that she stopped crying and started laughing.

"Kip, leave her alone," I said. "Down boy." But she didn't seem to mind, and when Kip did settle again, she finished her story. "I had parked in some trees. I thought I was safe there. Some men came and told me I had to leave. I tried to fight them." She flinched at the memory. "They just shoved me down and laughed. They said they would trade me the pistol for the van. I'm pretty sure it's not even loaded. They said 'it ain't' our fault you made a bad trade.' Then they laughed and drove away."

Silence fell again between, and because I had no idea what to say, I said, "I mean, it is kind of a cool pistol."

She started to laugh, and cry at the same time, and then she smiled up at me through the tears. "What did you say your name was?"

"Ralph."

"I'm Claire."

***

We drove for a couple more hours, and I learned more about Claire's life, and I told her a bit about mine. She told me she'd never seen a firefly—I couldn't believe someone had never seen a firefly, and promised to catch her one when it got dark. She told me about her life before the ship appeared in the sky, and the all consuming chaos after. Martial law. Chaos on the streets. Horror everywhere. No wonder her mother had told her to leave. Another smaller earthquake shook the ground when we stopped for a cold lunch. This time she reached out, and took my hand, clenching it tight till it passed.

Even though all we had was some dry sandwiches, it was a nice lunch.

After we ate, I gave her some of the spare clothes I'd packed, and she changed out of her dirty dress. When she came back, wearing my clothes, I was thankful Kip barked twice and put his paws up on her. I didn't know how to tell a girl, especially one in my old farm clothes, that she looked beautiful.

Then we got back in the truck. Claire was determined to convince me that I definitely shouldn't try and go and see the ship—not when half the US was currently trying to flee from it. She spent an hour listing all the reasons why it was too dangerous. I didn't stop her: I liked listening to her voice. She had agreed that she would come with me at least till Topeka, where she would see if she could get ahold of her mother and try to make a new plan from there.

"Stop!"

I slammed on the brake at Claire's voice, the two of us suddenly thrust forward against the seatbelts.

"What?" I said wildly, looking all around the road, expecting something terrible. "What is it?!"

She pointed to a small dirt road off the highway. There, hidden in a copse of trees so that I could barely make it out, was a camper van.

"That's my mom's van," she said. Then with anger, "That's my van!"

Her nostrils flared, and she suddenly opened the glove box and pulled out the pistol. "I'm getting it back. Right now." There was murder in her eyes.

"Woah, woah, wait a sec," I said, reaching out and taking her hand. She looked down in surprise at my hand on her arm, and I quickly let go. "Just hold on. You said they were open to trading, right? Maybe they'll trade."

"Or maybe they'll trade their lives," she said murderously.

"Or maybe something less likely to put us in prison," I said. "Just… let's go see if we can reason with them?"

I reached back behind me, pulling my rifle off the back seat.

She cocked a brow. "I thought you said we should reason with them?"

I shrugged. "Two reasons are better than one, right?

We spent a few minutes debating, but because I wanted to have a quick escape route, we decided to drive all the way up to the van. Then, giving Claire a nod, I honked three times.

It took several minutes, but finally three men stumbled out of the van. They each wore cutoffs and dirty shirts—a contrast to the van that was painted a sunshine yellow with daisies across it.

All three of them had guns.

"What now?" Claire whispered.

I picked up my rifle, holding it easily but not threateningly. "We ask to trade back." I opened the door and shut it heavily, striding across to the men.

"Afternoon, gentlemen!" I called out. "I was wondering if I could have a few minutes of your time." I winced at my words—I always got weirdly formal when I was nervous. And I was definitely nervous.

They laughed at this. The tallest of them belched and said, "What do you want, boy?"

"I want the van."

"Finders keepers," the tall one said. Then he gave an ugly leer back to Claire, who sat in the truck, with Kip. I knew her hands were wrapped around the gun. I just hoped if things got ugly, she'd remember how to drive.

"Oh wait," the tall man said, "I remember her. She traded with us, fair and square." The other two men laughed at this.

"Do you really want to cross the country in a van with daisies on it?" I said. My hands were sweaty on my gun, but I reasoned that they could have done far worse to Claire. There had to be *some* sense of humanity in them. "Besides, when the ship is gone, you'll be reported for grand theft auto, and things will get ugly. Why don't you just give the van back, and we can go on our way?"

It happened all at once; the tall man's gun came up, my rifle came up, and all at once we were at a standstill.

"Don't test me boy," the tall man growled.

"Don't test me," I said back. "I've been shooting since I could walk."

He smirked at this, and then, to my surprise, slowly lowered his gun. "You know, maybe we could help each other out." He glanced back at the van, and then across to my truck. "That's a *real* nice truck you got there."

My stomach dropped when I realized what he was suggesting. My truck was more than just four wheels and a cab—it was my ticket to freedom. To see the world. To adventure. I cast a glance back—and saw, there, in the window, Claire staring at us white-eyed, Kip beside her.

Maybe there are other adventures out there.

"The truck for the van?" I said hesitantly.

The tall man nodded, and after a moment, I lowered my gun and said, barely able to form the words, "Fine… It's a deal." Then I turned back to Claire and called out. "Claire, bring the keys!"

She made her way out of the truck, pistol in one hand, keys in the other.

"Ralph," she whispered. "Are you sure?"

I nodded, and then I waited until the tall man had tossed me the keys to the van, to toss him the keys to my beloved truck. He smirked as the two men climbed into my truck.

Then he turned back, gun pointed straight at Claire. "Oh, and one more thing. The dog too."

"My dog?" I said, my voice dry. "Why?"

"Need a good guard dog."

I swallowed hard. Claire's eyes were vividly angry, but I silenced her with a look. Stiff-legged, I walked to the back of the truck, opened the tailgate and called for Kip. At once he jumped into the truck bed, his loyal eyes focused on mine and his tail wagging. Always game for adventure.

"Sit boy," I said. He obeyed at once. The next word was harder to say, barely a whisper. "Stay." Again he obeyed. I shut the trailer and he began to whine as I took a single step back, then another and another. His whining grew as the tall man, laughing, slammed the door shut, and then took off.

With my beloved truck and my dog.

I watched them as they roared down the dirt road, headed for the highway. Claire slipped up next to me and took my hand in hers.

"Ralph, I'm so, so sorry."

As soon as they'd rounded the bend, I tossed her the keys to the van. "Come on, let's hurry."

She looked bewildered as she took the keys and started the van. I lowered my window and blew the dog whistle and said, "Don't worry about Kip. He should be running his ass back here any moment."

Sure enough, two minutes later, a black blur of fur crested the hill of the highway. He ran towards us, his tongue lolling out happily.

As Kip came closer, I saw a distant black cloud grow on the horizon—different from any storm cloud I'd ever seen.

"What is that?" Claire said, pausing on the edge of the highway.

I opened the door and Kip jumped inside. With the door open the sound grew louder, like an ocean wave, yet filled with terrifying chirping.

"Birds," I whispered.

We sat in stunned awe as the cloud of birds blacked out the sky, so many it sounded like a storm was raging all around us. The sky actually darkened from the sheer numbers of them.

Claire's hand reached out and wrapped around mine.

As suddenly as they'd come, they were gone, the wave of noise receding. I looked to where they'd gone, west, away from the ship, and then back east, to where I'd thought I was going this morning.

But seeing the ship no longer felt like the most important thing.

"Take a left, follow the highway," I said to Claire. "We'll go back to my house. It'll be safe there—we can try and get ahold of your mom. My parents have plenty of food and supplies."

"What about your adventure?" Claire said, staring at me with a frown

"I thought that was a pretty good adventure… I'm happy with my trade." I winked at her and the smile she gave me—well, I would have traded for more than a truck to see it again.

We drove down the highway, and when dusk grew, I had her pull over in an open field. It took only a few minutes before I saw it, blinking with light, then gone, then blinking again.

Claire suddenly shrieked—she'd seen it too. "Is that a firefly?" she gasped.

"Yeah." I smiled.

"Can we catch one?"

"Of course."

~

03

about the author

***Vee Lozada**, author and 2020 Watty Award Winner in Science Fiction, who lives to write stories that make the reader think beyond what's "normal." She loves losing herself in stories set in a future so close she can touch it.*

*Once called the **Cyborg Queen**, Vee accepted the title and proudly wears her Sci-fi crown.*

THE SURVIVORS

by Vee Lozada

CHICAGO, ILLINOIS, USA
AUGUST 28, 5:56 PM

My heart slammed in my chest. The panicked thumps became my world's soundtrack. Eclipse of the heart. Survival. One thump, two thump, three thump, four.

Giving my anxiety a name didn't change that we could've avoided this if Luna and I had just evacuated with everyone else.

Why did we stay again?

The sound of water sloshing in the streets increased. I flattened myself against the brick interior wall of Domingo's Corner Store, just two blocks from my apartment. With my cheek pressed against the cold slab, I glanced out the nearby window at the grey fog, and what seemed like forever-rising water.

Ah, Lake Michigan…

"Hey, George, I think we need to find cover, man. We got three minutes until the next pulse," a voice spoke outside.

Narrowing my gaze, I followed the outlines of three men pushing through the dark streets. Judging by the distinctive shapes in their shadowed hands, they were armed—weapons to attack those who remained in the city. Aliens hovered above us, but assaulting people who didn't leave was uncalled for. Sure, many of us broke into buildings, squatted, and looted, but we had our reasons.

The bottle of Tamiflu clutched in my grip was *mine*. *Luna's fever had to break this time.*

"Okay, George, George," a second voice spoke, higher than the first, and a little more panicked, "my watch says we've got two minutes. Two. We need to strap onto something or—"

The figure in front of the small group twisted in my direction. I jerked back from the window, my boots splashing against an overturned shelf. *Please don't let them hear me.*

The man didn't move for a few heartbeats, then pointed and spoke. "I saw someone, some guy, red hoodie, rain boots, a backpack—you know what our orders are." This had to be George. His voice was deeper than the other two. Obviously, the leader. Very commanding. Very observant. Very *motherfucker*.

"At this point, who gives a flying fuck about the orders?! I'm not trying to float to this ship like some fucking abductee. That falling shit fucking hurts, man!" The trailing man spoke, then spun and, headed in the opposite direction George had indicated. The middle man, *Mr. High-Pitched-And-Panic*, was hesitant but quickly followed the deserter.

George flicked a hand. "Fine, that's fine, I will report you to—"

I glanced at my father's old wristwatch. Cracked in the face, water drops trapped under the glass, the time made my eyes widen. *5:59*. One minute. Despite their actions, I hoped the two cops who'd bailed could latch onto something within the next few seconds. George could kiss ass.

And me? I needed to move. Fast. *Now.*

"Okay, okay, Max." I quickly scanned the flooded store and eyed my surroundings. Emptied shelves, rolling cans of vegetables, and generic ravioli bobbed nearby. Great. All things that, once floating in the air, could hurt if they hit me.

Never mind the water itself.

Clutching the flu medicine tight in my hand, I didn't have time to force the container into my backpack. The flickering light in the corner of the shop caught my eye, somehow surviving all of this sporadic electrical shit since the aliens arrived. The ENTER sign was battery-powered for all I knew, but the door beneath it held my attention.

Was there water behind it? Was it an entrance, like the sign suggested, or an exit? Why would a store have an enter sign on the inside? This place was backward.

"Nathan, hold on!" I recognized the second voice of the man who disobeyed George. They shouted, then flat-out screamed. Other voices, distant but just as distressed, followed. Energy shifted under my feet.

Run!

Clenching my jaw, I splashed forward, praying, hoping my feet would make it. With so much of the lake spreading over Chicago's streets, I'd gotten used to trying to wade through water and it never got easier. Now, running without gravity was ridiculous.

Yet, there I was. Flailing.

I should've been home fifteen minutes ago.

Nope. My feet left the ground. The water followed. Water morphed, floating in the air. For a child, this would be amazing. Large and small bubbles, bouncing off surfaces, merging and separating as if they were liquid toys, would've excited me, too. But when they got in the way, almost blocking my angled upward trajectory, not so much.

Stretching forward, I nudged a bubble away, and my fingers slid over the door's knob, just enough that I managed to drag myself down to the door. My hand gripped tight once I was close enough. *Fifteen minutes.*

I squeezed my eyes shut and held my breath as the surrounding water balled and bobbed around me. If I stayed braced in the doorway and directed them away, I wouldn't drown. Not that I thought it was possible, but it felt like it. Though it almost happened once, pressed against a ceiling in an apartment lobby flooded by water. The bubbles surrounded me then, and panic had me believing they formed a barrier, suffocating me in a circle void of oxygen.

Didn't happen, but man, when you're scared…

It took all of my energy to cling to that door frame. Never thought I'd find myself standing upside down on a supply run.

From my angle, I made out the time on my watch. *6:03*. Just seven minutes. *Fuuuck.*

"Arnold, hey, hey, I got you!" Mr. High-Pitched-And-Panic's voice echoed nearby, a little calmer now but still recognizable. They made it somehow. Good. I was glad. I never wished ill on anyone, nor would I start now. Yes, the aliens brought out the worst in us, but I was always the good, helpful guy; I would give my shirt off my back to anyone who needed it.

Maybe not their buddy, George…

"Ey, Nathan, there's a store! We can pull ourselves toward it!"

My eyes widened. A store? No, it couldn't be this one. They sounded close by, but they'd left the entrance side of the street.

I glanced up at the sign that lured me here. *This* wasn't an entrance, was it? It led to the alley. Shit. This meant that Nathan and Arnold—

"Just grab my arm and I'll pull!" This was Nathan, had to be. Fuck, the fact that I could tell their voices apart in a time like this had me biting back a snort. Heightened fear-driven senses would come in handy if I were running in the alley, sure. Not now, not while I was holding onto the door these cops were about to open.

"I'm almost there!" That was Arnold's voice. And shit, he was close.

My fingers gripped the knob tighter. If I held it, they wouldn't be able to turn it, right? Locking the door was out of the question without a key. I glanced at my watch. *6:08.* Fuck, no; had this much time passed? Two minutes left.

"Don't let go of me!"

"Did you get it? Is it unlocked? Shit!"

I held my breath. My fingers ached. I couldn't risk slipping and flying backwards. The knob turned. And jiggled.

I looked back at my watch. One minute. Maybe less. I wished the second hand wasn't obscured or I'd know more or less; if they managed to open this door while I was right here, I was *fucked.*

I was better off with the aliens. There hadn't been any attacks. *Directly.* Right?

"Shit." I let the door go. My body flew back, and I bumped into water bubbles, frantically batting at them away from my face.

The energy shifted. The sudden drop from the alien's pulse sent my stomach to the ground, and I braced myself for a fall; there were two overturned shelves on the floor beneath me.

In seconds, I slammed into the metal racks. I cried out as pain exploded through my side. Water fell to the floor, splashing like a gush from a water slide. Gritting my teeth, I squeezed my eyes shut and muffled my scream.

But the door opened. Water from the alley rushed into the empty store. With sweat sprouting on my brow, I stared up at the ENTER sign above me and wanted more than anything to kick it.

Lies.

"Nathan, I think we can wait in here until George—" My gaze fell on the two cops who'd been out in the streets. Fully dressed in riot gear, and wet from the city streets, streaks of water covered their helmets.

Arnold and I stared at each other. He was frozen, clutching the door, almost hesitant. I could see the debate in his eyes. Should he attack me? Should he come for me? The answer, according to George, would've been yes, but he didn't. He stood there, huffing, sucking in sharp breaths.

"Do you think George made it or—" Nathan looked at me next. His piercing blue eyes widened, and his jaw dropped. "That's the—"

Nope. *That's the—nothing.* I wasn't here—I was a figment of their imagination. I drew in a sharp breath, turned against the shelves, then looked down at my hand.

The Tamiflu stuck to me like glue. *Thank God.*

"Grab him! Hey! Freeze!" I didn't know who shouted, but I was up and limping, running in my waterlogged boots with the main entrance as my goal.

Luna, I'm coming. Hold on.

Something fell behind me as I reached the door. When I flattened my hand against it, I glanced back; the cops were throwing shelves out of their way. It would've been easier to jump over, but who was I judging? This gave me time to *go.*

"*Freeze!*"

I shoved open the door, heard the chime, then looked up and down the street. Scattered, overturned cars blocked the way I came originally. Shit. The other side was better, but where was *George?* I didn't want to escape these two, only to run smack into him and his gun?

The street seemed deserted.

Good for me. That meant I could get away, get back home, and take care of Luna's flu. It would take me longer to climb through the vehicles and debris on this side—another ten minutes—but if I moved fast, I would still be within my plan.

Just a few more minutes.

I pressed my hand against my sore side, and warm moisture met my touch. It should've been cold like the chilled water, but I didn't have time to check.

Moving through the flooded streets, I churned my legs as quickly as possible. Water splashed as I pushed forward. Behind me, the cops growled in frustration. They couldn't catch me, but I wasn't silent in these boots. I needed to hide. It didn't matter how far ahead I got, I wouldn't outrun them.

Getting away in the shop was a fluke. I couldn't count on that kind of luck again.

Still clutching my ribs, I looked at the SUV to my left. Dropped on its side with its passenger door wide open, it made for convenient cover. I took advantage. Water splashed into my boots, through my socks, and between my toes as I hunched behind it and ducked out of sight.

"What? No! Fuck, he has to be here." This was Nathan complaining, had to be. I wouldn't stick my head out to confirm. The longer I stayed hidden, the better chance I had of getting home.

"Let's just go, Nathan." I was right. Arnold was the next voice, huffing in retreat. His choice was better. Why make the effort to chase after me in these conditions? The world was wet. It was cold. And shit, the gravity pulse was over, but the ship itself left a constant headache.

Didn't it? Or was that just me?

"But George said—"

"Man, fuck George! He's gone, right? Where is he? The department doesn't pay me enough for this. I should've evacuated with my family. Fuck our duty. Fucking screw this alien shit. I want to live and make a sandwich right now. Let's go!"

I pressed my face against the SUV as I listened to Arnold. He'd described the mood of this alien situation. I wasn't a cop, and I agreed. Luna and I should've evacuated. We could've been out of the Twilight zone and somewhere safe, safer than here.

As their footsteps retreated in the opposite direction, I released a long, slow sigh. Time to go home.

***

The sun was setting. Not that I could see it, but the sliver of color lightened the western sky at the edge of the midnight craft above us. It gave a brief repreve from the murkiness that reminded me of death, of nightmares, of the scenes in horror movies that had a person cowering under their blankets.

When the aliens first arrived, I couldn't deal with the shock. Suffocated by my anxiety, I shut the curtains and feared going outside. At that point, despite what news reports said, Luna and I believed in the worst. We'd seen all of the movies. We knew the possibilities. Too many outcomes had humans dying.

So we hid. We refused evacuation orders. We remained in our apartment, silent as patrols swept through the buildings to find stragglers. And for a while, I thought it was the right choice. The government couldn't control our lives. Now, I wasn't so sure. It'd been over four weeks, and while my anxiety evolved from fear, turning into determination, I was tired.

So fucking tired. And the pain in my side, or these damn boots didn't help at all.

The tall four-floor yellow apartment building Luna and I called home was across the street. The ridges within the brick exterior were steeped in shadow, making the street darker than it truly was. Or was the brief sunlight fading already? After my supposed fifteen turned twenty-minute urban scramble, I couldn't tell the difference between reality and my exhaustion.

My vision blurred and I stumbled. I swiped a hand across my sweaty brow, wincing as the throbbing in my side intensified. All I wanted to do was collapse, to rest.

"Hey, hey, hey," a low rough voice came from my left, followed by rushed footsteps splashing through the water. I glanced sideways and spotted a thin, older man with his hands in front of him, pressing them together as if in prayer. I cocked a brow as he shot me a toothless grin. "Did you loot? Did you find food? Come on, can you help me?"

I inched back onto the sidewalk. The man's shirt was tattered, ripped where blood seeped through, but there weren't any visible injuries. He either took the shirt off of someone else or hurt someone. I didn't want to think he was violent, but danger surrounded us. For all I knew, he'd fought in self-defence.

Lethargy dragged at my limbs. I was too tired to defend myself again.

"Look, man—" I looked away from him, down at the water swilling around my heavy feet. Debris carried through the stream. Old Hershey's wrappers, muffin boxes, and a single yellow rubber duckie, equipped with sunglasses, hit my boots. The little toy made me smile for a moment.

Why can't I be cool like this little duck and just wade through the waters? Free, happy, and unbothered by this shit. A survivor.

"What's in the bag?" The man came closer.

The duck flipped upside down into the water. I watched it until he came within reach and I shot him a glare. "Nothing for you," I hissed.

"Come on, just a little something." The man grabbed my arm and pulled.

I yanked my wrist free and stumbled, stepping under the dead streetlight. My heart hammered. "Hey, yo, don't touch me."

"I'm hungry," he hissed. "It's been days, kid, days! Just—"

The world spun. When I looked down again to keep steady, I caught sight of my sweater; deeper red, darker, bloody. I gulped.

Did I injure myself that badly at the shop? Those shelves were sharp and my side hurt like a bitch. But I couldn't be bleeding that much. Home was right there.

I focused on the little duck as the man approached. His bootless feet were inches from mine. Yet, the sound of rapid footfalls caught my attention. And the man's because he stepped back in a hurry. I looked up just in time to see a blurry second figure reach the man and lift something long over their head.

"I just wanted food, miss, I—" The man's hands rose but that didn't stop the second person. The large object descended. The impacting thunk echoed, and a second thunk sounded, followed by a third. There were two more smacks when the man fell; this I saw clearly. The man, a gash on his forehead, and the second person. My person.

Luna.

When the man stopped moving, floating face up in the water, Luna stepped back. A quiet cry slipped past her lips. Her long, wavy black hair stuck to her face, dangled around her shoulders, and when she lifted her head to look at me, her flushed cheeks drew into a weak smile. Then it dropped as her eyes passed over me.

"Oh my God," she hissed, stepping over the unconscious man, "what happened? You're bleeding!"

I shook my head and cupped her face, my blood smearing on her skin. "Why are you outside?" I whispered.

"I was feeling better and decided to look out the window." Her large brown eyes peered into mine. "Then I saw you, but I saw this guy walking to you, and I…" She frowned, leaning into my touch. "I saw him rob a man this morning for nothing. Just… violent."

So, the blood on his shirt wasn't his.

"And I couldn't let him hurt you," she whispered.

Luna, the reason I stayed sane in this alien invasion. My purpose. I couldn't give up because she wouldn't. The aliens might march down our streets when that glowing blue number in the sky reached zero in two days, but I knew we'd be all right. Because she would make my world feel that way.

That was why we stayed. We opted to wait this out, because we had each other.

"Luna…" Her skin was warm under my hands. She may have felt better but her fever remained. I needed to get her upstairs as soon as possible, give her this medicine, and—

"We need to get upstairs so we can stop your bleeding."

The last of the sunset disappeared, and the skies darkened to that of the alien craft. The night was upon us now, and if we didn't get inside, who knew what other dangers would find us? "I've got your meds," I said, then I glanced at the building behind her. "Let's get inside and help each other."

"Don't we always?" Luna gave a faint smile. I did the same as I ushered her toward the door. Whatever our future held, we'd face it together. Always.

~

02

about the author

Wattpad's resident ghost, you may have seen ***Eli Gregory*** *under the floorboards a time or two. Writing about alien craft isn't exactly their forte, but they look out for any excuse to flex their horror skills.*

Eli has been scribbling on Wattpad since 2020, winning a Watty Award for horror that year, joining both the Stars and Creators program along the way, and jumping into a ton of fun projects (like this one!).

When they are not writing Gothic horror and paranormal fantasy, Eli can be found watching (debatably) scary movies, making another cup of tea, or getting slaughtered by rabid dogs in Bloodborne.

THE GRUDGE

by Eli Gregory

SUGARCREEK, OHIO, USA
AUGUST 29, 9:50 PM

Jacob leaned back and nursed a beer. It should have been an iced tea or lemonade, but Bess wasn't here to nag about it anymore. She meant well, but what his daughter didn't know wouldn't hurt her. He might have given more of a shit if there wasn't an unearthly large plate of who-knew-what floating above the sky, if the earth itself wasn't in total disarray about the whole thing, if the neighbours weren't screeching their heads off about this conspiracy or that one.

The evacuation notice had been the final straw for Jacob. They were all going to die, it was obvious. What difference would one beer make? Better to die with a happy, drunk stomach than scared and full of piss.

He drained the last of the can, crushed it against his chest, and hurled it across the street. It didn't take long for his taunt to be heard and answered. Within a minute, he could hear the stomping of overpriced boots and then the slam of a porch door.

Standing fifty feet away, *she* glared at him, hands on hips, hair held up by a towel. Did she know how stupid she looked? Jacob snorted and reached for another beer. The porch lights flickered and went out for a moment, coming back on to reveal Tammy or Toni or Terry (Jacob didn't care to remember her name) waving a shovel.

"What gives you the right to ruin my lawn, you asshole? I pay to live here!" She shook the shovel. "One more can, old man. I dare you!" Spitting on the dirt that she called a lawn, Tammy-Toni-Terry spun on her heel and thumped her way back inside, causing the lights on her side of the street to flicker with the force of her stomping.

"What gives you the right to be so loud?" mumbled Jacob. He rubbed his forehead aggressively. That dumb city-broad had been making more noise in the handful of months since she'd moved in than anyone else on the street had in the last fifteen years.

The noise was even more obnoxious since the *thing* had appeared, not that it made any sounds itself. Everything under it had died, miraculously. Bugs and birds and possums alike, everything unfortunate and small enough to be caught under the heavy gaze of the disk in the sky had been so disoriented upon coming back to land that it died sooner after a gravitational shift. Hell, he'd lost a few cows the first day the gravity went nuts, before he had the sense to lock them in the barn and pad the place with as much straw as he could pay Rico to pile.

Of course, Rico had quit almost as soon as he started. Good-for-nothing kid. Who was scared of a little anti-gravity and fucked up electricity? Jacob had grown up during worse. That was the problem with kids like Rico and Tammy-Toni-Terry - none of them had ever suffered through anything a day in their lives. Blasting music from her shiny new truck when nobody on the block owned anything their great-grandparents hadn't would be unthinkable if she actually worked on the land she claimed to own.

Jacob could have grumbled on and on about the music and the new generation of soft-backed wimps society called kids, but the clock on his phone (his only modern weakness) flashed blue and green, before reverting to its usual background of Bess and her kids on the farm. What did she want now?

"I'm not drinking, no need to worry."

"What?"

"Nevermind. What is it, hun?" He stole another sip and stood to go inside. No need to give the neighbor any excuse to eavesdrop.

"Dad, listen, you have to get out of Ohio. The news is saying you're in something called the Midnight Zone. It's not safe! Is it true the gravity is, what, *failing*? What in God's name does that mean? Carla and Kev are scared for you."

"Mhm." Jacob took a deep breath and tried not to roll his eyes.

Who could be expected to listen to that much that quickly? Just outside the house, he could hear the bounce of the beer can he'd thrown crash against the door. Fuming, he turned to fling the one he held back at the damn neighbour, but his daughter's screech of complaint made him stop and wince.

"*Mhm*? Really?" Bess' voice cut out for a minute before coming back in, admonishing him for being so careless about his own family's concerns. "...understand why you made Mom so mad. Can't you just drive out here and get back to your blissfully ignorant life when this freaky stuff passes? Better yet, *I'll* drive. Save you the excuse of not showing up."

"And go where? You have a house I don't know about in Kansas? Did that good-for-nothing loser leave you a fancy hotel in Las Vegas?"

Another can gone. Resisting the urge to launch it, he remembered what happened the last time Bess had found out he'd been drinking. On second thought, if they were going to die soon (The Midnight Zone - he could have laughed. Nobody in the old movies ever lived in something called the damn *Midnight Zone*), what was the point in avoiding his daughter's anger?

Compressing the can against his chest, he remembered the days when a good time involved a bunch of mellow-minded folks gathered around a field to sit on the hay, someone strumming a guitar while another handed out cold drinks. No speakers involved, no cell phones to ruin the natural ambience. No pushy daughters to ruin a perfectly good evening, alien bullshit aside. The ship above him, miles in the sky, could have been a Godsend.

"Is that a beer? Really, Dad? Why do I even bother…" When Bess' voice came back, she had finished her loud words and handed the phone over to one of her kids. It made for an amusing transition.

"Poppy? Mommy says you're a lousy drunk but I still have to say goodnight."

"Who's this little tyke?" Jacob smiled in spite of himself. Bess may have been a hardass just like her mom, but she and the crap-excuse for a husband she had the sense to leave had made for three sweet children.

"Abby. What's lousy mean, Poppy?"

"It ain't nothing but a bad word, hun. You tell your momma to watch her mouth for me, okay?"

"Are you going to die out there?"

"No, hun, I'm not going anywhere."

Standing in his kitchen in the dark, Jacob suddenly felt alone. He wasn't, was he? This was his house, had been his father's house, and his father's house before that. Nobody had left in all those years, not even when the war had come and gone or the money in the banks had dried up.

No, Jacob wasn't going anywhere. He sniffed and rubbed at his nose, cursing the allergies. The mess in the sky may have cleaned out the pollution from stupid trucks like the neighbours, but when the humming kicked in at midnight and set everything floating again, every flower and tree in the area tipped all of the damn pollen over the house.

"I miss you, Poppy. Carla and Kevin say you're - what? Leggin? Oh! - a *legend* for staying put. What's a legend?"

"I gotta go, Abby doll. You give your brother and sister a hug for me and go easy on your momma, alright?"

"Kevin told me he'll hit me if I touch him."

"You hit him back, darling. Good night."

Talking with Bess' kids always made him feel sentimental. She knew it, too, dammit. Grumbling to himself, Jacob angrily scratched his eyes and went upstairs to get ready for bed, trying to ignore the music that had started up across the street.

***

He woke up at 11:50, the humming louder than hell. Every window rattled in its frame and the silverware had started shaking. He looked at the clock and waited. It wasn't smart to stay in bed, but the beer had clogged his brain and made him sluggish. What was the point? He wasn't going to the west coast or the middle of who-the-fuck-knew-where Oklahoma just to avoid the mess that he was in. And he sure as shit wasn't moving in with Deborah again, not after he caught her with her boss in *his* bed.

"I told her, I'm staying put," he slurred, standing up and rolling himself into a bathrobe. He stumbled down the stairs, nearly toppling over when the humming turned unbearable, the very bones of the house threatening to burst free from their constraints. When they held, he snorted in triumph. "Good bones! Daddy made some good bones."

Before the gravity clicked off, Jacob liked to watch the black plate that passed as the sky for a few minutes. Anyone else would have locked themselves in the cellar with a padded coat around them just in case, or just driven out of town. As it was, Jacob and Toni were the only ones left. Toni made her presence obvious by the horrible noise coming from inside her house, something that Jacob vaguely recognised as some boy band bullshit. Bess had been obsessed with them when she was a teenager, and Jacob hated every word that came out of their mouths.

"Hey!" He staggered to the middle of the road and held in a belch. "You still alive in there?"

"What do you want?" The porch creaked and the dark-eyed Toni emerged, a bottle of Jack in her hand and an ice cream halfway out of her mouth. At least she had her priorities straight. For a second, Jacob considered asking her if she wanted to share a drink, but then he heard the stupid chorus of a song rattle her windows and he reconsidered.

"You think those idiots sound better in space?"

Toni gave him a hard look. "That's what you're interrupting my end-of-the-world time for?"

"I'm just curious," he answered, swaying in his fuzzy slippers. "You think we can convince our friends in the sky to throw a party for them?"

"The only party anyone's throwing is when you finally get sucked up and probed by the freaks." She smirked and stuffed the ice cream back in her mouth, little rivulets of caramel dripping onto the porch.

Jacob simmered. The disrespect! It could have been the beer that hadn't left his system or just the weeks of growing resentment but he had finally had enough. If the aliens were going to kill them all, if those stupid blue numbers that flashed on his phone every night and up in the sky were really counting down the days they had left, then what was the point in trying to make peace? Might as well get one last good memory stored away before he was killed in whatever dumb, sci-fi way the aliens had planned up their green asses.

He stalked inside and went straight to the fireplace, dry and unused since the summer had hit. A shotgun, cleaner than anything else in the house, gleamed in the night. Jacob was going to shoot that smug look off her face, and if he could get the bottle out of her hands, that would make it even better. He could die happy!

By the time he made it outside, though, Toni was gone. Jacob would have guessed she just went back inside to finish getting drunk before midnight hit, but her front door was still open. He walked closer and squinted. Her Jack was still on the porch, sitting down right next to her ice cream, as though she'd set one down and dropped the other where she stood.

"Oh, where'd you run off to now? Gone to blast some more music in my face?"

He raised the shotgun and tried to load a bullet, but the gravity made everything feel backwards, and it slipped from his grasp where it went… up. Straight up in the air, like a kid with a string had snatched it away. His gaze followed the little round and he saw the blue numbers, blinking bright enough to startle the remaining cows from even inside the barn. Their lowing could be heard way out here, panicked moos as they followed the same path as the bullet. The tip of the shotgun went up, and then the barrel, and then Jacob's hand, slowly. He stared stupidly at it, mouth hung open and eyes wide.

Was it really already midnight? The numbers on the big, dumb metal plate in the sky were too bright - he could have read the numbers if his glasses were on, but the glasses only got in the way. They were probably on his bedroom ceiling now, crushed under a chair or the bed. Along with the blue light, another set of lights were shining in his face in erratic swinging lines, but he was too distracted to pay attention. An alarm blared at the end of the street, a horn from some car some idiot hadn't locked up in the garage yet.

Jacob realised he'd been pulled up in the sky, too. He was floating! By God, he was really floating. The shotgun slipped from his grip and floated beside him, not rushing past like the bullet but going the same damn speed he was, somehow. Behind him (or was it under him?), his house had started up the rattling sound again, as though every bolt was straining to remain where it was.

That's a damn good house, he thought, even as he went up like a balloon. His slippers came undone and made their ascent in a peculiar circle around him. What did the aliens want with any of this shit? Were they making a mural of the good ol' American life in that huge disk of theirs?

As he continued, the lights that had been moving in a dizzying pattern became too bright to ignore. He turned his head to see the source of the car alarm, too: a truck, a familiar blue truck with wheels he had installed himself just last summer was speeding towards him, going up and up and up until there was no space left between Jacob and the headlights. As he braced himself for the impact, he heard a voice crying out, a sobbing voice that reminded him of his daughter. Before he could think about giving her one last call, the truck collided with him and carried him on its violent ascent into the sky, sailing past the slippers and the shotgun until all that remained was a faint cry in the distance.

***

Hunched in the corner of the ceiling, a pillow tied to her chest, Toni wondered if the old asshole across the street had made it inside in time. He might have been as annoying and stereotypically cantankerous as a human could be, but she didn't want him to die. Who was going to take care of the cows? Toni sure wasn't - she didn't know the first thing about farm life.

The rumbling went on for another ten minutes or so. When it finally stopped, the shower curtain fell slowly back to the floor, and Toni floated down with it. Even with the pillow, the air was still knocked out of her as she bumped into the rim of the tub, bouncing her stomach on the porcelain. Groaning, she made her way back to the front of the house, her porch lights flickering in the eerie darkness. There was no more sunset, not here. None of that beautiful country sky could be seen from under the ship.

She peered outside, but there was no sign of the old man. That was a relief. He'd been drunk and stupid to be out so late, so close to the shift. Toni looked around, hoping her whiskey had somehow got stuck in the rafters of the porch and been saved. There was no sign of the ice cream. She sighed and walked out a little farther, just in case the shift hadn't quite ended and wanted to snatch her when she wasn't prepared. Nothing. No noise came from the old man's house, either, not even the clatter of furniture that invariably came crashing down.

Toni stepped out a little farther and looked up. The clock on the ship, or so the news said, had been counting down for a month now. The number that blinked now said **2** in a great ominous blue. She checked her watch and saw the same thing. Maybe by the time it hit **0**, she would have wished she left town, but she couldn't give the son of a bitch across the street the satisfaction of seeing her leave.

The silence was deafening. No more crickets, no more mosquitos, no more cows. No more neighbour. Toni felt like she should have been happy about that, but when a shotgun came floating down just a foot in front of her, like a sign from heaven, she knew there would never be another sound across the street.

She moved to turn and head back inside for another Jack, but floating down right where the gun fell came a shower of blood, a thousand thick, dark droplets that fell hypnotically, slowly, until Toni was drenched in a silent bath of crimson mystery.

She blinked at the mess for a long time before turning wordlessly inside, red footprints dissolving into the dirt road.

~

01

about the author

Kristin Jacques *is an award-winning author of fantasy fiction for teens and adults. She currently lives in a small town in Connecticut with her partner, kiddos, and two trash goblins who think they are cats.*

When not writing, she's usually reading, or catching some excellent b-horror movies. She is currently working on projects full of magic, mystery, and delight.

BILLIE & THEA DON'T SAVE THE WORLD

by Kristen Jacques

SOMEWHERE IN HICK-TOWN, NORTHEASTERN US
PIT STOP #1: LOST IN PENNSYLVANIA

AUGUST 30, 7: 13 AM

Billie's morning grogginess broke when her head thunked against the car ceiling, the tires bouncing through a pothole large enough to drown a small herd of cattle.

Glancing at her passenger, Billie took a moment to admire the fine bone features of her companion, somehow still slack and smooth in sleep. Thea's cheekbones and thin, tip-tilted nose were impish, softened by the roundness of her chin and plush pink lips. Lips that were hanging open, a thin line of drool dribbling down her chin. Even that was cute.

Billie sighed. Three weeks on the road, and she still hadn't girded her tits to make the confession that spurred this whole blasted road trip.

The car coughed, the engine sputtering ominously in an irritable reminder Billie had pushed it too far and too long last night. Baby might look like a classic Caddy with the sea foam fins and trim, but her guts and bones were a butcher's operating table of whatever junkyard cars were mostly compatible. Frankenstein's monster brought to life by elbow grease and creative welding. If you didn't look too closely, it was a memorable drive-by experience. Driving Baby took a bit more finesse than the average vehicle, but Billie was the Frankenstein of this scenario, and she knew how to make those innards purr again.

Then there was the other problem.

This time of day, sunshine should be blinding her through the windshield, but it was muted as it was every day this month, while the great belly of the apocalypse hung in the sky with the same temerity as Billie's Born Again Aunt Judith on Christmas. Another sputter reminded her of the need for a pit stop.

"Hey, time to wakey-wakey, eggs and bakey," she nudged Thea's elbow. Her passenger woke with a snort, grimacing from hours spent sleeping up-right. Thea peered out the windshield, baby blue eyes wide.

"What time is it? Where are we?" Her jaw cracked when she yawned and stretched, one careless fist nearly clocking Billie in the cheek.

"Little after seven in the morning," said Billie, frowning at the shadowed greenery, broken up by sporadic strips of houses and businesses. "Best guess is somewhere in Bumfuck, Pennsylvania?"

Thea squinted through the window. "We're not at the coast yet?"

"Gurl, there is a lot of ground to cover. These states are huge, not like those piddly New England states that are a sneeze to get through," said Billie. Not to mention she was so, so lost. Pit stop first, *then* panic. "Once we push through to New England, it's a hop, skip, and a jump to the coast."

At least she hoped so. "See any good place to stop?"

Thea lifted her hands and peered through the circles of her thumbs and forefingers. "Ahoy there, Captain, I do believe that is a Wally World sign I see over yonder."

A Walmart sign peeked through the obscene amount of foliage on the opposite side of the road, the support pole listing to the side while the neon interior flickered, mostly blown out except for the familiar 'W'.

"Score," said Billie, cranking the wheel. Baby jumped the curve, thumping over the grassy divider with the wobbly determination of a hungover collegiate at a free breakfast buffet. The struts creaked in protest as they bounced down on the other side of the curb. Billie patted the dashboard, crooning how well Baby was driving while she maneuvered through the various abandoned vehicles strewn about the road. Honestly, the apocalypse made people so irresponsible, abandoning perfectly good parts like that.

There were more haphazardly placed cars in the store lot, though these looked less abandoned and more parked in a hurry, ignoring the faded painted lines. Billie clicked her tongue, pulling in smooth and straight in the free slot.

"This is a handicapped space," said Thea, pointing at the snapped sign on the pavement.

A frown teased Billie's brow. "You think they'd park here to loot?"

Thea shrugged. "Think they have any Funyuns left?" She rolled down the window to slither out of the car, since Billie had accidentally welded the passenger side door shut. Thea's neon yellow sneakers were eye-wateringly bright in the shaded gloom of the parking lot, wispy blonde hair mostly tamed by a matching scrunchie. Billie shrugged on her denim jacket and jammed her key in the driver's side lock, turning it back and forth three times before the 'automatic' locks grudgingly tumbled into place.

The sliding doors of the Walmart gaped open, a flurry of activity audible inside where the owners of the other cars scurried like rats through the aisles, pushing carts overflowing with pilfered goods. Thea and Billie ignored them, dancing across the linoleum to the 90's music that still cranked through the store's P.A. system.

Thea snagged a bag of Twizzlers. "I bet they still have Twinkies, sure as cockroaches."

Billie grimaced. "Two things that don't belong in the same sentence." She caught sight of her reflection with a snort—hair frizzed out in a brown halo like a chestnut dandelion puff.

"Both are guaranteed to outlast everything else." Thea grinned. "One with a delicious creamy filling and the other a cheap snack cake."

"Gross," said Billie.

"Protein of the future," Thea insisted.

Both women plastered themselves against the shelves as a cart barreled past, piloted by a wide-eyed man who looked like he hadn't slept in weeks, a teetering tower of toilet paper threatening to jump ship when he took a hard turn into the next aisle.

"What's got his tighty-whiteys in a twist?" Billie picked up a fallen pack of toilet paper off the ground. "Ooo, refill. Was getting tired of using leaves."

"Hey, leaves are eco-friendly!" Thea suddenly whooped, ignoring the flurry of background chaos as she made a beeline for the mostly ransacked snack aisle. "Funyuns!" Thea filled her arms. "They even have the spicy hot ones," she cooed.

"Yeah, yeah, grab your nasty snacks. I'm gonna go grab some stuff for Baby," said Billie.

Thea tore open a bag with her teeth, burying her face in the oniony contents with unbridled glee. "Funyuns," she cackled, the sound of muffled crunching emerging from within.

Billie shook her head, snagging a box of snack cakes on her way out. The sugar perked her up while she wandered into the completely untouched automotive aisle. Their fellow looters might be ransacking the shelves of food like raccoons at campground dumpsters, but Baby had needs. Billie scooped up a few quarts of oil and other odds and ends before she spotted the maps. Actual paper maps, a flipping miracle since cell reception had been spotty at the best of times and non-existent for days. She unfolded the unwieldy sheet of paper across the abandoned help desk, finding their actual location on top of a random receipt.

They were way off course. Somehow, the backroads sent them veering closer to Maryland than New York, piling more hours of travel time onto their already tight schedule. Bad enough most of the highways were a no-go but navigating the unfamiliar backroads with scant road signs added days to their original travel time.

Crunching noises announced the arrival of Thea. "What's the damage?"

Billie sighed. "Probably another three to four hours before we get out of Pennsylvania."

A moment of silence wobbled like a plate of lime jello between them, neither one wanting to acknowledge the total buzzkill hovering under the craft. Big, blue, and way worse than Aunt Judith, they'd both been awake when the number switched over to one.

Thea whistled. "Cutting it mighty close. Think we'll make it?"

Inhaling deeply, Billie flared her nostrils, catching the pungent scent of hot n' spicy Funyuns. "We'll get there before midnight." Because they had no choice but to reach their destination by then. "Oh snap, are those Swiss Rolls?"

PIT STOP #2: THE SIDE OF A ROAD, SOMEWHERE IN PENNSYLVANIA? NEW YORK?
AUGUST 30, 11:37 AM

Billie scowled at the map. Wide swaths of green fields gave way to more green fields. Bright green, even in the constant shadow that hung over their heads, the view mostly unchanged since leaving the ransacked Walmart behind. They had a trunk full of pilfered Funyuns and snack cakes. Baby was purring nice and smooth after slurping down a couple quarts of oil. Things were looking up, if they could escape the flatlands and zesty cow manure-scented purgatory of Pennsylvania. Or had they already entered New York? One backroad looked pretty much like the rest, but if they'd slithered into a new state, they were that much closer to their destination.

The bushes rustled. Billie cast them a speculative eye. "You done yet?"

"Never inquire after a lady seeking a decent place to pop a squat," said Thea.

"Least you have toilet paper this time," said Billie, a blush building when her mind stumbled over the image of Thea with her pants around her ankles. Thea had nice thighs and endless smooth, tan skin. Really, Thea had a lot of nice parts, parts Billie had wanted to explore and worship for years. Every time her mind turned that corner, she wanted to blurt out the words, only for them to stall and turn over like a stubborn engine. But a roadside pee stop was not the place for a love confession. No time or place was the right one. That would change when they finally arrived at the shore.

Billie's childhood memories of visiting New England were charitably foggy at best; long ago forgotten summers on seaweed-strewn beaches and slippery rocks when most of her formative years were spent in landlocked Nebraska. The ocean was cold there, a bone-deep biting chill that refused to dissipate until the very end of the summer season. Lucky for the end of the world to happen in the hottest month of the year, really.

When the ship arrived, looming over the country with the finality of tax season, and that ominous countdown began, Billie realized her chances to confess had drastically dwindled. Never the right time or place, but now the world was ending. And Thea wanted to see the ocean.

Nebraska was very far from any ocean.

"West coast, East coast, or Gulf coast?" Billie had posed while they poured over Google maps when their spotty internet allowed. In an ordinary summer, any direction would take them days on a highway but that was before people started trying to flee the craft. Pile-ups were left where they happened, choked with wrecked or abandoned cars. The backroads were another story, proven by the last two weeks scrounging for supplies, peeing in the woods, and generally having a grand old time.

"West coast is still the farthest," said Thea.

"Florida then?"

"Florida is full of swamps and Floridians," said Thea, and that settled the matter.

Billie had hesitated, a suggestion resting heavy on her tongue, as if she'd shoved an entire pack of Bubble Yum into her mouth until it was an ungainly sticky wad. The East coast covered a lot of states, and her idea was one of the furthest points away.

"There's this beach in New England I used to visit as a kid." She pulled up the directions.

Thea's expression went soft, the smile on her lips full of longing and secrets that Billie wanted to sink her teeth into and nibble away. "I had my first kiss on that beach."

The news slapped her in the face like a wet paper towel. An apparent false assumption that Thea had never left Nebraska. There were still things Billie didn't know about her decade-long crush, pieces to be discovered. Her gaze drifted upward to the proverbial elephant in the sky, the belly of the ship blotting out direct sunlight. She was not a fan of the doom and gloom flavor, putting off the sour mood by digging a snack cake out of the trunk. It was impossible to be mad while eating a

Twinkie. Like a party in your mouth, though Billie swore she truly did hear the faint strains of music filtering through the trees.

Thea stumbled out of the greenery; a couple of twigs lodged in her tangled blonde nest. "There's a *party* in the woods!"

Billie choked, spraying bits of Twinkie on the side of Baby while Thea slapped her on the back. "Seriously?" she wheezed out. "Who the hell is having a party *today*?"

"Dude, it reeks like skunk and Hurley's moonshine," said Thea. A wide grin split her face. "We're totally going."

Billie squinted at Thea, her eyes still blurry from the partially inhaled snack cakes. "Don't we have a schedule to keep?"

Thea dove into the trunk, hauling out their bounty of snacks. "You said the coast was only a few hours away. It's early. Plenty of time to celebrate and still get there before midnight."

Billie gawked at her, snatching her half-eaten box of Twinkies from the top of the teetering pile and tossing it back in the trunk. "What the hell are we celebrating?"

"Pfft, the end of the world, obviously," said Thea. She took off at a trot, spilling boxes of ding dongs and Swiss rolls in her wake. Flabbergasted, Billie followed behind, reclaiming their fallen snacks.

Thea darted through the green, a flash of neon and blonde hair like some mythical fairy of the munchies. The sounds of music and laughter grew louder, an otherworldly sensation swelling in the humid air, until Billie popped out of the endless green. She nearly collided with Thea's back, skidding on her heels in the dirt as her mind wrapped around the present tableau.

A collection of strangers in various states of inebriation stared back at them through a haze of smoke. Many were partially undressed, a solution to the sticky heat that hung over them like a wool blanket, exacerbated by the pungent smoke. One man was painted purple from head to toe. They sat on folding chairs, bed sheets, and pine needles, surrounded by a loose cluster of cars bearing New York plates. An old Chevy truck had its doors wide open, the engine idling so a mix of indie rock could pour from the cassette deck and speakers. They ranged in age from early twenties to maybe fifties or sixties by the gray in their hair. The weight of their curious collective stares made Billie clutch her snacks to her chest.

Thea dropped her load on the ground, holding up a bag of Funyuns in each hand. "We come bearing snacks!"

Through a chorus of cheers, they clambered across the clearing to envelop Billie and Thea into their apocalypse party. Over the crinkle of foil and ripped plastic, they introduced themselves in a flurry of names that went in one ear and out the other, but Billie plunked down next to Thea on a bed of pine needles. A grin stole onto her face and stayed there as she accepted whatever Thea handed her, the heat forgotten in the brush of Thea's knee against her thigh.

She let her mind marinate while she watched the others, enjoying the way some of them danced with their eyes closed, letting their bodies feel the rhythm of nineties folk rock. When the gravity sputtered out like a blown fuse, the dancers laughed, a couple grabbing tree branches for balance, riding out the weightless wave until the power came back on minutes later with a stomach-jolting internal pop. They swayed through the whole shift, their expressions blissed out. The purple man swam around them in a flawless backstroke, before he settled onto a heap of grungy pillows, blowing smoke rings around mouthfuls of cheap beer.

Billie itched to ask Thea to dance with her, but her friend was now deep in an animated conversation with the purple man.

Thea's grin would make a trickster blush. Billie tuned in as the purple man started speaking again with an exaggerated sigh. "It's true. If you humans took better care of your planet, it wouldn't have required such a conspicuous intervention."

Billie raised a brow, chewing on a Swiss roll while eyeballing the purple man. Thea nodded like a well-traveled sage. "Yes, we rather botched things up here, but do you think we can learn from our mistakes?"

"What's going on?" Billie murmured from the side of her mouth. She froze when Thea leaned back against her.

"Oh, Phil here is one of the aliens," she said, her smile wide and bright. "He's just telling me what we can expect at the end of the countdown."

The purple man's enthusiasm was infectious, the sort of bubbly nature that hooked in and reeled out a smile. "Humans are terribly complex creatures. You can be quite terrible to one another. The violence you inflict upon one another is breathtaking. War, famine, and hatred are a constant wound that leeches at your humanity, but amid all that bad, there are still pockets of good. Of wonder." The purple man smiled, black dye tinting his teeth and gums. "Of love." His gaze drifted over them in a knowing way that made Billie's ears heat. "For all the terrible things humans do, they are also capable of such beautiful, wondrous acts. And they dream of so much more." He sat back on his heels. "That… that might be worth saving."

Thea nodded along. "So, you think your people will what, select a few lucky souls to pony off this rock at the end of the countdown?"

One of the other men listening in on the conversation piped up, blinking bleary eyes at the violet-colored Phil. "That's not an alien. It's just a guy in purple body paint."

Silence fell around their conversational circle, while the rest of the group danced to the same tape of folk rock and unidentified insects chirped incessantly from the trees in the late afternoon gloom.

Thea leaned around Billie's knee to glare at the other man. "Duh, Carl. You're throwing off the groove."

"Yeah, Carl, read the room," said Billie.

"We discussed this, Carl. I'm a Purple People Eater." Phil graciously held up his hands, the purple paint flaking off his palms. "Now, now, let's not fight. There is no telling what tomorrow will bring. But if this is the end, what a way to go, right?" He clinked his bottle with the dubious Carl. They drank deeply until both men relaxed once again into the chill vibe.

Thea leaned back, chewing on her lip, lost in thought until Billie nudged her shoulder. "Twinkie for your thoughts?"

"He's right, you know," she said. Billie frowned, trying to puzzle out the reference until Thea's thumb smoothed the skin between her brows, sending all sorts of sparks and fizzes through her veins. "There's no telling what tomorrow will bring."

Billie blew her frizz out of her face. "The end probably."

Thea snorted. "Where is your boundless sense of optimism?"

Rolling her shoulders in a facsimile of a shrug, Billie pondered the question. "Left it somewhere in Pennsylvania, I suppose." All that methane and greenery likely sucked the joy right out of her. Not like Thea, who practically buzzed with excitement despite Armageddon quite literally looming overhead.

The car radios warbled a moment before her stomach went weightless, the swoop of a roller coaster that left her toes tingling as gravity continued to percolate and burble with increasing frequency the closer they came to zero. Was this another increase in frequency, or was it that much later in the day? So few hours left…

Billie wanted to lean against Thea until that warmth leached away the encroaching pall of inevitability. Her intentions were foiled when Thea rolled to her knees, snatching a half-eaten bag of spicy Funyuns on her ascent.

"Time to hit the road!" She declared, ignoring the squawks of protest from the others. "Thanks for the hang. The vibe was most excellent."

Billie blinked after her, struggling to catch up when Thea returned and pulled her to her feet. "Where we going?" Her brain stalled, refusing to brain after stewing for hours. Thea slung an arm around her shoulders, bodily hauling her back through the pocket realm they'd wasted the day in until they emerged beside her car.

Baby was untouched, and the sky was noticeably dimmer. Billie dreaded seeing the actual time but wondered why Thea bothered leaving now when she was so far from sober that she threatened to come out the other side. She slumped against Baby's seafoam-painted side, trying to keep her feet under her and her eyelids open while Thea wove in front of her.

"Keys, ma'am, you are in no condition to drive," said Thea, holding up her hand.

Billie clasped it, giving a vigorous shake until Thea's traitorous words registered. "Did you just 'ma'am' me?" She gasped, pressing both their fists to her sternum. "You wound me." She sniffled.

Thea giggled. "Such a drama-llama. Come on, I'll take a turn at the wheel while you sober up in the back."

Billie swayed, her knees choosing that moment to fold over. "Just leave me here to wither away from old age like the 'ma'am' that I have become," she said, still wrapped around Thea's arm.

Gently untangling their limbs, Thea crouched down. Somehow, she managed to wiggle Billie onto her back, probably through witchcraft, before she carried Billie around the car and deposited her into the passenger seat. The keys were in Thea's hand when she pulled away and Billie regretted that she was too pickled to enjoy the groping.

Her head lolled as Baby shuddered to life, the engine rumbling through her tingling limbs. Her gaze drifted upward, the shadowed underbelly of the craft tilting on an internal axis like waves in the ocean until the swirling motion dragged her down into briny dreams.

Memory bled into her dreams...

...the grit of sand between her toes, skin sticky from salt water and sweat, and blinding hot sunshine that slowly cooked her to a nice lobster red. Her body wavered between a shapeless child and the blooming curves of a teen as other kids chased her through the surf, faces flickering away until only one face remained. Teenage Thea flitted through the waves on her heels, clad in the neon green bikini she'd worn to neighborhood pool parties. That bikini was one of Billie's core memories.

Thea screamed and laughed, kicking off clinging strands of seaweed, her hands reaching for Billie, who sought the caress of those fingers down her sun-warmed skin.

The dream shifted until they sat side by side on the algae-covered rocks, thighs pressed together.

"I had my first kiss at this beach," Thea whispered. Her face was close, and Billie's hungry dream conjured the scent of her coconut sunscreen.

She'd never been to this beach as a teen, but she wished, desperately, she'd been Thea's first kiss. A lost childhood love to smooth the way for her now ill-timed confession. What was the point in confessing now, at the end? Or had she waited so long because she knew that if Thea rejected her, at least the heartache wouldn't last long?

The morbid turn of her thoughts burst the pleasant bubble of her dream, but that wasn't that dragged Billie back to consciousness.

"Billie, wake up. We've got a problem."

COASTAL TOWN IN CONNECTICUT
AUGUST 30, 10:00 PM

"How long have I been out?" The distant familiarity of the road signs in Baby's headlights told her how far Thea brought them while she drifted on seafoam dreams.

"A few hours," said Thea, nodding to the problem. "But we're not going to get much further like this."

Billie climbed out of the car, planting her hands on her hips as she observed the clogged road. This wasn't even the highway—only adjacent to it—but abandoned vehicles snaked over the asphalt in both directions. The culprit was further up the road, where an overturned tractor-trailer completely blocked the road, tree line to tree line. How long ago had the truck crashed that they hadn't bothered to clean it up to ease evacuations?

Unfortunately, this road and the highway were the only nearby routes in and out of the coastal town. She didn't possess the familiarity she needed to successfully navigate any other back road alternatives they might have. They were running out of time.

Billie gnawed her lip as she turned back to Thea. "Think we can hoof it?"

Thea made a face. "Maybe at a jaunty jog," she said.

"Crud." Billie scowled at the overturned trailer. She hadn't planned to arrive, sweaty and out of breath, at the beach in the dark, and it was very dark beyond Baby's headlights. There wasn't a single streetlight to break up the pressing night. The seconds continued to tick down while she waffled.

"Let's blow this popsicle stand," she said.

Thea's hand clamped on her shoulder. "You're leaving Baby?"

Billie swallowed around the sudden lump in her throat. "She'll be here waiting for us after."

A muscle ticked in Thea's jaw, the first crack in the good humor she'd displayed all day. Billie wondered what thoughts played through Thea's mind while she was passed out, but before she could ask, Thea seized her hand, tugging her into a run.

Their feet slapped the pavement, using the reach of Baby's headlights to weave through the cars. Lungs pinching and leg muscles twitching in protest, they pushed hard until they slowed to a limping trot, gulping air. When their bodies recovered enough, they resumed their punishing pace. Beyond the pitch-black road, some of the town's streetlights still functioned; the glowing circles were lighthouses in the abyss. Thea navigated them both through that breathless final run, until they turned onto a street they both recognized, greeted by the sound of waves crashing against the shore.

"How much time do we have?" Billie gasped out, clutching a stitch in her side.

Thea swiped the sweat from her brow, a glimpse of panic ghosting over her features. "Not much."

There was a hum of anticipation in the air, an internal clock that whispered in Billie's chest around her pounding heartbeat. No time. They had no time.

"Come on," Thea shouted, breaking into a run for the shore. Billie didn't think she had another burst of speed in her, but she would always follow Thea, right to the end. A lone street light lit up the parking lot beside the beach, close enough to the water to cast dark green shadows in the surf. Thea stumbled when she hit the sand, coming to a stuttering halt as she stood there panting, watching the nearly invisible surf. Billie caught up to her a minute later, unable to draw air into her lungs.

It was a full minute before either of them spoke, basking in the salty air that cooled their sweat-slick faces.

"Think gravity will give out at midnight again?" Thea straightened, her hands lax at her side.

Billie had never seen her look so lost, but these were unique circumstances. Steeling herself, she stepped forward and slipped her hand into Thea's, tangling their fingers together.

"Maybe." Would it hurt? Would the end be instant or lingering? If she were the sort for brutal honesty, she would be a babbling wreck, not at all ready to go. Not when she'd barely begun to live. There was so much to say. To experience. She glanced at Thea, memorizing the lines of her face. This was the last sight she wanted to see. "There's no one I'd rather see the end of the world with than you. You're my person."

Thea's nostrils flared. She bared her teeth at Billie. "Oh, *now* you say it. You have the worst fucking timing—"

The breath swooped out of their lungs, the air around them vibrating with the now familiar sensation of gravity turning off like a switch. A regular occurrence now, but one they'd always been somewhat sheltered for, sheltered inside Baby or surrounded firmly planted trees, not out in the open like this. Not at midnight, on this day, the last day.

Thea spun off balance, catching Billie's hands as they both lifted off the ground, floating upward.

"Don't panic," said Billie. "It doesn't last that long, remember." Except this felt different, and as the seconds ticked on and on, and their bodies began to float out and over the water, Billie knew this was it. The End, and here they were floating like balloons that'd broken free from a five year old's sweaty fist, bobbing over the ocean.

Too much time had passed and gravity remained absent. Billie knew she should be feeling dread or terror at what was coming, but there was none of that. Not when her heart beat between their clasped palms. Thea's grip tightened.

"Look," she whispered. Below them, the sea glowed a faint aqua green, the color pure and warm. "What's doing that?"

"No idea," said Billie, her voice equally reverent when rippling balls of seawater broke off the thrashing waves and rose, floating beneath them, around them, surrounding them. She locked eyes with Thea, both laughing amid the levitating sparkling bubbles.

That aqua green glow highlighted the planes and hollows of Thea's face, and sparked in the tears knotted in her lashes. "You're my person, too," she said, her words drawn and weighted with awe.

Billie's heart rumbled in her chest. No, the very air hummed, vibrating through their bones. They looked upward, gasping at the sight of the massive ship filling the sky. It almost seemed close enough to skim their fingers along the hull, a looming, crushing presence about to drop on their heads but Billie could only smile.

"Well, we weren't here for a long time, but it sure was a good time," quipped Thea.

Rather than crash down, the ship began to rise, lifting higher and higher, while the rumble intensified, until Billie thought her teeth would rattle out of her skull. The watery globes shivered and scattered in Pollack-equese sprays through the atmosphere. Billie drew a breath, bracing herself.

A great sucking noise, like a vacuum in reverse, filled her head, the pressure nearly unbearable until she heard an audible thwap between her ears. The ship vanished from the sky, moving faster than her bewildered vision could register.

Billie barely had time to register what happened when gravity returned with a vengeance. "Oh shit—"

Thea yelped as they plummeted straight down. The sea seemed to reach up to catch them, the risen dollops of sea water coalescing in a foaming cushion. Billie's shoes kissed the sandy floor. She pushed up, her sodden clothes weighing her down, strangling her until she broke the surface. Blinking rapidly through the stinging saltwater, she sputtered for air, treading water while she flailed for Thea. Where was Thea?

Thea's sodden blonde head burst out of the water beside her, coughing and cursing and alive. They were alive. The ship was gone and they were alive.

"That's it?" Billie spat out a mouthful of seawater, staring at the empty sky. "What the shi–"

Thea burst out laughing, the sound lapping against the shore. "Come here," she said, her voice broken, giving the smile on her face a ragged edge when her hands slipped around Billie's waist to haul her closer.

Billie forgot to breathe all over again when Thea's hands framed her face, brushing her dripping hair out of the way. Their mouths slanted against one another, warmth that crackled like fireworks in her belly as she tasted salt and sweetness on Thea's lips. Proof of life in the sensations that flared and overwhelmed her until tears of joy and relief mingled with the ocean water dripping down her face. Their knees bumped together as they tread water, pressed chest to chest so close they could feel one another's hearts hammering against their ribs, knocking like impatient neighbors.

Overhead the night sky was clear, studded with stars so bright and close, they sparkled like shards of glass caught in black cloth. Moonlight shone in Thea's smile. "You never know what tomorrow will bring."

No, she didn't, but Billie didn't care, because they had tomorrow. And the day after that. And the day–

A cluster of shouts grew in volume, their proximity sudden and alarming, until they were abruptly swallowed by the sea. Water splashed over them, Billie and Thea sharing a bewildered look when several disgruntled men in oddly colored camouflage floundered to the surface around them.

Coughing and sputtering, they glanced around in confusion when one of them caught sight of Billie and Thea staring at them in open bewilderment.

"Excuse me, miss and… miss, did you happen to see where the ship went?" He was awfully polite despite the strand of seaweed plastered across his forehead.

Thea pointed upward. "They left."

"Left? They *left*?" He flapped his arms, glaring at the night sky. "This is going to be so much paperwork."

Billie and Thea remained quiet while the soldiers dragged themselves ashore with a great deal of grumbling, before mutually deciding to put the encounter firmly in the apocalyptic shenanigans box and move on.

The water was warm, the tepid bathwater of summer's end, and the night was full of possibilities. Billie and Thea leaned back to float side by side, holding hands in the ocean's embrace.

"Think any diners might be open?" Thea piped up. "I'd kill for a stack of pancakes."

Billie shrugged, the water gurgling against her ears. People craved normalcy. Even at the end of the world.

"There might be a Waffle House nearby."

~

00

about the author

Ben Sobieck *is an author, inventor, entrepreneur, and Reuben sandwich enthusiast. He read Jurassic Park at far too young an age, but it seems to have worked out. He resides in Minnesota, USA, where he has three kidneys.*

THE LAST TESTAMENT OFTHE WAFFLE HOUSE HERETICS

or

THERE IS NO LETTER Z IN THIS STORY

by Ben Sobieck

DUMFRIES, VA - AFTER

The Waffle House quiets as the scribe opens the door and steps inside. Heads turn and lights flicker, and the 24/7 restaurant finally pauses. Someone whispers something to someone else, but there's no reply. Even the music in the overhead speakers takes a breather between songs.

A hostess breaks the silence, breezing by the scribe to say, "Pick a seat."

The scribe takes a seat at the counter and pretends to look over the Waffle House menu. He knows what he'll order. He ate here many times before, especially in the days leading up to the mysterious craft's final countdown. In fact, it used to hover right above this very Waffle House only a few weeks ago.

"Nice weather today," the scribe says to the customer seated next to him. The customer slides down to the other end of the counter.

The restaurant resumes its chaotic hum, and a server approaches the scribe with the vacant look in her eyes that everyone carries around these days. The odds are 50-50 that she'll be overly friendly or outright hostile. There isn't an in between anymore. Everyone processes what happened in their own way, and almost no one talks about it. In five years' time, the scribe supposes, all manner of conspiracy theories will claim an event everyone on Earth experienced never happened.

Thankfully, the server gushes with friendliness, adjusted for a Waffle House. She asks the scribe, "Whatcha want?"

"What's good here?" the scribe says, more out of conversation than curiosity.

"I ain't got time to make decisions for you. You came in hungry, didn't you? Pick something," the server says.

After he places an order he'll ignore later, the scribe pulls out a pen and a notebook. Someone needs to write down what happened to them as a testament. It's not to make money or to brag, the scribe tells himself, but for the sake of understanding. No one understands what happened after the countdown, or why the craft appeared in the first place, or what any of it means. Maybe, someone in the future will, but only if there's something to consider.

"Why do I have to write it? My experience is so strange," the scribe asks himself under his breath. The ocean of vacant eyes in the Waffle House settles his doubts. The world is still too rattled to commit to remembering, floating like amoebic automatons. Stimulus-response. Stimulus-response. Hungry-eat. Eat-pay. Pay-leave. Leave-sleep. Sleep-shit. Shit-hungry. Repeat.

The scribe puts pen to paper and starts to write.

***

CH. 1, VERSE 1 – THEY don't believe HIM anymore. THE OBJEKT, that baffling and beautiful bullet in the sky—that *was* the sky—is gone now. Finished with its countdown from 30, it simply vanished the morning of August 31. It took with it so much, and left even more, but mainly—to the chosen few people known as THEM or THEY or TheY, since the last letter of the alphabet was forbidden to THEM—it took THEIR belief in HIM. However, it was not always that way, and it is of incredible importance that you understand why.

CH. 1, VERSE 2 – In the beginning, THEY believed HIM when HE healed that kid in the parking lot behind Waffle House #1243 in Orlando, smashed to pieces by a car and then put back together by HIS miraculous touch many months ago. No one remembered seeing any of this, but that didn't matter. All anyone needed, HE'd said, was to believe. And so the first few of HIS followers believed HIM, and these followers became THEY and THEM.

CH. 1, VERSE 3 –THEY believed HIM when HE disappeared for exactly three days and came back with that beard and that hair and those shoes and that accent and that propensity to hear voices at just the right times and HIS strange methods to make friends of enemies and that way HE'd look at you when HE spoke truths into you. Oh, that look! Piercing deep down to the soul HE'd go to swim and wiggle into a pregnancy of peace and love and understanding and justice and the fulfillment of every broken promise to every broken person. And that smell, that sweet aroma—like roses in water, like orange blossoms in the wind, like God's own aftershave—that followed HIM around like a drunk puppy to kiss HIS feet and bathe in HIS attention. THEY believed. Oh, THEY believed! And so THEY grew in number, and THEY believed.

***

"Whatcha writing?" the server asks the scribe as she refills his coffee for the third time. It's been a long time since he's had the courage to drink the brew. He forgot how incredible it tastes.

The scribe looks up from his pen. "Oh, nothing."

"You a writer?"

"I guess."

"You ever publish anything I've read?" the server asks.

"Maybe. Have you heard of Wattpad?" the scribe says.

"Sounds like I need to," the server says and walks off to greet another customer.

***

CH. 1, VERSE 4 – THEY believed when HE drew pictures of HIS magnificent visions that arrived only at the peak of writhing, sweating ecstasy. This, the symbiotic nature of THEIR relationship to HIM: HE the swollen cow that must be milked, and THEY the hands at the udders thirsting to drink.

CH. 1, VERSE 5 – THEY believed when HE overlaid the locations of Waffle Houses in the United States atop the living Earth's living arteries of living energy, called "ley lines." THEY believed when HE required more visions through more writhing and sweating and ecstasy. And so THEY writhed and THEY sweated and THEY explored every last corner of THEIR writhing, sweaty bodies. For it was the Waffle House that held the locks, and HE the key, and THEY the belief that these things combined will yield an epiphany. For even HE acknowledged, as anyone would, while laying breathless on the floor of an RV parked outside a Waffle House, that there must be a reason to all of this beyond mere mortal indulgences of flesh and French fries. A final purpose. A conclusion. And so THEY grew in number with every stop they made at every Waffle House, until the RV turned into an overhauled school bus.

CH. 1, VERSE 6 – THEY believed HIM when HE said HE could turn water into gasoline when the bus shuttered and sputtered and slid onto the shoulder. THEY believed HIM when HE said this transformation could only work if THEY shut THEIR eyes for a long time on the bus. And because THEY believed, and because THEY followed HIS directions, the bucket of water HE brought with HIM into the wilderness turned into gasoline. A miracle! Oh, how THEY believed HIM then.

CH. 1, VERSE 7 – THEY believed HIM when HE said THEY must remove the last letter of the alphabet—which cannot be written here out of respect for HIS beliefs—from THEIR vocabulary, either verbal or written. For to do so would be to acknowledge that there is an end to anything, and language is the descriptor of reality. Nothing could ever come to completion, HE said, until the arrival of some great, history-crushing event that no one on Earth could possibly ignore. HE referenced this event often, but HE never could put a name to the event, because HE said HE wasn't allowed to, because THEY were not ready to hear that part of HIS message. And so it was that the alphabet ended at Y, and THEY and THEM became TheY as well, because HE sayeth this pun sounded cool. Any of THEM caught using the other, forbidden letter at the end of the alphabet would be smote with the ferocity of a Waffle House knuckle swap at midnight.

CH. 1, VERSE 8 – It took such a midnight Waffle House knuckle swap for HIM to give a name to the event in HIS visions. A customer threw a chair at a cook, and the cook accidentally threw the chair at a different customer—who had nothing to do with the altercation—and that customer ducked, and so the chair careened toward HIM and HIS plate of All-Star Special™, and HE grabbed the chair with one hand without so much as missing a bite of HIS bacon. The entire Waffle House fell into silence, and HIS satisfaction in bringing the melee to a stop was so profound that HE was blessed with another vision. In that exact moment, at that exact table in Waffle House #1302, HE announced to the entire restaurant that the world may resume using a 26-letter alphabet after THE GRAND REVALASHUN occurred, for that singular event would mark the completion—the whole point—to all of this. It is now forgotten why HE chose to spell THE GRAND REVALASHUN in such a manner, but THEY believed the quirk only added to how informed HIS latest vision proved to be. For THEY believed—oh, brothers and sisters, how THEY believed!—that no one would be so moronic as to intentionally misspell "revelation," whether for lack of education or lack of care, given the gravity of HIS proclamation.

CH. 1, VERSE 9 – None of THEIR belief, however, could possibly come close to what THEY felt and experienced when THE GRAND REVALASHUN took place as HE foretold. For the stirring deep in THEIR souls transcended mere belief, becoming something even more powerful, as the whole world watched THE OBJEKT appear. THE OBJEKT, being massive in both form and spirit, struck the globe like a blacksmith's hammer and forged a new reality. Few on EARTH could claim they were prepared psychologically or spiritually or physically for such an event, and of those few even fewer boiled the heavens with the fever of their elation as THEY did. For THEY no longer believed. THEY knew. Oh, brothers and sisters, how THEY knew! The only thing THEY needed was for HIM to confirm that THE OBJEKT surely was the embodiment of THE GRAND REVALASHUN.

CH. 1, VERSE 10 – And so gathered all of THEM at exactly midnight in the parking lot of Waffle House #1011 to coax new levels of immortal vision out of HIS mortal body. Such a vision arrived after three hours and three minutes of such coaxing, bare bodies chaffed and chap from the writhing and sweating and ecstasy. And HE revealed the vision that confirmed THE OBJEKT truly was THE GRAND REVALASHUN, and so not one of THEM slept for a solid day after this pronouncement out of raw respect and revelry.

CH. 1, VERSE 11 – "Teacher, may we now use the forbidden letter? The one that used to mark the end of the alphabet?" THEY asked HIM. And HE replied, "We may not until we know THE OBJEKT." And THEY asked HIM, "Is that not THE GRAND REVALASHUN?" And HE replied, "It is, brothers and sisters, but I say unto you, to know is to experience. So we must go to THE OBJEKT, and we must experience THE OBJEKT for ourselves, for there is a sign about it that did not originate in one of my visions." And THEY begged and THEY begged for HIM to reveal what this meant. So HE told THEM, "Foolish beggars! Charity has already filled your wanting palms. Have you not heard the news? THE OBJEKT rests in permanent midnight above Waffle House #1041. A Waffle House! Should not this embolden your faith?"

CH. 1, VERSE 12 – Upon hearing this, THEY begged HIM forgiveness for THEIR ignorance, and so HE made THEM go bare into a ditch to be punished for THEIR lack of faith and most irritating demeanor. When HE finally reached satisfaction and THEIR transgressions were made whole, HE proclaimed, "Behold, while the rest of the world cowers in fear and hides on four legs, we stand firm on two legs with the spirit of the Waffle House!" And out of the ditch arose a cheer, for Waffle Houses do not close unless and until the world is ending, as it is written in the Waffle House Index. Then HE declared, "We must go to this chosen Waffle House #1041. Surely, brothers and sisters, this is so much more than cosmic coincidence. This is our moment!"

CH. 1, VERSE 13 – So it was that THEY journeyed with HIM in the bus to Waffle House #1041 beneath THE OBJEKT, bringing with THEM THEIR knowing and THEIR belief and THEIR cash money, for all the credit card processors were down, but that was not enough for the Waffle House in question to cease tableside service of waffles, T-bone steaks, hashbrowns, cheese 'n' eggs, country ham, pork chops, and grits to both the frightened and the faithful.

***

"You seem familiar. Have we met before?" the server asks the scribe.

"We might've," the scribe says and sips his coffee. "What were you doing during the—you know—the thing."

This rattles the server. She looks back at the kitchen. "Oh, OK. Yeah, um, let me grab something quick. Just a minute."

The server doesn't come back in a minute, or five minutes. The scribe keeps writing.

***

CH. 2, VERSE 1 – And when THEY arrived at Waffle House #1041, HE needn't visions any longer, and THEY had no use for visions, for the air was so pure it tasted like the breath of life itself, and the permanent midnight outlined the warm glow of the restaurant like a lighthouse against a dark shore, and the aromas of grease and griddle and grits and goodness went straight to THEIR stomachs like mana.

CH. 2, VERSE 2 – And when HE first set foot in Waffle House #1041, a man in a suit sitting in a corner leapt to his feet and shouted, "Hark! This is what I've been waiting for this whole time!" And HE sayeth to the man in the suit, "It is, brother. You are now THEM and THEY and TheY. Let us celebrate. I sayeth unto you—nay, to this entire eatery—that the food is on me. For soon we will have no use for food, or of money, for we will be among the stars with our galactic family, basking in perfect harmony with the universe on the craft above our heads, where we will let the recitation of that forbidden letter at the end of the alphabet be our annunciation. So mote it be!" Oh, brothers and sisters, how THEY rejoiced and filled THEIR bellies with cheese grits and biscuits. Two more joined THEM as well, having come down from the roof of the restaurant to partake in the food and celebrations. Even the chef in the back of the Waffle House cried out with tears in his eyes, "Eat all you want, you Manson-lookin' hippies. If the food is gone, maybe they'll finally close and I can go home." And sayeth the server responsible for dispersing the food to HE and THEM, "You freaks might not have any use for money, but I still do. You better pay for all this shit." And HE laughed and patted the server on the head, and the server slapped HIM, and so THEY smote the server with THEIR fists, and so a group of customers smote THEM with their fists as well, and so the chef grabbed a chair and a knife and threatened to bury all of them beneath blood and bruise. "Fuck this, I quit," sayeth the server. And so the server left, and THEY were made glad, and the chef cooked food for everyone, and HE was made glad. It is said the food was not as many as the mouths, and yet no mouth was left unsatiated.

***

The TV on the wall of the Waffle House switches to a news program. The chyron on the top story mentions something about satellite data taken during the time of the craft—or THE OBJEKT, as the scribe would write it.

"Turn that shit off. I'm so sick of hearing about it," someone from the other side of the Waffle House shouts.

The scribe watches as the server flips the TV to a baseball game.

***

CH. 3, VERSE 1 – All of the events hereto told occurred when THE OBJEKT hovered fresh in the sky. 'Twas a month ago. THE OBJEKT shone numbers in the sky, and those numbers counted down from 30, with a new number each day. HE assured THEM that HIS promises of harmony with the universe would be fulfilled once the number on THE OBJEKT finished its countdown. On the Earthly calendar, such a date would read as August 31. In the days prior, the staff of Waffle House #1041 turned over 54 times, and THEIR outstanding bill increased 327-fold as the food dispersed unabated, and the number of HIS followers quintupled, and HE was made glad.

CH. 3, VERSE 2 – On the morning of August 31, THEY could be seen in every corner and crevice of Waffle House #1041, so much so that the chef could barely prepare breakfast. Sayeth the chef, "Give me some space or there's going to be a grease fire." And HE laughed and HE said unto the chef, "I've no concern of fires, for today is the day." And the chef sayeth, "Yeah, it's the day one of you gets their fucking face melted off in a grease fire. Everyone out of the kitchen. I don't understand why they don't close this place." So HE led THEM out of the kitchen and into the parking lot to revel once more at THE OBJEKT that surely would take THEM to the next level of existence, and to prove THEIR worthiness for such an adventure by making bare of THEMselves and writhing and sweating and eating Toddle House® Omelets. But hark! Hark! Rays of sunlight fell unto THEM for the first time in a month, and it burned THEIR ashen bodies, for 'twas no more midnight than a waffle is a crocodile, and HE was not made glad, and THEY were also not made glad.

CH. 3, VERSE 3 – So it must be that HE and THEY ran—oh, how THEY ran!—back into Waffle House #1041 and turned on a television mounted to the wall. HE demanded the staff tune this television to the oracle known as the Cable News Network, and HE demanded THEY be quiet as the president of the United States of America animated the oracle.

CH. 3, VERSE 4 – Sayeth the president, "My fellow Americans, and to all members of the human race, I want you to hear it from me first. The craft that mysteriously appeared over our skies has just as mysteriously disappeared. I want to lay to rest any rumors: this is not the result of military action. The international community, including scientists from every continent, conducted research as quickly as possible. However, whether we did something or did not, the craft ended its countdown and left our skies. We have no indication it's anywhere near Earth, or even in the solar system. Now, I'm not one to turn this into a partisan moment, but had Congress passed the budget I proposed earlier this year, we would've had far more resources at our disposal to expedite our research in this limited amount of time. Folks, the fact is this Congress is one of the most obstructive I've ever worked with in my 35 years in Washington. I urge every American voter to turn your frustration into action at the ballot box this November. As for what to do today, let me give you some advice: E.T. went home and now you should, too. Does anyone remember that movie? Yes? No? Ah, forget it. OK, time to take questions from the press."

CH. 3, VERSE 5 – How sad that those words from the president would mark the end of HIM and THEM as each knew it to be. For THEY turned to HIM and THEY said, "Blasphemer! THE OBJEKT is gone, yet we are still here. We believed in you, but all we have to show for it be herpes and heartburn." And this was disagreeable to HIM, and so HE smote the man in the suit in the eyes with the pepper shaker, and HE sayeth unto THEM, "Heretics! It is clear to all that one of you broke the sacred commandment, that of not using the forbidden letter at the end of the alphabet. You have proven us unworthy of The OBJEKT's intentions, and so it left us here. How dare you!" And there was much disagreement after that, and a melee took about.

CH. 3, VERSE 6 – Then came out the manager of Waffle House #1041 to break up the melee. The manager's words, not fists, ended the scuffle. The words be, "You heard the president. Time to go home. You all have been eating here on an open tab for a month. I've got the bill right here. Who's going to pay it?" Though the manager be not familiar with magical incantations, the words took the effect as such, and THEY drifted away from Waffle House #1041, until only HE remained. And HE smote the manager with a chair, and the manager smote HIM with a chair, and the chef smote both of them with a carafe of hot coffee, and then an ambulance came to treat HIM for burns, thereby adding to HIS outstanding debt.

CH. 3, VERSE 7 – Yet before the ambulance carried HIM away, the manager told HIM with glee that HE had failed in HIS mission. And so HE reached to the sky from the gurney one last time and doth proclaimed, "Failed? No. To know the presence of mystery from beyond our skies is beautiful beyond description. It is its own success. For is it not mystery that fuels us? Is it not the pursuit of answers that makes us human?"

CH. 3, VERSE 8 – And the manager, looking back at the wreckage of Waffle House #1041, sayeth unto HIM, "Uhhhh, sure, but that pursuit sure can leave behind a big mess." And HE sayeth unto the manager, "It can, but it's the friends we make along the way that matters the most." And the manager sayeth unto HIM, "Friends? Buddy, all your friends left when it came time to pay the bill." And so HE passed out in the gurney.

CH. 3, VERSE 9 – This be the Last Testament of the Waffle House Heretics. So mote it be!

***

The scribe closes his notebook and leaves a nice tip for the server on the counter. She smiles and then takes a step back.

"Hey, I know you. You cut your hair, didn't you?" the server says.

"I don't know who I am. I don't know anything anymore," the scribe says and pushes away from the counter.

~

the end

ACKNOWLEDGEMENTS

This collection of stories couldn't have happened without the support (and endless patience) of the WritersConnX Discord community.

Seriously: they had to sit and watch this group of writers form and plan and then do some more planning. There was so much planning that people either got excited and wanted to be part of it... or they just got tired of the chaotic energy and eventually muted us. Hell, I would have muted us too. There is quite nothing like getting 317 notifications on one channel after being gone for one hour.

The thing is that the general community saw only a few hints of what we were planning as we tried to gauge interest with a little tease here and there. In private, we were having all of these discussions about logistics, the big story and how it would all work together.

Clarissa North was crucial with her feedback that helped to turn the initial pitch of "30 Days to the End of the World" to a more forward-thinking "30 DAYS TO SAVE THE WORLD". The last thing we wanted to do was have a whole lot of stories of doom and gloom, because only a tiny fraction of readers would actually want to read that.

The first piece of anything ever created for this anthology came from AW Frasier (Fray). It's the cover art that you see, the illustration of the woman with the guns and the enormous braid. We had no idea what the cover was even supposed to look like, no full concept apart from the image I had found on Canva with the blast of light from the heavens hitting the earth. That was just the developmental image, and all Fray had to work with was the idea that "of course, people will be fighting back" so art was created. It was an act of pure faith that we would work together to create the best image for the cover. So HUGE thanks to Fray for their creativity and talent.

AB Channing was a chaotic force to be reckoned with, a brilliant strategist and observer of human nature; he took a look at the entire layout of events on the calendar, rubbed his hands gleefully and said, "let's make it worse", so yeah... I'm not entirely responsible for all of the chaos.

Before they even got involved, though, the planning started with the loose team we had formed to complete the rollout of the previous anthology "Monstrous Love". It had previously been just Van Carley and myself (although to be honest, I had wanted nothing to do with planning the anthologies, and yet somehow, here we are), but then along came our chaos twins: Eliza Solares and Iveto (sometimes Ina) Ramos. If you ever want to know who really keeps my personal brand of chaos in check AND organized, it's those two. Van is our enforcer, and she makes sure everything is on track and moving along, especially as we move into the reader engagement part of this release. I cannot thank them enough for listening and correcting some of the wilder ideas that I brought. And they were wild.

Now you would have thought that we would have thought of absolutely everything. I mean for the first time, we actually had contracts, (a necessity since we were going into official print and general release) thanks to Jane Peden, the lawyer in the community. We had a development plan, a release plan and an idea of how we could pull off a Kickstarter campaign. The stories started to come in almost immediately, and I quickly realized that my main strength in editing was for developmental story edits. My strength is knowing the big picture and how everything fits together. Kind of like a showrunner on a tv-series, which was essential for this type of anthology. The stories aren't directly connected, but they are all in the same world and believe me, that counts for a lot.

Melody Grace Hicks, Cardin Watts, Fiora Voss and Debra Goelz all stepped up to help us through the editing process. They each brought their experience and talent to the process and collaborated quite well in working with each of the 39 authors. The main goal, as it is with the best editors, was not just line corrections, but to help shape the stories into the best versions of themselves. I continue to be impressed with each of these wonderful editors and cannot wait for the chance to work with them again.

And now we've reached the writers.

My gods: *so many writers.*

I had sworn never to include so many writers again, after all, we had 36 (count them: 36!) of them on "MONSTROUS LOVE," and that was an undertaking, so the total number was going to be capped at 30. Period. Only a 30-day countdown, right? No way we could go over that. Oh, but wait: we had to include the prologue, but that was okay, because we'll just set that before August; still, that was one more writer… Then there was August 31, but that was fine… Just add an epilogue, after the countdown type of thing. Now we were up to 32. Except…

Somewhere along the line, I had miscounted, and more writers were asking to be involved. Do you know how hard it is to say no to people who are excited to be part of your project? The fact is, in most anthologies for one reason or another, people are going to drop out, and we had to be prepared.... That didn't quite happen. Not with this anthology. The concept had caught on fire in people's minds. We had a variety of writers who had never even considered writing anything close to Science-Fiction before. Romance writers, Historical Fiction, contemporary, and horror... so the first thing we had to make everyone understand was a simple concept. They didn't have to know anything about science, or space or alien biology or warp engines. That wasn't what science fiction is about. Science Fiction at its very core is about people and how they adapt in the face of the extraordinary. Science fiction could have all of those elements involved, after all, human beings go through a range of emotions and develop relationships in the strangest ways. So we wanted to see real stories in the face of possible annihilation by the biggest alien spacecraft we could think of.

And the writers delivered. Of course, they did: I mean, have you seen who we have involved in this thing?

Thank you, to all of the writers for being patient with us and enduring the editing process, and most of all, for believing in the idea and lending us your talent to make this anthology as great as it can be. I have HUGE respect for each of you. For some, this was my first time meeting and discovering their work, and I am beyond impressed. I keep telling people about the wonderful community of writers on Wattpad and the sheer talent available on the platform, and I'm glad to be able to offer a showcase of some of this talent.

We have big writers here with HUGE platforms, and some with barely 1000 followers, but followers don't make you great. Most times, some of the best talent is just not visible to the public. Anthologies like this one can make them more visible.

Do yourself a favour: follow each of the writers in this book and read at least one book from their catalogue. I promise you'll be well entertained... and have a huge reading list that will take you into next year.

Or at least until the next anthology...

Rodney V. Smith
Editor-in-Chief *(I actually get to use this now)*
WritersConnX

special thanks to

Curtis Ardourel
Membership Chair
Marin Amateur Radio Society

Printed in the USA
CPSIA information can be obtained
at www.ICGtesting.com
LVHW050420050124
767800LV00107B/333/J

9 781738 018406

"I *am* thinking about them, Martha. The economy is crashing right now. This is one of the best-paying jobs in the market. Like ten times what they usually pay. I'll be ahead of the curve when things settle down."

"I'm not the one you need to convince. Talk to your wife, Gary. She might seem fine when you talk to her on phone breaks, but she's definitely putting on a brave face. Your family needs you more than you realize."

"I know, I know. I'll talk to her about this today, okay? But you don't need to worry about that because *you're* starting the long trek to Nevada." he tried to smile. "I'm going to miss you, Martha."

She shook her head. "Stay safe, Gary. Take care of yourself." She reached forward and wrapped her arms around him, her head thumping gently against his chest. For a moment, the air was fraught with emotion, and Gary nearly considered packing his bags then and there.

But the moment passed, and the old woman was composed as she stepped away. Gary watched her short figure stride determinedly down the hall, becoming a silhouette in the exit door's meager illumination. Gary collected himself and started the twelve-level hike up to the makeshift comms center.

The thud, thud, thud of his footsteps echoed in the cold concrete rectangle, each step placed apart like a metronome playing the beat for the melody of Gary's rushing mind.

When the mysterious ship first arrived, Gary had only planned to stay for ten days. Get in, do some coverage, and get out before things went sideways. By the tenth day, though, nothing *really* bad had happened yet.

Sure, there was the endless darkness, the satellite difficulties, and the tiniest of gravity displacements now and then. But directly under the spacecraft hadn't been the chaotic center of catastrophe he'd always seen in the movies, and even the glowing blue number had become disturbingly commonplace to him. Whatever was going to happen wasn't going to for another fifteen days. Why not stay a little longer?

But more and more of the crew was feeling otherwise. The taste of normalcy yesterday had shaken up people more than Gary had expected, causing the already tense atmosphere to bubble over. Martha would be the fourth reporter leaving since this started, and the team was already a skeleton crew, down to essential positions. How many more people could leave before they would have to fold up the sidewalk and go dark along with the rest of the East Coast?

Pushing past the solid metal door, Gary walked down the hall on the twelfth floor, making his way through pockets of darkness punctuated by emergency lights that flickered in and out of life. The buzz of the single space heater reached his ears before he entered the communication room.

A desk was situated against the far wall, near the covered windows, and on the edge of the desk, perched a laptop with several wires running down to various power boxes under the table. Shane Huang, a middle-aged Asian, sat in front of the laptop and faced the studio switchers. They wore headphones, laughing and talking to someone. Garett noticed a young adult on the screen before he glanced away, not looking to intrude on the personal moment. He instead stared at the space heater working its hardest in the corner, idly taking comfort in its orange glow. What a contrast it provided against the cold blue numbers suspended in the sky.

After a couple minutes, they closed the video call and removed the headphones with trembling hands. "Hi Gary, didn't see you there."

"Hi, Shane."

"Your turn with the comms, huh?"

He nodded.

"Enjoy it," Shane murmured, shaking their head. "Fifteen minutes is only long enough to make me miss them all over again."

They patted Gary's shoulder as they trudged out of the room. Gary settled into the worn leather office chair in front of the computer. Taking a few deep breaths, he navigated quickly with a few clicks and connected the call.

"Papa! Papa!" A mop of curly black hair popped into the frame.

"Sofibear!"

"Mama, Papa's here!"

Carmen's voice echoed from somewhere off-screen before she entered the frame and settled down beside Sofia. A warmth buzzed in his chest as he absorbed her heart-shaped face and warm brown eyes. Even though it had only been two days since they spoke, Gary deeply missed his wife of nine years.

"Hi, Carmen," he whispered.

"It's good to see you, Gary." Her lips quirked into a smile, but it didn't reach her eyes.

"So, where are you guys?" he asked. "Are you guys still in the hotel in Hobart?"

"We've been staying with Tia Rosa in Austin since the evacuation orders a couple days ago. For once, I'm glad to be in Texas."

"That's really good," Gary breathed. Relief washed over him. They weren't alone. "I'm glad you're with family. "

"It's not the *whole* family," Carmen murmured.

An awkward silence hung in the air. Or maybe Gary was simply imagining the tension from his own guilty conscience.

"I watch you on the TV every day, Papa!" Sofia blurted out excitedly.

"Aww, Papa thinks of you every time I go on camera."

"What number was it today, Papa?"

"*Quince*," Gary answered, flashing five fingers three times. Sofia mirrored him, pressing her chubby hands against the screen. It had become a ritual every time they video-called, and Gary had come to cherish the routine.

"How big is the number today, Papa? Is it bigger than a house?"

"Much bigger than a house."

"Is it bigger than a castle?"

"Bigger than the biggest castle."

"How big was it, Papa?"

"It was as big as a whole city!"

Sofia wriggled on the couch, giggling. Carmen's lips were pressed in a firm line, and she didn't join in the laughter. Gary could see the worry etched on her face, and Martha's words echoed in his mind.

"Sofia, go see Tia Rosa. She has a snack for you," Carmen said softly.

"Okay. Goodbye, Papa! See you again on the TV!"

"Goodbye, Sofibear," Gary smiled and waved, his heart fluttering as his daughter toddled off-screen.

There was a moment where they stared at each other. He felt the tension growing like a crawling itch on his spine, and wanted to say something reassuring, but what could he say that hadn't already been said?

"Gary, when are you leaving that place?" Carmen broke the silence.

Gah. He wanted to bring it up to her, but not like this.

"Carmen…"

"You've been up there for over two weeks now!"

"Trust me, I don't like being away from you and Sofia. But it's really good pay. It's my first big project and they've promoted me to one of the head reporters on the assignment!"

"Because the others have been leaving, Gary. They're going home to find their loved ones."

"Carmita, what if the world doesn't end? When whatever this is finishes up and goes away, we're going to have so much put away. We'll actually have enough for Sofia's college fund."

"*Are you listening to me?* They're leaving to be with their families because the world is ending."

"They're trying to leave… but all the highways are jammed with traffic. The tent cities aren't helping either. Even if I could go, Carmen, it'd be God knows how many days before I could reach Texas."

"How do you think you're going to settle your affairs in just five days? What if the world does end, and you wasted all this time in a box under a UFO?"

"It's not like that, Carmen. What I'm saying is, here is one of the few spots I know I have consistent communication with you guys. If I tried to head out there, it could be two days before I even get out of the midnight zone. Then trying to navigate through all the tent cities and crowded highways—because I do check the other news about this." He laughed, picking at the corner of the desk. "It could be easily five or six days with no contact, maybe longer. It's a complete madhouse out there. Neither of us would know if the other was okay."

"Then why are you pushing it off?"

"I just… I haven't seen anything to think the world is ending, yet? I've been covering this event since it started and nothing's really *happened*."

"Nothing? That little light show yesterday was *nothing*? The giant freaking number in the sky that counts down every day is *nothing*? The huge thing in the sky that's blocking out a whole side of the United States *is nothing to you*?"

"But what's *happened*? It just sits there. There haven't been any other bad effects. In fact, the air around here has been easier to breathe than usual."

"And what if something does happen, huh? What if the circle in the sky suddenly decides one night to shoot down radiation, or simply crashes down to the earth below? Will there be time enough for you to leave then?"

Gary ran his hands through his hair, tugging on the messy curls. "But nothing like that has happened, Carmita. And I need to focus on what I know, the facts I've seen, and keep hoping for the best. I have to. I'm a reporter, it's who I am."

"Do you even hear yourself, Gary? I need you. Our daughter needs you at the end of the world. *Dios*, Gary, there's a freaking *alien ship* above your head and you're putting your job before us! Come *home*!" Carmen's voice cracked like a pane of glass. The shards lodged in Gary's chest as the tears threatened to spill from her eyes.

"It's not the job, it's about building our future even in the middle of all this uncertainty. If I can just keep doing this work, keep reporting what's *actually* going on and not what everyone is afraid of happening, maybe I can help other people build toward their future. I can help other children feel safe, children like our Sofia." He twisted his wedding ring frantically, trying to keep his voice steady. "I miss you, Carmen. So much. You and our child. And if I thought the world was ending, I would rush out in a heartbeat. But I have absolute faith that it's not, and you have to trust me on that. *Please!*"

Silence.

Carmen sat unmoving on the screen, saying nothing. In the background, Sophie was a frozen blur of black hair, caught in the act of running.

"...Carmen?"

An alert popped up in the corner of the screen:

Your internet could not be connected. Try troubleshooting your network.

"No, no, no…" Gary slammed his hand against the table.

How long had the line been dead?! Had Carmen heard anything that he'd just said? Had she left before then? Did it even matter?

Gary bent down to check the cable, shaking fingers ready to jam the bloody thing back into position. And he found what the issue was.

The cable was floating. So was the computer it should have been attached to. As Gary looked around, he noticed just how many things hovered a few inches above the concrete floor.

He felt weightless. Cold. Nothing was where it should be. The gentle, unyielding pressure causing the ground to slip away from him was almost comforting in its relentlessness.

Everything around him hung in the air, keeping pace with his own suspension. It wasn't a dangerous height, not more than a couple feet, but it was still a completely foreign feeling. But not as terrifying as it should have been.

Instead, the sensation reminded Gary how completely helpless and alone he was. There was nothing to reach for, nothing to hold onto, nothing else he could do.

He could only keep on keeping on.

He shut his eyes and took a deep, shuddering breath.

"Gary?"

Gary jolted in the chair. When did everything come back down? How long had he been up there? It mustn't have been more than a few minutes. Was it even more than a full minute?

A cameraman called from the other room, "You're back on in five."

"Got it!"

There was always another day. He could call her back then, explain things to her. Or he could start packing up tomorrow.

~

14

about the author

Mikaela Bender *has been a Wattpadder since 2012 and has been sharing her stories with readers since 2014. She is a fantasy and sci-fi author who loves any chance to write about aliens or fairies.*

In 2019, her Wattys-winning novel EXPIRATION DATE was turned into a pilot for SYFY. Born and raised in Florida, she knew she had to be the one to tell the FLORIDA MAN story.

She now lives in New York where she works in publishing.

THE FLORIDA MAN

by Mikaela Bender

JACKSONVILLE, FLORIDA, USA
AUGUST 17, 8:32 PM

Crouched in the back of his boat, Cletus Mac knew two things for certain: the big dark alien ship of impending death in the sky had shifted its number from fifteen to fourteen and his wife Beth had left him to screw one of those darn alien creatures. They probably had a forked tongue and two dicks. What human could compete with that?

He had to reach past Perch, the baby alligator he'd found as a hatchling in his retention pond, to grab his wrench. Perch opened his maw and made a sound that sounded like a blaster in one of those video games his nephews had made him play.

"Hush." He waved his hand at Perch, dismissing the gator's thoughtful contribution to how he might have sped things along. "I'll be done soon."

Perch squawked at him again.

"I'll feed you before we leave... What's that?" Cletus looked at his watch. "There's plenty of time." There were still over three hours till midnight when he had to be in position to take advantage of the witchcrafty thing the gravity did every night.

As he hooked the wrench around a bolt, the static sounds of a radio drifted through the quiet night. He was used to hearing bugs chirping, having them buzz around his forehead and arms. But over the past few nights, those sounds had softened until he rarely heard them now. The radio waves carried the voice of the cult leader who had enraptured his wife. Cletus had told her not to listen to the man who called himself Pippin. He had turned off the radio each time he'd caught her, but then one morning, she was gone.

Cletus jerked his elbow side to side as he tightened the bolts, attaching the poles onto the back of his boat, and Perch crawled along the rubber boat's edge to avoid Cletus's deadly elbow.

Cletus rolled his eyes. "I wasn't gonna hit you, but maybe if you didn't practically sit on top of me when I worked, it wouldn't be an issue in the first place."

Perch made the gruntiest of grunts, a disgruntled one, and glared.

Cletus glared back for almost a whole minute before returning to work.

The edges of the wrench pressed into Cletus's calloused palms, but he hardly felt it. Pain didn't matter if he got Beth back. When he had realized she was gone, he'd immediately gone to the cult's compound but was told his wife wasn't there—that she had already gone to find her way to the aliens.

Above him, attached to the poles was a yellow canvas that blocked out his view of the alien ship. The hang glider had belonged to his wife, though she had never used it. Positioning it on the boat had been difficult as he had had to avoid the propeller he had salvaged from his buddy's abandoned airboat.

The sound of the radio grew louder, and two women, draped in gray robes walked down the street. Their hands were pressed together before them as if they were in the most devout of prayers to their alien masters. Hanging from the wrist of the one was a portable radio. Gritting his teeth, forced to listen to the voice of Pippin, he continued tightening the bolts.

Perch opened his mouth and hissed, and Cletus rubbed two fingers down his scales in praise. "Good boy."

He was glad Perch hated listening to Pippin as much as he did; Pippin who was content to lead hundreds, if not thousands to their deaths, as long as his pockets got lined. It wasn't clear if he was accepting cash or only things that would be useful once the number above them hit zero.

The women turned and walked up his driveway. "Good evening, weary traveler," they said in unison.

He couldn't tell them apart. They both had long blonde hair and skin as pale as the white of his buttcheeks.

"Unless you have news about my wife, you have five seconds to get off my property." He didn't have much in the way to threaten them with right then so he picked up the baby gator and held him out before him like Perch was some ravenous creature.

Perch hissed, really selling the act.

Backing up a couple of steps, the two women glanced at each other.

"Pippin sent us," one said.

"He thought you may wish to follow in your wife's steps," the other said.

"If I become brainwashed and enslaved to those snake-tongued aliens, then who is there to save me?" He stabbed outward with Perch like he was a fencer. "En garde, you doughy-eyed charlatans."

As one, they titled their heads to the side. "Doughy?"

"Doughy." After all, they looked like deers in headlights before the might of Perch. "You can tell Pippin that when we meet, I'll be kicking his offer up his ass."

Perch hissed again, and the two women scurried off.

"Yeah, you get on out of here, you lizard-loving disciples."

They picked up speed after that, and Cletus set Perch back down, feeling smug.

"And that's how you get rid of a cult."

Perch stared up at him.

"You really should be writing all this down."

By the time he finished attaching the hang glider to his boat, the two women were long gone. Now he just needed to load up his truck with the necessary supplies and pour his remaining supply of gas into its tank.

He set his wrench in his toolbox and vaulted himself over the edge of his boat. The trailer it rested on was rusty, nearing the end of its usability. He had planned to replace it in the next few months.

He crouched down so his shoulder was in line with the edge of the boat. "Come on, Perch." And just like that, the baby gator crawled onto his shoulder and hung on to his shirt, hence Perch's name.

As Cletus walked up his driveway, Perch's claws continued to dig through his shirt and into his skin, but Cletus was used to it by now. He bent down, pulling two keys from his pocket, and unlocked his garage, first undoing the latch on the main lock and then on the deadbolt he had installed a few days ago. His muscles strained as he rolled the door up, and the overhead light flickered on, illuminating the forms of long-dead bugs stuck to its clear surface.

For a moment, he could imagine that tonight was like any other night he returned home late from a long day of work. It was like he could hear the TV set to the Hallmark channel. The white fridge near the door leading inside seemed to tempt him to open it and check for leftovers of the dinner Beth had either made or had delivered. On nights like that, he'd pop the leftovers in the microwave, and as the timer counted down, he'd go into the living room and kiss Beth's cheek from behind.

But she wasn't inside. And the TV was definitely off. He had made sure of that. Earlier today he'd chucked the remote at the screen and shattered it. That was after he'd gotten fed up with the news anchor trying to reassure his audience that everything was going to be all right when it all very clearly was not going to be all right. They were probably going to die and anyone who survived would have to pull out any and all skills they had learned from *The Walking Dead*. A segment like *You've Survived the Apocalypse, Now What?* is what they should be featuring.

Cletus had tried turning off the TV, but no matter how hard he jammed his finger down on the power button, the news anchor kept staring into his eyes, practically whispering sweet nothings to him. So he chucked the remote at the screen, put a nice spiderweb in the glass, and yet the anchor's voice still came through the TV. But now he looked distinctly like the AI Cletus had always suspected him of being, all pixelated and all evil. After that, the only thing left to do was to chuck the TV in the retention pond outback.

Cletus opened the fridge, but not for himself—rather to grab a couple frog legs for Perch. The gator swallowed the first down in only a few gulps, so Cletus grabbed a handful of them and stuck them in his pocket.

In the corner of his garage was a large metal cabinet. He'd recently attached three padlocks to it. After all, inside was one of the most precious commodities known to mankind right now.

Not toilet paper.

Not weapons.

But gasoline.

Three jugs of it. It would be enough to get him to the St. Johns River.

Above the gas and up on a shelf were his remaining cases of beer. Long ago, he and his buddies had figured out a way to make their boats run on the stuff. That way if they ever ran out of gas while on a fishing trip, they had a backup.

Frowning, he pulled the first case off the shelf and walked it to his truck. He'd probably never find another can of beer after today. The stores had run out back on day three. But he always had a hefty supply. Especially since Beth didn't even drink the stuff. She preferred ciders or rosé.

He might never again taste the sweet nectar of alcohol, but for vengeance, he would sacrifice every last drop. And if he got his wife back, they'd ride off into the sunset (he wasn't yet sure on what) for whatever little time they had left.

He hesitated as he went to open the back door of his truck. What if being with the cult and its alien overlords kept Beth safe when the countdown struck zero? What if rescuing her was wrong?

"Shit, Perch." He set the case of beer on the roof of his truck and pushed back his trucker's cap, running a hand through his sweat-dampened brown hair. Perch shifted uneasily, trying to maintain his balance. "Am I making a mistake?" What if rescuing Beth was really only sentencing her to death?

Perch stared up at him with those beady black eyes of his.

Letting out a growl, Cletus yanked open the back door of his truck. "You're right, Perch. Of course, you're right." He shoved the first case of beer inside the back row of his truck. "We're gonna get your mom back."

What had he even been thinking just then? Those hadn't been his thoughts. Those had belonged to the cult leader who had convinced his wife to give herself to the aliens. If he survived rescuing Beth, his next step was paying Pippin a visit. "What kind of a name is Pippin for a cult leader anyway?"

In response, Perch tilted his head.

Cletus finished loading in the cases of beer, keeping an eye out for any thirsty neighbors. It may not be the zombie apocalypse—or the vampire apocalypse—*yet*, but he wasn't going to act like his neighbors weren't dangerous. Most had evacuated, but some remained—those who weren't as lucky or as prepared as him to have gas on hand for emergencies.

Cletus wouldn't call himself a doomsday prepper. At least not a serious one—his wife would never have let him. But he did like to keep a few necessities on hand at all times. He returned to the garage for the gas and grabbed two of the jugs and poured them into his truck's tank before going back for the third.

His truck guzzled up all the gallons his three jugs offered and still could hold more—the greedy monster truck that it was. Lowering the last jug to the ground, Cletus took a moment of silence to mourn the abrupt end of any and all Monster Jams. The world would end in only a few days, and it seemed highly unlikely that January, the month he had tickets to attend the show in, would ever come again.

Fall also probably wouldn't come. He and a group of his friends had planned to chuck pumpkins with a catapult and a canon this November. He hadn't heard from any of those friends since day four.

He locked up his garage and climbed into the front seat of his truck. As the engine rumbled to life, his headlights flickered on, illuminating the parts of his driveway the lights on his house didn't reach. He tucked Perch in his cup holder and scratched his head. "Your mom will be back soon." Cletus gave him a few more mushy frog legs.

As they drove through the suburbs of Jacksonville, they passed very few cars. In the beginning, there had been a mass exodus. Those who had stayed were the ones who knew they wouldn't have had enough gas to make it out of the Twilight zone. Most of those who had left were probably stranded, still under the ever-present shadow of the ship.

Cletus and Beth had stayed mainly because he had been certain the ship would disappear in a few days, that it wouldn't actually stay for the entirety of its countdown. It had seemed likely it would move on to another country, another continent. But that number staring down at them every day seemed to say that the aliens wanted to pass judgment on their country. And who did they think they were to judge them? They weren't gods. They were probably made of slime or goo. Or maybe they looked like cockroaches. Cletus had killed enough of those to no longer be scared of the pests.

The gas stations they drove past looked like the apocalypse had hit them. Overturned and broken barricades were strewn across the concrete from when the military had taken over the stations. Gas handles lay on the ground. Bags, marking a pump as empty, only covered a few nozzles even though no gas remained in any.

Some of the gas stations and convenience stores had signs tacked to the walls that said, "CASH ONLY." Credit had no value when the world was ending. Cash would have none either for any survivors who made it through the month. Goods would be the only thing that held any value. A bartering system would be formed. Food. Supplies. That's what would be needed. People had to eat. People had to have shelter. Paper labeled with numbers would have no value because everyone would finally have to give up the illusion that it ever had.

He'd have to figure out what he'd be willing to trade. That was if he survived till tomorrow.

Out front of the last gas station he passed before his turn was a man sitting in a purple camping chair with a red gasoline jug chained to his wrist. A sign was propped up against the jug that said:

Gas
1 Gallon = $100

The man waved at him, and Cletus slowed down.

"Need gas?"

"Does it look like I need it?"

"Well you do have a mighty big truck. And you've got to fill up that boat somehow."

Perch crawled up Cletus's arm to see what was causing the holdup. When he saw the man, the gator let out a hiss.

The man's eyes widened.

"As my associate here has so nicely put it, we don't need your watered-down gas, we've got beer!"

Perch hissed again, and Cletus floored it, his tires squealing as they took off, leaving the man with only the smell of their exhaust.

A mile later, Cletus turned down a dirt road that ran parallel to the St. Johns River, his headlights and the giant blue fourteen in the sky were the only sources of light to illuminate the way.

Ahead, there was what looked like a log in the road, but Cletus knew better. He swerved and threw his arm down, holding onto Perch so the baby gator wouldn't go flying. Cletus narrowly avoided the gator's tail. If he hadn't seen the gator in time, the jolt of going over it would probably have been the thing that finally did his trailer in, not to mention that Perch would be highly offended.

He finally reached the boat ramp, the only bit of concrete to be seen in miles. Lining everything up was second nature to him at this point, and he backed the trailer down the ramp slowly until he heard the light splash of his tires hitting the water. He eased back a few more feet before he threw his emergency brake on and opened the door, grabbing his flashlight and putting Perch back on his shoulder.

He walked down the ramp and into the murky water. The air clung to his skin as beads of perspiration formed. Still, something about the air felt cleaner. *Smelled* cleaner even through the scent of dirt and brine. But even by the river, the bugs were far too quiet. He hated it.

He shined his light over the trailer, making sure everything was where it needed to be before he began loading the boat.

It didn't take long to finish. He made sure to strap one life vest and two parachutes under one of the chairs. The only way he imagined him and his wife getting off the spaceship was by jumping. He had a third parachute, but this one was much smaller than the others. Perch squirmed and wriggled as Cletus tugged it on him.

"Hold still. You don't want the aliens to think you're unprepared, do you?" Perch made the blaster noise. His parachute wouldn't actually deploy, but Cletus didn't want Perch to feel left out. During the jump, he'll have already been safely tucked into a special strap on Cletus's parachute.

In the past, Cletus had always had at least one other person around to help handle either the boat or the truck, but tonight, he wasn't particularly worried about leaving his truck parked on the ramp. After releasing the boat from the trailer, he gave the boat a good push before hauling himself carefully over the rubber side. The boat swayed under him as he made his way to the back and pulled the first beer from its case. He popped the lid of the can and froth foamed at the opening with a hiss. He was tempted for one sip, one last sip, but resolutely he held it away from him and poured it into his boat's tank. One after another he emptied what could be considered a substantial portion of the world's remaining stock of beer down the drain.

At least it was going to a good cause. No more sticking it to the man. It was time for the man to do the sticking and stick some aliens.

The tank was full before he ran out of beer, and he carefully stacked the rest of the cases to the side before moving to stand behind the wheel. It was off to the side of where he'd sit later behind the bar of the hang glider.

The motor sputtered as he backed the boat away from the ramp, and he glanced down at the map taped to the wheel. It would guide him to the spot he'd designated for his lift off. Fitting this would happen on Florida's east coast. It wasn't like NASA had figured out how to get rid of the giant thing of death floating over their heads or even how to make contact. He was going to do what they could not.

In the corner of the map, he'd taped a photo of Beth. He'd gotten it from her Facebook profile picture. He kissed two fingers and pressed them to her face.

"We're coming."

His red checkered shirt was cut at the shoulders and yet still not one single mosquito had bit him. It felt wrong. Especially being on the water. He used to come home covered in light pink bumps that Beth would patiently put ointment on. Sometimes they'd sit in silence. Other times she'd chastise the bugs, not him. Those were peace—

There was a plop from out in the water. Probably an alligator dipping below the surface. The wind felt good on his face, though he found the all too quiet of the river eerie. He'd been out late on this river plenty of times but never without another person.

"It's just you and me, Perch."

The gator made that video game blaster sound again.

When they reached the spot marked X on his map, the clock showed they had fifteen minutes until midnight, but they would already have to be moving before the clock struck twelve. On the bank of the river, cattle grazed, most likely abandoned by their farmer. They stared at Cletus while chewing their grass, and Cletus saluted them. After all, he was about to embark on a dangerous mission.

Taking a deep breath, he grabbed his headphones and tugged on one of the parachute vests, buckling the straps across his chest. Next, he carefully tucked Perch inside the strap at the front of his vest, fastening the little gator in place.

"Nice night we're havin'."

Cletus startled. If Perch hadn't been secured in, he would have dropped him. An old man wearing a straw hat rowed his wooden boat alongside Cletus'. A piece of straw hung from his mouth bounced as he chewed on it.

"Could be better. What are you doing all the way out here this late?"

"Fishin'." The man stroked his long bushy white beard thoughtfully. "Why are *you* out here?"

Cletus pointed to the sky. "I'm saving my wife."

The man looked him up and down. "*You* have a wife?"

Cletus flipped him off. "She was hypnotized by those aliens."

The man shrugged, nodding his head, unbothered by Cletus and his middle finger. "I wouldn't worry too much about her. I've seen a lot: bigfoot, lizard people, cattle mutilations." Hopefully the cows didn't hear that. "Yet I'm still here. When the aliens are done with your wife, they'll return her. I'm sure they're just probing her. I went through that back in the 60s, and I'm fine."

Cletus saw red. "So they *are* screwing my wife!"

The man continued to chew on his straw. "Nahh. They're just poking her brain."

Cletus didn't like that either.

He checked his watch. He only had a few minutes left to get set up. "Well, I'm going to be carrying on with my rescue mission... if you could just steer clear of my boat."

The man tipped his hat to Cletus and rowed his boat closer to the bank near the cattle.

Cletus added a few more cans' worth of beer into the tank until it was full again, and at a minute to midnight, he started up the propeller. His headphones did little to drain out the intense, heavy noise that the blades created.

He took a seat behind the bar of the hang glider and hit play on his MP3 player, an old model that held up better than any of those newer generations. *Don't Stop Me Now* was queued up and ready. He took hold of the bar and pushed his foot down on the lever he'd connected to the gas pedal.

The old man was off to the side, fishing in the shallow water, paying no attention to Cletus as he started gaining speed and the propeller grew louder. His watch struck midnight, and Cletus pulled the bar toward him. His boat rose into the air as the old man and his rowboat and the cows on the bank floated up as well. The cows kicked their legs side to side, in and out, trying to get down as the old man grabbed his straw hat and waved at Cletus.

The propeller blades whirled, and he climbed higher and higher into the air, leaving the cows and the old man behind. "Yeehaw! We did it, Perch!"

Perch opened his maw, but whatever noise he made was lost to Cletus.

The numbers above grew larger and when he looked down over the edge of the boat, the river was so dark he couldn't make it out. But in the distance, he saw the glittering lights of downtown Jacksonville. Not as bright as it would have been a few weeks ago. He would—

The boat dropped, and Cletus gripped the handle, his stomach lurching into his chest. The propeller slowed, and he let out a cry. "No!" Not yet. The ship was still too far away even with the hocus pocus that gravity was doing. He pulled back on the handle, urging the wind to catch the tarp of the glider and lift him back up.

But the propeller continued to slow, and as it did, he could hear the wind whipping past him. It swiped at his face and whisked his hat away, but the wind wasn't strong enough to take him higher, the gravity wasn't light enough. None of it was enough to keep him airborne.

His boat continued to fall.

He needed to abandon ship, but doing so felt like he was giving up on his wife. Cletus looked down at Perch. The baby alligator stared up at him.

"You're right, little buddy," he agreed. They couldn't save her if they were dead.

So Cletus stood from his chair, holding tightly to the bar, and in doing so, caused it to go up and down, changing the direction of the glider and making the boat bounce.

He had one chance to clear the boat. Once he'd let go of the handle, he'd probably become airborne, and he couldn't release his parachute while under the glider.

"Hold on, Perch!" His warning to the gator was lost to the wind.

With a last glance at the ship above, Cletus shoved himself away from the bar and barreled over the edge of his boat. He yelled, and the wind shoved its way down his throat. He grappled for the release, his hands brushing against Perch, and after a few dizzying seconds when it looked like he wouldn't manage to grab it, he at last snagged it and pulled down as hard as he could. Immediately, he was yanked up into the air as his parachute deployed.

For a brief moment, he thought that maybe it would work like a hot air balloon and take him and Perch up to the ship.

But, instead, the Florida Man and his gator hovered in the sky caught in the magical doodah going on with the air while his boat fell to Earth and a big shiny thirteen now glowed above them. The wind whipped past them, and something smacked Cletus in the face.

He reached up, peeling away the piece of paper that had formed around the shape of his nose.

It was his picture of Beth.

Surely this was a sign. A sign that she was waiting for him, that she didn't want to be with the aliens any longer.

Cletus placed his hand on Perch's head, shielding the gator from the wind. He had to make sure that nothing would stunt Perch's growth so that if they made it through the apocalypse, he'd have a nice big gator to go visit Pippin with.

"This isn't over, buddy. We'll try again tomorrow with–" Cletus racked his brain. "A jetpack! You hear that, you gooey-dick wife stealers? I'll be back! Cletus Mac will be back!"

~

13

about the author

A home baker by day and a writer by night. ***Jovi R*** *is the author of the Wattpad novel The Other CEO, which won a 2014 Watty for being the People's Choice with now over 50 millions reads.*

She leans more into writing contemporary romances with a soft spot for brooding men in suits.

THE NEIGHBOUR

by Jovi R.

VILLAGE OF WINNEBAGO, ILLINOIS, USA
AUGUST 18, 8:57 AM

If there was one thing I hated to do more than anything, it was asking for help from a neighbor I hadn't spoken to in three years.

Kade Sterling, the neighbor, had ruined my marriage.

But now was not the time to wallow in sadness. The world had turned to shit, and there was no guarantee that we would survive this. I was preparing to go outside for the first time since the alien ship had arrived. If I could, I would have kept hiding behind my sealed doors and windows like I had been for the past two weeks. But I needed my damn portable generator to work. There might be electricity now, but for how long?

I took my dark-colored hoodie and stuffed a paring knife inside my pocket for my protection. Despite the low crime rate in this area, looters had gone rampant. An alien race ambushing us didn't scare me as much as people who thought killing each other was the only way to save themselves. It was the most vile scenario in which I might die. I shivered at the thought.

After locking my door, I scanned to see if anyone was out being suspicious. The stretch of houses on my street seemed quiet for now. The skies were no longer visible; however, low light still passed through during the day, giving us a small amount of visibility. We were situated in the Twilight zone directly under the gigantic alien craft that hovered thousands of feet overhead. I looked up to see it in its actual size. Peeping through my sealed windows hadn't really materialized the weight of the situation.

Like I said, the sky was gone. The ship had replaced the sky.

"Fuck." I whispered in dejection.

I hurriedly trudged to my lawn to get to the other side of my neighbor's house. His motorcycle was nowhere to be seen, but I knew he was home. I had heard him loudly grunt at night, hoping to the heavens he wasn't doing what I think he was doing.

I got to his door and checked to see if anyone had appeared nearby. Today was the day I would not get jumped by someone I knew in this village. With a deep breath, I raised my hand and knocked on the door. There was no answer after a few tries, so I started banging a little aggressively. I almost started to wonder if he had died inside when the door opened abruptly.

"What?" he grunted in anger.

Although he had fury in his eyes, we both knew we couldn't raise our voices in order to avoid others from discovering that the houses were occupied. Most people who had enough money to evacuate had already left; those who had stayed were getting desperate and dangerous.

"Hey, neighbor!" I whisper-yelled, sounding chipper.

"You have avoided me like the plague for the last few years, Ember. Drop the act. You need something?"

I guess he didn't buy it. "Okay, yes, that's why I'm here. I need help to fix my portable generator."

"What makes you think that I'm going to help you? Find somebody else."

"Wait! Please. I'll do anything."

"Go home, Ember." He said with finality, about to close the door on me.

But I wasn't ready to give up. As I gave him a quick once-over, I noticed his rough appearance and pale complexion. He looked like he hadn't eaten a full meal in weeks, and had been suffering. Glancing lower, I saw his leg was covered in bandages, dried blood seeping through.

"Are you okay?" I asked, concerned.

"It's none of your business."

He let out a subtle grunt of pain, and I knew something was wrong. I pushed the door open further, and found out that he was leaning on crutches.

"Okay, I've seen enough. Here's the deal, Kade. You get a full meal, maybe a few extras, and I'll help you clean up your wounds. In return, I get my generator fixed." I offered.

I could see on his face that he was inwardly fighting to reject my offer, but we both knew it was too good to pass up. With what this entire country was going through, it had probably been weeks since he had a good meal. And everyone needed to eat. Eventually, I saw his shoulders drop in defeat.

"Fine."

"I knew you'd say yes. Let me help you get to my house."

We walked back to my house in slow steps. I let him put his weight on me to ease the pressure on his leg and prevent any more bleeding. It was a challenge, but it wasn't like I hadn't lugged enormous boxes of liquid detergent to the basement on my own.

I secured the locks to my house. We'd be safe here. There was everything anyone needed to last months—including a basement overflowing with inventory from my couponing addiction. Once we were locked in, I situated my neighbor onto the couch. He groaned in pain as he tried to bend his knee, but I encouraged him to lie down and stretch his legs out.

"Now, relax. I'll be in the kitchen to cook us some brunch."

Kade grumbled a thank you and I immediately got to work. The basement was my comfort zone. Rows upon rows of canned goods and bottles were lined up on shelves, neatly labeled and organized into identical piles. I had gotten into food canning last year, and the colorful jars stood across repurposed bookcases, each shelf dedicated to preserved meats, fruits or vegetables. It was my corner of order in the middle of all the chaos, and the reason I had survived for the past two weeks.

Who was crazy now? Extreme couponing wasn't as useless as everyone told me.

People had judged me for hoarding a bunch of food and products that I could never use up in time before they expired. But I wasn't that selfish. What they didn't know was I would donate a portion of my stock to my local food banks and homeless shelters. It helped many people, plus it was just a great way to get amazing deals for a small price. I never guessed my neighbor would be one of the people I helped with my coupon stock, though.

I decided on cooking pasta, having a few spaghetti boxes left. I would use my homemade tomato sauce and cooked chicken breast that I successfully canned a few months ago. My house was silent; the only noises heard were the water boiling in the pot and the sizzling of minced onion and garlic in the pan. This was what it had been for the last few years: silence and loneliness. The loss I'd suffered was something I could never recover from, and the silence was the only thing loud enough to muffle the wailing of my heart.

Glancing away, I glimpsed the locked door at the end of the dimly lit hallway. The cheery robin's egg door always invited me in to visit, but I hadn't stepped foot in the untouched nursery for a long time. I had tried to convince myself several times to just get over it and do a deep clean. But a big part of me would never be ready.

My thoughts were in the dark again, and I nearly forgot I had company over. The smell of the delicious meal reminded me I had a guest, so I set two plates on the table and toasted some frozen bread slices. Kade looked quite dehydrated, so I got him a Garotade from the food pantry. After setting everything, I helped Kade off the couch to the dining table.

When he sat down and saw the food, his eyes lit up. Then he sensed I was watching him, and set his face back into a stoic expression as he looked up.

"You can go ahead. Enjoy it if you want." I told him.

"How did you keep them fresh?"

He sounded bewildered. I didn't blame him. Some shops had closed the moment the alien chaos began. Food deliveries had ceased and consumer goods were scarce.

"You'll think I'm a lunatic if I tell you."

"Between aliens and you being crazy, I don't think there's anything more that could shock me at this point."

"You're right. I'm known for being the crazy coupon lady who does food canning at home."

"No judging here. But food canning? What for? You can buy those in the store."

I was about ready to fight him. People hadn't really seen the positive side of what I was doing. All they believed was that I was insane for inviting botulism into my system. But I had to give my neighbor a chance. He was just being curious.

"I get great deals in a farmer's market when I buy in bulk. I can't finish them in one go, so I put them in a jar and do a pressure canning process."

"That's too much work," he commented whilst stuffing another bite into his mouth.

His reply irked me. "Well, the hard work I put in just saved you from dying of hunger."

"Fair enough."

We continued to eat our brunch in slightly tense silence. He was an asshole, although I never really knew him. But I needed to keep my temper at bay if I still wanted him to help me.

As I calmed myself down, I was in the mood again to keep my end of the bargain, and settled him back into the living room. Before I could treat his leg, I needed to get him clean with a towel bath.

"We need to remove these bandages, apply antiseptic, and wrap them in new ones. It's going to hurt for sure." I told him.

Treating his wounds took longer than expected. The bandages had not been changed in a while, and blood had crusted over them. They stuck to the wound too, which never got the chance to heal properly. It was a gruesome task, but it was nothing compared to what I had to clean up at the preschool. Kade was quiet, trying hard to fight through the sting.

"So... what happened to you?" I asked while wrapping his leg in bandages. "Why didn't you evacuate like everyone else?"

"Motorcycle accident. I didn't break anything, but I got a pretty bad road rash which resulted in a skin graft. I just got home when the alien thing happened. No groceries, no medical supplies, and no one to help me around the house. I couldn't really leave. I've been in terrible pain since."

So, that was the loud grunting noise at night.

"It must have been—" I didn't get the chance to finish my sentence when Kade interrupted me.

"Hey, Em. Look."

His eyes were staring directly at my TV. All the screens that were found in my house lit up at the same time at noon. We tuned in, knowing what number was going to appear today.

13

Whoever ran the ship was trying to communicate something. For the optimistic, it could be a countdown to be the biggest welcome party of the century. For me, *Megadeth's Countdown to Extinction* had been my anthem since it all began. Who was right? We would never know.

"Any idea you have on this, Kade?" I questioned.

"Not a clue. There's no point in finding out. Leave that to the conspiracists," he said with no interest.

"We have a lot of time to guess."

"Aren't I here to fix your generator?" He retorted, looking annoyed.

I guess no small talk then. "Right. Are you able to go down the stairs?"

"I feel a bit better, but I'll still need help. Thanks."

I slowly led Kade into the basement, making sure he didn't suffer too much. It had already been a long morning for the both of us.

When we got to the bottom, he gave a long low whistle as he saw the mother lode of supplies. "Damn, Ember. You weren't joking when you said you're the crazy coupon lady."

"I'll take that as a compliment," I chuckled. "Let's get to work."

Since he couldn't crouch, I got him to sit on a small platform cart so I could easily wheel him around if he needed to move. The dusty old toolbox, which had been kept under the dark stairway, found its purpose. Handing him a flashlight, Kade got to work.

I knew Kade worked as an auto mechanic. My ex-husband used to take our cars to get checked a few times at the garage. I'd taken the chance to ask him for help as a last resort, assuming he knew how to check generators. He hadn't said that he couldn't do it, so I was more hopeful.

"Didn't you have this maintained?" His voice was muffled by being hunched over.

"Uhh. I didn't know that I had to?" My voice was unsure. Nobody told me about these things. My ex-husband was the handy one.

Kade heaved a sigh. "Where's your husband?"

"Excuse me?" I asked in disbelief. His innocent sounding question had triggered my trauma. The fuck was he on about.

"What? Did I say something wrong?"

Was he for real? There was no hint of remorse at all. "We already got divorced three years ago," I reminded him.

He stayed oblivious. "Shit. That sucks. I didn't know, sorry."

"You really don't remember?"

"Remember what?"

"You're the one who ruined my marriage!" I hadn't meant to scream, but this was all a fuckload of bullshit.

"Ruined? How?" His brows furrowed in confusion.

The ugly crying had started, but I needed to release this pent-up anger. It was time to confront my demons. All this time, I was the only one who had been suffering. These men might have been entitled to an exit ticket to freedom, only having to feel the pain in their heart. My husband apparently hadn't been able to withstand the loss of our stillborn child, and left me with a house I could barely afford on my preschool-teacher's salary.

But as a woman, that loss had been a part of me, growing for a full cycle of nine months only to be welcomed into this world with not a single breath of life. It wasn't just the heart that suffered. Losing such a big part of myself was the ultimate destruction that made me question my existence. What was the point of this life if I couldn't share it with my baby?

After I managed to calm my tears, I faced my neighbor.

"You told me he cheated."

Kade had the audacity to laugh awkwardly at my pain.

"That wasn't what I implied. I only told you I saw him with someone and asked if you knew her when they came to your house while you were at work. Was this the reason you were mad at me? I never intended to ruin your relationship."

"I talked to him about it that night. He told me you were lying."

He sighed and looked me in the eye. "I didn't want to meddle, but I saw them kissing in the driveway, and I knew something wasn't right. There was a high chance the bastard manipulated you."

"No..."

"Em... I might not understand your situation, but I know what I saw."

All those memories of us shattered. The warning signs that I tried to ignore rose up like angry red flags.

"He–he couldn't... He said he would never… We were going through such a big challenge and it was so easy for him to forget about me..."

"I'm sorry. You didn't deserve any of it." Kade put a hand on my shoulder to offer his comfort. The simple gesture took off the heavy weight that I was dealing with emotionally. He didn't know how much I had went through, but it was enough. Kade Sterling had been a friend all along.

The tears that I had to pour out today were the last time I would grieve for my ex-husband. As I took a deep breath, I let go of the pain. It was time to move on. I grabbed the neckline of my shirt and wiped the tears and snot off my face.

"You good?"

I could only nod in reply.

"Well, the good news is I'll be able to fix your generator. Bad news is... we'll need to do a supply run to get the parts we need."

"We should probably figure out how we're going to go out safely. For now, let's call it a day." I told him, feeling very tired. There was still a risk of what could happen to us out there, and I had dealt with enough outside for one day.

"Your call," he shrugged.

"I'm sorry about everything, Kade." I blurted out. He needed to hear my apology.

"Don't worry about it. It was just a stupid misunderstanding."

I laughed softly because he was right. We were facing a worldwide phenomenon allegedly involving aliens; my problems didn't feel so big and important against that, and I needed a friend with me.

"You can stay here until everything blows over, Kade. I honestly don't want to die alone."

We shared a look, and no words needed to be said. He had my back, and I had his. It was going to be one hell of an adventure fighting off this invasion together.

~

12

about the author

Sam Camp *is a Venezuelan chef, lawyer, and writer who specializes is comedy and existential horror -- which he would argue is the same thing.*

You can find him everywhere as @sam_le_fou

THE FULL METAL MAIDEN

by Sam Camp

BOSTON, MASSACHUSETTS, USA
AUGUST 19, 1:15 AM

It is a cold, dark night—as every fucking night is thanks to that flying saucer overhead—when I step into the clandestine casino with a plan, a bag full of TP, and nothing to lose.

The tables are hot, and the waiters are hotter. That's the draw of Doctor King's Prudential Palace of Pleasure, at the top of the Prudential Tower. You can make your wildest dreams come true, provided you have the moolah to pay for it. On the far wall is a blackboard full of bets, the most lucrative one being: what will happen when the eerie blue countdown in the sky strikes zero?

But that's a long-term bet. If I wanna get out of here in the twelve days remaining before that flying saucer decides to finish the job, I need to make it big, and fast. I bee-line it to the highroller's table, Black Jack, a six-pack of Charmin on my belt, ready to paint the town red.

I toss a roll to the dealer, taking a seat between a gimp and steampunk lady. "Cut me in."

The dealer silently deals me two cards. A ten and eight. Not bad. Time to make my move.

I take out my calculator, ready to math out this bitch. I am gonna card-count my way to victory. "Okay, hit me."

The dealer looks at me with horror, as well as the people at the table. In fact, everyone in the casino seems to be staring at me. Do I have something on my face?

"What?" I ask, before a gloved hand grabs me by the shoulder.

I do get hit, but not with a card, but with a fist, squarely in the chin. Turns out, casinos aren't very keen on you taking out a calculator between moves. The only prize that gives you is being dragged to the backroom and tied up while someone practices boxing with your skull.

My head tilts back as my new friend gives my face a high-five with a closed fist. Every blow measures the karats of his diamond rings.

"You fuck—counting cards is legal!" I yell, earning me a backhand to my left cheek.

The person hitting me in the face repeatedly doesn't have the courtesy of replying. His seven-foot frame blocks anything besides his body, and the blood-red scarf and sombrero combo don't allow me to glimpse their face. He is a wall of pain, and I am the stress ball being hit against that wall over and over again.

The man wears a poncho, with a holster holding a slingshot—efficient, no bullets needed, economical, good for an apocalypse, a weapon not for amateurs—and a camping knife. He looks like some LARPer with a Wild West fetish. You can't negotiate with those weirdos. Looks like I am not going to sweet-talk my way out of this one.

"Look, I learned my lesson, okay?" I tell the man as I spit out a tooth. Damn, my upper left incisor. There goes my root canal. "You can take all the TP on me. I'll go away, never to return, and we can just ignore all this happened, *comprende?*"

You would think stuff like medicine, canned food, weed, or gasoline would be the currency for the apocalypse, but no. It's always fucking toilet paper. People didn't learn about bidets during the pandemic, and now we're paying the price yet again.

The price here depends on the ply. A roll of scratchy-ass single-ply public toilet TP would get you a hot bowl of chowder around the Fenway Park refugee camp. A four-pack of two-ply no-brand nonsense can get you a warm bed for the night at the Park Plaza, provided you're not intimidated by the Southie gang taking control of the area.

But a Super Mega pack of Charmin Super Soft toilet paper? That's gonna get you places. More importantly, a ticket out of this fucking mess.

The man grabs me by the neck, pulling me so close to him that I can smell what he ate for breakfast. Baked beans and shakshuka. He must be on a bigwig's payroll. That ain't no canned shit. He turns me around, showing a one-way mirror behind me. Above the one-way mirror is a small speaker. It zaps to life, all treble, no bass.

"I don't think you comprende," says a voice, muffled and dry, like a southern biscuit. *"See that mirror? We have ten people betting which bone you'll break first."*

Beside the mirror is a girl dressed in a maid outfit, but with cat ears, wearing a headpiece. Next to her is a blackboard, with different bones and odds attached to it. The fingers are two to one. The bridge of the nose is four to one. The vertebrae is two to twelve.

I'm the main attraction. How flattering. Thing is, I kinda like my body whole, thank you very much. Some of the first rich dickwads who got out of town were the doctors. Even a simple cut will mean game over if you don't have the TP to pony up to some goth bitch with healing salts and best wishes. I'm not gonna be the one here leaving with stitches.

"Yeah, no, that ain't happening, chief," I tell the voice, giving him my best shit-eating grin.

"You don't seem to understand where you are right now. You ain't making it out of here alive."

"I know where I am," I say, grasping the hilt of the knife on the cowboy's belt, "and that is within pick-pocketing distance!"

With a swift motion upwards, I cut the rope binding me. The cowboy barely dodges the knife swipe, pushing me away from him at the last second.

You absolute dipshit, that's exactly what I wanted.

I use the momentum to combat roll away from him and into the cat maid. A twist of the arm and a knife to the throat, and now I have a hostage.

"Sorry, doll, but you're my ticket out of here," I tell the girl. "Now, just do as I say, and nobody gets hurt."

The bandido stays put for a minute, before giving me some creep fuck vibes. In the blink of an eye, he reaches down to his slingshot, puts a pebble on it, and draws a bead on me. Quick motherfucker.

A similar girl dressed as a maid, but with a princess tiara, comes out of a door behind us. She strides to the blackboard and flips it upside down, writing three new odds.

Death of Maid - 1 in 4

Death of Prisoner - 1 in 2

Death of Guard - 1 in 20

Motherfuckers, I have the girl in my grasp. How in the everloving fuck am I a safer odd than her?

"That will not be necessary," says a muffled voice, the same as the intercom, but now, it sounds like it's coming through several layers of clothes.

Suddenly, a smell. A *stench.* Like something foul crawled up Satan's butthole and died in whatever the opposite of cruelty-free is supposed to be. It is rank, stale, and yet oddly familiar. My eyes water for a second. Not necessarily from the smell, but from the mess of neon blues and yellow stripes assaulting my senses all at once. What appears behind us is a furry—a blue wolf with a yellow striped scarf and vest combo, and a lolling tongue. It stands as soon as it enters the room with a loud, and very distinct crinkling sound.

It's then that my brain finally processes that the smell, alongside the crinkling sound, is the sign of one thing and one thing only—the furry is wearing a diaper.

Now, when you've been in my line of work for long enough, you find out that there are three kinds of people you can't trust: people who use dark glasses indoors, people who still use Yahoo email, and suspiciously wealthy furries. I just don't trust no-one who hides the whites of their eyes, or doesn't use Gmail like normal people.

The furry claps twice, muffled by his furry paws. "I will let you out, but please, let my employee go."

The door where the maid came from opens, no resistance, no one to stop me, nothing. It smells like a trap and baby piss. But what can I do? If I stay, I would have a desperado breaking my bones for the amusement of some rich massholes. I had to take a calculated risk.

But as you know from the calculator incident, I suck at math.

The second I turn around to see the door, the cowboy lunges at me, hands ready to wring my neck. The hostage is useless at such close quarters. I toss her out, swiping the knife toward the cowboy's face. If he is dumb enough to lunge head-first at a knife, then that's self-defense.

Unfortunately for me, he dodges it at the last second, swiping away the hat instead. What lays beneath the hat isn't a LARPer with a Wild West fetish, but a woman.

An angel.

Seven feet tall, straight black hair, covered in a ragged cloth that only lets a few pieces of body armor shine through. A blood-red scarf wraps around her mouth and ears, only showing a pair of obsidian black eyes, like a dog taking a shit and looking at you with shame. A full-metal maiden.

She is breathtaking—in the way girls who punch you square in the gut and knock you out tend to be.

***

"Let's try this again," says the furry, now sitting in front of me with his legs closed while he fake-licks his paws. "Hello, my name is Dr. Jeremiah King Fluffybottoms the Third, the patron of this fine establishment. But you can call me Dr. King."

Needless to say, I am bound yet again to a chair, being watched over by the angel

"And you can suck my—" I begin to say, before being backhanded by the girl.

"Now, now, it is rude to interrupt while someone else is talking, Mr…?"

"...Jack. Just call me Jack."

"Jack. Wonderful. How wonderful," says the furry. "You already know my right-hand woman, Queenie…"

She, naturally, says nothing, being the stoic angel that she is.

"She made quite an impression on me," I say. "So, now that we're buddies, you mind tellin' me what the fuck you want with me?"

Dr. King strokes his face comically, clearly enjoying all of this a little too much. "Tell me, Jack. What do you want more than anything?"

An easy question. But he is clearly leading me somewhere with this. I have to play coy. "I want what everybody wants, Doc. I'm up Schitt's Creek without a paddle."

"I see. I take it you, like many of your peers, are striving to get away from the city before whatever happens, happens."

I take a sip of my coffee, making eye contact with his fake eyes. You gotta let 'em know who's boss here. "Ain't we all?"

"Not at all," he barks without skipping a beat. "This is the wild, weird west. The last frontier, forgotten by God and country. No federal oversight, no one telling us what to do. We forge our own path forwards."

Great, he's not just a furry, but a *libertarian* furry. I swear, if he starts quoting Ayn Rand…

"Whatever, Doc. You do you."

"I will, my friend, don't worry," says the furry. "And for me to live my life here to the fullest, I need your help."

Until now, they've had my attention, given that I am going nowhere, fast. But now, they have my curiosity.

"Now, why would the powerful patron of this fine establishment need the help of a pickpocketing lowlife such as myself?"

To that, the furry leans forward, grabbing my hands with his paws and rubbing them. "I saw what you could do with your hands, and let me tell you, I'm impressed. I could put them to good use."

I look back at the angel. She refuses to meet me in the eye while Clifford, the big blue weirdo, is fondling me. I can see where this is going.

"I see. You want me to jerk you off."

Doc places both paws around his snout in a sign of surprise as the girl, beet red, slaps me across the head.

"Hey, what you do that for? I wouldn't be opposed!"

"Jack, I don't--"

"I mean, if you give me enough lube and you change your diaper…"

"Jack…"

"But I won't suck you off. I have standards!"

Dr. King makes a motion with his hands, and next thing I know, I am being punched by the angel. She packs a mean punch. I think I love her.

"Okay, okay. I will suck it. But only the tip!"

"Jack, I don't want you to suck me," says Dr. King, leaning forward on his seat. "I want to use your pickpocketing skills for a job. A job that will give you enough TP to get you out of the city in style."

One minute, I am fighting for my life, and now, I am being hired for a job. I can't get a read on the furry, other than that he stinks to high heaven. "What kind of job?"

"Oh, nothing too hard," says Dr. King. "All you have to do is rob a truck. You, my friend, are gonna make me a lot of dineros."

***

WASHINGTON STREET
AUGUST 19, 4:55 AM

Gotta hand it to the Doc, he's a crazy motheryiffer, but he ain't a dumbass. Any other man would see the Winter Hill Gang and dare not even enter their territory. Dr. King wants to rob them from right under their noses.

"In one hour, a truck carrying a few tons of TP is gonna drive through Winter Hill territory and onto their hideout. Our plan is to sneak behind the truck carrying the load and… liberate the rolls before they reach their destination. Of course, you will all get ten percent of all proceeds, so it will prove to be a very fruitful enterprise, indeed."

My part of the mission is simple: dress myself like a homeless man, achieved by ransacking the nearest North Face store, and pickpocket the key of the truck lock from the driver. All I have to do is bump into the right man, at the right time during rush hour, and I'm golden. Then, Queenie and I would empty the truck into a waiting van and get the hell out of there before we got spotted.

Now, how could two people unload a ton of TP in a few minutes without machinery? Easily, thanks to our lovely neighborhood flying saucer. Whatever fuckery is afoot at that thing shifts gravity at 6:00 AM on the dot. Swiss watches be damned, that's the only consistent thing in this wasteland. We have eight minutes free of gravity to move as many rolls as we can. It's gonna be tight. Lucky for us, I have the fastest hands in the East coast.

Dr. King knows from coerced sources that the driver loves to wait the gravity shift out by having breakfast at one of the Dunkin' Donuts speakeasies commanded by the Cosa Nostra. Hey, America runs on Dunkin, and ain't no flying saucer gonna rob us from our blueberry munchkins.

One thing the apocalypse seems to bring out of people is the desire to cosplay. I buy the biggest Americano they have—costing me half a two-ply roll, the opportunistic fucks—and it is just a matter of whoopsie-daisying-it all over the man right as he's about to enter the speakeasy. He isn't hard to spot. He's the only douchebag wearing Crocs during this cold ass weather.

"Whoops," I say in my most monotone voice, spilling coffee all over the man. "Shit man, I'm sorry."

"My vintage Crocs!" yells the man. "You fucker. I'm wearing socks underneath!"

I take out a handkerchief from my back pocket, and gently, softly, I grope him all over. "Shit, bro, I'm sorry. Here, lemme clean this off."

"Get your filthy hands off me!" he yells, waving his sawed-off shotgun at my face. "Gonna go all day with some stank-ass socks. I've killed people for less. You're just lucky I haven't had my coffee."

I bow at his generosity as I skip away, conductor key in hand. Fastest hands in the East coast, baby! I do my part. A few seconds of work for a ticket out. Easy.

I press the button on my walkie-talkie, cracking alive with sound. "Jack to King. Got the key. I bribed the barista, so we should have eight minutes until he comes out."

"Rawr, copy that, Jack. Go to step two. Queenie will meet you there."

Next, on to step two. Open the back of the truck and get as many rolls as possible. Easy peasy.

Queenie is waiting in a van the next street over. Slowly, but surely, she pulls right behind the truck.

We move like one, latching tethers on the inside of the truck. Things are gonna get really squeamish in a second.

"*Five, four, three,*" chants Dr. King as the fated hour approaches, *"two, one, Hallelujah. You have eight minutes. Begin."*

The buffet shrimp churns in my stomach as the gravity eases off. The truck, the TP, Queenie, and everyone floats gently above ground. Time to get a move on.

Queenie is like a fierce orca, swiftly moving in zero gravity, and I am a brainless jellyfish, hopping and bopping out of her way, but secretly hoping she might take a bite out of me. We open the back of the truck and begin to unload twelve pack after twelve pack with practiced ease. We throw pack after pack into the van, absorbing the recoil thanks to our tethers. Who would've thought a rope, a magnet, and some duct tape would be the only thing keeping us from floating away?

"*T-minus one minute!*" yells the walkie-talkie. Or the standy-yelly, if we go by dumb naming conventions. "*Pack up and get the fuck out of there as soon as you get gravity before you get spotted.*"

I drift out of the cab as soon as the contents of my stomach decide to stop doing the macarena, cutting our tether with a knife. Gravity will be back to normal any minute now. Somehow, we managed to move every single roll. Not gonna lie, I didn't think this plan would work.

And it doesn't, a fact made known to us by the shotgun blast aimed directly at my head as I'm closing the cab.

The blast connects, alright, not with my head, but with Queenie's chest. She's used her body as a shield. Thankfully, most of the bullets hit the metal plate on her chest. It sends her tumbling backwards through the air, as it is a point-blank shot.

Queenie uses the momentum of the impact to reach the brick wall, twist around, grab a cracked chunk of brick, and slingshot it at the now-careening in one fluid motion. However, the driver shoots sideways, using the recoil of his shotgun as a propulsor to jet out of the way at the last second. That sneaky bitch!

I jump toward Queenie to assess her wounds, but she launches away from the brick wall, grabbing me mid-air. It would be a very touching and romantic moment, just two people dancing in zero gravity, embracing each other, were it not for the fact that our momentum puts us in a collision course with the van. Still, the redirection is just in time, as the shotgun sprays pellets where I hovered just a second ago.

"*Jack, I hear gunshots. What's happening?*" says Dr. King from the screamie-hidey.

A window gets shot up, glass shards exploding into deadly floating tiny knives spinning and churning around us. Queenie simply takes this as another opening she can use to rain suppressive fire. "We are under fire, sir. And Queenie…"

Every glass fragment she throws flies a little more sluggishly, a little weaker. Blood drips from her biceps in crimson balls, leaving a trailing stream in the air. She's been hurt in that initial volley. And yet, there she is, clinging to the van to keep from flying away, still fighting like a knight in crimson armor, while I am a small and nubile squire.

"*I see. As soon as gravity returns, leave her behind to lay suppressive fire and drive to the rendezvous point.*"

My blood runs cold for a second. Me? Leave my angel? The one who's just saved my life? Impossible. I'm only some pickpocket lowlife. My life is not worth it. And yet, she risked it all to save my ass. There's no way I'll leave her behind.

And yet, it isn't my decision to make. Queenie takes the van keys and thrusts them at my chest, giving me a solemn nod.

I take her hand in mine, holding it close as lead and glass litter the air around us in dangerous constellations. "No! I will not leave you behind. Come with me. We have enough TP to last us for years. We can buy our way out of this damn city! I will not let you die!"

To that, she smiles. Or at least, I think she does. Queenie squeezes my hand gently while removing her scarf. What lies beneath shakes me to my core.

It is a mess of tangled braces, the old-timey, medieval torture kind, that went all around the mouth and head. Her plaque-filled teeth are exposed for me to see, alongside multiple sores and cuts from the wires in a cute, squirrel-esque overbite. In a toothy, slippery voice, Queenie speaks to me, for the first and last time, with added waterworks.

"Shorry, I can't go wish shoo. I need new brashes, and Doctor King promised to remove theshe."

Of course. The depravity, the wealth, and his continued stay in the city. Dr. King is no doctor, but a *dentist*! That's why he didn't leave with the rest of the *real* doctors.

Queenie gives me a toothy smile, as there isn't any other she can give, as gravity returns amongst a rain of glass and lead, she sprints away from the van, shooting volley after volley of pebbles at the man. For her troubles, she gets shot yet again, square in the chest.

"Queenie!" I yell, running towards her, but her outstretched hand stops me.

"Go!" is all she says before continuing to shoot suppressive fire.

She is bloody, beaten, alone, and yet, fearless. She isn't a killer, or a cowgirl, or some hero. She is just a girl, looking for affordable healthcare. An angel sent to this world. There is no way I am gonna let an angel die for some TP.

They want me to drive? I'll *drive*.

Straight into the man.

I hit reverse, full gas, no brake, and slam the rear of the van against the driver. His body and the back of the van melt in a slush of blood and gas, sparked by the grinding of metal against the speakeasy Dunkin' Donuts. Whoops.

You know what bursts into flames faster than a van? A van full of flammable TP. Luckily, I manage to crawl out of the wreckage before I recreated a high school prank.

All the TP is gone, but I saved my angel.

I rush towards Queenie, holding her sides as she stands there, watching everything caught in flames.

"Jack, did my cute little wolf ears hear a fucking explosion?" says the calmy-seethie.

I sit next to Queenie, watching as the ball of molten metal and flesh roasts the coffee beans inside the Dunkin'.

"We kinda burned every piece of TP in the van, sir," I say with a smile.

Then, silence. A pregnant silence. Eight months along. That awkward *finding out you're going to be a father to your one-night stand* kind of pregnant silence.

"I see. You do realize I now own your ass, right? You will be working that debt off until you die. Every single ply."

I look at Queenie, sighing in relief as she bandages her arm with her scarf. She risked it all for me. I will risk it all for her. I'm a good-for-nothing pickpocketer, but a debt is a debt. Dr. King is willing to let her die, so I will be her shield for as long as I can.

"That's fine by me, Doc. That's fine by me. There's only so much time left in the world anyway..."

~

11

about the author

***Mhavel Naveda** is a writer, an artist, and architect originally from Peru, known as the land of the sun. Now residing in Arkansas, known as The Natural State. Writing has been a part of her life for as long as she can remember, but she only started publishing her work online a few years ago on Wattpad.*

Through Wattpad, she has gained valuable experience in grammar and editing. Her fantasy-humor book in Spanish won a Watty award.

She indulges in a passion for sci-fi-romance writing while working in an Architectural firm.

Happy endings? As only a book can deliver...

THE EVACUATION

by Mhavel Naveda.

BENTONVILLE, ARKANSAS USA,
AUGUST 20, 4:30 PM

"Do you think the aliens are cleaning the environment so they can come down to populate the earth?" asked my little sister Casey, watching the TV. I hadn't seen her blink.

I sighed. The news would not stop broadcasting about the damn ship and everything that happened. "Well, the air in the cities, at least, but the air in the forest surrounding us already seems clean enough to me. Anyway, I don't know what they're planning."

Since nothing changed overnight, despite the massive ship in the sky with a countdown ticking off the time to doomsday, many still posted memes—as if they were excited about humanity's possible extinction or just wanted to ease their fear.

Some people might think we architects weren't so necessary after the world's end, but we knew how to make construction documents by hand. Why? A wise professor said that if the technology failed or if one day the world ended, we could draw by hand and rebuild civilization. Ironic. My boss had made us continue working. He wanted our projects finished before something happened, although the day-by-day increase in empty desks and huge number eleven in the sky today told me it was time to look for a hiding place.

Being in Bentonville, NW Arkansas, we were very close to that thing. You could see the edge of the craft in the distance by going to the nearest mountaintop.

"I called for you, but you didn't answer," Casey said.

"I went for groceries," I replied. At least what was available. Food was scarce, reminding me of the pandemic. Each day, it had gotten worse as I went to buy what I could and stood in line for hours. A nightmare. "We're going to put everything in the car, and then we're going to go south to see Grandma."

It was more than time for us to escape. Every day I returned from work, more neighbours had left, leaving a darkened house behind. Although I heard a few muffled sounds, I hadn't dared knock on any doors.

The phone rang, and I jumped to answer it. It was my other younger sister, the one in the middle—Camilla.

"Hold on to your tights because I have an idea."

I chuckled despite the tightening in my chest that had been building as each day passed. I wasn't laughing much anymore.

"What is it?"

"A colleague from my work went to hide in one of the many caves in the forest. We should do that."

"Oh no, thanks. I don't want to go to sleep with Big Foot."

"If the aliens get off their ship in eleven days, the first thing they will attack is the cities. Moreover, people are speculating that perhaps they are already among us or have already spoken with the president. I don't know. We can not wait any longer."

"Knowing me, I'm going to eat all the food on the way before reaching some cave, with how anxious I am."

"No, well. We have to ration the food, and you'll deal with it."

"We'll see." I wasn't so convinced. "We should have bought plane tickets before prices skyrocketed beyond what we could afford and left for Peru."

Although, my country was so bad that, honestly, it sounded better to hide here than travel there and perhaps lose the opportunity to return to the US, if hopefully, everything improved one day. Still, Mom had also insisted that we go back to Peru. It was my fault we'd lost the opportunity. Even though it didn't happen, I'd been afraid that they would attack the planes or something while we were flying. And, well, Camilla and I needed to work, needed to continue to bring in money to our family.

"Yeah, what's done is done. I'm coming to the house."

***

My little sister kept watching the live feed from the ship. It didn't seem to be doing anything, but she had forgotten her other distractions like checking social media or following content creators. "Maybe they've come to pick up the Chupacabra, Big Foot, and all those weird animals."

"Oh, yes, I wish," Camila scoffed, coming through the door with bags in hand. "Ready. Let's go. The more days we wait, the worse it will get out there."

She lifted her shirt to show me a gun tucked into her waistband but then hurriedly hid it, giving Casey a sidelong glance.

I swallowed, my stomach churning, but we were three girls. Realistically, we would have more challenges and need protection if we ran into problems.

People were scarier than the ship itself.

I was grateful not to be in the Midnight or Twilight Zones under the ship. People out there were more scared, and fear did terrible things.

"Good. Let's go to the forest. To one of the caverns."

"What if they are already occupied by people?" I asked.

"We'll go where my coworker went with his girlfriend. Hopefully, we'll support each other."

"Wow. They can have threesomes with the Wendigo."

Camila laughed, but insisted, "Carla, we have to go. At least we can wait there and see what happens when that countdown runs out."

"What if the ship falls or blows something up? We are very close, in my opinion."

"So? Do you want to drive like ten hours to get to Houston? Fuel is expensive, scarce, and people are dangerous on the roads."

A muffled snuffling sound had us turning. Casey was crying quietly. We went to her, and I hugged her as Camila rubbed her back.

"We'll be fine. It's okay," I said.

The phone rang with my mother's number on the display. "Hello, mi'jitas. Camila told me you are going to the forest. Be very careful," she said in Spanish.

"Yeah. As long as there is a cell signal, we will try to call you. How is everything there?" I said. The news reports from Peru had not been good. Even though it was far from the ship, the people had rioted. Many other countries were in the same situation, despite being on the other side of the world. If the aliens were starting our extinction, it would eventually reach all of humanity.

"Ugh, you know how it is here. There are no more things in the markets, and several Members of Congress have disappeared with money from the country. The President is under surveillance in case he wants to escape, too."

"Bah. Well. I hope you ration your food in case it all runs out. We have to go before it gets late. Let's try to stay in contact," Camilla said, and the rest of us added our goodbyes.

After packing, we quietly took our things—including three large clothes-stuffed suitcases—to put them in the car, not wanting to attract attention. A subdued crash from the supposedly empty house next door had my head jerking around.

"Hey," I whispered to Camila. "There are always noises coming from that house. Do you think the neighbour got trapped or something?"

"Well, he would have died by now if that was the case, wouldn't he?"

"Yeah, well. Maybe he left the dog behind." The idea of that had me gazing at the house for a long moment, but a shiver up my spine made me turn away. I wouldn't go knock to find out the truth.

Casey came downstairs with her stuffed animal. She had already packed a backpack with her things.

"Do you think teenagers are training to save the world at the last minute, like in the movies?" she asked.

"Pft!" Camilla scoffed.

"Yes, of course, " I said, then we laughed.

"Let's go now," Camilla urged.

A neighbour, one who had never displayed good manners toward us, had come out of his house and watched us. I hated people looking at everything I did, and I hadn't wanted anyone to know we were leaving.

"Casey, get in the car already," Camila requested, exasperation in her tone. Our little sister obeyed.

"Are you guys leaving?" asked the nosy neighbour.

"Mind your business," Camila replied curtly.

The man advanced menacingly.

"We must all await the punishment fate has prepared for us." He swayed on his feet, the overwhelming stench of alcohol wafting through the air to surround us. At that moment, taking advantage of the distraction, another neighbour opened our trunk and snatched a box of canned goods.

"Hey!" I yelled, but it was too late.

The drunk grabbed another box and ran in another direction. Annoyed, Camila leapt from the car to chase them.

"No, Camila! Let them go!" I yelled.

She shook her fists at them, but halted. My heart in my throat, I trembled. She could get hurt or worse.

"Leave them and let's go!" I fought the sinking sensation in my gut, but gaped, frozen for a second as the situation got worse.

One of the neighbours had returned with a shotgun in one hand.

"Camila!" I squealed, and she turned to look.

She ran, of course, and I darted in the opposite direction. Could I confuse the gunman? I slammed open the door to the empty house and caught sight of Camila dashing back to the car. Casey hugged her stuffed animal, sobbing.

"Not so brave anymore, are you?" the gunman yelled.

He approached the car. Was he going to steal more food? I hid, smacking my palms on my thighs. Why? Why couldn't we have gotten away without notice? My pulse pounded in my ears as my muscles shook.

When I watched movies, I always criticized the protagonists when they didn't act the way I thought they should in a tense situation, but now, I understood. My mind spun and I could barely think, could barely move. A knock on an interior wall made me jump. Yes, there was definitely someone or something in this house. I rose and ran towards the noise. If it was a dog, maybe it would scare or distract the neighbours.

I found a locked door with a shelf shoved in front of it. Groaning, I strained to push it sideways and opened the door, not caring if someone heard me. A stairway led downwards, fading quickly into darkness.

"Hello?" I spoke to whatever was there. "I need help!"

I drew back with a scream, startled as footsteps pounded up the stairs fast, then darted past me. I chased after it, seeing only a silhouette framed against the outside light. A moment later, my eyes adjusted. A girl stood there, long, ashen hair matted and tangled in bare feet and dirty, pale clothes that clung to her lean body. She glanced to the side, eyes widening and mouth dropping open. Raising her hands, she fell onto her side, then covered her head.

Skidding to a halt, I spotted what she had been cowering from. The neighbour had dropped another box of stolen canned goods and now aimed his gun at her. Despite the roaring in my ears, I heard the girl cry out.

"Don't shoot!" I yelled.

"She's an alien!" the gunman yelled, clearly an idiot.

"What is this?" Camila was a couple of steps behind us. “What's going on?”

"Don't come any closer." The drunk man continued aiming at the girl. "Look! She is an alien! People are right that they're here with us!"

"No!" the girl cried. "I was trapped. I was trapped! That man had me trapped!"

Wow. That neighbour had always been a weirdo, but this was just something else. With the media focused on the ship, the darker side of humanity had burst free in recent days. Too worried about our own survival, nobody paid attention to the evil among us.

"She's just a regular person! Look at her!" I yelled back.

"Lies!" the other neighbour insisted, approaching the drunk's side. "She's wearing a damn spacesuit!"

She wore a strange white suit stained with dark spots.

"She must have killed Roger!" added the drunken neighbour, waving a hand to indicate the empty house surrounding us, the owner nowhere to be seen. "Her hair is almost gray!"

"No!" the girl squealed, trembling. "He dressed me up and dyed my hair! Then he lost his mind even more and abandoned me!"

"She's an alien! Shoot her!"

The man trembled and tightened his grip on the shotgun but didn't shoot. My heart thudded, breath rasping. My little sister's cries for us to come back to the car had me torn.

"Carla," Camila was closer now. "Let's go. Let's not get involved."

That was humanity. People were easily influenced by their beliefs, by the media, and by their own concerns. No one could tackle it all and we were forced to be selfish, to take care of ourselves and those important to us. It was too easy to lose it all.

Ship or no ship, we all were like this.

At that moment, the gunman took a step, and a shot cracked. I jumped and screamed. But it was Camila who'd pulled the gun from her waist and fired. The man cried out, clutching his thigh as blood stained his fingers. Camila met my gaze, and then, as one, we ran.

"Run! Run!" the unknown girl shouted and took off in another direction faster than I would have thought.

"No!" I yelled to her. "Over here!"

"Leave her!" Camilla insisted. "She is already safe. We must go!"

Safe, but for how long?

BOOM! The shotgun blast was way too close and made up our minds for us. We jumped into the car, and Camila accelerated, tires spinning for a moment in the gravel, and then we sped away.

Terrified, I peered through the rear window and spotted the neighbours retreating to their homes. One limped badly. Camila didn't stop or slow down. She had learned to drive in Texas, and there, they all drove fast.

***

I was able to breathe a little easier when we reached the winding forest paths through the mountains.

"Do you think she's going to be fine? It's gonna get wilder outside."

"Well, we have to look for ourselves. Hopefully, she is okay. You got her out of that house."

Camila turned on the radio and, as was the custom these days, all they reported was the situation within the country, around the world, and the alien ship.

"Countries on alert since the disappearance of missiles from military bases."

"That's how it is. Fear and tension have increased. Was it the work of many spies in various countries, or is it due to extraterrestrial action?"

"Where are those missiles?"

Casey held her breath, then said, "The aliens are disarming us."